Etienne van Heerden

Kikuyu

Translated from Afrikaans
by Catherine Knox

KWELA BOOKS
in association with
RANDOM HOUSE

Other books by
ETIENNE VAN HEERDEN
in English translation:

Ancestral Voices
Mad Dog and Other Stories
Casspirs and Camparis
Leap Year

Original title *Kikoejoe*
Copyright © 1998 E R van Heerden
Copyright English translation
© 1998 Catherine Knox and Etienne van Heerden
Published by Kwela Books, 211 Broadway Centre, Foreshore,
Cape Town, South Africa
in association with Random House South Africa (Pty) Ltd,
Johannesburg, South Africa

Cover design by Karen Ahlschläger
Set in 11 on 13 pt Plantin and
printed and bound by National Book Printers,
Goodwood, Western Cape, South Africa
First edition, first printing 1998

ISBN 0-7957-0079-2

Deep in Africa, at the foot of a mountain, lies a holiday farm. The stuffed heads of antelopes are mounted on the veranda walls. In the cicada summers, bats surge from the gable of the big house at dark and, as the fierce, frosty winters set in, swallows huddle on the telephone lines. They look northwards as they tip and tumble in the wind.

Some distance from the main building – exactly how far I can't remember any more – stand ten rondavels, each with two windows and one door. At Christmas, the High Season, balloons are blown up and a sheep braaied on the spit. The trail of a half-dry river bed winds its way close to the buildings and when grace is said, before and after meals, mercy and rain are mentioned in one breath. A bell announces meals to the guests and afterwards they snooze the sultry afternoons away. The stomachs digest lamb and sweet pumpkin and steamed pudding while the bodies sweat the rondavel sheets clammy.

At the desk just inside the front door of the big house stood a bunch of plastic flowers which were all the rage that year – 1960. A framed postcard of a Dutch woman with wooden feet stood propped up against the flowers. It was one of the cards that Tant Geertruida sent regularly from Amsterdam, where she was busy doing research.

Tant Geertruida came to visit every Season. When she left, the window-sills were blue with Delft windmills and dolls, and all of us, willy nilly, sounded as though we had extra tongues in our cheeks when we spoke Afrikaans.

"Geert's Dutch accent sneaks in under your tongue. One-two-three, before you know it," Ma always said, "you're talking with a mouth full of cheese."

The first guest to book for the summer of 1960 was Tant Geertruida. She rang months too early from Amsterdam to say that she needed a summer Christmas. The sparrows flipped on the line as her trunk call came through. The frost still lay white across the Karoo, but, she said, she was sitting with rolled-up sleeves on the Leidse Plein, reading.

"I'll take my usual rondavel," she said. "And I have some interesting news for the family."

"God forbid," said Ma. "What Geert considers interesting news usually only spells disaster for the family. What's interesting to the Dutch is only bad news for the Latskys here in the Karoo. Very bad news." Ma poured herself another little brandy where she stood behind the reception desk beside the plastic flowers, recording Tant Geertruida's booking in the ledger. "We'll have to paint the Wilhelmina."

Each rondavel had a name. There was the Wilhelmina which Tant Geertruida took every Season. Then there was the Camdeboo, the Kudu, the Windsor, the Bitter Aloe, the Utrecht, the Van Riebeeck, the Verwoerd, the General De Wet and the Zane Grey.

The wind changed direction with Tant Geertruida's call, the plastic flowers seemed brighter, the sounds of the afternoon splashed like water. At the end of winter, I knew, waited a Season. Then the rondavels and the stoep rooms would be full and the Borgwards and Cadilacs and DKWs and Studebakers would stand under the pepper trees, cooling off after the long road through the Karoo.

Tant Geertruida was mad about Amsterdam and London. Every year she went to London for the English autumn. She stayed close to Marble Arch in the Queen's Guards, took long walks in Kensington Gardens and did her research in the British Museum.

She ambled down Oxford Street, window-shopping at the jewellers and fashion boutiques, sniffed the fresh English autumn air and had a cup of tea in Regent Street.

In the late afternoon she could eat fish and chips in a London pub without causing a stir – a woman on her own, with a foaming pint at her elbow (and a second to follow), attracted no attention. "The villages," said Tant Geertruida when referring to rural South Africa – because of the narrow-mindedness, the curiosity.

But as soon as the English weather got too much for her,

Tant Geertruida caught the ferry over the channel and hied herself as quickly as possible back to Amsterdam, "where overcast has a different tone."

She would take a room over a canal – each time a different canal, because "Amsterdam has so many faces" – and place her table and lamp under the window.

It was in Amsterdam that Tant Geertruida wrote everything down. The rest of the time she sat in libraries and doodled those cross-hatched lines of hers with an obssessiveness that only now, years later, I recognise as mine too. This meant that by December every year, she had a thick wad of papers to bring with her to the Wilhelmina – the rondavel furthest back that looked out over the rolling Karoo.

"God only knows what she's bringing with her this time," sighed Ma. "Tant Geertruida isn't terribly feminine," Ma always said, patting her bun of hair, smoothing her frock and shuddering. And when Tant Geertruida's call was followed up by a telegram delivered by the bicycle messenger from Halesowen, Ma tossed the telegram down beside the plastic flowers.

I grabbed it and read. *Arriving 10 December. Please reserve the Wilhelmina. Remember vegetarian.* That "vegetarian" was an affectation, as Ma called it, because Tant Geertruida only had to get a whiff of the mutton chops the first evening, and all her scruples melted away.

The Wilhelmina was the prettiest of all the rondavels. It stood a little back from the others and the front door opened on to a view of the far ridges. From the one window you could see the orchard. A set of kudu horns hung above the rondavel's door and the furniture inside had rounded profiles. Above the bed hung a photo of Wilhelmina, Queen of the Netherlands. It had originally been a humble black and white photo but Hepburn and Jeanes in town had painted in colours, so that Her Majesty now gazed out of it regally.

Above the writing desk hung a portrait of Doctor Verwoerd, our Prime Minister, but every year when she moved in, Tant Geertruida took this down and put it face down in the shoe cupboard.

"Not at all, Fabian, love," she'd say to me as she stowed the portrait. "Even if he was a born Hollander. No, not at all."

Tant Geertruida was fond of doing things in the same order. "That's because she's a genealogist," said Ma. "It's precision research, tracing the blood of the family's women. If you take one wrong step, you can cause a family scandal."

Each year when she arrived, Tant Geertruida parked her Borgward under the same bluegum tree, put the same two deck chairs out on the little stoep in front of the rondavel and sat so that she could keep an eye on the other guests as they moved around the rondavels, the stoep rooms, the ablution block, the tennis courts and the swimming pool. If she wanted anything, she would ring the little bell at her elbow. When she booked in, Ma always gave her the bell, a mosquito repellent lamp, suntan lotion, a candle, a box of matches and the latest *Reader's Digest*.

When the tinkle of Tant Geertruida's bell came drifting over the lawn, Reuben, our head waiter, had to run immediately to the Wilhelmina to take her order – usually a whisky and soda, a slice of toast with radishes, or a cup of English tea.

Now Ma stood near the plastic roses, fiddling with the telegram and leaning towards the Veteran who had a hole in the heart and lived as a permanent guest in the Van Riebeeck. Ma didn't think I could hear, but I had my ears pricked.

"Do you know," Ma whispered, "my husband's sister – that's the one in the telegram – she was only twenty-one when her research showed her that cancer of the female parts and the breast ran in the family. So she went on her first trip to London and had everything cut off and taken out.

"She went over to Amsterdam, to the shows and to visit the museums and got up to all sorts of things at night and then she came back with that bossiness of hers, the men's pants with the turn-ups and the Stellenbosch blazers and the snuff, and she was twice as clever as ever before."

Tant Geertruida had booked into a hotel in London. She'd unpacked and called room service. She invited the waiter into her room and then took off her blouse so that her erect young nipples stared at him like a rabbit's pink eyes. She begged him,

4

offered him money, promised him her body, if only he'd take the knife and cut off the rabbits that pressed their snouts against her bra. The seeds of the cancer were sown in them, she pleaded with the waiter. Cut them off. The waiter refused and fled, confused, from the room, down the stairs, dropping his tray in the foyer, and he refused ever to serve the woman in thirty-three again for the rest of her stay.

Tant Geertruida flipped through telephone directories and visited medical practitioners. Finally, in Gower Street, she found a doctor whose voice and bedside manner met with her approval. She donned her pillbox hat, pulled on her gloves and walked down Oxford Street without a bra, turning into Regent Street where jewels lay gleaming in the windows.

She walked fiercely because the two rabbits strained at her chest. The tips of her nipples tingled as they rubbed against her blouse. In her lower body, below the navel, behind the pubic hair, pulsated the hedgehog of her womb, that little creature that would also have to go. She decided while she waited at a traffic light for a red bus to go past, she'd have it out too.

She called on Arthur Maylam, Doctor of Medicine (Oxon). And Tant Geertruida felt lighter when she left the hospital two weeks later, more confident. She bought a new jacket and a filter for her cigarettes. She stared people straight in the eye, making them look away. She decided to visit Amsterdam – for the art and theatres, for the free thinking. But not to linger too long now, rather to return later. Because the circle of canals could also become stifling, she realised. It was 1938 when she boarded the Dover ferry; the Great War lay ahead, and more than twenty years would pass before the cars rolled up that 1960 Season for the city families' fourteen High Days on our holiday farm.

Children scrambled from the cars, flattening the geraniums and the rock gardens. The city dogs rushed around madly, drunk from all the wild animal smells they didn't recognise.

2

On the tenth of December I was up early. I Brylcreemed my fringe carefully, a dab more than usual. I combed it to one side the way the young chaps in Utrecht and Oxford combed it – I knew because Tant Geertruida often sent cuttings from Dutch and English newspapers. In the evening, when the guests had settled down, the whole family would sit reading them in the lounge.

While Pa shaved pieces off the biltong, Ma would read the clippings carefully, one after the other. She pushed some of them over to Pa, some to me. She was careful only to push over to Pa the clippings that would not disturb him – reports about damage to the dykes in Holland, the tulip harvest, snowfall figures from London.

But the reports of Harold Macmillan's Winds of Change speech that he'd delivered in our Parliament – about the Winds of Change that were blowing over Africa and would change the continent irrevocably – she gave discreetly to the Veteran, who stroked his medals with his fingertips as he read.

I got the clippings about universities and schools in Oxford and Leiden: blurry pictures of long academic processions, little reports about regional achievers, sometimes a postcard with a band of smiling students. Ma wanted me to study in England. "She wants to turn you into an English gentleman," the Veteran always teased.

But Tant Geertruida had decided I must go to Holland. "Your great-grandpa studied law in Leiden," she said.

"She wants to make you into a seventeenth century Dutch trader," grinned the Veteran.

But now it was the tenth of December and we were expecting Tant Geertruida's Borgward. She had steamed into Table Bay harbour aboard the Windsor Castle, picked up the Borgward where it was always waiting for her with friends in Tamboerskloof and had driven as far as Laingsburg the first night.

"God, the wide open spaces," she had said over the phone to Ma. "The stars." The following day she had pushed through to Graaff-Reinet where she greeted family. And today, at dawn, she left there with only Wapadsberg and a hundred miles of gravel road between her and the Hotel Halesowen.

I pulled on my best short-sleeved shirt and fastened my belt with the inlaid copper work. Standing in front of the mirror, I pulled my socks right up to under my knees and then I made my way down the linoleum passages to the veranda. Ma stood near the geraniums in her floral frock with her hair combed out loose. "By all standards," Pa would always say, "she's a beautiful woman. And intelligent, too."

Ma swung round to me and clapped her hands. "What Fabian! Socks too! And in the middle of summer!"

When she hugged me close, I could smell the jasmine from the little bottle of perfume the Veteran had brought her from town the last time he'd gone there.

"For the Sunday lunches," he'd said when he gave it to her.

The Veteran had on his best uniform – the one he always put on for dinner on the terrace. "I could have worn my Action Working Dress," he said, "but I heard this is an important visitor this. You must spruce yourself up for a clever woman. Vrije Universiteit no less. And Oxford. A cosmopolitan."

At the time, I wasn't too sure what a cosmopolitan was, but I assumed that it had something to do with what Ma always referred to as Tant Geertruida's "inclination for travel".

"Travel, books and bad weather," said Tant Geertruida, "that's the secret of accomplishment. The travel keeps your mind open and the bad weather forces you indoors, back to the books. Not like here in the Karoo, where the sun never stops shining and even at night people have to stay outside to cool off. The houses are so dark and stuffy! The Afrikaners never learned to build facing north. You lie baking under the iron roof and even thinking about reading makes you feel queasy. And outside the sun is too bright and the hands too sweaty to hold a book. That's why Karoo people have such strong legs and those small heads – just like lizards.

"No, give me a drizzle over a canal, any day – and a strange little Dutch hotel with a book store on the next corner. Then I feel as grand as her Majesty."

"Far from home . . ." Ma would then say dryly, pouring herself another drink.

". . . sentiments go astray," Pa would add, peeling an orange.

But Tant Geertruida never answered. I would keep an eye on her: the broad strong shoulders and the man's shirt with the snuff box, the notebook and the Parker that made a bulge in the pocket over her left breast. The other side was flat. I thought my way into her naked upper body. Pink scars marked her chest where the breasts had been cut off – eyes like you get in wood when you've sawn through it. As big as the palm of your hand.

But while I listened to her, I forgot her wounds. She had a voice as luxuriant as the curls she combed back from her forehead. She bought her flannels in the men's department, with turn-ups above the shining lace-ups – the sort you can only buy in London, she said. And she crossed her legs like Pa – ankle over the knee – and she read her newspaper with widespread arms.

Before I ran to the gate to wait for Tant Geertruida, I checked the Wilhelmina quickly. The door and windows had been thrown wide open to let in the fresh morning air. It smelt of fresh soap and fly poison. Doctor Verwoerd's portrait was still hanging there, because Ma didn't want to take it down in front of the cleaners. "It's bad politics to denigrate the Doctor in front of the labourers," said Ma. "I'm just going to leave him there. Let Geertruida take him down herself. Next thing I take him down and the servants think they can take over the guest house. Can you just imagine the stoeps crawling with children? Oh no, rather let the old Doctor stay there and maintain some law and order."

I ran to the yard, saluting the Veteran on the terrace, and took up my position at the gate. Waiting for the shining bonnet of the Borgward, I reminded myself to call Tant Geertruida by her name.

"Don't *tante* me, Fabian," she'd say. "My name is Geertruida. Or, if you'd rather, just Geert. I actually prefer that. I don't like names that end in a. They sound too tentative."

I sat on the gate-post, leaning on the big board that declared: *Hotel Halesowen. Family holidays. Lunches. Reasonable tariffs.*

Everyone had a different name for our place. The Veteran talked about the Guest Farm and swept his cold cigar to his lips with an extra flourish of the elbow. He had a hole in the heart and wasn't allowed to smoke. Ma called the place Hotel Halesowen and when the telephone rang on the counter, she'd put her drink down carefully, rest her cigarette on the ashtray with the Johnny Walker man, stretch the corners of her mouth with her thumb and forefinger so that you could see her nice teeth behind the lipstick. Then she'd toss the curls back from one ear, pick up the receiver and say in a radio voice: "Hotel Halesowen, hello."

Miss Marge Bruwer, Tant Geertruida's friend who worked in the town library, called our place a "vakansieplaas", speaking the word severely in her heavy English accent, as though it were our fault that other farmers ploughed and harvested, earning their daily bread by the sweat of their countenance, while at our place it was all just the tap of snooker balls, lamps twinkling among the pepper trees, mesh doors creaking on their hinges, guests snoring in their hammocks and waiters trotting about amongst the rondavels with their trays.

Tant Geertruida spoke of "The Farm" or "De Boerderij", depending on which foreign city was freshest in her memory. Ma believed that Tant Geertruida saw our place as a haven of spiritual refreshment. Because she came here every year, apparently to "sort out her research".

"Sort out what research?" said Ma, "Geert just wants to nurse her whisky under the bluegum and wiggle her toes in the cool kikuyu and listen to the Fish River running over the pebbles. She wants to get away from her cities and her books and all those men-women she is friendly with. Here she can just be Geert and put her feet up without anyone asking an intelligent question. At our place anyone can kick his shoes off,

9

let his sins hang free and no one will make a fuss about it. Enjoy! Enjoy! Hotel Halesowen, hello.''

Then Ma would swing her hips as if she swung a hula-hoop, wink at Pa or me or the Veteran and flip through the register. Ma was worried that the unrest among the blacks would affect our business. But: "Our bookings are looking good. We're running a full house!''

But soon her mood would sink again and the midday drinks trickle sourly from her bladder. She'd get that dazed look she always wore between tea-time at four and drinks at six, stick her pencil behind her ear and open the latest *Reader's Digest*.

Pa called the place Soebatsfontein or Moordenaarskaroo, or, when politics got him down, Kaffirland. If he'd just got to the end of one of Zane Grey's cowboy books, he'd talk about Dodge City.

"And you're John Wayne," Ma would tease with a dreamy look in her eyes. "Oooh, that cowboy Wayne can leave his boots under my bed any time."

At last the shiny bonnet of the Borgward swerved around the furthest thorn trees. I looked back to the house, and waved. Ma waved back and Reuben came trotting out without his tray. He stood at the ready to take Tant Geertruida's bag to the Wilhelmina. The Veteran appeared behind him, straight as a candle. The medals flashed on his chest. The guests' children stopped playing ball on the lawn. Their faces turned towards the gate.

Usually I'd open the gate and Tant Geertruida would drive straight in. She'd always toss me a coin from Holland or England. Then I'd close the gate and race back to the terrace where she'd greet me.

Today she pulled up and got out. Her jacket was draped over the passenger seat. Her hair was shorter than before and brushed back. She took off her dark glasses. "Fabian, my boy!'' she cried. "But you've grown!'' She didn't kiss me or shake hands but just stood there with that big smile. "So, don't you have anything to tell me?''

I put one foot forward. It was difficult to drop the *Tant*. "Hello . . . Geert," I said bashfully. She laughed.

"Hello, Fabian, old thing," she said. "Look what I've brought you." She pulled out a large book. "Have you ever heard of the painter who cut off his ear?" I shook my head. "Well then, you've got some education coming, boy! Dammit, it's good to see you. Jump in. Let's go! Look there's the whole crew waiting."

3

Miss Bruwer lent forward, her elbows on her knees. Her lips were parted and her nostrils seemed wider than usual. I couldn't hear her breathing because the Wilhelmina's windows were closed and I was peeping through a tiny crack so I could hardly even hear the faint voices. But I could see her chest rise and fall, rise and fall.

It was late and I had climbed through my bedroom window to wander among the rondavels. Miss Bruwer's car was still parked under the pepper trees, but the terrace was deserted. Even Reuben had gone to bed. As head waiter, he had to stay up until all the guests had retired to their rondavels or outside rooms.

Miss Bruwer's cheeks were red and she tugged at her collar.

"Geertruida," she said in her heavy English accent, so it sounded more like "Gertrude", "do you also feel so inspired by Olive, old girl? By her bold challenge to her society?"

Tant Geertruida sat in her flannels with her knees far apart. She wasn't leaning forward like Miss Bruwer, but relaxed back in her chair, either with one ankle resting on the other knee, or she would drop her foot back to the floor and sit the way Ma said a lady should never sit.

"My dear Marge, I've never ever bothered," she told Miss Bruwer, "with what you call 'society'. Frankly, up theirs. Not so? I don't ever put a telescope to my blind eye." She stroked her chest, rubbing through the shirt against the pair of pink eyes. "I had my breasts removed when I realised they were a threat. I got rid of my womb. God help me, my uterus and all my womanagix. I took it out and I'm freer than Man or Woman, without the pressure of balls or the bloody business that women have to put up with."

Tant Geertruida took a pinch of snuff and looked, watery-eyed, at Miss Bruwer who reached for the sherry bottle and topped up their glasses.

Miss Bruwer took a sip, carefully, as if she were tasting a thought. She closed her eyes and threw her head back against the Morris chair. She spoke Afrikaans now. And Tant Geertruida spoke English.

"God," said Miss Bruwer, "just listen to the night sounds. Only the Karoo sounds like that on a summer's night." She moved her head back and forth so you could see her voice box, and the big artery in her neck, throbbing.

"And desire?" Geertruida asked after a little while, with the sherry glass raised before her. She gazed through the sherry at the lamplight as an actress might.

Tant Geertruida flicked specks of dust from her flannels. "Desire," she said, "is controllable in the middle years. Earlier . . . Well, then it was impossible."

Miss Bruwer stared directly at Tant Geertruida. Her eyes looked dreamy; sherry swirling in a glass.

"Is that why you always travelled to London and Amsterdam, all those years?"

Tant Geertruida was silent for a moment. She fondled her sherry and her eyes wandered round the room.

"Marge, can I lick your pussy?" she asked, putting her glass down and looking towards Miss Bruwer as though she'd offered her another biscuit. Miss Bruwer went deathly pale. Her hands fluttered round her head. She put her glass shakily on the table.

"Oh, God!" she groaned. "Oh yes, Lord, yes!"

4

You're really just scratching and scraping when you're trying to look back through the eyes of childhood at a summer which you've placed in a specific year, more for convenience than anything else . . . Maybe you're taking on more than you should, because your own experiences have already settled over those of your parents, calcified layers that you now scratch at in your determination to break through to that summer, so different in your memory, as though it were the only summer season in all those years.

Perhaps the things I'm telling of didn't happen in the summer of 1960, but over many summers. Perhaps, when I extend the telescope of memory and try to focus it sharply, the events of many seasons shift into one another and it's the occurences of many years that are re-enacted in the lens by Ma and Pa, Tant Geertruida, Reuben and Tsitsi (we're still coming to her), Charles Jacoby, Hendrik Verwoerd (hang on), the Veteran and all the others who are proffered in my story.

Perhaps, in addition, the memory will reveal itself a sly director, an unscrupulous or sneaky presenter of imaginings, probabilities, yearnings: fragments stitched together and mutilated on the pattern of our own times – the sort of construction that the French call *bricolage*. Because to arrange the happenings of those days, as I sit here today, is to take up a controlling position.

You look back, you judge with the insight of experience, you pre-judge so easily, compassion can slip through your fingers so quickly, and reduce your people to figures or puppets.

Perhaps it's really just a case of fears and yearnings which are propped up as a story, feeding, I know now, on the memories of what may have been an imaginary summer, that Halesowen summer at Soebatsfontein.

Reuben was the head waiter.

"He is a white kaffir," Ma said. "As decent as they come. I swear he must have some coloured blood in him. He speaks the most beautiful Afrikaans and he washes every night."

"No," Pa insisted. "He's as black as the King of the Kaffirs himself."

"But he's so trustworthy!" Ma looked at Pa. "I even trust him to give out the rondavel keys." She glanced at me. "Isn't that so, boy?"

"He's a bit too clever for my liking," said Pa. "He reads. He steals the old papers which we put in the waste paper baskets."

"Yes, I know he pinches something to read now and then," said Ma. "But I can forgive him that. Where else is he supposed to get anything to read?"

"A clever kaffir is a dangerous kaffir," said Pa.

"That's true too. I worry that he gets contaminated by all the unrest."

"I'll keep an eye on him," promised Pa. "We won't put up with any nonsense. Maybe you should check now and then on the books lying around in his room. Ask the maids to bring the books to you when they go to sweep."

Reuben lived in a small room next to the donkey. The donkey was made out of a colossal tank from a petrol lorry that had overturned at Dynamite Krantz. The tank stood on stone pillars with the place for making the fire right underneath it. A long pipe stretched upwards like a flagpole on top of the tank.

Reuben slept next to the donkey because he had to stoke it up early in the morning. The pipes began to hum at five as Reuben made the fire and, by six, the boiling water was spluttering out of that flagpole pipe. In the winter the steam fluttered like a flag above Reuben's pole.

It was the same story in the evening. At four, when tea had been served on the terrace, Reuben had to start chopping wood and loading it in and by six you could smell the white hot pipes that ran along the back of the stoep rooms and down to the ablution block. If you brought your face up close to the pipes, you could feel the heat against your cheeks and see the insects that had died there. Then the guests could bath in time for supper on the veranda.

"If I could make it a rule," said Ma, "every guest would bath and dress for dinner. Look what a good example the Veteran sets in his dress uniform with his medals, night after night. You'd never guess he had a hole in the heart. After all, ours is a decent establishment, isn't it?"

I wasn't allowed too close to the donkey because Pa was afraid the petrol tank wasn't up to taking the pressure of the steam. He'd bought the wrecked petrol tanker and dragged it here, thought up the contraption and welded the donkey together.

"That thing is going to explode one day," he said, "and then you had better be far from it, Fabian."

I'd sit about fifteen paces away every evening, chatting to Reuben as he fed the donkey the thorn-tree stumps and ran his hands over the pipes to make sure they weren't shuddering too much.

"Reuben is the only one who really knows that tank," said Pa. "He's trained the donkey to his hand. Any other stoker would heat the thing up too much and then it'd explode."

"Oh, heaven forbid," said Ma. "Can't you stay away from there, Fabian? Hopefully one day the Fish River Valley will get electricity, if the Verwoerd dam scheme works out, and then we can also stop worrying."

"Soebatsfontein," said Pa. "Moordenaarskaroo."

"Oh, go on with you," protested Ma, glancing at her watch to see whether the Boeing had come over yet.

I sat against the bluegum's trunk, breaking the dry leaves in my mouth to taste the medicine, and watched Reuben sweat in his white shirt and black bow-tie as he served tea on the terrace. I could smell the musty steam and the thornwood that smouldered and then burst into flame. The sun sank redly over the plains and the vervet monkeys called down near the river.

The evening starlings, gorged on figs, came chattering by in a flock to settle on the reeds. At the kitchen door the screen door whined continually on its hinges and the crockery and pots clinked against one another.

"Kleinbaas Fabian?" asked Reuben, and wiped the sweat from his forehead.

"Yes, Reuben?"

"What is the equator?"

So I told Reuben what the equator was.

"Kleinbaas Fabian?" said Reuben.

"Yes, Reuben?"

"What is a volcano?"

So I told Reuben about volcanoes.

"Kleinbaas Fabian, what is gravity?"

Then I told Reuben what gravity was.

I sat there until close to dinner time when the roof of the big house began to creak as the dusk evaporated the day's heat from it.

"What else did you learn at school?" asked Reuben.

I lent him my school books, telling him he should hide them under his mattress because the maids had been instructed by Pa to look for books in his room. Reuben tucked them under his waiter's jacket and read them all through in one night. He loved the Geography and Biology.

"I'm looking with new eyes at grasshoppers and earthworms," said Reuben. "I still don't know what's going on in their heads, but now I understand the little holes in their bodies and their strange habits."

"Reuben," Ma always said, "mixes the best drinks this side of the Cape. You can order any cocktail. In a flash he's into the bar and out again and you find the guest sitting there, completely satisfied. What on earth would we do without Reuben?"

I sat with Reuben, watching him stoke the donkey and split the white flesh of the thorn wood with his axe. He threw a stump in and waited awhile with his ear close to the tank. Then he'd nod and stoop to chop another stump.

Or he'd look up at the flagpole and, if the boiling water began to bubble out, streaking the iron of the house roof with white hot splashes, he'd drag two stumps out with the fire iron and leave them smouldering to one side for later.

Reuben called the donkey his train. When it began humming, he'd say, "Listen to my locomotive, Kleinbaas Fabian! We're on the way. Full steam ahead!"

"Where to, Reuben?"

"No, you decide, Kleinbaas Fabian!"

I rattled off the names. Reuben took each one as though it were a gift: "Klipplaat, Kommadagga, Cookhouse, Mortimer, Halesowen, Daggaboersnek, Baroda, Fish River, Conway, Rosmead, Noupoort . . . Alicedale, Pearson, PE . . ."

"Faraway places," said Reuben.

"Ag, Reuben," I laughed, "the furthest one is only two hundred miles away. When we go down to Cape Town, that Volkswagen has to travel four hundred miles!"

"Doesn't the engine get hot?"

"Ja, but we take a break in Beaufort-West – shit-house number six."

"Hey, Kleinbaas Fabian, the miesies is going to say I'm teaching you to swear."

"Then we stop under shady trees and Ma gets out the biltong sandwiches and pours herself a quarter tot because the road ahead is still long."

Pa sleeps the last bit past Beaufort. Once we can see the Du Toitskloof mountains in the distance, Ma wakes him up. The blue mountains bring tears to her eyes – the peaks and the vineyards, and the memories of her childhood in the Boland. I told Reuben all about it and he shook his head. He'd never been further than Cradock, our nearest town.

"And Miss Geertruida," I said. "Do you know how far she travels?"

But Reuben shook his head and said the donkey was now running full steam on its tracks and it was time for him to take up his position at the stoep door for dinner.

Night after night, as the guests came out for drinks and

17

dinner, Reuben stood alertly there. You'd never say he was not completely happy. A guest had only to raise a hand or snap his fingers, and Reuben would jump to attention with the speed of a cocked trigger. "He speaks so politely too, that Reuben does, and he knows whom to call Baas and Mister and Miesies; he has an eye for people, an instinct," Ma always said. "He twigs straight away who's who and what's what. Phew, if I only had ten Reubens, Hotel Halesowen would be a four-star establishment. Instead, we're just a flea-pit battling to keep out of the red."

"Ag," Pa would say then, "you're dramatising again. You're imagining you're still on the stage."

"All the world's a stage," Ma would say, and she'd get her tot measure out of the cupboard when she felt that her hand had been getting a bit heavy again, of late.

Or she'd brew a big pot of tea, get out her fortune cup and sit in the deserted dining room drinking tea and reading the tea leaves until dusk settled and Reuben stood behind her to ask for instructions about dinner.

Reuben didn't like talking to Tant Geertruida. He didn't even want to discuss her with me. When she arrived, he just nodded and carried all her baggage out and gave the instruction that the garden workers should rinse the worst of the dust off the Borgward with the hose pipe.

"Ag," Ma said, "the blacks have their own prejudices about females. It's her manly airs."

If I wanted to tell Reuben about Tant Geertruida's travels to London or Amsterdam, he looked away. I brought the book with the big colour prints of Van Gogh's paintings out to the donkey. I waited until the steam flag waved and Reuben put down his axe. "Have a look at this, Reuben."

I showed him the paintings, paging past the pavement café, the potato farmer, the yellow chair, the still-lives, the pair of boots, the portrait of Dr Gachet, the chief superintendent of Saint Remy, the bedroom at Arles, the colourful self-portrait.

"This boer's gone mad," said Reuben, taking hold of his axe. He split the thorn wood and threw it into the donkey's red mouth. The tank shuddered and the steam spewed out over the roof. "He is mad!" he shouted. The sweat ran down Reuben's neck. "The boer is mad!"

6

I chewed the bluegum leaves, savouring the Vicks taste in my mouth. I looked out over the plains as the coming night lowered coolness on to the whole of Soebatsfontein, the wisps of red evening mist lying over the plains. The wild geese called up the river course.

While Reuben's train spewed out steam, the guests walked up over the kikuyu round their rondavels, self-conscious in their freshly pressed clothes. The smell of their aftershave and perfume filled the air over the lawns, the footpaths and on the terrace. You smelled soap and hair oil and powder, and everyone spoke in lowered tones because the frogs had started croaking in the river, the lamps on the stoep were lit and, way in the distance, in the huts, you could see the flicker of workers' cooking fires.

"Evening brings such sweet sadness," said Ma, putting on a record. The waiters carried round drinks and the light sparkled on the polished glass. The children couldn't do as they did during the day – roll on the lawns or romp in the lucerne bales in the barn – and they hung about in their clean clothes, chatting among themselves and eyeing me.

I don't catch their eyes. Once Reuben's train was on its journey and he moved over to the stoep, I whistled for the dogs and set off for the orchard. It had a special night scent. The heat of the day hung trapped under the canopy of trees. As you walked from tree to tree you moved from coolness into warmth, coolness into warmth.

I circled further out, closer to the workers' huts, and smelt the maize porridge and offal that they were cooking and saw candles being lit on windowsills. I went past the milk shed and between the rondavels, standing empty now. From each rondavel emanated the smell which each family had brought with it from home.

With the dogs, I wove amongst the rondavels and approached the stoep rooms, but when I saw the guests' children playing there, I veered off past the kitchen and across under Pa's bedroom window with its tightly drawn curtains, and when I arrived at the stoep, Ma already had on her red earrings and her hair was smoothed back in a tight bun, gleaming in the light.

The Veteran appeared in the stoep light, as upright as a Christmas tree. He wore his dress uniform. Tant Geertruida sat at her usual table, with her back slightly turned towards the Veteran, so they didn't have to talk unless they felt the need.

Ma almost never sat still, flitting in and out of the kitchen and the bar, always ready to answer a question about this or that – mosquito bites, sunstroke, lost tennis balls, flat tyres or heartburn.

"Thanks goodness for Reuben," she sighed, walking back and forth from the kitchen through the main entrance to the stoep, busy with orders and requests: extra gravy here, a small salad at that table, a little dash of something there.

"Take this, Reuben," she'd say. "Stand in for me over there, Reuben." She'd go in and come out again. "Perhaps we should ask Reuben," she'd say. And: "Reuben, you never put a foot wrong, my Jack. Thank God."

Then Reuben would wink at me and stand stiff as a poker against the jamb of the stoep door, with his white napkin over his arm, the shiny tray precisely under the middle button of his jacket, and look far over the people's heads, away to the furthest hill.

But let so much as a finger stir, and Reuben would be there. Unless it were Tant Geertruida. Then Reuben would be as blind as an elderly dassie on a sunny peak of Dynamite Krantz.

"It's something we're just going to have to live with," said Ma. "Please bear with us, Geert."

Tant Geertruida waved her cigarette holder.

"Nothing surprises me any more," she'd say. "I am not at home in the world."

7

One night Pa and Ma and I saw the Beast. We'd been into town to see a John Wayne film at the Odeon and on our way home I had swaggered out like a cowboy to open the gates in the light of the Volkwagen's headlamps. Pa and Ma laughed and asked me where my six-shooter was.

"Atta, cowboy!" Ma called out as I climbed back into the car.

On our way to the last gate, right near the Scanlan irrigation canal, the half-human, half-orang galloped obliquely into the ring of light and then disappeared into a belt of thorn trees.

Pa stopped immediately. He switched off the Volkswagen's engine. The lights flickered feebly over the gravel road that stretched before us. We could hear ourselves breathing. The veld was black around us.

"Careful," Ma whispered.

"God . . ." Pa murmured. He opened his window and the smell of dew and the Karoo scrub came wafting in. The hair on my neck stood on end.

"What was that?" I asked.

"Let's go," Ma said suddenly. "Let's go!" And as we drove on, she whispered: "I saw him in my fortune cup . . ."

Everyone knew about the Beast, but this was the first time we'd seen him. He was very furtive and never left complete tracks, but if you could read the veld, you saw the half-moons of strange palms, the heel-print of an alien foot, the knuckle-marks of a half-man. One spoor was always deeper than the other. The Thing is lame, the farm workers always said. Or there were snapped branches, pig's ear succulents that had been dug up and half eaten.

The hotel waiters called the Beast Kikuyu, because some mornings bites had been ripped out of the kikuyu lawn round the furthest rondavels. The kikuyu runners that had been torn loose and half eaten lay scattered under the trees.

The waiters were afraid that the secretive Beast, who was obviously a loner, would come to catch himself a wife from among the young women in the huts. The farm workers' daughters dreamt feverish dreams under their jackal karosses. There were no unexplained pregnancies, but the men kept a watchful eye on all their women nonetheless.

One afternoon, when the Veteran and I crouched at the river to drink, he said the Beast could be a dream that had escaped someone's mind.

"Probably a nightmare, corporal," he said, grabbing hold of me and pulling me against the rough material of his tunic so that my cheek was pressed against his medals. Sometimes the Veteran wore his medals when we went on patrol, but usually he only pinned them on for dinner. From the time we had seen the Beast and Ma had told him about it, he wore the medals more frequently on expedition.

"Probably only a nightmare," he whispered against my ear, his whiskers tickling my cheek. "A nightmare, maybe escaped from the frightful dreams your poor confused daddy lies dreaming in his bed. Little dagga dreams, you know."

8

"Fabian, lovey," said Ma. "Get those three old *Reader's Digests* from the lounge and give them to Reuben. He's sitting there on the stoep in front of his room staring into space as though he's completely alone in the world. Shame."

Pa looked up sharply. "What are you up to now?" he asked. "Developing a reading culture among the workers? You've heard what's been going on with all the marches, and the burning of passbooks, and the Poqos are just here over the Kei and they are wild kaffirs, I tell you." Pa stood up. "It's because of education. The communists give the kaffirs books and then we end up with egg on our faces."

"Ag," said Ma, "what would we do without Reuben? To begin with, who will stoke the donkey? Every morning he polishes the guests' shoes. In all these years there never has been one complaint from the guests about their shoes. And the drinks he mixes! I sometimes wish I were also a guest who could snap my fingers and say, 'A dry Martini, stirred.' Or 'A Bing Crosby on ice.' Hell, man."

"That's still no reason to educate him," Pa muttered. "What does he want with a *Reader's Digest*? 'I am John's gall bladder'. Why would a waiter at Soebatsfontein want to read about the anatomy of a gall bladder? Or about how Hillary and Tenzing climbed Everest? Or about orang-utangs at the equator?"

"Maybe he'll recognise his family," laughed Ma, shooing me away to get the *Reader's Digests*. "And what's more," I heard her telling Pa as I scuttled off, "Geert thinks it's a scandal that the man sits there on his own day after day and has to steal newspapers out of the bin."

"I thought sister Geert was behind this," grumbled Pa. "It's those Dutch liberals again. They're forever messing around with Geert's head. Where's it going to lead to?"

I ran round to the back stoep where Reuben was watering the pot plants.

"What is Poqo, Reuben?" I asked. Reuben almost dropped the watering can. He turned his back on me and gave the hydrangeas a second watering. He loved those hydrangeas that Ma had brought from Cape Town. "What does Poqo mean?" I asked again.

He turned back and saw that I had the magazines. I could tell he didn't want to answer so I held the magazines out to him. "Ma sent these." I shook the magazines, but he didn't take them. "She said you're all alone in the world. They're for you to read. Take them, Reuben."

Reuben put down the watering can. He wiped his hands on

his pants and checked that they were dry. He went down on his haunches so that he was my height. He held one hand out to me, palm upwards. With the other he held the wrist of his outstretched hand. This is what the blacks do when they are very grateful. The giver can see both hands, there's no danger that the one hand will take a gift while the other holds a spear behind the receiver's back.

Reuben stood up with the magazines in his hands. "Poqo means we are going forward alone," he said quietly, then added in English: "We go it alone." He wiped his nose. I was surprised by his English; I'd never heard him speak English before.

"So you speak English, Reuben!" I cried.

He smiled and said: "Tell your Ma Reuben says thank you very much. Tell her Reuben will read them and maybe that will help him to be a better waiter."

"But, Reuben, you can't get any better. Ma says you're the best waiter in the world!"

Reuben's eyes brightened. "The meisies says that?"

"Ja. And Pa thinks so too. And Tant Geertruida."

"They say so?" Reuben carried on watering the plants.

"Yes, of course they do."

"Why don't they tell me, then?"

I looked at Reuben. "I don't know," I said. "But I think there are plenty more *Reader's Digests* where those three came from."

Reuben said nothing. He turned his back on me.

9

That night, the candle burnt in Reuben's room until the small hours.

"Reuben is on the road to education," Ma teased him next morning when he took up his position at the doorway with his white napkin and his tray. She came closer. "What did you read last night, Reuben?"

Reuben groped behind him and produced the three *Reader's Digests*.

"Here you are, missus," he said. "I read all of them last night."

"Good heavens!" cried Ma. "Are you sure, Reuben? Geertruida, Fabian, come and hear this. Our Head Waiter read three *Reader's Digests* from cover to cover in one night. Fabian, my boy, do you hear that? But Reuben, we must get you over to Kaizer Matanzima so you can lend a hand with the homeland Doctor Verwoerd wants to give you people."

Reuben turned away.

It was the first time he'd ever turned his back on Ma, in all the years.

Later, Pa said: "It just goes to show. Three *Reader's Digests* and the kaffir thinks he's white. Haven't you and Geertruida heard what Verwoerd said about Bantu education?"

Ma called out after Reuben. "Jack! Where are you off to now, my boy Jack!" Jack was the name white people called black men. I don't know why Ma decided to call Reuben Jack at this moment. I went and stood in front of Ma. I swallowed and wiped my mouth.

"Ma, Reuben must be tired after all that reading."

Ma looked at Reuben and then ruffled my hair. "That's probably it, Fabiantjie, and on top of everything, he has to keep the shoes shiny and stoke the donkey morning and evening and he's the only one who can offer a decent bar service and we always pick on him when the other waiters are drunk. Let's give him a break."

Ma glanced at the clock above the plastic roses. "Has the Boeing passed yet? Ag, no, it's only breakfast time. But it's panic stations already, hey, Fabian?"

She poured herself one for the nerves from the half-jack she kept near the phone book for emergencies. "Ag," she said, "these blacks can be so hard headed. I'm glad the Doctor wants to give them a homeland of their own. Then they can be hard headed towards each other to hell and gone."

She sipped from the brandy and looked at me. "But what would we do without our Reuben?" She sighed. "If blacks could only save, I'd have helped him save for a radio or a car, or something. But you know what they're like, Fabian. Just like children, these dark ones. Children of the night. And the Doctor speaks so beautifully."

Ma raised her drink to the sun. "A Commonwealth of Southern African countries, can you believe it? Everyone will look after himself and the show can go on."

She looked back to me and tilted her head. "Ag, man, you're still so young and those eyes of yours are like saucers, my boy. With all those questions and you stare, stare, stare, stare. Sometimes you remind me of a praying mantis, rubbing his little paws together and keeping an eye on us all.

"Okay, run along now, get out from under my feet. Run along and play. There's a good boy. Reuben, is breakfast ready? Morning, morning, have you had a good night's rest? Good day, good day. My but you're up with the fowls this morning. The usual table? Two English breakfasts? Mealie porridge for you? Hey, come on, this is the Great Karoo! There's pan-fried soft biltong. Just try it. And to follow, kudu kidneys and Leghorn eggs."

I went through to the kitchen and found Reuben at the wood stove where two dozen eggs sizzled in the big pan. He stood watching the egg whites bubble in the hot oil.

"Reuben . . ." I whispered. "Reuben . . ."

Behind us, the cooks banged and clattered, water hissed on pans as they boiled over and we were engulfed by the smell of dirty dishwater, vegetable peels, creamy milk, bacon and kudu kidneys. "Reuben!"

He turned to me.

"Kleinbaas Fabian," he said in a shaky voice. "You must steal some more books for me."

Pa issued an Order.

It wasn't every day that Pa summoned Reuben to give an order.

Pa usually stayed in the background, reading his Zane Grey Westerns. "Ma is the front man," he'd always say. But today he sent me to call Reuben. "Run," he said, "and tell Reuben to leave the guests' shoes. He can shine them later."

I rushed round to the back stoep where Reuben was sitting beside the donkey, buffing away at the guests' shoes. The shoes were laid out pair by pair. Reuben would start by rubbing polish into every shoe. Then he'd place them to one side in the sun so the polish could soak in. After a while he'd give each shoe another good brushing to spread the polish well into the leather. Then the shoe would go to one side again. Once they were all done, he'd go back over each one, rubbing it with a ball of scrunched-up newspaper until it shone. The finishing touch came with his special polishing cloth which put a sheen to the shoes. If the Veteran's boots were there, he'd spit on the toe caps and buff them until they looked like shaving mirrors.

"You can see your face in Reuben's toe caps," Ma would say. "He really is a faithful old soul."

"One of the best," said the Veteran. "He reminds me of the fighter kaffirs we used in the desert against Rommel. Our unit had the shiniest boots in the Africa Corps. Montgomery said so himself."

"Reuben," I called. "Pa says you must come to the reception desk."

"What about the shoes? Kleinbaas Fabian, the guests will start coming out for breakfast now-now. It's half past six."

"Doesn't matter, Reuben. This is an Order."

Pa was standing on the terrace with his feet well apart when I showed up with Reuben.

"Reuben!" he barked. "Unlock the Utrecht. See that you spray the flies. And switch on the ceiling fan."

Reuben sprinted off. "Fabian," said Pa, "go and get your aunt Geertruida out of bed. I want to speak to her in the Utrecht before breakfast."

I rushed off to the Wilhelmina. I knocked softly so as not to wake her too suddenly. She opened the door, drowsy and unsteady on her feet. She wore striped men's pyjamas and her hair was tousled from sleep.

"So what's happened to Reuben and the shoes this morning?" she asked, running her fingers through her hair. "Is one obliged to take one's English breakfast barefoot?"

"Could you . . . um . . . could you come now?" I ventured.

"Right now?"

"It's Pa," I murmured.

Tant Geertruida looked at me for a moment. She seemed to be waking up. "My poor old brother," she said finally. "Right. All right, I'm coming. It's obviously an emergency."

The guests were hanging out of their bedroom windows to see whether Reuben was on his way with the shoes. The fragrance of bacon and eggs, kudu kidneys and fried tomatoes came wafting over the lawns and the guests' toothpastey mouths watered.

Reuben was actually too busy getting the Utrecht ready and the guests were forced to shuffle out bashfully in an assortment of sandals and slippers over the kikuyu to the breakfast terrace. Some of them came barefoot on snow-white feet that obviously never saw the sun normally.

Ma made the best of a bad job. "Never mind, never mind," she soothed. "Take a seat, take a seat. A minor hiccup. After all, one doesn't eat with one's shoes. Two eggs? Merino kidneys on the side? Orange juice? Marmalade or honey?"

As she hurried past, she whispered to me: "Pa is furious. This is a showdown."

Ma only used that word when Pa went off to see the Neighbours or the Station Master or the School Headmaster or the Water Bailiff or the Magistrate. I knew that "showdown" meant days of phone calls, letters and squabbles. And, usually, tears for Ma.

Pa would stay in bed and you could hear the springs creak as he turned over. That was all – for days. He'd send his food back to the kitchen and wander round the big house with a candle or torch at night and Ma would lie wide-eyed, waiting to hear whom he was going to ring and whom he was going to see next.

We all waited until Reuben had thrown the Utrecht windows open. From the terrace, we could see the ceiling fan turning inside. Reuben swept the Utrecht's stoep steps and then marched up to the terrace with his broom over his shoulder. Pa emerged from the big house and made his way through the guests. Reuben escorted him back to the Utrecht to make sure all was in order. "Luckily," Ma said, "the Utrecht's Seasonal visitors are only due here tomorrow evening. Otherwise what ever would we have done with them once Pa got it into his head that he wanted to confront his sister Geert in the Dutch rondavel?"

Confront? I wondered. Tant Geertruida came walking over the lawn from the Wilhelmina. At the door of the Utrecht, Pa nodded to Reuben and went inside. Confront? Tant Geertruida looked up at us on the terrace and changed tack. She went into the Utrecht, closing the door behind her. We heard Pa's dark voice falling and then Tant Geertruida's hand appeared, pulling the windows shut. Reuben stood guard at the Utrecht door with his hands clasped behind his back.

"Listen," said Ma quietly, "it's a family conference. Let's turn our eyes away, Fabian, and let the brother and sister fight it out between them."

"What's it about, Ma?"

Ma looked at me. She looked at the guests and then down at the Utrecht. She drew a deep breath and pushed the curls back from her eyes.

"About Antjie," said Ma.

"Antjie?"

"Antjie Provee," said Ma, then she flapped her serving napkin in my face. "All right, that's enough, Fabian. This is big people's business. Go and sit down, sonnie." She turned back to the guests. "Would you like a boiled egg? And what about an extra spoonful of sugar in that coffee this morning?"

11

"I will not tolerate it," boomed Pa. He stood under the Utrecht fan. "Excise it."

Tant Geertruida sat wide-legged on the bed. Her hands rested on her thighs. They didn't meet each other's eyes because they were both furious.

"That'll be the bloody day," she said.

"You come and ensconce yourself here in my rondavel," blustered Pa, "and you suck this stuff out of your thumb."

"I'm a paying guest," warned Tant Geertruida, shaking a forefinger at him. Then her hand rolled into a fist, again on her thigh. Her fists were nearly as big as Pa's.

"Whether you're paying or not isn't the point. The point is . . ."

"It's ethical scientific research," yelled Tant Geertruida.

Pa swung round. He was deathly pale.

"If you bring this dirt out in public, Geertruida, that's the end of everything between us. You'll never set foot on Soebatsfontein again."

Tant Geertruida stood up. "But what on earth is the problem?"

Pa answered slowly, through clenched teeth. "It is not our culture."

Tant Geertruida went to stand at the Utrecht's window seat. She could see the aloes on the ridge from there.

"Our culture? What is our culture?"

"Our people's customs."

Tant Geertruida turned on him. "Those cowboy books you read – is that our culture? That cowboy singer who's on his way to do a show here in town? The Bible puncher in room

30

seven with his American fall-down Christianity? The Zephyrs and Studebakers parked out there? The bluegum from Australia? The plastic flowers on the reception desk? You and your wife's Bing Crosby records . . . are they our culture?"

Pa drew a deep breath. "Our language," he said. "The Afrikaans language."

"Just listen to the way your own wife talks," said Tant Geertruida. "Every third word is English. Although she was a so-called defender of the language when she was an actress. Is this the culture you're talking about? That doctor of yours with his New York line on psychedelia? Are these the things you want to keep pure?"

Pa sat down on the bed. He was as white as the sheets. Tant Geertruida yanked the Utrecht's door open and nearly sent Reuben flying. I saw her coming across the lawn up the terrace where Ma and the Veteran and I were waiting for the family conference to finish. She was wearing sandals, and behind her, through the open door of the Utrecht, I saw Pa sitting with his head in his hands.

Tant Geertruida was out of breath as she went past me. She didn't even greet me. She came to a halt in front of Ma. "I'm going to town for the morning," she said. "You lot can do your thing here." She turned on her heel and stumped off towards the Borgward under the bluegum.

Ma called after her, "But Geert, won't you even have just a little egg and a sliver of bacon?"

"I'll eat at the Masonic. And Fabian must come with me to open the gates."

Ma hesitated at first, but then gave in. It would be better if I were out of the way because she had to get Pa from the Utrecht to the breakfast table, and calm him down – and that with all the guests hanging about taking a keen interest in the family row.

Tant Geertruida grabbed my hand and we were in the Borgward before I could even greet her properly. She shoved a peppermint into my mouth. "For that foul taste in the mouth," she said, popping one into her own cheek.

We drove to town in silence. I hopped out to open the gates, waiting for Tant Geertruida to drive through, sullen behind the wheel. We drove along the Dynamite Krantz. The Collets were cutting lucerne in their back field. At the Barbers' someone sat working in a windmill's head piece. The eight o'clock train rumbled up and the passenger windows flickered past.

"I wish I could go to PE," I said.

"You must go to London, Fabian," snapped Tant Geertruida. "Or Amsterdam." She looked out the window. "You must stop thinking the world ends at Cookhouse or Noupoort."

Along Dynamite Krantz, where the road, the river and railway line ran close to one another at the foot of the slope, eagles hung in the air above their nests. The dassie sat staring blindly at us, drowsy in the early sun. At the Hennings' farm, the ostriches started running down the fence as we came up. By the time we passed them, they were rocking full speed on their funny toes.

"They want to race us!" I shouted.

That made Tant Geertruida smile. "They put their heads in the sand if they're frightened," she grumbled. "They reckon if they can't see anyone, no one can see them."

At the Karoo Café in town, Tant Geertruida had me jump out to buy the morning paper. We parked under the pines in front of the Masonic and went inside.

"Two English breakfasts, please," she said at the reception and we went and sat at a table in the big dining room with its white cloths and little yellow balls of butter in silver dishes.

"You see, Fabian, this is what a proper hotel looks like," said Tant Geertruida. But then she ran a hand over her mouth, took my hand and said: "Sorry, pupiltjie, sorry. I didn't mean it that way. Would you like some orange juice? I don't know whether one can order ice cream after breakfast, but we can try."

I rolled the ball of butter round on my toast until it started to melt. Then I spread it flat. I had already had breakfast at home, but I didn't tell her that. Our bacon and eggs came and

Tant Geertruida tucked in hungrily. I waited until she'd wiped her plate clean of egg and bacon fat with a piece of bread.

"Who is Antjie Provee?" I asked then.

12

Tant Geertruida called the waiter before answering me.

"Ice cream for the young man," she said. "And for me, a nice cup of coffee."

She leaned back, took out her holder, stuck a cigarette into it, slipped her notebook and Parker from her breast pocket and arranged them in front of her. She looked me up and down, blowing smoke to one side.

"You're growing up fast, eh, Fabian? This summer's full of things. Your head is probably spinning already."

I didn't answer, just played with a toast crumb on the tablecloth. It was sharp under my soft fingertip. Tant Geertruida sat forward and put a hand on my arm.

"You know, I think you're old enough now to know about certain things. I could avoid your question and say: let's rather go and see whether White & Boughton have any new books in, or we can go round the corner to the Karoo Café for Oros. But I think I'm going to tell you what your Pa and I were arguing about this morning."

I still didn't answer, just played with the toast crumb under my fingertip. I thought of the eagles circling above Dynamite Krantz. I thought about the way they'd drilled holes in the rocks there. I smelled the whiffs of gunpowder that smoked from the holes.

The sun was hot on the shoulders of the man holding the drill. As he finished each hole, he pushed in the sticks of dynamite. He fumbled and strained and sweated, cursing, but the wall of rock had to be opened. The trains and cars had to get through here. The land had to open up to the interior. The earth had to part.

The man straightened the fuses from the sticks and carefully attached them to the long fuse. He led the long fuse over the rocks and down the slope to the river bed. He had his workers stand back. "More, more," he gestured. "Back."

The workers withdrew with their picks and shovels over their shoulders. They looked up the rock face into the sun. The cicadas screamed in the bush at the river's edge. Crabs hid under the river pebbles. They would die from the tremors of the massive explosion. The cracks where dassies live would collapse, and they'd eat each other from hunger.

The man struck a match and held it momentarily above the end of the fuse. He turned and laughed at his workers. Then the flame leaped to the fuse and the spark ran up the rock wall like a shining lizard. The workers drew back further and their heavy boots threw up bright splashes as they stamped through the shallow waters. The man gestured to them and looked up to the sun.

Suddenly the rock broke and the dull thud made pigeons flutter to the sky for as far away as Kleingannahoek and Green Acres. Boulders rose up into the sky, blotting out the sun. Then they sank down again and the man's arms weren't good enough to stop them. Dust continued to settle and the smell of cordite hung in the air and the earth lay open, shamed and angry, while the workers scrambled back up the gravel and rocks with their picks and shovels, bewildered, calling to the foreman.

They looked up at tender tree roots that hung like pink snakes from the broken earth. Inside, the rock had all sorts of colours. The river water turned brown from all the soil that slid into its bed.

In time, people miles down, even as far as Golden Valley, could see from the river water that a huge catastrophe had taken place upstream.

"Pupiltjie?" asked Tant Geertruida. "Aren't you going to eat that ice cream?" I shook my head and Tant Geertruida's voice came from far away, through the daze.

"As I was saying, research is a strange business. Sometimes

34

it leads you to places you don't want to go. But that, Fabian, is the whole excitement of research. One minute, you still believe that one equals one, then suddenly you have three in front of you." She leaned forward. "Do you understand me, Fabian?"

I nodded, flattening my ice cream with my spoon. I didn't feel like eating it. I wanted to be out of the Masonic, back at Soebatsfontein. I wanted to go and sit with Reuben while he chopped the thornwood. I wanted to breathe in the nice smell of the wood – the smell that curled in my nostrils. I wanted to run off into the warm veld, feeling the sun bite the skin between my shoulder blades. I wanted to watch Ma as she wiped the corners of her mouth with her thumb and index finger and then shook her curls back from her cheek before picking up the phone.

Tant Geertruida put her hand on mine. "Often research shows you things you don't like." She looked at me. "And Antjie Provee is the kind of thing the family isn't going to like. A person isn't always what they think they are; you are those things you hide. It's the same with a nation." Tant Geertruida leaned back in her chair again. "Go on, eat your ice cream, boy." I took a mouthful of the ice cream. "See! I knew you'd be surprised. The old Masonic is famous for its condensed-milk ice cream. No one can get the recipe out of them."

I scraped my bowl while Tant Geertruida read the newspaper. And since she sat behind a page I licked the bowl clean with my finger.

She dropped the paper and stood up. "Fabian, it seems to me you've heard enough. If you want to know more about Antjie Provee one day, just ask."

I looked at Tant Geertruida who stood over me. "Does this mean we're coloureds now?" I asked.

Tant Geertruida looked at me, dumbstruck. Her mouth opened and closed again. "My world," she said. "But you're a fast one. You've guessed it all." She took my hand as we left the room. She pressed the money into the waiter's hand. "Keep the change," she told him. We went into the shade of the pine trees. "Just a touch of the tar-brush, pupiltjie," she said gaily. "Only adds spice."

We got into the Borgward. It smelled stuffy from being closed up. We drove through town and took the river road to Halesowen. Tant Geertruida's eyes swept over the lucerne fields. The river wound gleaming into the distance. "Ag, the Karoo is so beautiful. One feels as though one were living between the morning and evening stars here. Why do I always have to travel?" she asked, winding down her window so the wind could blow through her hair.

Below Dynamite Krantz she looked at me. "Great-grandma's great grandma," she said. "I came across some documents in Amsterdam. She was brought on a Dutch East Indiaman from Java to the Cape. She was a slave."

"Was she pretty?"

"Apparently as ugly as all hell," giggled Tant Geertruida.

13

Towards evening, I sat with Reuben as he stoked his train. The tank shuddered and steam spat from the flagpole. I watched Reuben's black forearms. He'd rolled up the sleeves of his white shirt, and the muscles knotted like rope round his arm.

"Do you know where Java is, Reuben?"

"No, Kleinbaas," he answered, resting his axe. "Is it beyond Noupoort?"

"A bit further."

"Do you take a train or a car to get there?"

"A ship, Reuben."

"A ship! But then you have to get to the sea first."

"Ja," I laughed.

Reuben bent to split another stump. I put a bluegum leaf into my mouth and watched a flock of white tick-birds drift slowly over the veld. The sky was already pink behind them.

Then I got a whiff of Tant Geertruida's cigarette. I swung round to find her standing behind me. She was watching us. Reuben saw her too.

"Miss Geert," he greeted her. She smiled and turned away. The screen door squeaked shut behind her.

I looked at Reuben in surprise. "You're rather friendly towards Tant Geertruida today, Reuben. Most days you won't even greet her. I suppose because she wears men's things."

Reuben threw another piece of wood into the train and glanced at me. "I've given the train a name," he said with a wink.

"A name! What name?" I picked another bluegum leaf and drew closer.

"No, stand back, Kleinbaas Fabian," warned Reuben. "Go sit there, in your place under the bluegum. The train is running very hot today."

"But what name?"

"Antjie Provee!" screamed Reuben, throwing his head back. He laughed until the dogs barked uncertainly. The bats came tumbling from the gable of the big house. They bubbled out, dipping and spreading through the air.

"Antjie Provee," laughed Reuben again.

14

Pa had to take his dose of LSD every day. Ma would send Reuben to the huts to call the son of our head cook, Boe. Willempie had to go out on the farm with me. Then Ma would lock their bedroom door and administer Pa's dose.

Some days the big house shook with Pa's nightmares. He rode on chairs into outer space. Under the bed, he visited a world beneath the sea with a kaleidoscope of fish, starfish and silver seahorses. He lay reciting wondrous songs and then wept, terrified, amongst Ma's dresses in her wardrobe.

Afterwards – when it was all over and he was asleep – Ma sat staring at the dim light of the lamp from the wind-charger. She'd sit in the dining room at table seven, among all the empty tables, content that all the guests were in their rondavels or stoep rooms and that Reuben had cleared up so beautifully.

She'd take a sip of brandy, staring into space, maybe fiddling with the knives and forks near her hand, and then lean over the dream book in which she wrote detailed reports for Dr Clark in Cape Town. There would be a red lipstick stain on the cigarette burning in the ashtray beside the lamp.

Dr Clark's instructions were that Ma should report on Pa's every dream to the best of her ability. In spite of her drama training and experience on the stage and at the reception desk, it must have been difficult for her to find words for the dregs of sentences, the dream colours, the shrieks of anxiety and the soaring flights.

But she would do anything to avoid that Pa should be coupled to the volt-machine at Mouille Point again. She never wanted to think again about how his eyes bulged out white, how the veins swelled on his arms and then hardened into impossibly thick knots, how his legs strained against the shackles, how his back arched and his chest sobbed out curses.

She did not want to imagine, months later, that she could smell gunpowder on his wrists and ankles.

It was going very well with Pa's dreams. In the evening Ma would sit and write continuously. Now and then she'd get up and go to the dining-room window to look out towards the rondavels in the dim light. She'd stand smoking and watch the moths – attracted by the lamp behind her – bounce against the window screens. Sometimes she saw the Veteran standing in the doorway of his darkened rondavel, his long, thin upper body naked, his shoulders crooked, and his face shrouded in shadow. He would grasp the mesh door of his rondavel as though he held it between him and the woman who stood smoking in the dining room.

Every evening, once done, Ma would stow the dream book behind her brandy in the drinks cabinet that stood beside the reception desk. One night I came upon the Veteran, crouched in front of the cabinet with the book in his hand. "I'm stealing brandy, Fabian," he lied and we stared at each other, both equally shocked.

The following year, Verwoerd was to break away from the Commonwealth, and – along with the other children at our school – I was to get a gold Republic medal and a small Republic flag.

15

The Veteran and I would often go for a walk together of a Sunday afternoon, with our walking sticks, our knapsacks, my many questions and his answers. We never encountered the Beast in broad daylight, although we were both prepared for a skirmish. Once we came upon a pile of canvas sacks under the karee thorns, from those robbers who got busy at night while the trains waited for the signals at Halesowen station. "Look at the booty," said the Veteran.

"We must go and tell Pa."

"No, corporaltjie, leave it be. We must allow others their adventures." The Veteran came upright and swung his knapsack over his straight back. He took up his stick. "Do you know the tale of Robin Hood, Fabian?"

We walked on and I cast one last glance over my shoulder. As we went down into the dongas near the river, the Veteran asked, "Does your father smoke dagga, Fabian?"

"No," I answered. "He works for America."

"Admirable," said the Veteran, showing me a splash of pee where something had relieved itself against the red wall of the donga. "Be prepared," he warned, tousling my hair, "Yankee soldier!"

16

Pa sat upright in bed.

With his hands he pushed the colours away from him.
Glowing paint dripped from his eyes, his nostrils and his ears.
Pink cotton candy foamed at his mouth. It fell on his chest in
flakes, sticking to the black hairs and melting on to the sheets.
He spread his wings and rose slowly. He circled round under
the ceiling. He lost his balance.

"I am a parrot," he said.

17

Unlike Ma, Tant Geertruida figured that Pa had drawn the
short stick with Dr Clark, the flamboyant Cape Town psychiatrist.

Eventually she found out from Ma that Dr Clark had studied in America. He'd just returned from New York before he
saw Pa for the first time. He'd visited clubs at night over there,
getting to know writers who were to become famous later: the
declamatory Ginsberg and the hitch-hiking Kerouac.

He had also experienced the wonder substance that could
cause a paradise to bloom in you and make the moon as pick-
able as a narcissus in the garden.

Armed with new ideas, Dr Clark had returned to South
Africa. One of the first patients to occupy the brown leather
chair before his desk came from the Fish River Valley – a
farmer whose eyes spun like two windmills in the dusk.

They sat opposite one another in Dr Clark's spacious consulting room. They could gaze through the window across the
lawns and past a couple of windblown palms this side of the
low wall. They could see the gulls, hanging in the wind, and,
further, the open sea, with the streaks of foam and kelp that

tossed restlessly on the swell. Far away – while they sat opposite each other and mostly stared out of the window – ships floated by like butterflies over the ocean.

Above Dr Clark's head there was a poem about New York City, printed in the shape of an apple. Pa sat looking at this over his brown forearms while he rubbed his eyes. He knew he had to say something. His sigh was like a breath of wind among dry leaves.

He would say anything that would keep him away from the volt machine in the armoured room in the furthest corner of the hospital, forty paces down the red polished passage round the corner from Dr Clark's office.

The foghorn reminded him that he must say something. Not far away children were packed together on the trucks of the model train. The engine driver – a grey-haired fellow – sat comically on the locomotive with his knees practically behind his ears, as the train rode round and round.

"You're very sad," Dr Clark said finally. "Do you want to tell me about it?"

Pa nodded and thought about his wife and child in the Volkswagen beyond the Hex River mountains, driving home to the guest farm at the foot of Buffelskop in the Fish River Valley.

"You've got six weeks to get me right," he told Dr Clark. "Then the harvest has to be brought in."

Dr Clark leaned forward. "If you're willing to walk a new road with me."

Pa made a slight movement as though this went without saying, and took his pipe and tobacco pouch from the pocket of the bright purple paisley dressing-gown that Ma had bought at Greatermans in Adderley Street. He filled his pipe with the slow deliberation of a countryman. When the blue tobacco smoke had filled the room and the calmness of the nicotine had settled on him, he could meet Dr Clark's eye.

Four hours later he was running naked over the lawn to the sea. The kelp was my head and Ma's head; the farm implements, which were waiting in the shed for the harvest, travelled past on the surface of the water. Ma floated upside down above it all, just like the figures on the Chagall postcards that Tant Geertruida always sent from Amsterdam.

Three male nurses with flapping white coats pursued Pa over the lawn. He was making for the sea, hell for leather. People on the pavements stopped to watch, forgetting to lick their ice creams so that vanilla melted and dripped down their knuckles.

Dr Clark stood at his office window, watching it all. He was surprised by the pinkness of the nurses' hands and forearms. They must spend very little time outdoors.

Dr Clark sighed and turned back to his desk to make a note in a file. "Euphoria," he wrote, "does not guarantee happiness."

18

On his arrival at Soebatsfontein, the Veteran had introduced himself as "Heathcote MacKenzie Esquire OBE, Veteran El Alamein." That had been two Seasons earlier. He'd been riding the north-bound train that passed Halesowen. While the train waited for the locomotive to drink its fill of water, the Veteran had fallen into conversation with the station master.

"What is that belt of trees down there in the valley?" he asked Station Master Ferreira. They stood and looked together at the brown plain that shimmered in the heat; wisps of mirage drifted in the lower parts, and the train lines ran to a single shining eye in the distance. The cars creaked in the heat and passengers leaned out the windows on their elbows, or went to get a drink of water at the tap under the pepper trees beside the platform.

The station master looked at the man beside him: the thin, almost ravaged face, the crooked nose, the black hair combed back from the high forehead. He recognised the bent wings of a crow in those shoulders and the hands were those of a man who had already undertaken many journeys and could get by with very little.

But that mouth . . . Although it was thin-lipped, there was a sensual curve . . . a hint of lustfulness.

"Ja, I had a good look at him," the station master said one day to Ma, "and I could see he was an interesting chap. Not a troublemaker, but a citizen of the world. A bird of passage. Quite different from the usual riff-raff that comes past here by rail, with their greedy eyes roaming over everything looking for something to scavenge. So I recommended Hotel Halesowen. He looked travel-weary."

The two men on the platform stood looking at the avenue of trees on Soebatsfontein. One could also see the green seam of the river. "It's a holiday farm," said Station Master Ferreira. "Cheap accommodation. There's a swimming pool and tennis courts, too. We always have Christmas and New Year's day dinners there, the wife and I. They braai an ewe on the spit."

The Veteran clambered back into the train, fetched his knapsack and his large shabby old leather suitcase, staggered back out on to the platform and asked the station master for a taxi.

"A taxi?" said the station master. He screwed his eyes up against the sun. "Does this look like Johannesburg to you?"

Carrying his baggage, the Veteran took a short cut through the veld and the dongas to the clump of trees in the valley bed. He battled to get it all through the fences and over the rocks, and Karoo scrub scratched the bottom of the suitcase, so that he had to carry it high, with a bent elbow. The sweat trickled into his eyes and a long greasy black curl flopped down over his face. He glanced up at the sun, reminding himself that he was a veteran of the desert, of the dune divisions, of sandstorms and quicksand and the blood and petrol smell of a war under the sun.

At the Scanlan canal, right near the Soebatsfontein gate, he sat down under a tree to rest. He pulled off his shirt and washed at the furrow. He pulled a comb through his hair and cleaned his nails with a thorn plucked from the tree. "Heathcote Mac-Kenzie," he practised quietly. "Heathcote MacKenzie."

Then he picked up his suitcase and knapsack again, and now more slowly than before, but still upright and as dignified as possible under the circumstances, made his way down towards the barking of dogs, the inquisitive faces of the kitchen staff at the windows, and Reuben who waited at the edge of the terrace holding his shiny tray like a shield.

In the course of time it became clear that the Veteran had no intention of leaving Soebatsfontein in a hurry. This was confirmed when he screwed a little sign to the door of the Van Riebeeck. He'd painted it himself. *Heathcote MacKenzie, Esquire. King's Brigadiers (Veteran El Alamein)*.

He paid his rent every month in shining shillings which he sent in a small envelope with Reuben to the reception desk. It became an entire ritual. On the first morning of each month, Ma would send Reuben to the Van Riebeeck at exactly eleven o'clock with a tray of tea.

Then Reuben had to ask the Veteran whether he had any special requests – perhaps a box of matches? Or the latest *Reader's Digest*? Or a peeled yellow peach, chilled in the fridge?

This was the signal for the Veteran to count out his shillings and to lick the flap of the envelope with his purple red tongue. On the front of the envelope he wrote our surname followed by *Proprietors*. On the back, his own name and *Esquire*.

Shortly afterwards, Reuben returned with the envelope of shillings on his tray. Because the Veteran always paid his rent in advance, Ma would then say to Pa: "The Major will be staying on for another month, thank goodness. That takes care of my cigarette and brandy money."

She'd go off and lock the shillings into the drinks cabinet with the dream book behind the bottles. From the beginning she and Pa had agreed that the Veteran's rent shillings would be her pocket money. For women's magazines, for bath salts, now and then, for cigarettes, the Oude Meester, for earrings or new summer sandals. And for the unexpected – perhaps for the day Tant Geertruida invited Ma to come with her to London to visit the theatres of the West End, if Pa felt better, and Ma could find someone to relieve her at the front desk.

"My nest egg," Ma would say, letting the shining shillings slide into her palm. She stroked her fingertips over the shillings. Her fingertips slid over the Veteran's shining medals, pinned to his heaving chest.

To seal the contract anew, Ma would send a plate of crackling and toast, biltong slivers with fresh white bread, or a bowl of apricots, burnished gold by the summer sun, down to the Van Riebeeck.

This was Ma's token of appreciation of the man who had become part of our family during the long lonely days between Seasons. In later years, two years after Pa's death, she would marry the Veteran, in spite of the fact that he had serious problems with his prostate. When I hid behind the door of the ablution block, I could hear how he groaned and urinated drop by drop.

Those were the groans of a man who had loved many women and now, in his quieter years, had to pay for his indiscretions. For some reason or another, Ma fell in love with him. Pa's death, years after the season of 1960, relieved Ma and the Veteran of the burden of hiding their love from the world. It was only I – wandering between the rondavels, or lying on my stomach on the cool floor next to the reception desk – that knew early of their love.

And, in the Season of 1960, I – like them – already realised that Pa's increasing feverish hallucinations would eventually drive him permanently into the nightmare paradise where he could gallop for eternity through dream landscapes.

No one was visible to Pa in his last years. No one died lonelier than he. You could see it in his eyes during his last stretch. Even though he still breathed and although his eyes were still open, he saw no one and nothing.

His eyes were as clear as a Karoo morning, as clean as the wind across the plains.

"I was in love, once," the Veteran recounted.

It was winter and the Veteran, Pa, Ma and I sat in front of a crackling fire in the family lounge, next door to the guests' bigger sitting room. Tant Geertruida's call had come through that afternoon: we must reserve the Wilhelmina – she needed a Karoo summer.

Now the Veteran was telling us about his first love.

"Every morning," he recalled, while his cold cigar hung from his fingers and he sipped his brandy, "I'd ride through the little town on my bike to get the paper. The doctor had recommended this exercise for the hole in my heart. And for the war wounds." He looked at his cold cigar. "At that time I smoked too, on top of everything else. A youngster has limitless faith in his body."

"Which little town?" I asked.

The Veteran waved his hand as though he wanted to wipe my question out of the air. "Ag, corporaltjie," he said.

"Fabian," warned Ma. "Rather chuck another log on the fire. Come, come, the hearth is your responsibility."

The guests laughed in the sitting room next door. One of them had told a joke. The Veteran got up and closed the door. His crooked shadow sneaked over the wall. Pa looked at it, caught my eye and looked away again quickly. He chopped biltong, piled the slivers on a board and passed them round.

The Veteran sat down again. He looked at the game of patience he had laid out before him.

"Ja?" asked Ma.

"It was a wonderful experience to cycle through a town like that in the early morning. People were hurrying off to work. Some workers were already standing in front of their shops waiting for managers to open up so the day could begin. There was a feeling of energy and expectation.

"She appeared on the pavement with a guide dog. She had the confidence of one who could see everything – and more.

The dog was a tired old Labrador. At first glance she wasn't really pretty.

"But it was her smile."

The Veteran straightened the cards before him. Pa sent the biltong board round. "Ja?" asked Ma.

"I was immediately, irrevocably, in love with her smile." The Veteran ran a forefinger over his medals. "I cycled past. We were moving in opposite directions. We were close only for a second or two."

The Veteran looked at me. "The blind smile differently from other people. They smile inwardly. They are not distracted by the things they see around them. How wonderful it would be to love a woman like this! I thought. A woman who lived by smell and touch and the tone of a voice. A woman who'd forgive me my hooked nose, my untidy mustache, my crooked crow's shoulders and who'd feel that my skin was as soft as a baby's and that my touch could be as tender as a woman's."

The Veteran stroked his forearm. His long fingers slid over the crooked veins on the back of his hand. I looked at Ma. She was leaning forward and had forgotten to eat the biltong in her hand.

"Ja?"

"A woman who would inhale, with my body odours, the smells of army expeditions, of glorious victories, of terrible suffering, of heroism. One who would listen to my dreams and realise that, trapped in the broken body of a wounded war veteran with a heart defect, the heart of an Apollo may lie concealed."

The Veteran fell silent, waiting for Ma to ask again: "And then?"

"A woman who would not insist on the visible wealth of the world, but who could lose herself with me in the hum of bees in blossoms, the sting of broken dreams, Grieg's music, the poetry of the balladeers. A woman like this would value the touch of my breath on her cheek more highly than a new car, my voice more than brand new clothes . . ."

"And then?" Ma prompted.

The Veteran was silent again, staring into the flames.

"Ja?"

"I have to admit it. I began to follow her. She was the switchboard operator at the magistrate's court. Every day she sat there with voices buzzing in her head like a swarm of bees. She only spoke to me once."

"Ja?" asked Ma.

"Are we getting to the point yet?" asked Pa, using his teeth to tear a strip of sinew off the remaining biltong.

"I was still healing from my wounds and I couldn't walk fast. I limped. My heart also remembered the stresses of the battle-field. But as soon as I was on her tracks, a new energy took hold of me. The dust clouds of the Western Desert were forgotten. Gone were the grindings of tank gears, the groans of the wounded. Every morning, she and I wove through the morning streets. We were like angels on wings."

"Oh, how lovely!" said Ma, swaying her body as though she had a hula-hoop round her hips.

"We wound our way through the people, I a little way behind her, so that she never heard me, and the Labrador, a messenger of the gods, up front."

"In the winter months, clouds of condensation bloomed from our mouths. In the summer our skins glowed like apricots. I was never closer than five paces behind her, but it was close enough to breathe in her fragrance. The light scent of her sweat was as fragrant to me as a thousand roses; like vitamins for my exhausted body. My blind love!"

The Veteran leaned forward, staring intently into the fire. The flames flashed on his medals. He felt the cards with his fingertips as though he couldn't see the pictures. Gently he traced the outlines of the King of Hearts and the Queen of Aces. He shook his head.

"Ja, and then?"

But he only shook his head.

"She only spoke to you once?"

The Veteran sighed. He gathered the cards into a pack and

48

divided them in half, placed them close together and shuffled the cards so the two piles melted together. He did it so fast you could scarcely see his hands move.

"One morning, the morning before Heroes' Day, the day that commemorates the heroes of the war, she suddenly stopped on a street corner. By then I had been following her for seven months, morning after morning, without ever speaking to her. My body and soul were too broken to approach her.

"For hours on end, I had stood behind her, in the doorway of her office in the court building. I had watched her fleet hands that had kept up with a thousand requests. Her hands darted like butterflies over the lights and holes of the switchboard. And she sat there like an angel with a smile on her lips."

The Veteran's shoulders were hunched up over his medals now so that the row of eyes were in shadow. He stared down at the floor.

"Just once?" Ma asked quietly.

"She stopped all at once on the street corner. I had to stop short so as not to bump into her. She turned to me slowly. People hurried past us – businessmen with newspapers under their arms, school children with heavy satchels. A pall of exhaust fumes hung in the air because so many cars idled at the stop signs on that corner.

"She turned her face to me. Her half-closed eyelids fluttered. I could see the whites of her eyes behind her eye lashes. 'You started following me on the second of December,' she said. 'It was a Tuesday.' That is what she said first."

The Veteran sighed and looked at Ma. "And then?" asked Ma. Pa was also sitting forward.

" 'You must stop following me now. I can smell that your healing is nearly complete. At the beginning there was the smell of wounds and ointment and scar tissue. But it's over now. You smell like a healthy man again. I can hear from your footsteps that you aren't limping any more. I can hear from your breath that our morning walks have made you fit again.'

" 'Is that why you walked faster and faster?' I asked. She nodded."

The Veteran sighed again. "She didn't smile while she talked to me. 'You must understand fully,' she said quietly. 'I do not love you. You must live your own life now. It is over.'"

The Veteran looked at Ma. "And then I boarded my first train," he said.

Ma gazed at him for ages.

"There were many trains, over many years. People forget their war heroes."

"Until you got here," said Ma.

"Until I got here," he nodded.

Pa got up, handed the biltong board to me and walked out.

20

It was a moonlit summer night. Tant Geertruida and Ma had sat up late, talking. The pepper tree leaves stirred silvery in the night. The bluegums threw scraggly shadows. The guests' cars gleamed under the thorn trees, and the whitewashed lime-stones that marked out the parking places looked like balls of crunched-up paper.

Ma stooped over Pa and noticed that a string of drool hung from his sleeping mouth down to his neck, creeping over his shoulder and down to form a damp patch on his pillow slip. She lay for a long time looking at his face. She had her memories, she comforted herself, and now Pa's face was the cinema screen where other, better days were replayed. But she was amazed at how little she remembered. There was only the clear scene: Pa cycling into Jonkershoek in his Stellenbosch blazer, far ahead of her, teasing her because she was so tired. "Have you lost your breath?" he'd call to her over his shoulder, his jacket lapels standing pointed in the wind. It seemed he could rise, soaring over the green-blue valley, over the vineyards and the hazy mountains, her Karoo prince full of promises and declarations of love.

Ma's dreams flickered out over Pa's face. The clear pictures melted away against his cheeks. She saw only his sunken eyelids, his eyebrows like hairy caterpillars, his teeth gleaming, slightly slimy behind his parted lips.

She threw the sheet back and swung carefully out of bed. She felt the cool floorboards under the soles of her feet. The night dress sucked against her soft body, full of static. She knew that she smelt of night cream and bath salts, but she was too accustomed to the odour to smell it herself. She knew that she had passed up too many chances. The evening's brandy was already sour in her throat.

She sat and waited until the two o'clock train came past under Buffelskop, the mosquitoes stopped circling and hung, light-footed, from the ceiling. She heard the roof creak again as it cooled down and a last breeze rustled through the pepper trees.

The night held its breath and all was still except for the alarm clock's minute hand that jumped forward every sixty seconds. Time pressed down on her, trying to smother her, press her back against the bed. Sitting there, she was conscious of battling against a heavy body that panted over her, wanting to have its way with her. She just didn't know what it was. It pressed against her, this thing with no name. But it had a breath, rank against her cheek.

Then, as though she'd made a decision, she stood up. She didn't need to be too quiet: few things roused Pa from his remedy sleep. Dr Clark had prescribed a dark gold sleeping remedy and Pa's head fell lifelessly to one side within minutes of his taking it.

That made Ma worry about our being alone in the big house – specially out of Season – what with the unrest among the blacks. Instigators were busy on the trains and nipped over the Karoo fences at night. "They'll come and murder us all one of these days," said Ma. "Like the Mau-Mau did in Kenya – they even cut the cattle's tendons. Only a black can be that cruel to a dumb animal."

She threw her dressing gown over her shoulders. It billowed

for a moment in the warm air; a cloud of satin. Then gently, with a sigh, it sank over her shoulders and took on the shape of her body.

The passage floor was even cooler. Reuben thought that a water course must run under the passage. In the rainy season he would kneel with his face right down near the floor, and point out specks of mildew on the wall. "There's water running under the house," he would say. "We could sink a borehole right here in the room." Then Reuben would laugh and hurry back to the stoep with his tray.

Ma smelled moisture and coolness in the passage. At my bedroom door she paused to make sure I was breathing peacefully. I was the one she had to think of now.

Then she crept to the hallway and through the dining room to the side door. On the stoep she felt the gravel under her feet. It was a pleasant feeling. Then she was on the kikuyu and she was free.

She moved quickly and the dressing gown made a bell of air round her. It was transparent, so her body movements were visible: the breasts which had already sagged a little, but were still attractive; the hips still firm after only one son; the sway of her back, bowed inwards and danced into strength during school ballet and the movement classes of her drama training at Stellenbosch; the dark triangle at her groin; and her hair which streamed out behind her as she hurried along – a shining flag in the wind.

Not one of the dogs – neither ours nor the guests' town pooches – raised a head. No monkey barked a warning from the cliffs near the river. The trees looked the other way as Ma moved over the kikuyu to the rondavels.

She heard only the grass whispering against her bare feet. The Veteran's rondavel door was open. The windows had been thrown open too. The shutters stood wide.

Through the mesh door she saw a dark form on the bed. She grasped the cool handle of the door. All the mesh doors at Hotel Halesowen squeaked. She knew he would wake up if she opened the door. She hesitated. His medals shone from their resting-place on the red velvet cloth. The gun barrel gleamed against the cupboard.

She hesitated.

Suddenly he touched her shoulder from behind. She swung round. He stood there in his old coat. The moonlight carved sad shadows over his face. She realised that the dark shape on the bed was only a shadow – a spell cast by the moon and the night. They said nothing. Neither did she turn to him. Her fragrance engulfed him and she inhaled the gun oil and Brasso smell that always hung about him. There was also a faint flavour of wet canvas, as though it had penetrated his skin during his days in the veld. She felt his eyes running from her neck and down her back. She felt completely naked and then she turned round, pushing him out of the way and disappeared into the orchard.

He stood on the steps of the Van Riebeeck's stoep, surprised by his own calmness, but once she was gone, his breath started rushing in and out over his tongue, as though it were a physical thing. After a while it steadied a little. He opened the mesh door and went inside. He lit the oil lamp and while the lamp chimney warmed up slowly, he cupped his hand round the curve of the glass. He watched the little flame gleam in his red hand. As it got hot, he had to withdraw his hand. He pressed it against his lips. It was the first time he had kissed Ma. Her mouth tasted of the orchard and he brushed a peach leaf from her hair. She was surprised by his lean, sinewy body and the veins that writhed like snakes over his arms, his legs and his lower body. In the moonlight, they looked like black worms feeding on him.

She shuddered when he raised his body and she saw the shiny penis head just before he shoved it into her with a gasp of breath and she felt the forgotten pleasure in her pelvis.

They were unsure of each other's bodies. It was the first time and there was no rhythm in their movements. Their breath searched here, fumbled there; their hands were surprised and disappointed. They smelt strange smells and eventually rolled as far away from one another as the divan allowed.

They lay staring at the roof of the rondavel, waiting for the first word to fall.

21

Dr Clark with the lightning-blue eyes and tousled fringe sent a telegram saying he could be expected the following Wednesday. Decent, private accommodation should be reserved and the bill sent to The Superintendent, Mental Research Division, Somerset Hospital, Mouille Point, Cape Town. Ma had to use promises of a reduced tariff begging the guests who had already moved into the Bitter Aloe to move into one of the stoep rooms.

The Bitter Aloe was the most private of the rondavels, and the stoep rooms were packed in, stuffy and close to one another, right near the terrace.

The guests moved out sulkily when Ma told them it was a booking error, but they felt better when Ma sent Reuben with a sack of kudu biltong. "Ag, what the hell," said Ma, pouring herself an emergency tot, "they're staying for a song now. Where else in the Karoo could you get all this for so little? Plenty of water, tennis courts, a swimming pool, a bar service to die for – thanks to Reuben – and these gorgeous evenings on the terrace with the stars so close you feel like you could pick them and hang them from you ears."

Ma stood for a long time with Dr Clark's telegram in her hand. She leaned over the reception desk and sniffed absent-mindedly at the plastic roses. She clean forgot to offer the customary glass of Oros to the station messenger who had ridden the two miles from Halesowen Station on his old bone-shaker to deliver the telegram.

I went to the kitchen, poured the orange Oros into a glass, added water and went to the paraffin fridge for ice. With the ice blocks clinking against the glass, I brought the drink to the man. He was Station Master Ferreira's son. His mother was drinking herself to death in the shack under the thorn trees, just behind the station building.

Ma was still standing there holding the telegram. "Ag, my boy, what next?" she asked, going for the emergency-tot bottle.

Her hand shook slightly as she poured. She took the first sip with her eyes closed. "Aitch-a-aitch," she said.

Then she became aware of me, standing at the door biting my nails.

"Cheer up!" she said. "There isn't anything that you and I can't handle. What do you say to that, Fabiantjie?" She took another sip and looked at the station messenger, the boy with the bow legs. "But just out of the blue, he wants to come here!" she said. "And that while a very, very busy Christmas lies ahead and we might even get the cowboy singer too."

"Ja," I added, "and the Pastor in room three."

Ma nodded and looked at me. "Ag shame, sonnie," she said, "you're being forced to grow up so young. You're a real hotel kid." She got that dramatic expression left over from her days on the stage. "A child of numbered rooms." She came up and pressed me close. She bent over me. Her breath smelt of brandy.

"You mustn't think that life is just a row of hotel rooms, Fabiantjie," she said quietly. "Passing through is not all that life offers. You can put down roots, sonnie. You only need to find the right place to do it."

But I had already freed myself from her embrace, slipped past the reception desk and out the door. I whistled for the dogs, blew my nose out over the grass in the way that Ma forbade, and sauntered off to the Van Riebeeck.

It was a lazy morning and the door stood open. He lay on his back on the divan with his eyes on the ceiling. His tunic was unbuttoned and for the first time I saw his white skin – as white as dough. A few hairs sprouted round the wrinkled nipples. There were ridges on his skin as though it had been pinched. I remembered his stories about the battles, the clatter of machine-gun fire and how hot lead is when it comes out of the barrel of a gun. "It melts through your flesh," he'd said.

I didn't knock but stood watching him awhile. On the bed-side table lay Montgomery's biography and a book called *Operation Desert Fox*. A crumpled rag with finger stains on it lay beside the Brasso tin. The row of medals were laid out on the red velvet cloth. The 303 stood propped up beside the cupboard and that was all there was to be seen – only the table and chair with the lamp, the mosquito lamp on one windowsill, and the candle in a candlestick on the other.

The Veteran never referred to his rondavel as "my room" or "my rondavel" like the other guests, but as "my barracks". Or sometimes "my quarters". And he kept it as spick and span as a barracks in a military camp. "Spick and span!" Ma always exclaimed when she did her rondavel rounds to see what the cleaners had been up to. "He Brassoes the door-knobs himself."

If Pa started complaining about the Veteran's perpetual presence – even in the evening in our family rooms – Ma defended him by referring to his habits. "At half past five sharp, summer and winter, he goes over to the ablution block," Ma would say. "The man is disciplined. You can tell he was an officer, a major."

Pa blinked and he was in a boat on the Mouille Point sea. The boat took him into currents and winds that we did not know. It jerked and bobbed and glided on stormy waves. Kelp tangled round the boat and Pa was not alone there. The body fell against him as the sea tossed and it was he or Pa. They wrestled and Pa felt dank hair brushing over his face, the strong, muscular body that pumped against him, the hairless stomach and the erect penis. The devil's paws trod on Pa's bare feet and he felt he was being overwhelmed. It was as though the breathing over him were drugging him. Consuming his breath. Pa let his head sink back and Ma bit her finger. Her eyes darted to the drinks cabinet and then, guiltily, at me.

I felt the same thirst stir in me. Pa's darkness surged in me as I walked alone along the river paths among the river reeds. The clammy smell of the river banks and the frog slime was in my nose and vervet monkeys romped mockingly in the trees. They knew me; I didn't carry a gun. I came to sit here to quench my thirst, to ask questions like Tant Geertruida's sharp questions when she stood with her feet parted and her hands on her hips.

"Things are getting tough here at Hotel Halesowen, Fabiantjie," said Ma, swaying on her feet. She'd had a little too much to drink because Dr Clark was on his way and there were rumours that the blacks were going to overrun the country. She went to the reception desk to do her crossword. She could only think standing up, said Ma; a habit you developed in the theatre. Pa went to lie down, whimpering softly on his bed. I stood watching him and saw how his eyelids fluttered. I picked up the smell of medicine that hung about the room – the remedies that Dr Clark and Dr Lyell in town had prescribed for Pa: for his insomnia, for his temper tantrums, for his sadness, for his stomach ache, for the stabbing pain in his chest, for his heartburn and his migraine, for his nightmares and for his anxiety attacks.

Beside his bed stood the pile of *Path of Truth* booklets which Pa always read with his short pencil in his hand. The booklets bore witness to the redeeming power of Jesus Christ. Every month – along with the *Beano* comics Tant Geertruida had subscribed to for me in London – a new *Path of Truth* booklet came from the Halesowen station. When Pa sighed, Ma would always ask, "Have you worked through this month's *Path of Truth* yet?"

And when things got as rough as they did during those days leading up to Dr Clark's arrival, with Pa and Tant Geertruida barely greeting each other over the Antjie Provee affair, Ma would ask me, "Have you read your comic through yet?"

Tant Geertruida had said I must read comics "because humour is good for a young man from the Karoo. Karoo people are too stern. English humour is the best. If Fabian can learn to laugh at the Bash Street kids, he'd be free of the other humourless kids at his school who just want to thump each other on the rugby field and the enemy on the battle-field."

Pa had nodded when Tant Geertruida had asked if she could subscribe to comics for me. "As long as he also reads Afrikaans," he'd said. "Have you read *Stinkie en sy maats*, Fabian? And *Patrys-hulle*? And what about *Seuns van die wolke*?"

"Stinkie and Patrys," snorted Tant Geertruida. "When the whole wide world is waiting out there for Fabian. With his noggin he can go and study overseas."

"First our own," said Pa.

"Quite so," said Ma.

"Ag, the Nationalist crusade," Tant Geertruida sighed.

"SAP," snapped Pa, walking out.

I sniffed Tant Geertruida's suitcase with the labels from many lands. It smelt of platforms and ships and airports and foreign hotel rooms. It was a smell I couldn't quite place. Did it stink, or was it a nice smell?

I thought about Dr Clark who was on his way. I'd already heard so much about him, but I'd never seen him. We'd been to drop Pa at Mouille Point and Ma had helped him move into his room, and when they had come out he was in the new dressing gown that I hadn't recognised.

"I'd like to ride on the little train," I said.

"No, Fabian, we have to leave immediately," said Ma.

"But I want to ride on the train." I had looked at the children fluttering on the miniature train like happy washing. I saw their parents standing at the fence and waving. "The little train!"

"Fabiantjie, boy," Ma said fiercely, "we must stick together now."

"The little train!"

"Pull together, son."

"Ride the train, ride the train!"

Ma and Pa's faces were wet when they kissed each other. Pa stood in the wind under the palms. Wind clouds boiled over the mountain.

"The sea is so grey," said Ma as we drove off. "We'll sleep over in Laingsburg tonight." When I looked round to wave to Pa, there were two men, one standing on either side of him.

"H-A-H," said Ma, catching my eye in the rear-view mirror.

"Hang on, arsehole, hang on," I answered.

"Fabian!" cried Ma tearfully. "You're impossible."

22

Dr Clark rapped his knuckles on the front desk. The plastic flowers trembled. "The remotest rondavel," he said.

Ma and Reuben had to go across to the Bitter Aloe with him so that he could inspect it before moving in.

Tant Geertruida sat at her table on the stoep and looked him over in silence. "A New Yorker," she told me. "You can smell them a mile off, pupiltjie. The Beat Generation. They say they're going to turn the world upside down. But I think he's going to get his come-uppance here at Soebatsfontein. He looks like a bit of a lightweight to me. You know how the men are in our family. There's no stopping them. Horribly spoilt by their mothers and rejected by their fathers. They think they're generals but they can't understand why the war is so fierce."

"God forbid," said Ma when she and Reuben walked past us to where Dr Clark waited on the lawn with his luggage. Ma escorted Dr Clark. The Veteran watched the proceedings through an open window in the Van Riebeeck. Ma was wearing her powder-blue summer dress and her hair was fastened high in a bun. She had no idea what Pa might already have told Dr Clark about her. She felt defenceless, forlorn. Betrayed. It's unfair, she thought, this man knowing things about me, and me not having a clue what he knows. Maybe he even knows the most intimate things.

Tant Geertruida gestured to Reuben. "Ag, Reuben, old chap," she said, "bring me a beer with a good head on it, and very cold, mind. And let Fabian have a taste of the lemonade from the guests' fridge for a change. With ice, you hear?"

"That must go," gestured Dr Clark in the Bitter Aloe. "And that, and that thing too. This too, please. And that object. There, too, yes, there. That one too, if you don't mind."

"The stuff that had to be removed, was all the clutter," Ma told Pa later, "although I'd also say it was everything that made the place homely. And then the apple had to be hung up – a kind of picture in words. Reuben had to make it snappy, the little doctor knows exactly what he wants. The apple above the bed – in place of the Pierneef print – can you believe it?"

In preparation for his sessions with Pa in the Bitter Aloe, Dr Clark pointed first to the painting of Blood River, with the Voortrekker rifles spitting fire and wounded Zulus writhing in the water like ants.

Dr Clark must have been afraid, I thought, that the painting would distract Pa into talking about the Black Threat and History.

The second picture that had to go was a print of the Narrow and the Broad Ways – which hung in all the rondavels and stoep bedrooms. "It's a necessary wall decoration," Ma always said, "to remind us of our ups and downs."

Beside the Broad Way, carafes of wine were depicted along with flowers, baskets of fruit and beautiful woman who guarded the road. The Narrow Way headed in a dead straight line to the gates of heaven with only a couple of faithful cherubs hanging about. If you looked at that little road, you could imagine that it ran through the hills and aloes to where the light burnt white in the summer heat.

"The Gideon Bible too," requested Dr Clark, and Ma remarked later that it was his New York habits that prompted him to make that request because the good Gideon Brothers had seen to it that there was a Bible in every hotel room in the country. "Why does the little doctor suddenly want it to be removed?"

Ma looked to Pa, but he didn't answer. "It's not as though we're a bunch of Bible punchers." Ma swirled the ice in her brandy, "But its comforting to know that Joseph, Rahab, Joshua, Noah and Rebecca, or whatever their names are, are within easy reach, ready to be picked up. All those beautiful stories!"

She looked at me where I lay on the stoep with my cheek against the coolness and my nose right up against the geraniums. "Isn't that right, Fabiantjie?"

I spat small drops and watched the thirsty stoep ants run up to the pearls of saliva to drink. Periodically, Ma would remember that religion was also part of upbringing and then she'd throw pious sentences at me, like: "When did you last page through your New Testament, Fabian?" Or, "Do you remember the first verse of Psalm twenty-three? Those lovely words, 'The Lord is my shepherd'?" Or, " 'I will lift up mine eyes unto the hills, from whence cometh my help'?"

Pa was the religious one. But he never set foot in the church at Cradock and the dominees and parish council were frightened to set foot on Soebatsfontein when it was their turn because Pa was always argumentative. "The virgin birth?" he asked. "Are you crazy?" Or, "Do you really think God walked through that garden where Adam and Eve were kafuffling? God? Does He wear sandals? Walking around there like the neighbour? And since when can a snake talk?"

"Blasphemy!" and they fled through the farm gate.

They said Pa's *Path of Truth* booklets were sectarian. Dodge City was too dangerous for them. "John Wayne has chased the deacons out of town again," Ma would say, swaying her hula-body and winking at the Veteran.

Now the dominee and the parish council and the deacons never came by. But Pa prayed for hours. When the nights were humid and the dogs stirred restlessly outside and the workers made a drunken racket at the huts and the guests were asleep, he sat by the oil lamp and shook his head when Ma offered the dot of LSD or the sleeping remedy.

He lay with his eyes closed and if a nightmare woke me and I stumbled to their gloomy room Ma would gesture that I must be quiet, because Pa was talking to his Lord.

And the plastic flowers that Ma had sent down specially to the Bitter Aloe from the reception desk should also be removed, indicated Dr Clark. "Obviously for emotional purity," Ma grumbled, but Pa had stopped listening a while ago to the list of things Reuben had to carry out of the Bitter Aloe. He sat there on the terrace listening to the guests' cars tick-tick-tick as the shadows moved over the metal.

Eventually, Ma came to sit beside Pa. "What a day!" she said. I crept over the cool grass and under their chair legs. Ma's calves shone and tiny spikes of black stubble dotted her shins. I stroked gently over them.

"Ooh, Fabian! You're tickling!"

I ran my fingers through the hairs on Pa's calves. "Any fleas?" he joked.

My saliva made stripes on the shale that had been bedded into the lawn to form part of the shale path. As I lay under there, they couldn't see that I was using my saliva to draw little pictures.

"Bitter Aloe!" Pa shouted unexpectedly, jumping up. His mood had changed out of the blue and he gave Ma and me a fright, she from her emergency tot and I from my saliva patterns.

Dr Clark had finally settled into the Bitter Aloe, the guests were busy in the pool and on the tennis courts, dinner was still an hour or two away, and Reuben was chopping wood round the back near the donkey.

But Pa shouted "Bitter Aloe!" glancing this way and that. "That word's still going to become a curse at Soebatsfontein. Bitter Aloe!"

Then he went inside and we heard the clink of his night-remedy bottle against the glass.

"But why's he taking his own remedy today?" Ma was shocked. "And in broad daylight!"

With the scent of fear and perfume around her, she hurried into the big house, leaving only her gold sandals there beside the red geranium. They were her special summer sandals that she'd bought, years earlier, at Greatermans, along with Pa's purple paisley dressing-gown.

Near the sandals, my drawings were drying up quickly. The ants looked for more moisture and then scuttled off in disappointment.

I turned to see that the Veteran had brought his folding chair out and was sitting in front of his rondavel. He was a good hundred paces away, but I could see how those black eyes glistened in his face as he looked at me.

23

My earliest memory is of an evening when Pa carried me. My head was on his shoulder. I was crying. His neck, against my face, was wet with my tears. We were walking up and down in the short passage that joined their bedroom to mine. With his dark voice he sang one of those Caruso songs he loved so much – songs that still echo in my mind as I sit now in the afternoons and look out over the hills, waiting for inspiration.

Something must have given me a fright that night. Yes, that's what it was: a bat had come tumbling out of the chimney in Pa and Ma's room. Pa was naked in bed with Ma, in their room that smelt of withered roses, sleeping remedy and pipe tobacco. He grabbed the tennis racket and pranced about on the double bed, trying to swat the bat from where it whipped back and forth round the lamp.

The whole spectacle was too much for me: my hairy Pa's bobbing penis and his wild swipes with the racket, the shadows dancing over the walls and ceiling, Ma lying giggling with the sheet pulled up to her ears, and finally the closed little gnome face of the dead bat in the white washbasin in the corner of the room, blood trickling from its sharp little teeth on to the porcelain.

I ran to Pa's handkerchief drawer and groped amongst his socks and handkerchiefs and gripped tight in my fist his molar which he'd kept there for years because there was a gold filling in it.

It was a family joke: in times of anxiety, Fabian grabbed Pa's wisdom tooth and held it tight in his little fist.

The incident became a family legend which Ma recounted over again to Tant Geertruida every year. It was a legend for everyone because of Pa's naked leaps with the tennis racket; for me because of the grimacing snout of the dying bat, that hybrid animal, abandoned by evolution somewhere between mouse and bird.

24

Years later, as a lone traveller, I landed up beside a Spanish couple in a Florentine trattoria, close to the cathedral.

She was one of those fascinating women who seem to be timelessly suspended between forty and sixty, with a thick mane of hair and brown skin, leathery from too many years in the sun.

I was first struck by the loads of jewellery on her long, strong fingers. Rings that would have made another woman look cheap and tarty, but which were dwarfed by this woman's magnificent spirit. She was as earthy as a gypsy, but she also exuded the world-wearinesss of a forgotten baroness.

Don Quixote would have looked just like the man, if I could have dictated to Cervantes: a bony, elongated head, eyes hooded by melancholy, lazy lids, bristling eyebrows, as hairy as his hands, long fingers that moved over the table like a spider's legs – over the spoons and knives and forks, over the woman's rings, over the napkins, and over the bread which he'd broken on the cloth beside his plate, Italian-style.

Our tables were close together, but my Spanish was so weak that their conversation remained no more than music to me, a tide rolling in and out of a little bay, over the smooth sand of her vocal chords, over the tidal gravel of his.

Florence bewitched me, that old city with its fragrance of tanned leather, its face of stone and marble, the lazy river and the cunning gypsies who lay in wait for tourists in the shadow of the Uffizi Gallery, that palace of genius.

The man with the long head – he was at least six foot four – and the woman with the extravagantly curly hair, became aware of me at the next table. Their voices sank lower and lower until they were no more than the soft sigh of wavelets over shell gravel.

And then – as often happens on travels – our eyes met, and we fell into conversation. She was a writer of books, she told me, and he was a professor at a Spanish university. He was in

Florence to do research on the bats that lived in the bell towers and old villas around the Ponte Vecchio.

I stared at them in amazement. I acknowledged that I was also a writer, travelling on a grant from a foundation in my homeland, digging around for themes, in the hope that I'd get lost in Florence's streets and finally reappear with a story in my head.

They smiled with polite understanding, but their eyes were sceptical. Even in Florence, two novelists in one trattoria was too much of a coincidence. I left it there. They invited me to join them and I entertained them with the story of how a dozen gypsy children had ambushed me in a lane near the Ponte Vecchio, robbing me of everything, except, mercifully, my passport.

"They even took my self-respect," I explained to the laughing couple, "and my American Express travellers' cheques.

"Will I ever get them back?" I asked them.

When the laughing professor explained to me that he thought it unlikely, and that the incident was probably a warning from the gods about the inner restlessness that characterises those who love to travel, I saw, deep in his dark laugh, the glistening gold at the back, nearly in his throat.

25

The Beast stood astride our lives. The Beast barked in our dreams at night. His paw stroked Pa's hallucinations and his saliva dripped over the book where Ma wrote up Pa's nightmares – recording them on Dr Clark's instructions to help the cause of International Psychiatry.

At night the Beast snuffled in the door jamb of the Veteran's rondavel, so that he woke, red-eyed and alarmed, staring, later, at Ma's legs as she moved amongst the breakfast tables.

The Beast followed Tant Geertruida down Oxford Street

and into Regent Street. He followed her without her seeing him. He trailed her through the streets of London. Growling, he wove past a taxi's black snout. He pranced like a monkey when people pointed at him. He kept her always in his lustful eye. He mounted guard under the brass plate that read *Arthur Maylam. Doctor of Medicine (Oxon)*. Darkness fell early here and the light from the consulting room window gleamed on his pelt. He sat sulkily, shifting from one buttock to the other.

Inside, Dr Maylam was surprised by the young woman's strange request. The Beast heard the soft mumble of voices, Tant Geertruida's speaking urgently and long. He scratched his groin and fondled the pink head of his pizzle. It stood erect and then sank back into the hair and rose again, following the rhythm of the thoughts eddying through his head.

At the beginning of the Season, when the stream of cars began to arrive, the Beast would sit on Buffelskop, keeping an eye on the city dogs who leapt from the cars and ran in crazy circles in the yard. Later, once they were confident of the yard smells and satisfied that they knew where their people had moved in, they began to venture further. The Beast growled softly when they came upon his rank odour on the branches of the river scrub, the hair bristling on their backs before they ran yelping back to the lawn between the big house and the rondavels.

The Beast watched the multi-coloured people and cars scattering like sweets, children romping in the trees, at the rondavels, the river like a shining wet scar fringed by the dark river bush.

The Beast sniffed over the red verandas of the hospital at Mouille Point, raised his head when the foghorn bellowed, considered whether to answer because there was something in the clamminess and mist that he recognised, but then he plodded down to the room whose door bore the sign *No entry. Patients strictly forbidden. Electro-therapy room.*

He pushed the door open and had to stand on his hind legs to sniff at a red light. He scratched at the letters under the light. For him they were ants, strangely ranked in neat lines. He sniffed the letters and tried to scratch them off, striking them until his claws had worked the fastenings loose so the little board sagged from one screw. The following day one of the patients was diagnosed by the Superintendent as displaying destructive tendencies.

The Beast slunk about amongst the rondavels at night, and if there were an open window, he stole things, carrying them round in his mouth. He dropped the books and pens and bottles on the kikuyu and pissed on them, uttering groans of pleasure. His urine smelled like nothing else on earth. It gave off steam and the stench drifted through the night, past the terrace with the upturned, sleeping chairs, past the moths fluttering round the stoep lights, past the city dogs that crept in under cars, whimpering.

It drifted down to the river and the sleeping troop of vervet monkeys stirred restlessly. They began chattering and jumping about and shaking the branches. Some lost their balance, tumbled into the reeds and began scrambling about in confusion, crashing into one another, tripping and scrabbling out of the way.

I leapt out of bed, banged against my open wardrobe door and stumbled on sleepy legs to Pa and Ma's room, where the night light flickered low and opened my shadow like the wings of a giant bat, then folded them as I plunged into the warm gap between their bodies.

26

And then the Veteran had himself converted.

One night he and the Pastor sat in the breakfast room and polished off two bottles of whisky. It was our turn to use the irrigation system and the shiny lanterns swung like fireflies in the dark lucerne fields. The fragrance of water set the frogs croaking and the turtle doves were surprised right out of their feathers and sat cooing in the night's bluegums.

Pa went out to Scanlan to make sure the sluice gate was completely open and to measure the strength of the flow, because if it wasn't right it meant farmers upstream were stealing water. Then Pa would phone the bailiff and there would be a hell of a palaver and Ma would have to stop him and bring pills and rub Pa's back to stop him from jumping into the Volkswagen and going to bugger up the farmers upstream.

"It's those black Latsky eyebrows again," said Ma. "They predict only bad temper and no mercy."

The whole night the farm would smell of wet earth and water and the irrigation-workers' gumboots would squelch behind their shovels as they opened furrows and raised banks. The hungry earth drank.

Our water came from Commando Drift dam and Lake Arthur and when it was our turn to use the water, it was like Christmas. Before the time, the bailiff from Lake Arthur rang and then the Scanlan bailiff pitched up and he and Pa had a discussion. On the appointed day, the water was released from the storage dams on the other side of town. Even though the water took half a day to reach our side, by early morning the farmers were already standing in the furrows near their sluice gates eyeing their watches jealously.

"This is the day when the most friendships go sour, and the Fish River Valley loses its sense of law and order," said Ma. "There should really be a prayer service for this bunch of farmers before the furrows are opened."

No matter how much the farmers threatened, the black children still swarmed into the Scanlan canal. Sometimes one drowned and then there had to be a funeral. Ma always cried when the little corpses were laid out in the wagon shed. "Will these blacks never learn to swim?" she'd ask. "And always just the little picaninnies. Once they're grown up, they're afraid of water, and it's a fear that stays with them through life. It is one of the tragedies of Africa, dirty bodies."

I had to give up a pair of pants, a shirt and socks. They were carefully washed and ironed before the little corpse was dressed in them. "They have no sense of judgement," said Ma, "and then Harold MacMillan wants to put them in charge of the country. Winds of Change, hmph, that'll be the day."

The tears streamed down her cheeks as Ma dug out a pair of pants and a shirt from my cupboard. "No sense of current or depth," she said. "No judgement. Oh, Fabian, oh, my boy . . . that tiny fellow with his shiny little face always opened the gates for me." She stood with my pants and shirt pressed to her chin. "There's tragedy ahead for Africa," she said. "That people's lives can be worth so little, even the little children's. We must keep ourselves apart from all this dreadfulness."

We all waited for news of the Verwoerd Dam which would be the biggest dam in Africa, after the Kariba and the Aswan. We were the first farmers in the valley who had heard about the Verwoerd Dam because Pa's oldest brother, Uncle Boeta, was high up in Pretoria and he'd phoned in a whisper one night. "Do you think the exchange operator is listening in?" he'd asked.

"She always listens in," said Ma.

"I've got good news," said Uncle Boeta, "but it's for your ears only."

"Then you must send a letter," said Ma. "There aren't any secrets in the Fish River Valley."

When Uncle Boeta's letter with the government crest arrived, Mr Ferreira rang from Halesowen station. "There's a letter here from the Mister in the Union Buildings," he said. "I'm sending the messenger on the bike right away."

Pa couldn't sleep a wink that night. "Water!" he kept exclaiming. "Just think, water whenever you want it. We'll tame Africa by farming."

"Are you going to drink a toast to that with me tonight?" asked Ma, pushing a curl back from her ear.

"Water!" Pa kept saying. "Water!"

Now everyone in the valley knew that Doctor Verwoerd was going to have a dam built on the Gariep. It was going to keep the world moist from Teebus in the north to Gamtoos in the south.

"We'll be the larder of Africa," Uncle Boeta wrote from the

Union Buildings. His letters were bundled with Tant Geertruida's postcards and fastened with rubber bands and stored in the top drawer of Pa's desk.

"When the Verwoerd water comes through," said Ma, "we can lock up the rondavels and sit back to watch the lucerne and the mealies grow. Then we'll also be stoep farmers and Pa will feel more cheery. It's the wind and tumbleweed and the stock losses that affected his moods so badly. If it weren't for the great drought and the smell of his own dead lambs Pa would still be the man I married. And then this whole hotel business wouldn't be necessary to keep body and soul together." Ma wiped her face. "Drought is a bitter thing," she said. "Fabiantjie, you must never even think of farming, sonnie. Promise?"

On irrigation nights a light burned in Pa's eyes. When the worst of the bloody-mindedness was over and he felt satisfied that we were getting our share and that the sluices above us were tightly shut, then Pa felt much better.

And it was on one of these irrigation-nights that the Pastor from room seven chose to treat the Veteran to a laying-on of hands. The foundations of the big house shook until late at night as the Veteran jabbered on in his parade-ground voice.

"Glossolalia," said the Pastor to Ma, still flustered, in her slippers and dressing-gown, when she brought them coffee in the breakfast room early that morning. She returned to Pa, still in bed. He was exhausted from going out to the fields periodically throughout the night. I stood in their door, also flustered, hugging my pillow against me. Ma looked totally thrown off balance. She smoked nervously and tugged at her hair.

"The Pastor says the Gifts of the Spirit came to the Major last night," she said. Apparently he received three gifts: prophecy, speaking in tongues and, on top of that, understanding of both."

"God help us," said Pa and turned over to stare at the wall. Wandering through the irrigation lands had left him completely worn out. He switched on the radio so we could listen to the farmers' programme. The rooster crowed over the transistor and then we heard "Calling all farmers".

But the Veteran's voice rose again and tugged at the window

frames and door jambs. "Glossolalia," said Ma cautiously, as though she were tasting the word. I couldn't understand anything the Veteran said.

Pa threw back the sheet angrily. "What are the guests going to say when they pitch up for breakfast just now?" he asked.

"Ag, wait a bit, just wait a bit," said Ma. "Just give them a chance. I'm sure they're nearly finished . . ."

I went to sit with them on the bed. Ma smoked and looked at herself in the mirror. "There are two empty whisky bottles on the breakfast-room carpet," she said.

"And you stop me when I want to go and give them what for!" said Pa.

Pa didn't think very highly of the Pastor's theology. "Anabaptist," he'd say as the Pastor took the dusty path through the veld to the Halesowen station with his Bible in his hand. There, on the platform, in his dusty funeral clothes, the Pastor waited for one of the passenger trains that ran between PE and De Aar. The conductors knew him as a man of the mission and let him ride free in the conductors' van.

He would ride away past Mortimer and sometimes as far as Cookhouse. Or his calling took him north, past Baroda to Noupoort. He would walk up and down the train corridors knocking on the door of every compartment. He knew the people were sweaty and irritable, that they were sitting stewing in their compartments behind closed windows, because if you opened a window, the steam engine's soot blew into your face.

The black people's carriages were the nearest to the locomotive, but even here in the white carriages, where the Pastor did his missionary work, there was plenty of soot. And that was why, if someone opened the door of a compartment, he had to act fast. "Revelation promises Doomsday in seven months," he'd say. Before they could slide the door to in his face, he'd warn, "The Rapture is upon us. The Millennium awaits believers. Unbelievers will be cast into darkness."

To me, he always said, "Satan rides with me on every train, discipletjie. He sits on every train. Even the train of life."

What else could the passengers do but invite him in?

"I knock them off like flies," boasted the Pastor as he sat drinking red cool drink on the terrace after a hard day. He looked tired but satisfied, holding the ice cubes in his cheek, and sucking on them, before he spat them back into his glass. He'd shake the glass so the cubes could melt a little, sipped the little water and then took the ice cubes back into his mouth. "Why did the young God have to bleed?" he called as he looked up. Dr Clark reached for his notebook and made an entry. "Blood as multiplicatio," he murmured. "The psychic bleeder."

Ma shuddered and said she wished the Pastor wouldn't spit into his glass like that. She gave Reuben instructions that the Pastor's glass must be kept apart, specially for his red cool drink when he came back from the trains in the evenings.

"They fall like flies in the corridors of the passenger coaches," recounted the Pastor, "slain in the Spirit. God rides with me on that train. We kicked Satan off at Baroda so hard he saw his ass. Praise the Lord, Jesus, Prince of Peace, oh Saviour, Almighty Majesty, John Ten Verse Sixteen, be praised! Praise! Praise! Praise!"

Some waiters would run inside from the terrace and kneel down on the kitchen floor. Reuben looked elsewhere, standing stiffly in the doorway and edging his body halfway in behind a potted plant. "Reuben would never abandon his post," said Ma. She stared into the distance when the Pastor went on like this, and if there weren't many guests, she'd kick off her sandals and stick her feet under the cool geranium leaves.

But that morning, when the Veteran and the Pastor came out of the breakfast room, pale and trembling, everything was at sixes and sevens. The news of the Veteran's conversion had travelled round the rondavels and spread to the stoep rooms like a veld fire. Even the kitchen staff came to stare.

Tant Geertruida stood with her feet well apart on the stoep, watching Pa. Pa went to sit at the corner table, as he always did when he didn't want to be disturbed. At the other end of the stoep, with his back turned to Pa, sat Dr Clark. He looked up when the Veteran and the Pastor appeared on the stoep, dishevelled and noisy. He put on his little round spectacles.

"God be praised!" the Pastor bellowed out over the terrace, as if the entire farm should come to a standstill.

"Do you want bacon and eggs?" asked Ma, shooing the kitchen women back into the big house.

"Sventoe svitari sojano serengeti shaman shibboleth bitikitiki kontiki," said the Veteran, turning in the sunlight.

"The Gift of Tongues!" crowed the Pastor. "Jesus be praised!"

"Whisky," muttered Tant Geertruida, turning her back on them. She lifted her nose and sniffed the water smell that stirred over the farm from the cultivated lands. Everywhere it gleamed in the furrows and herons and white tick birds waded through the fields.

Dr Clark took a notebook from his pocket and, as fast as he could, scribbled down everything the Veteran said. Ma saw to it that Pa got coffee and pointed out to him how lovely the water looked, sparkling in the fields, and then she darted to the Pastor and the Veteran, got them seated at a table and had them served black coffee in large mugs without delay.

"With brown sugar," Ma whispered to Reuben. "Quick-quick, my Jack. Quick-quick." She put the heaped teaspoonsful in herself because she reckoned brown sugar was good for the system. She stood over them while they drank it.

Then came the bacon and eggs – four eggs each with rashers of bacon, kudu sausages, lambs' kidneys, fried tomato and toast and marmalade.

"Two English breakfasts!" called Ma and stood by to make sure that they ate everything. She wanted to stuff them. Eggs, especially, Ma always said, dampen the spirits and stop thoughts from going haywire.

And indeed, a calmness descended on their table as they ate. Only now and then the Veteran looked up, wiped the gleaming bacon fat from his mouth with his sleeve, and said something: "Vladivi, vladiva, vondisi, brindisi, gladiatori oh glory!"

"Be praised!" the Pastor would shout and then they'd bend over the lambs' kidneys again. They ate sloppily and the egg ran yellow down the corners of their mouths. The bacon fat gleamed on their faces and they slopped coffee and scattered bread crumbs round them on the stoep. The Veteran's hair stuck out on one side of his head and his crow shoulders looked skinnier and more crooked than ever.

He still wore his dress uniform with the medals because he'd put it on to go with Pa to open the Scanlan sluice. The Veteran never passed up an opportunity for a bit of pomp and ceremony. "This warrants a salvo of gun fire," he'd said as he and Pa set off, but Ma warned: rather not. Next thing the bailiff would think that Pa was arguing with the neighbours again about whose turn it was to have the water and he'd call the police.

Ma asked Reuben to sweep the stoep paving round the two eaters' feet. She worried that the affair would disturb the guests who'd come here for a rest.

"The guests are here to forget the cares of the world," she always said. "We don't ask any questions at Hotel Halesowen. Here you can get away from the hundred and one questions of life. Here we kick our shoes off, unfasten those step-ins and braces and gaze out over the plains. Give the veld a chance and wait for it to suck the nonsense out of you. The veld can drain you of your miseries."

Then Ma would raise her drink and talk from experience. She was a Bolander who'd married the Karoo. "In the Boland the mountains are always around you and you're never far from shelter. Now you come here to the plains and you think: Oh, Lord in heaven, just look at the bareness. There are only dust devils and aloes here. But," and she would sip her drink, "you must give the veld a chance. It takes its time with you. It lets fresh air and space into your moods. It has no voice. It has no questions. It has no answers. What you see is what you get and that's the way you'll become too. Stoic – long suffering."

"Soebatsfontein," Pa would say then, intoning the names of the farms: "Allesverloor. Genadebrood. Wurgdroogte. Kainsdeel. Godverlaat. Moedverloor. Amenslaagte . . ."

But Ma would make out she hadn't heard Pa. "Yes, Fabiantjie," she'd say, hugging me close. "You're also one for the plains, aren't you?"

Then I wouldn't know what to say because Pa would say the open spaces wrung blood from a stone. "The sun is drawing blood!" he'd shout when the heat mirages shimmered as we drove to the family in Graaff-Reinet in the Volkswagen. "Witches' water," Pa called the mirages that danced round us. "God's eye," he'd say, pointing at the sun. "The devil's fist," he'd point to a rocky peak with a boulder on top.

"What do you say, son?" Ma'd ask. "This really is a holiday farm, wouldn't you agree?"

But now Ma was standing there waiting over the Veteran and the Pastor's table. Once they'd finished eating, she bent to them. "Go now and sleep in Peace," she whispered.

"No, sister," said the Pastor. "We want to go to the workers' huts now. The Veteran received a Vision and a Calling that we must go and tell the workers about the Revelation."

Pa stood up suddenly. No one messed about with his labourers. He swung round. Dr Clark sat upright and glanced at his watch. His notebook lay before him. Tant Geertruida stood up, folding her arms. She positioned herself so she had a good view of Pa.

"Bloody nonsense," said Pa in that Latsky voice. "You're going to sleep off your hangovers. Almighty God doesn't allow Himself to be buggered around."

The two struggled up out of their chairs and tottered down the stoep steps. The Veteran was trembling. It was all a bit too much for him.

Ma had to soothe Pa because he was also trembling. Dr Clark bent over his book and made an entry. Tant Geertruida beckoned me.

"Come, pupiltjie," she said. "Let's go and look at the wet fields. Nothing smells quite as good as a wet lucerne field in the summer, wouldn't you agree?"

Tant Geertruida and I walked down to the lucerne fields. I battled to keep up with her long strides.

"Gallipoli," she sighed as we stood at the first fence and she

drew a deep breath. That's what she called Soebatsfontein
sometimes.

Then she turned to me, wiping the tears from my cheek.
"Fabiantjie," she said. "Never mind, darling. Never mind."

27

"You know, corporaltjie," said the Veteran, "we keep on sear-
ching here at Soebatsfontein, but for all we know Kikuyu has a
lair on Dynamite Krantz. It's the ideal place to hole up in, you
know. My military instincts tell me that Dynamite Krantz is as
good as a fort. From up there you could look down on the
Collets' farm and the Barbers' and the Van Rensburgs' fields,
past the Reitzes' and you could see right as far as the water
tank at Halesowen station.

"On top of that, you have plenty of drinking places, close at
hand. And you could keep an eye on the trains and the cars
because everything has to go through the bottle-neck of Dynamite Krantz together. All those dassies! Can you imagine! If
he's a flesh-eater, as I believe he is, it must be like Christmas
up there in the gullies. What say you, corporaltjie?"

I rubbed my airgun with the oil rag. Today was Ammunition and Firearm inspection. I had to polish my airgun first
and then lay out all my pellets in lines of a hundred on the
floor of the Van Riebeeck. The Veteran had already polished
the 303 and it lay gleaming on a white sheet, beside twenty
rounds.

"Come on, corporal. You must lay out your catapult and all
your hand weapons too. Where's your Joseph Rodgers? Your
stick? And you still have to polish the rondavel windows for
barracks inspection. Just look at that washbasin. Oh no, corporal, this isn't a holiday farm, this is a military base. And
what about that pair of shoes?"

The Veteran didn't let Reuben get hold of his parade boots

every day. On days like today I had to polish, spit and buff. The toe caps had to shine like the Volkswagen's wing mirrors.

Inspection did not take place regularly – sometimes once a week and then nothing for a fortnight, or maybe two days in a row. "It all depends on the campaigns," said the Veteran, "on the movements of divisions, on strategy." He rubbed my hair. "You can't keep equipment in tip-top shape in the desert, corporal. It's only when we return to base that we can afford to get everything out and polish it."

Today was such a day. I had to get everything ready. I even missed lunch, but Ma let that pass. I polished and unpacked and dusted. The Veteran lay on the divan. His hole-in-the-heart was playing up. The Beast's carryings-on had upset him. He wasn't accustomed to this kind of guerrilla warfare. Conventional battle was better because you could see your enemy.

"Did you know, corporal, that the Boers thought up guerrilla tactics during the Anglo Boer War. And now the Beast is using the same tactics on us, attack at night, lie up during the day."

The Veteran rubbed his chest. "It feels to me as though my heart were pumping mouthfuls of air," he said. I was polishing his bandolier. "Keep going, corporal, until you can count your teeth in the reflection."

He sighed and moved his head on the pillow. "I never realised religion was so exhausting," he said. "Just one night of speaking in tongues and I feel I've spent a month in the advance trenches. So much so that I went to call on the Pastor last night to inform him that the Gifts were better suited to someone with a tougher constitution."

The Veteran coughed with a hand on his chest. "Remember the medals," he said, "but shine up the cartridges first. We don't go on parade with grimy ammunition. It's an indication of weak discipline and ours is no Uhuru army."

Once everything was clean and orderly, the Veteran got up. I had to straighten the bed behind him and plump up the pillow. He buttoned his shirt, asking if today he might conduct the inspection without the medals on his chest, due to unfavourable circumstances. I nodded and he went out. I checked that everything was okay. He gave me a minute to make last-minute adjustments and blow away any stray dust.

Then he coughed outside and that was a sign for me to leap to attention, calling out:

"I-i–n-s-s-s-pe-e-ction! Platoon, a-a-atten-tion!" The Veteran appeared, his back as straight as a rod. I saluted and shouted: "Ma-jor!" and he answered more quietly: "Corporal."

He wore a snow-white glove on his right hand. He came in and while I stood frozen to the spot, he ran a white-gloved fingertip over the windowsills, the door jamb, over the plumbing pipes, the legs of the divan and the picture frames.

Then he picked up the airgun and held it casually. He stroked the polished wood with the white glove, broke it and squinted up the barrel. His fingers touched the pellets briefly. His fingers touched the pellets briefly.

He sniffed the bandolier leather. I could hear his heart thudding dully in his chest. And when he bent over I could smell his sweat. His blood sounded sticky and red. His wings creaked, his bill hovered over the bullets. Then he straightened, shook his feathers and stuck a paw under my nose.

"Do you call that clean?" he asked.

As always, I hung my head. I must take my punishment like a man. "You smell like your mother," he said quietly. I rushed through the door and over the lawns. "Remember," he called after me, "we launch our next offensive against Dynamite Krantz!"

Dynamite Krantz! Dynamite Krantz! Dynamite Krantz! Dynamite Krantz!

28

When the Spirit started following the servants through the billiard room, the breakfast room, the kitchen and pantry, the dining room and the lounge, the games room and down the stoeps and over the lawns, the Veteran deemed it necessary to take a plaster of Paris impression of the Beast's spoor.

The first sign of the Spirit had been the arrival, in a dusty Austin, of the Pastor with his greased-back hair. At first Ma hadn't trusted him, because in those days greasy hair had been associated with ducktails, cars with big tail-fins and Elvis the Pelvis films.

When the Pastor parked his Austin between the limestone markers under the pepper trees, climbed out and slowly ran a comb through his hair while he looked Soebatsfontein over, then stuck the comb back into his sock, Ma had said: "Now what have we here – without so much as a telegram let alone any other advance warning?"

Bitter experience had put Ma on her guard if people didn't book in advance.

Not that there was no space. There was always a shake-down at Soebatsfontein, except during the Season, of course. "The Golden Days," as Ma always called them. But we had never turned anyone away.

"That's Karoo hospitality for you," Ma was fond of saying, and even though sometimes it meant rolling out sleeping bags in the dining room, we were never officially fully booked. "The more the merrier," Ma said, swaying her imaginary hula-hoop, and on the summer evenings guests would drop off to sleep with the fragrance of flowering lucerne, the cry of jackals on Buffelskop or the crazy scream of a monkey having a nightmare, and the sad whistle of night trains on the long tracks that stretched north and south.

And it was a good couple of weeks to Christmas when the Pastor drew up in his Austin, stuck the comb back in his sock and said quietly: "Praise His Name."

Pa couldn't stand the Pastor's perpetual "Praise His Name."

"Like a dassie farting," Pa would say. "What praising is this all day? Why would God be so dependent on our admiration? It's actually very big-headed to think that God needs our worship. Didn't He perform the wonders of Creation in absolute silence and on His own initiative? No, man, it's just Anabaptist sales talk."

Then the Pastor popped his head back into his Austin and

brought out his guitar. At the reception desk, Ma straightened her hair and said: "What have we got here? A crooner? A lounge lizard?"

She stubbed out her cigarette and shoved her is-the-Boeing-over-yet drink out of sight, into its special hiding place next to the Eno's Fruit Salts. The Pastor pushed the screen door open and a smell of Brylcream and the awesome odour of sanctity oozed in over Soebatsfontein's threshold.

His eye fell immediately on the plastic flowers. He stroked his hair back. "Praise His Name," he muttered as he came in. The screen door whined shut behind him. He was not the first guest to notice the flowers on booking in – many a guest before him had marvelled at such a modern novelty here, so far from any city. And so life-like and, even more amazing, not a drop of water was needed to make the flowers bloom.

"Eternal blooms," the Pastor said. "If only people were like that too, hey sister?"

Ma looked at him, taken aback. She wondered if there was a ring of brandy in her tone.

The Pastor came and stood in front of the reception desk. "God never sleeps, sister," he said. "We must extend the Kingdom. Work hard in His Mercy. Salvation awaits us. Praise His Name."

Then he introduced himself. "Joe. Joe Muller. Apostolic. Pentecostal. Of the Prince Jesus Movement, Port Elizabeth Central. Sent out as a missionary, Praise His Name, God Jesus-s-s Chris-s-st!"

Ma worshipped the big city. Anything that came from Cape Town, Port Elizabeth or Bloemfontein was for her "blessing enough". And she'd always pussy-footed around religion. "I look upon matters of faith with caution," Ma said.

Although she was not exactly a woman of faith, she was clever, and she knew that you could never predict when you'd land in deep water, and then you'd be sorry if you'd spoken too hastily about gods and faiths.

The Pastor had thus impressed her on two points and she put him in room seven on the stoep – a nice, large room, cool in the summer, and it attracted few mosquitoes from the river.

"And the guitar?" asked Ma. "Do you play the Hallelujah accompaniment, Pastor?"

"Oh yes, at the revival services I don't hesitate to accompany Hallelujahs to the Lord on my strings." And right then he asked, "Do you have regular prayer services at the hotel?"

Ma dropped her pen, grabbed for her drink nervously and cried "Oops!" guiltily, and put it down again and then blurted breathlessly, "Not regularly enough, Pastor, but now that you're in number seven . . . ."

"Trying times are ahead," said the Pastor, tapping a finger on the bookings register, at the last column where the booking-out date was to be written. "Keep it open for now. I'll look around a bit and see how the Spirit moves me. Then I'll let you know how long I'll stay over. These things can only be decided through prayer."

He wriggled his shoulders and wiped back his greasy hair. "Do you have any baby powder, by any chance? For the back and limbs. These dirt roads made the Austin shudder with pain. And my body feels it, too, hey."

"Shall I have the donkey stoked for a bath, Pastor?"

"That would be heavenly salvation." He had leaned over the reception desk to Ma. "And tell me, sister, do you hold purification services?"

"Purification services?"

"To chase out demons." He leaned even closer to Ma, preparing to impart something confidential.

Then Pa appeared in the door, wearing his paisley dressing gown, with his hair flat on one side from sleeping and on the other side standing crazily on end.

"I'm ready to be crucified," said Pa. He let his dressing gown slide from his shoulders. Like a slippery black skin, it peeled silently from his body and lay in a heap behind his feet. He stood there naked. "Golgotha! Dodge City!" he cried.

"Cleanse us!" Ma shouted, knocking her drink over.

"I'll perform a laying on of hands, but later." The Pastor

stood frozen to the spot for a moment, and then hurried out-side, deathly pale.

While Ma gently led Pa back to his bed with clucking noises, I crawled slowly on my stomach along the linoleum floor. I slid up to the guitar where it stood against the front desk. It was of gleaming, white-painted wood. I drew so close that my breath misted the shiny wood.

"Will you sing for me, softly, will you sing for me?" I whis-pered.

29

Tant Geertruida stood in front of Ma, her arms akimbo. She gave Ma the kind of look that made it clear that whatever Ma might say wouldn't count.

"Things are getting a bit too much for Fabian," said Tant Geertruida. "I want to take him away with me on a trip."

Ma was in the kitchen, drying her hands on her apron.

"Ag, no, Geert, that's too drastic." She looked over her shoulder to see whether any of the kitchen staff could hear. "I know it's heavy going with Clark here, but it's not that serious."

"The child wanders about nights among the rondavels. He doesn't sleep any more. I've sat up working the last three nights and I saw him outside every time."

"What?" Ma wiped over her face. "But where does he get out?"

"Well, obviously through his bedroom window or the dining-room door, which you leave open in any case every night because one of the guests might want to come in and get a glass of fridge water."

"And what does he do outside? He doesn't go to the blacks?"

"No," answered Tant Geertruida. "He spies on everyone."

"What?"

"Ja, and that's not a healthy sign in such a young child. Just think of all the things he's seeing at night: Dr Clark in the Bitter Aloe with his New York Music, the Veteran's late-night parades – hup-hup there in his rondavel. Left-right-left-right, turn, salute, like a maniac, well after midnight . . . You people up here in the big house have no idea what goes on in the rondavels at night."

"Goodness, I didn't realise, Geert." Ma rubbed her eyes and then hid her hand in the folds of her apron.

"I can show him the wide world out there," said Tant Geertruida urgently. "Lord, just think." Tant Geertruida put a hand on Ma's arm. That made Ma feel uncomfortable. Tant Geertruida made her nervous, she always said. "Think what it could mean for him! London, Amsterdam, the museums of Florence, Venice . . . Then he can forget about what's going on here. It's not healthy for a child so much on his own. Especially as you don't like him to play with the black children . . ."

Ma cut Tant Geertruida short. "He sometimes plays with Boe's Willempie. The labourers are drunk at the weekends and some evenings, you know that, Geert. It's no place for a white child. You know how they fight. It was only last week that I had to rush a split head to the hospital again."

"Just give me the chance . . ."

"Geert . . ."

"He's at such a receptive age . . ."

"But he's still a raw child!" Ma cried. "He's just a kid."

"You'd be surprised at all the things children know. Don't think he isn't aware of what's going on here. And, small as he is, he's carrying his Pa on his back like Virgil's Aeneas. It isn't right."

Ma bit her lip. From where I stood behind the pantry door, watching her and Tant Geertruida through the crack between the hinges, I saw how she wrung her hands under the apron.

Say yes, Ma! I prayed. Take me away, Tant Geertruida. Yes, Ma.

Suddenly Ma turned towards me. There was a moment's

silence while she stared at the door. "Fabian!" she said. "I know you're there behind the door. Come out, boy." I felt faint. "Come out, I say."

I came out from behind the door and stood staring at them.

"Do you see what I mean," said Tant Geertruida, quietly, without looking at Ma. "The child is watching everything. It isn't healthy."

"Do you feel okay, Fabian?" asked Ma.

I didn't know what to answer. My pocket was full of peach sweets that I'd pinched in the kitchen for Reuben and me to eat while he stoked the Antjie Provee at sunset.

Actually I wanted to ask: what is the CIA?

30

"Ag, that Geert," Ma always said. "No fixed abode! One minute the postcards come from the Museum in Pretoria, then from the Archives in Cape Town, then from Amsterdam, and you have to look at all the water and the boats; and then from London, and it's the English way of doing things. Not to mention those postcards from Spain stained with red wine, and the bravado, or the snippets of news about museums in Florence. No, no healthy family could keep a decent household with a toughie like old Geert."

But the moment Tant Geert let us know that she was on her way to put her feet up here at Soebatsfontein, Ma got very excited. She took dresses on appro from Verbruikers, and me and Pa and the Veteran had to sit on the stoep while she tried them on and showed us the dresses, one after another. She bought the dresses with the Veteran's shillings.

"Too short," said Pa.

"Perhaps too bright." The Veteran ran his fingertips over his medals.

"I like it, Ma!" I nodded.

Then Ma nipped inside and came out again wearing something else.

We held a fashion show and the waiters, who were as morose and silent as anyone would be from the boredom of all standing around on the terrace before the Season, now ran backwards and forwards happily bringing cold drinks for me, whiskies for the Veteran and cream soda for Pa. Once the Boeing was well and truly over, Ma's brandy and water came out on Reuben's tray and then one thing just led to another.

At dusk it was the turn of the box with the cocktail dresses and Pa asked: "But for heaven's sake, where are you going to wear these fancy-dress costumes?"

"Maybe the Collets or the Cawoods will have another party," said Ma. "When the Fish River is full, the English farmers always throw fancy parties, you know that. Or perhaps a minister will visit the town and there'll be a dinner at the Masonic."

Ma looked pleadingly at Pa.

"Fine," said Pa. "But only one. It's no good having five cocktail dresses hanging in your wardrobe and the only places you ever go are the John Wayne films at the Odeon or the church bazaar."

"And the parent-teachers' association," added the Veteran, his black eyes creeping like beetles over Ma's bare shoulders.

"And also perhaps the farmers' association dance," said Ma. She looked at Pa. "Although it's been four years since we were last there." She looked at me. "They send those lovely invitation cards every year, but your Pa says he's sick of the river farmers and the plains farmers, and the plot owners on the other side of the Dynamite Krantz and the Swaershoek crowd and the Mortimer bunch; not to mention the sheep farmers north of town . . ."

"That'll be enough of that," said Pa.

Ma sat a little longer in the cocktail dress. She lit a cigarette. Tonight was another of those nights, I knew, when she'd sit alone in the sitting room, playing her records one after another.

Her eyes glazed over and her hand went limp on her glass. The Veteran retired to the Van Riebeeck. Pa remained on the terrace in the dark. Reuben wiped a last table, up-ended the chairs and disappeared silently to his room. One last guest walked carefully over the kikuyu to the ablution block.

"This was not meant for me, Fabian," said Ma while the record turned. "Life is brief. Age comes as suddenly as frost bleaches the pastures. You think it's still a long way off and suddenly the winter's on you."

Ma had turned the lamp down low and we sat there looking at the shadows of the furniture against the walls.

"It isn't the way I planned it," Ma whispered.

I wiped the seventy-eight with a damp cloth and turned it over.

"The Pastor says glory awaits us in heaven," I said softly. "He says all our dreams and longings will come true."

"Ag, Fabiantjie," Ma sighed.

I stroked the short stubble on her calf. Her toenails were enamelled pastel pink. Pa didn't like it but Ma insisted it made her feet look more dainty. "A woman with ugly feet," she said, "has no grace."

"Right," said Pa, "if you people do it that way in Cape Town, I suppose I have to accept it. But here in the Karoo we think it looks cheap and tarty."

It was when Pa used the words "cheap and tarty" that Ma got up and walked out, straight to the little cabinet in the bathroom where she kept the half-jack for emergencies. She slugged the emergency tot so it burnt like fire inside her, dousing the frustration.

"Desperate! Desperate!" Ma muttered and said, "The miserable geraniums, the stunted hydrangeas, the scabby animals, the frightful plains. Why, in God's name, did I forsake the theatre and come to live here, to hell and gone?"

Then she turned to me and said: "Why're you crying, Fabiantjie? All couples fight, you know. And you must know, whatever things are like with Papa, I still love him. Its not Christmas all day and every day – with a man who suffers from bad nerves, you must understand that, sonnie. Come, let's get you a nice piece of biltong from the cold room.

"Or what about fifty extra pellets for your airgun? Then you can go and blast those starlings out of the fig trees. I'd hoped to make fig preserve before the Season, but those birds come down on the trees like starving kaffirs. Pitch black and arguing in Xhosa, just listen to them. What will it be, sonnie? Biltong or pellets?"

If Tant Geertruida were on the way, Ma would recall her days as an actress and she'd become aware again that there was a big world there on the other side of Buffelskop, and then she'd drive into town for the big white boxes from Verbruikers' "on appro" department.

The clothes would be wrapped in tissue paper and smell of the shop. "Take a sniff, sonnie," Ma would say then. "Smell the big world. We must go to the boys' department and buy you some new shorts and a pair of braces because Tant Geertruida likes a bit of style, for all her men's pants. Look at how she writes on her postcards about the Italian fashions and recipes. Look what she writes about the Spaniards' late-night escapades. Style, that's your Tant Geertruida, even if she does give a person the creeps with her flannels and her snuff. She is, after all, a woman of the modern world. And she knows something about everything. Not like this bunch of Karoo farmers who only know five stories.

"Come, let's buy Pa some new pyjamas and slippers, then he won't look like a ragamuffin when he comes out for lunch. And for the major, perhaps a pot of Brylcream for his hair or a bottle of Brasso for his medals? Come, Fabian, let's go shopping."

Ma was an actress and when Tant Geertruida was on the way, she'd sprinkle her sentences with English words, hula-hoop her hips, do her hair up and persuade Reuben to trim the kikuyu runners back from the terrace. She had once toured with famous people: Graaff-Reinet, Beaufort West, De Aar, and as far southwest as Oudtshoorn and Knysna. They'd played before the most eminent of audiences, mayors, ministers, school boards, doctors and farmers.

Ma had kept her trunk from her stage days on top of the cupboard in the bedroom, and when she heard Tant Geertruida was on the way and she got sad, she hauled it down and opened it so that she and I could breathe in the smells of stages and imaginary characters and forgotten applause. We stuck our heads in to the smell of dressing rooms and powder and gravel roads between small towns.

Ma took the dresses out carefully. She stood at the mirror and held a dress in front of her and called, "Gosh, Fabian, from the day you were born I started gaining. If only I could squeeze into this little frock and go back on stage! Do you know, people would sit as quietly as mice listening to your Ma. You could have heard a pin drop. And, do you know, it was our great aim to promote the Afrikaans language and dramatic art. That's what we did, sonnie. You should have seen the parties after every performance. All the most gorgeous farmers danced with us, and at night in the boarding house, or hotel room, I had to write dutifully to your Pa on the farm and promise I was still his.

That was after Pa and Ma had completed their studies at Stellenbosch and Pa, in terms of the trust, had begun farming. Ma had gone on tour with the company and they would only marry three years later.

"Wow, I almost went on tour with Wena Naudé, but then I got measles and my part went to that Angela de Witt girl, the one with the ugly cheekbones."

Ma's stage name was Joey Versluis, and once we'd finished smelling and touching the dresses, we got to the bottom of the trunk – below the fake jewellery and wigs and moth-eaten gloves and the scarves – and there lay two posters.

Joey Versluis in romantic mood! shouted one in curly script. *Joey Versluis in lost love,* promised another. *Drama, heartbreak during the locust plague. Our own Wena Naudé!* There was a drawing of Ma with her hair in a bun on that poster.

"Fabiantjie," said Ma, blowing smoke rings from where we sat cross-legged on the mat before the trunk, "can you imagine your Ma, on the stage, with the lights shining on her?"

31

Tant Geertruida was wearing her spectacles. We sat silently on the terrace. The Lister generator was off already and the flame flickered in the paraffin lamp. She was reading poetry out loud. Ma, Pa, and the Veteran and I listened attentively. Pa and them didn't see him, but I heard Reuben come and sit quietly on the step in the shadows. Candle flames flickered in the windows of the rondavels. Some doors stood open and the far-off sound of voices came wafting over the grass.

"Read it again, Geert," begged Pa. "Read it for Fabian. Specially for Fabian." He stretched out a hand and took one of mine. "This is just one of many summers," he said quietly. "Try never to let a summer pass you by, Fabian. Pick each one as though it were a ripe apricot. And God bless you, big boy."

While Tant Geertruida read it again, Pa went to his bedroom. Would I ever see him again? When was he going to die?

Reuben stirred slightly in the shadows. The moon hung in the thorn trees. It was, as Ma always said, a Halesowen summer second to none.

Or as Tant Geertruida often said, when everyone was sitting round gossiping about the Beast, "A Bluebeard summer."

32

The Pastor asked Ma if she could let the Lister run a little later than usual tonight.

"Until the diesel runs out," said Ma.

But she had Reuben top it up anyway. "The Pastor wants to plug in his electric guitar," Ma told Reuben. "He needs electricity."

The Pastor unloaded a square case from the Austin under the pepper trees. He took the blanket off it and stood it on the stoep. He removed one of the red globes from the veranda roof and plugged a wire into the socket. He brought his electric guitar from his room. The evening lights flashed on his white guitar that was as shiny as enamel. His black hair was oiled, not a hair was out of place. He wore a ruby ring on his little finger and, with his sleeves rolled up, you could see the crucified Jesus tattooed on his forearm.

Everyone made themselves comfortable after the waiters had removed the dirty dinner dishes. Pa sat wrapped in a bedspread because he'd caught cold during the irrigation. The Veteran's service medals gleamed on his chest and, behind us, the waiters and the kitchen women leaned against the doors with their white tea towels over their shoulders.

The Pastor took up his position beside the geranium with the big red flowers. Behind him the night lay deep and black and a cool breeze came up from the river. We imagined we could smell rain, and I listened to the frogs at the dam, the night crickets and the lowing of an ox behind the cow shed.

The guests had stopped chattering and sat lost in thought with drinks at their lips. The holiday had already started doing them good – their faces were burnt red, their eyes were clear and the faint smell of Karoo shrubs, kikuyu, suntan lotion and Lexingtons wafted over the tables.

The Pastor's fingers – spiders' legs – stroked the strings. Our eyes shone with expectation as the amplifier started to boom out deep, mournful sounds. We were surprised by the great wave of sound that swept over us and took possession of us. The guests' dogs darted under the cars. Pa's eyes narrowed to pitch black slits.

Ma stroked her forearms as the Pastor began to sing.

> Come bo-ow down in worship,
> Bo-ow down in wor-ship
> Bo-ow down and wor-ship
> Chri-ist the Lord!

The Veteran filled the song with curly sounds that made our feet move and our chests tremble.

Pa wiped his eyes.

"Goodness, Geert, I'm so touched," said Ma.

Tant Geert pushed her chair between Ma and Pa's. She took each of their hands and sang along with gusto.

The servants behind us threw their tea towels open on the stoep. They kneeled on them and gazed with upturned faces at the Pastor.

"Jesus-s-s . . ." he began to hiss.

"Jesus-s-s . . ." answered the kitchen women.

"God!" shouted the Pastor, his face shining in the light. His one forefinger trilled on a string. "Drive the demons away! Reveal the demons in us God, Lord, Jesus, Prince of Heaven and Earth, even of our dry Karoo. Drive the Power of Darkness out God Send your Spirit now Reveal the Satan to us that we can be released Oh God Father Prince let us come to you shining and purified Show us the devil now Show Now Now Show us Satan now . . .!"

"Jesus-s-s . . ." moaned the kitchen women.

Slowly the Pastor began to move. His one hand was stretched out before him and the other twanged away on the bass string that growled over the loudspeaker. Ma leaned forward, a hand to her lips. The Pastor came walking slowly between the tables so that the guitar string never hooked on anything. He descended on Pa.

"Jesus-s-s!"

He stood before Pa. His arm that was stretched out to Pa trembled. Pa sat frozen, with his eyes jet-black.

Tant Geertruida jumped up. "Cut it out!" she shouted shoving the Pastor away.

Pa slid from his chair.

"He has fallen in the Spirit!" cried the Pastor. Then the Lister gargled as it did when it was taking its last gulp of diesel. The lights flickered, grew dim and finally went out altogether. We sat dead still in the darkness.

Then, from far in the river dongas, from out of the thickest river reeds, we heard the moaning call of the Beast.

33

At the weekends the workers went wild, getting desperately drunk, making a racket and throwing all caution to the winds. They could have been sacked any day because of the drought, and found themselves back, broke and without a future on the dreary gravel roads. Pa sat up behind drawn curtains until the back of his head left a greasy spot on the wall above the bed. Ma stood at the reception desk, the silent phone at her elbow, filling in crossword puzzles or scanning "The Matchmaker" column in the *Farmer's Weekly* with a wry, sad smile at the corners of her mouth, as if she took comfort from the longings of others.

One below the other, she wrote the names of the characters she'd played, while the Veteran lay sweating in his rondavel. The screen door was propped open with a stone, and when you walked past you could see the shiny 303 cartridges where he'd drawn them up in divisions on his bedside table. He surveyed them with an expert eye, consulted his army handbooks and shifted them, drawing them up against one another, calculating the casualties in a never-ending war game, while he waited for Reuben to ring the dinner bell on the terrace.

In an isolated place, like the small valley at the foot of Buffelskop in a bend of the Fish River, so little happened that every day became a repetition of the day before. In this way, a ritual was made of the most mundane of chores, bringing the cows in for milking, the evening starlings swarming together at a certain time, the release of the wind charger when the milk buckets were tipped into the big shining cans, Reuben taking up his place on the terrace with his tray as regularly as clockwork every evening, the clink of Pa's sleeping-remedy glass against the medicine bottle, followed shortly by the snuffing of candles, one after another, in the rondavel windows.

And then, at the beginning of the night, when the couples in the rondavels rolled towards one another, holding their breath, careful not to wake the children who lay sleeping on mattresses on the floor, the holidaymakers discovered bodies they'd forgotten in the trying passage of the year. Afterwards, embarrassed, they hurried barefoot to the ablution block to wash off the evidence of their holiday passion.

All these rituals were so deeply ingrained because day after day, night after night, they took place according to the same patterns. Months after we'd seen it, a John Wayne film at the Odeon still swirled in our minds and in our talk; the couple of tightly-rolled magazines that had arrived from Cape Town or London became beacons in time and were read and re-read repeatedly. A visiting family who had moved into one of the rondavels for a week or so during the Off-season, formed part of the field of reference for years to come. Do you remember the woman's odd shoes, the man's habit of sighing, how those naughty children of theirs went and upset the cows in the milking shed so they wouldn't let their milk down, their car with the dent in the bumper, their stories about life in PE?

A rain storm that blew over would be remembered and described over and over again, long afterwards. Ma would ring the neighbours to fix exactly where the downpour occured. The readings from every rain gauge between town and Mortimer would be entered in her record book, so that you could always go over it again – Klein Gannahoek: ten points, Kranzplaats: only seven, Hasimara: twenty points, Green Acres: enough to moisten the dust.

Ma loved keeping records. This was her way of giving names and numbers to the endless blur of the days and nights outside the Season, to the growing intensity of Pa's depression, to the thing that stirred between her and the Veteran, coming and going like a water snake that lifted its head out of the dark waters now and then only to disappear again.

She kept records of politics, of the Doctor's speeches and of the demands of foreign nations that South Africa should change its bad habits; she wrote up the money that she secretly held back every month for Reuben, for his old age, so that he could perhaps one day buy a radio or maybe even an old second-hand Ford; she kept lists of my school marks, writing down every test or exam mark; Pa's medicine consumption was written down, as well as the gallons of petrol used by the Volkswagen every month; as were the days when the wind dropped and the windmill didn't move and no little stream of water splashed into the cement reservoir; the sicknesses of the worker's children, the birth and death dates of the workers' extended families.

Ma arranged a whole row of books in the wall cupboard under the calendar beside the reception desk. There they stood, in her effort to bring order to all our lives – a thankless task because the stirrings and paradoxes and fears and longings were aroused in the blood and the genes by the chaos of memories and the anxiety of premonitions. Ma kept an eye on the lot and wrote every change down as though she hoped that she could finally draw a graph from all the collected statistics, and that the graph would move upwards – a rising line, I reckoned, which would lead her away, away from the low plains of the Karoo out to the rarified air of the Boland, to the blue mountains that brought tears to her eyes when she so much as mentioned their names, and to the bays and rivers whose memory softened her eyes and tossed a curl over her forehead.

Ma, so brave there at the front desk, so frightfully lost.

Are my memories of her true? She is, alas, no longer here to be interrogated. And, anyway, she would never have answered. She'd have raised her brandy to the sunlight, or to the moon, or to the bulb of the standing lamp, and she'd have dropped something, a phrase from one of those songs from her seventy-eights or a snatch of dialogue from her stage days, or she'd have stood up, old and stiff from the arthritis now, her voice husky from the drink but her mind still as sharp as a razor, and make that hula-hoop movement of her hips to let me understand that you must look forward in life, that you must never look back, and that you must bear within you, without complaint or murmur, all that was past and could not be changed – keeping the lid on the deep, secret sediments of the days and nights, of your life, of that which had been given to you and that which had been denied you.

Perhaps it was only when you were alone at night that you

could lift the lid and peer into the pit of bats and dead carcasses and shrieks and dancing shadows and nightmares and other terrors of a Karoo life.

"Tomorrow," she would say until the end of her days, while pouring another finger into her glass, "tomorrow is another day. The show must go on, and this girl's a showgirl."

34

"It's going to be a Christmas to remember," said Ma. "Pa will be feeling better by then, I'm absolutely convinced of that; and you and I are always in high spirits, anyway, Fabiantjie; Pa and Tant Geertruida are talking again after their showdown about the Malay skeleton in the family closet; Miss Bruwer is coming to share Tant Geertruida's rondavel until after the festivities – can you imagine it? Two old ladies together in the summer stuffiness of the Wilhelmina! Dr Clark has booked the Bitter Aloe until after New Year, the Pastor is content there on the back stoep, the Veteran's new uniform has come in the post and he looks quite the thing in it . . . Charles Jacoby in the Zane Grey . . . and the rooms are overflowing. Sonnie, looks to me like we're going to have to put up tents like we did in 1957.

"The whole Bay is headed for Hotel Halesowen, and Pa reckons there'll be unrest early in the new year, the roads will be rotten with stone throwing again – ag, those blacks, the children of the night – and there's a good chance that everyone will be stuck here until well into January."

Ma looked up at the calendar where the December page showed a nice picture of a snow scene in America. There was a typical American farmstead, with a barn, a log house, horses peering over a wooden fence, and snow lying white over everything. To one side, a cowboy stood with a hand on his hip looking at the camera. In a corner of the picture was written,

"I'm dreaming of a white Christmas – signed, Bing Crosby."

Ma stroked my hair. We were standing at the front desk. "We have to keep our cool, Fabiantjie. I have a feeling that 1960 is going to be a knock-out Season. Happy, happy!"

Between the river reeds, he scratched his hairy belly, groaned and snorted. His belly was something between that of a cow and a donkey, but when he stood up on all fours, he was more a baboon; and then, suddenly, he stood on his back legs, half like a person, swaying back and forth on his hips as he gazed over the reeds. His bark echoed on the river banks, making birds fly up in fright, and weavers chirped anxiously at the mouths of their pot-bellied nests. The vervet monkeys scrambled through the river bed and drops of water splashed up like a hail of gunfire around them.

They couldn't tell whether they'd picked up the scent of a person or an animal. They were confused about the Thing that sometimes looked like a person if you glanced at it quickly, but then, in the open, limped like a great ape or something whose scent they had never smelt because as a dropping fell, he dug a deep hole, kicked it in and covered it with soil.

They'd already seen him trap a female monkey in a donga and saw her scrabble desperately against the bank, but he'd been too fast for her, so nimble with his ungainly body that it gave them a fright. He flipped her over there in the loose sand, splayed her open and pumped his hairy buttocks over her. Then she bit him in the neck, in his shoulder, where the veins showed pink through the thin hair; she scrambled up and ran away with long, crippled strides, slightly dragging a foot over the sand, crying while the troop's males drummed frustratedly on their thin chests and swore at the half-person Thing while they swayed in their branches at a safe distance.

The Thing rolled on to his back, in the same moment that the crying ape had rolled away, found her feet and began running. The white seed spurted from his penis, jerking in long arches over his belly hair, to the warm river sand. By the time he got to his feet, growling in fury and touching the bite on his neck, the whole troop had disappeared into the vegetation.

They knew he'd be back.

"Fabian?" Ma's perfume tugged me back. She bent over me, concerned. "Is everything okay, sonnie? Are things getting you down again? Do you know what you can do for your Mama? Go and get your bicycle pump and ask Reuben to delegate two waiters and then you can start blowing up the balloons. They must be hanging up by the time Charles Jacoby arrives. I want him to pick up a Christmas feeling when he gets here. And please remind me to hang mistletoe from the Zane Grey's ceiling light. It's only plastic mistletoe, but that's the next best thing, wouldn't you say? Come, come, don't daydream, run along, get your pump." Before I was round the corner, Ma called after me, "And ask Reuben if the stable is ready for Mr Jacoby's horse!"

Reuben stood on the terrace. Sometimes he could stand so still, half behind the pot plant, that you had to look twice to make sure it was he. "Like a statue," Ma always said, "carved from wood. Will we ever know what these blacks think?"

I stood close to him. "Hey, Reuben," I whispered. He stuffed my new school reading book behind his belt, under his waiter's jacket.

"Is there more to read?" he asked.

"No," I whispered, "that's all. And you have to find another hiding place. Pa has asked the maids to check under your mattress."

Reuben didn't bat an eyelid.

"Ma says the balloons must be blown up. I must get two of you to help me."

Reuben turned to me. "Have you run out of breath, then?" he asked sharply and walked quickly inside. I stood on the threshold, listening to his footsteps through the dining room. Reuben never walked so noisily. "He moves like a little breeze down the passages," Ma said, "like a breath, as faithful as my shadow. God bless his soul."

In the dining room, the two waiters and I sat with the heap of floppy balloons that Ma had shaken out there. "They still smell of last year's Christmas," said Ma. "Gosh, but time flies, sonnie. The clock never stands still."

She also brought a new packet of balloons that she'd bought at Verbruikers. "Look! Each year the colours are brighter! People really are getting clever. And all the shapes and sizes! Look at this yellow one with dots. I wonder what it'll look like once it's blown up? Come, come, get to work, sonnie, don't just sit there staring."

The two waiters sat cross-legged and puffed away with balled cheeks, while I put the balloons on to the bicycle pump and inflated them up. When Ma had gone back to the reception desk, they made lots of jokes about the balloons. They thought I didn't understand, but I saw one gesture with a long balloon between his legs, and the other spread his hand lustily over the bum of a round red balloon before he released it to one side, unexpectedly gentle, so that it bounced between the table legs and a draught blew it here and there in the empty dining room.

At last a heap of balloons of all shapes and colours were drifting before me. The waiters had gone back to their other chores and I stayed sitting cross-legged with the balloons. I blew gently into them. They rose and bounced and rocked silently, with a patient grace, swaying dreamily away, falling back again, shifting through sun patches and shadows. When I blew again, harder this time, they swept about, surprised, separated from one another and the floor and table legs for a minute before they drew back together again.

It was so beautiful that I closed my eyes and just felt the warm bodies of the balloons stroking against me, with the waiters' breath and the warm air of the bicycle pump inside them.

The smell of plastic and fly poison drugged me, along with the smell of sweet potatoes and carrots and the bredie that the waiters had started carrying in. Then I looked round from where I'd sat with my back to the rest of the dining room and I was surprised to see guests already seated.

I hadn't heard them coming in. They sat there, strangers from PE and Bloemfontein, from Queenstown and Aliwal North, from Graaff-Reinet and Murraysburg, and they smiled at me, friendly and approachable, but not without those slight question marks people always had in their eyes when they looked at me.

I jumped up and ran out. The sun was shock white. The door of the Bitter Aloe stood open. I stared at Dr Clark's back – he was leaning forward, writing. Books were stacked beside him, a glass of water stood at hand and there was a big apple full of words above the bed. Otherwise the walls were bare. He must have heard me because he turned round. Perhaps he heard my panting breath or the grass against my feet. He looked at me without a word. He seemed to be waiting.

And I waited for him, perhaps to say something. He was used to waiting – you could see it in the way he always chose a table to one side and waited for someone to decide whether to sit with him or not. Or if he were introduced to people, he always waited for the other one to speak first. Now he looked at me.

"The people in the huts say the Beast's name is Kikuyu and he has a row of shining eyes." The words slipped from my mouth. Then I turned and rushed off while he called out his nickname for me, "Huck Finn!" But I rushed through the orchard where the perfume of blossoms overwhelmed me and the deafening hum of the bees rolled over me like the sound of a huge train bearing down on me. I ran until my flight no longer had a name or a direction, until, eventually, exhausted, I collapsed on the river sand and dipped my face in the water.

35

With a white mane streaming in the wind, tail flowing with the breeze, head held high to the front, neck haltered into the ride, thick green dung tumbling from his arse when the train reached top speed beside the green, winding seam of the river. Eyes rolling when the locomotive seemed to scrape too close past Dynamite Krantz. On the snake's back while the cars zipped, muffled, through the lucerne fields. Flocks of starlings clattered from the reeds. Startled white tick birds flapped from the trees.

Charles Jacoby came to Halesowen and an open truck on the train was filled with straw for his stallion, Valour. At Halesowen the station master came running out to where we waited on the platform, and said he'd just received information, the train was leaving Cradock, Valour was safely in the truck and Mr Jacoby was sitting with the conductor in the guard's van enjoying a cup of tea and sandwiches, with the compliments of the SAR&H.

I wanted to climb up the signal pole so I could see them coming, but Ma said I should rather go up the water tank. "But not right to the top, sonnie. Only twenty rungs, Fabiantjie, or next thing you'll break your arm." I rushed over the shiny tracks. "Only twenty! Count them as you go up."

It had been arranged that the train would come to a standstill so the guard's van would be exactly opposite the doorway to the station building. Ma had arranged balloons and streamers. They were fastened to the fire buckets and window frames of the station building. Pa had a mounted springbok head under his arm. Ma had asked him to present it to Mr Jacoby as a token of our esteem.

Pa practised the words that Ma had suggested, "It is a proud day for the Hotel Halesowen that the Cradock Cultural Board has decided that our hotel would be the best place for you to stay during your visit. It is indeed private and peaceful, and you must not worry about autograph hunters and other disturbances. We are at the service of you and your stallion."

Valour lifted his nose, whinnying in the breezes of our valley; his eyes drank up the fields, water furrows and dams that flashed past his gaze, and, in the distance, the backs of hills that flew with him like the brown haunches of mares.

Twenty-two rungs brought me so high that I could see right over the thorn trees and as far as the station master's house. The tracks ran shiny and straight through the plains, then joined the river bush and followed the bends in the river and stretched past the forbidding scowl of Dynamite Krantz.

I waited with bated breath. From here I could see the avenues of Soebatsfontein clearly, the bluegums clustered round the farmstead, the lines of pines down to the cultivated lands, the pepper trees round the tennis courts and the thorn trees down near the riverbanks. The roof of the big house shone. The sun flashed on the cars under the trees.

Ma had decided to welcome Mr Jacoby to Soebatsfontein with a Country 'n Western theme. The stoep was festooned with cowboy hats that we'd been able to borrow from Verbruikers because Ma was friends with Aunty Susie Williams, the manager of the clothing section. The Zane Grey was decorated with an American flag. Reuben had nailed it up above the bed, hastily, because Mr Jacoby's visit was somewhat unexpected. He was to have stayed at the Masonic in town, but on his arrival in town he had pointed to Valour and said, "We're inseparable."

Ours was the only hotel that could offer stabling facilities. The chairman of the Cultural Board, Mr Crafford, who was also the manager of the White & Boughton book store, rang out of breath and Ma had to go and sweet-talk the people who had already moved into the Zane Grey.

"Soebatsfontein," Pa teased Ma, as she helped the people move to the back stoep room, beside the Pastor. "You can stay for nothing," Ma said, and added: "Just pay for your meals. That's all. Ag, what a carry on!"

All Pa's cowboy books were sent down to the Zane Grey and arranged there. At the Odeon, after a hunt in the projector room, Ma had got an old John Wayne film poster and it was hung up opposite the bed.

"Right," Ma had said once she was done fitting out the rondavel. "Now we must just carry in the small wall cabinet, so that Mr Jacoby can lock his guitar up. Just imagine, Fabiantjie, what would happen if that guitar got legs and walked?"

"Is he really a cowboy? Does he know John Wayne?" I had asked and Ma had put a hand on my head.

"Of course, Fabian," she said. "He's from the real Wild West." She looked dreamy and pressed her thumb and forefinger against the corners of her mouth. "Home on the range," she crooned. "I feel as though Hotel Halesowen should be re-christened Hotel Hollywood!"

From the rungs of the water tank, I looked at Pa, Ma, the Veteran, Reuben and the station master on the platform. Ma was in earnest conversation with Station Master Ferreira. Behind them the lines stretched straight as an arrow into the distance, disappearing among brown hills and aloes, there where the heat shuddered and everything started to swim and move in the water that only consisted of light and imagination – as Pa always said, just heat and deception and never water.

Ma and the station master gestured thus and thus. They were planning exactly how the train would pull up and who should stand where as Mr Jacoby got out.

I shook my head to clear the heat from it and climbed up one more rung. Far away I could see the town shining between the brown hills. Then, quickly and angrily, with a frown on its forehead, the train came gliding round Dynamite Krantz and aimed directly for me. It toot-too-tooted and its steam puffs shot up into the air. They looked like white doves, released only to melt suddenly in the blue.

"He's coming," I yelled to Ma and them. "Here comes Charles Jacoby!"

"Hold tight!" Ma called to me. "Don't fall off."

Behind the black locomotive, in the open truck, the white horse lifted his head. He tossed his mane in the wind. I heard him whinny and smelt his saltpetre sweat. I could feel his warm breath on my hands. I am astride him and we race over the plains. No Red Indian can catch me! Behind me, the shacks of Dodge City get smaller and smaller. I am headed for the Wilderness. I close one eye and take aim.

He stalked them out of the night where they grazed in the sun on the prairie. He gored a buffalo with one stroke of his paw, so that the animal stumbled a little way with its innards dragging on the ground, and then sank to its knees. He moved in on it, taking his time. The buffalo looked up into the sun and the darkness of bright light struck him. He drew the intestines out of the buffalo's belly wound, dragging wet red stripe-marks in the dust. Green stomach juice burst on the grass. The buffalo bellowed and screamed, its eyes rolling, and the fiery sun burnt white over the prairie as he thrust his wet paw into the buffalo's body cavity, reaching up to grasp its heart and wrench it out. The buffalo looked at his own heart in the Beast's paw, in the clear sunlight, before he died.

The sun tipped when I opened my eyes and I could no longer hold the rung near my face. I slid. The black head of the train thundered down on me and Ma screamed, "Fabian!" and I woke up, lying on my back, on warm cement. To one side stood a cowboy with frills on his sleeves and a broad-brimmed hat.

36

Ma and Pa bent over me and Ma said: "Fabiantjie, you almost broke your arm, sonnie. Didn't I tell you only twenty rungs? And now you've gone and spoilt Mr Jacoby's arrival with your naughtiness. You're going to have supper in your room tonight. I'm very cross!"

I felt cold and closed my eyes and smelt horse dung and platform cement. Station Master Ferreira came to bend over me, too. I couldn't see him, my eyes were shut, but I could smell him through my eyelids: his station-master sweat, his black jacket, his stamp ink, the grease he used for his signal boom, the ingrown hairs where his cap had dug a ridge on his forehead during years of wear. I heard what Ma and them were saying. She wanted Mr Jacoby to give a terrace concert for the guests. "If you aren't too tired," she added hastily. "And our Pastor has also got a guitar – he can do the backup vocals."

I opened my eyes when Station Master Ferreira's smell was replaced by the smell of aftershave. The cowboy bent over me again where I lay on the platform. The white hat blocked out the sun. A sheriff's star shone on his chest. He wore lots of rings and there was a gold chain round his neck.

"Are you Fabian? I'm Charles Jacoby." I battled to keep my eyes open when he moved his head and the sun was right in front of me. I heard someone laugh and I turned my head and I wanted to keep my eyes open but I battled. I felt the cowboy pick up my hand and press something into my palm. I held it tight and told no one about it.

I was helped to the bakkie after Ma had examined me thoroughly and had asked Pa whether he thought Dr Lyell should give me a good once-over. Pa reckoned it was just the fear of heights that many Latskys suffered from – that's what had made me feel faint – and so it wasn't necessary to call in a doctor.

"Fabian isn't going to be the sort that needs doctors," said Pa. Ma looked at him quickly, then hurried to Mr Jacoby's side. He was shaking hands with the conductor and the station master and waving his white hat to the passengers who leaned from their windows.

"Be good!" he called to them before joining us. Our procession departed slowly while Station Master Ferreira, the train driver, the conductor and the stoker waved to us from the platform.

In front, Reuben led Valour, Ma followed in the Volkswagen with Mr Jacoby beside her. He kept his white hat on his head and filled the whole cabin. He sat with his elbow out the window and his hand on the car roof. His rings flashed in the sunlight. I knew Ma was talking business with him. It was about the evening concert and whether he would be willing to perform or not.

The station messenger followed the Volkswagen on his bone-shaking bike. I didn't know why he had to come along, but Ma had said, "We need a messenger, just in case. Next thing that horse breaks loose and bolts into the veld. Thank goodness Reuben understands horses. He can take care of the stallion because Mr Jacoby wouldn't like our going on ahead and his horse following behind. I'll talk promotions with Mr

Jacoby while Pa and Fabian and the baggage bring up the rear."

"Oh yeah," Pa had said the day before Mr Jacoby's arrival. "Calamity Jane is going full tilt."

"Dodge City, here I come!" Ma had laughed. She had pumped me with her elbow. "Hey, Billy the Kid!" She pointed to Pa. "And there's old Buffalo Bill."

"It's a showdown," said Pa. He took Ma into his arms and there were tears in her eyes. He breathed deeply of her perfume and they flashed by on bicycles, through a green valley. The sun flickered on the spokes. It was a summer valley with vineyards and his jacket lapels flapped in the wind.

Ma could smell medicine at the corners of his mouth and she found it impossible to look into his black eyes. They stirred like river water when you wade through it.

"Darling," she said, turning away, shaking her curls and taking a deep breath.

"How the West was lost," Pa whispered. He turned on his heel and made for his bedroom.

That summer his footsteps grew heavier in the passages. They echoed through the empty dining room. Everyone stood still to listen. The servants waited with their trays and kitchen towels over their shoulders, the waiters tilted their heads, Reuben lifted his head and the Veteran drew his breath in quietly. Pa was going to his room.

Ma and I looked at each other. For once, she was at a loss for words, and looked desperate in her muteness.

Then all at once when the copper curtain rings in the bedroom tinkled as they were drawn to, the moment passed and everything went back to normal. The servants hurried between stove and pantry, or to the dining room with trays piled high with cutlery and pressed serviettes, or to the rondavels with sun-fresh bath towels. The waiters straightened the chairs on the terrace and sprinkled water on the pot plants. Ma took a book down from her shelf and made an entry. The Veteran sighed and flipped open *Operation Desert Fox*.

I went dawdling among the rondavels to see what Tant Geert,

the Veteran and Dr Clark were up to. Or I followed Reuben onto his rounds between the bar and the terrace, the donkey and his room, the stoep rooms and the dairy, until he turned and said to me, "Kleinbaas Fabian, I think you'd better help me stoke the Antjie Provee tonight. We're going to ride that train all the way to Cape Town."

Then I laughed with Reuben and forgot about everything and I could whistle for the dogs again, and I made a turn round the guests' children, past the orchard, across the fields, into the dongas to where the river trails smell wet and musty, and the shadows pin down swarms of mosquitoes. I stretched my hands out to the calcified shells encrusted in the river bank, reminding us that this was all once sea and, as Pa always said, will be sea again, in God's mercy, in God's own time, at the End, the time of Resurrection and Hope.

37

Ma shook her curls and called out as if to Pa's back: "The show must go on!" She stroked my head. "Mr Jacoby is an Entertainer and we must be prepared for every eventuality."

And she'd arranged everything, to the last "jot and tittle".

She'd told Reuben earlier that the labourers could also come and listen to Mr Jacoby's terrace concert, as long as they stayed beyond the circle of light and didn't get out of hand. "They mustn't pitch up full of kaffir beer and they must applaud when I give the sign. And they should leave their kids behind in the huts."

Ma made the minutest of plans about where Mr Jacoby should stand so the light would fall on his guitar and catch his spurs. "People should be able to see his hands, Fabian," she told me. "A musician's hands must be visible. Those rhythms come from God. And perhaps we could bring Valour up from the stable and he could be tethered to the veranda rails while

Mr Jacoby sings," Ma reckoned. "That'll be charming, the cowboy and his horse. Just think how it will amuse your Pa."

Ma got out the home-movies Kodak and checked that it was still working. "We used it so long ago. Since Pa's nerves got so bad we never shoot movies any more. And we've never shot anything at night. But it's worth a try, even if I waste a film. I'll just have to write a note to the lab in Port Elizabeth explaining that it's a night film and that they must give it special care. It isn't every day that we have a star performer at Hotel Halesowen. And so close to Christmas! This is turning into a bumper Season, sonnie."

In the days leading up to Mr Jacoby's arrival, Ma had started peppering her speech with English words again, swaying her hula hoop and hurrying about with a pencil behind her ear. Forgotten is the heavy hand on the tot measure, and that faraway look in her eyes. The suitcase stayed locked on top of the wardrobe while she considered sending me off with Tant Geert to London and Amsterdam for what she called "a grand culture tour".

Excitedly, she planned everything down to the finest detail, with the procession from the station to Soebatsfontein as Act One.

Pa and I followed behind the station messenger's bicycle in the truck. The Veteran sat on a bale of lucerne in the back, holding himself straight as a poker, his medals shining like Mr Jacoby's rings. He gazed into the wind like a combat general on a Jeep.

The balloons bobbed on the Volkswagen's wing mirrors and, just past the first gate, where the farm road turned off and a sign indicated *Guest House Three Miles Overnight Accommodation Teas Tennis Swimming*, there was a banner stretched across the road with *Welcome Charles Jacoby* painted on it. "The Halesowen Guest House welcomes you, Mr Jacoby," said Ma, her hands gripping the steering wheel, her eyes fixed on Valour's rump.

I sat beside Pa. "Do you feel any better, Fabian?" he asked. "What happened up there on the tank? Now that we men are alone you can tell me, kid."

I shook my head and glanced at the back to make sure the

Veteran was still on his bale. He gave me a victory sign. Pa didn't ask again and we drove the three miles to Soebatsfontein in silence. "You can smell the veld properly when you drive this slowly," said Pa. "And just look at the tracks of the smaller animals. Look there, those dragging marks. What do you think went there, in under the thorn tree, past the anthill?"

We stopped first at the Scanlan furrow gate. It was still four hundred paces to the house. Mr Jacoby got out of the car, straightened his stetson, slipped on his silver spurs, took his guitar carefully out of its box on the back of the truck and slung it round his neck. Reuben held Valour steady as Mr Jacoby swung nimbly into the saddle. He rode up front and Valour dropped these fat turds on the gravel road. They lay steaming and Pa said, "Look. Golden droppings. It's a wonder Ma doesn't scoop them up as souvenirs."

"Memorabilia," giggled the Veteran. "Showbiz memorabilia."

Pa and the Veteran laughed together. It wasn't often that they shared a joke. There were usually long silences between them. Not uncomfortable silences, but an unspoken acceptance that things were the way they were. The Veteran waited patiently and Pa knew too, that time would catch up with him: the time would come, was the silent understanding between Pa, Ma and the Veteran, when Ma wouldn't have to make a choice because circumstances would already have made it for her.

I couldn't understand why Pa didn't put up a fight. Perhaps he was already so done in, eroded like so many dongas, trampled so limp by his demons that it didn't matter to him any more. Perhaps he saw the Veteran for what he was, and enjoyed his revenge before anything had even really happened.

I'll never know, but I do remember that one morning when the Veteran thrust out a skinny arm, his crow's wing, and placed it on Pa's shoulders, while the glamorous cowboy singer rode away from us, leaving behind those steaming horse turds at Ma's feet.

Ma got back in the car, and we into the truck. Reuben hopped up beside the Veteran. The station messenger steered his bike carefully round the droppings, bent over them momentarily as though he wanted to establish what Valour was fed on, and then proceeded on his wobbly, dusty way, behind the Volkswagen.

When we reached the last gate, we could see the guests, waiters and cleaning women grouped under the trees, on the lawn and the terrace. Mr Jacoby waved his hat as if he were acting in a film. Ma tooted the Volkswagen's hooter enthusiastically and Valour pranced so that Mr Jacoby had to hang on for dear life.

For a moment we thought Ma had made a helluva mistake because the squeaky hooter and the bucking horse had roused the town dogs and they rushed up, barking. To make things worse, the guests started clapping and children came running over the field from the huts. But Mr Jacoby was an experienced horseman and we were spared shame and disgrace when Reuben shooed the dogs and the black children back to the furthest bluegums and the horse calmed down.

Ma got out of the car and came towards us all shiny-eyed. "That was close," Pa reprimanded.

But she didn't hear him because she had good news. "He's agreed to sing!" She grabbed Pa round the waist. "Just think of it! Charles Jacoby on the terrace at Hotel Halesowen! And you, Fabiantjie, do you feel better? Just forget about the accident, sonnie, what do you say?"

I opened my hand to look at the thing I'd clasped for the three miles from the station without peeping at it once. My fingers were stiff. The sheriff's star had dug deep marks into my sweaty palm. On the back it said *Country & Western Products, Arizona State.*

Pa teased me: "Go get 'em injuns, cowboy!"

38

The curtains were drawn. The brass rings had sung over the brass rod and their ringing hung in the room afterwards, shrill and pained. It was quiet outside. The last guests had retired, and there was only the faithful Reuben's activities to be heard on the terrace as he tilted the chairs up against the tables so the dew wouldn't collect on the seats.

If you listened carefully, you could just make out the faint gurgle of the pipes which led from the donkey and ran along the walls to the washbasins in the rondavels and the showers in the ablution block. A small transistor radio in one of the stoep rooms managed to pick up faint melodies in spite of the height of Buffelskop. The voices of the singers drifted over the kikuyu to the end of the terrace where Reuben stood now, letting his eyes run over the cars to make sure all was in order. And then he looked down over the lawns to the dim lights behind the rondavel windows. As he stood watching some of the lights went out.

He gazed up at the stars, strewn like crumbs across the sky, and twitched his nose. Was that the smell of rain? Was there another smell on the evening breeze, something other than the faint smell of manure from the cattle pens, the grass smell rising from the kikuyu as the first dew fell? Was it a smell other than that of the damp sandbanks at the river and the peach trees behind the huts?

At this time of night the heavy, dank smell of soap and steam wafted on to the terrace from the ablution block, the smell of Jeyes Fluid and shampoo and aftershave. But there was something else that Reuben couldn't place. It was a smell that was familiar and strange at the same time. He raised his arm and sniffed absent-mindedly at his armpit – Ma was very strict and made sure that every waiter got a Mum roll-on every month. No, it wasn't him, although he recognised something of himself in the odour.

He turned and looked at the homestead. It was already dark – only the night light in the passage at my door gave a faint glow and in Ma and Pa's room there were figures whose slow movements were etched against the curtains. Reuben turned away, looked over his terrace again, sighed, thrust his hands into his trouser pockets and took the cement path past our bedroom windows to his room near the donkey.

He pushed his door open, fumbled for the candlestick and matches and, once the flame had sputtered to life, shut the door and then, like every night after every long day, he was alone in his room. Pa preferred him not to go to the huts too often. He hadn't forbidden it, but he knew Pa preferred to have him up here, close to the big house. He knew Pa and Ma had given him a particular position, and that they regarded him as different from the others who made a racket round their fires and in the small huts round the yard until deep into the night – drinking, fighting, laughing raucously and, once the beer started working on them, urinating against the walls inside the huts.

Reuben pulled off his shirt and sat down on his bed. He relaxed, going over the day. He counted his tips: the farthings, ha'pennies and a single sixpence. Then he got up on to his bedside table so his hands could just reach under the low ceiling. He pushed the loose plank to one side, taking care that no bat droppings should fall and betray his hiding place to the other servants. He thrust his hand into the dark ceiling space and drew out his book. He shifted the plank back, moved the candle to the bedside and propped himself up against his pillow. With his lips sounding the syllables, he began to read. *Seuns van die wolke*, he read. "Sons of the clouds," he whispered, resting his head on the pillow. "Sons of the clouds."

39

The brass rings sang over the brass rod and the sound still trilled in the room. Ma and Pa sat on their bed. The paraffin lamp threw their shadows big against the wall. Ma had the dab of

LSD on her fingertip. She'd taken it up off the paper strip that had come from the parcel Dr Clark had sent by registered post from Mouille Point. Every evening she first wet her finger tip on her tongue, touched it to the almost invisible dot of powder and then held her finger up.

Pa pulled himself upright a little and his shadow slid over the wall. The lamp flickered. Pa's slight movement stirred the air round the room. It was a completely ordinary room with a double bed of dark wood, a chest of drawers with a mirror, a wardrobe and Ma's dressing table with its huge round mirror. A faded wedding photo and portraits of Pa's grandma and grandpa hung against the wall. There was a painting of the Cape mountains – Ma wasn't sure which ones, but she thought it was Simonsberg taken from an unusual angle. Pa's *Path of Truth* booklets were piled up at his bedside and a few *Reader's Digests* lay on Ma's side. A bare bulb which was powered by the wind charger hung from the ceiling above the bed. Ma didn't like turning it on, she preferred the lamp. It was only some nights that Pa asked for it to be left on, and then she'd sleep with her face in the shadow of his body while he sat upright with his head against the wall.

Pa's tongue was warm and wet on Ma's finger. Ma remembered other times, moisture and warmth and love. Pa, as a young man, over her, his desire erect. Such a strong young man. His voice, his humour, his movements.

Then Pa toppled backwards and the powder took hold of him and he jerked and trembled. He began to crawl like a spider over the white sheets, over the dressing table, over the chest of drawers, against the walls, across the ceiling. "The music is blue," said Pa. He looked at Ma. "I'm melting," he said.

"Yes?" Ma asked conscientiously, and bent over her dream book. Around them stretched the endless Karoo night, and the small constellations of light from towns like Cradock, Graaff-Reinet, Murraysburg or Aberdeen were insignificant interruptions in the massive open landscape, the swirling nothingness that lay stretched out under the stars, under the milky way, exposed to the soft hand of the dew or the cold eye of God, or the night breezes that pushed smells unhindered across the landscape, stirring the lukewarm air that had dammed up in the hollows, pushing it out over the plains, further, further, away to the emptinesses that grew bigger and bigger, the horizon that still beckoned as Pa dripped off the end of it and became landscape and stood spinning on the bedroom floor, explaining hesitantly, "I melt from the edge of the Camdeboo, I drip, I drip . . ."

Ma wrote it all down, as fast as her pen would go. She'd found that it was sometimes better to sit writing like this with Pa, better than going later into the empty dining room amongst the empty tables to write up what she'd heard. Here at least he was beside her, she was not so alone.

Ma wrote and the Veteran stood in the doorway of his rondavel, looking up at the big house, up at the lit bedroom window. In the Wilhelmina, Tant Geert sniffed at her fingertip, thoughtfully, while she lay reading and murmured, "Marge". In the Bitter Aloe, Dr Clark sat cross-legged trying to achieve his karma. "Ahu-u-mm, a-a-h-u-u-mmm . . ." he sighed rhythmically. In his stoep room the Pastor wished out loud, so that the people in the room next door stirred restlessly in their beds and resolved to make a formal complaint at the reception next morning: "Oh Spirit, oh, Holy Spirit, enter the lives of the people on this holiday farm . . ."

Pa sat on the floor with his face turned up towards the ceiling. "Fuck the shit," he said ecstatically. "That's my conclusion, fuck the clearbright shit."

Ma's pen hovered above the page. Should she write this down too?

40

"B-i-i-ig station master, tee-ee-ny siding," Ma said of Mr Ferreira. Since he'd arranged for Mr Jacoby to come to Soebatsfontein by train, Mr Ferreira thought he was the bee's knees.

"No, for heaven's sake," said Ma, swirling her fortune cup anti-clockwise three times and tipping it over the saucer. While she stared thoughtfully at the tea leaves in the bottom of the cup, she continued, "Now it's suddenly charges on delivered postal items and no train waits for anyone, and every now and then a phone call to hear how it goes with the Entertainer."

That's how Mr Ferreira referred to Charles Jacoby. And he called the horse The Steed. Every morning at crack of dawn, the phone rang while Ma stood at the reception desk still fuzzyheaded from the last night's tots, trying to gather her thoughts for the day that lay ahead.

"How goes it with The Steed?" Mr Ferreira wanted to know. "And with the Entertainer? Did he sleep well?"

"Look, Ferry, old chap," said Ma. "I haven't even had my first cup of coffee yet. Reuben is still feeding that white paradise donkey. My husband hardly slept a wink last night. It was all too much for him, yesterday. And the child had to fall off the water tower, on top of everything else. And you're asking me about the welfare of a horse!"

At that hour of the morning Ma had to show people to their breakfast tables with one hand, while she signed out tennis rackets and balls and swimming towels, as well as issuing warnings about suntan oil, snakes in the river reeds and scorpions under stones. With the other hand, she worked out the day's menus, and on top of that she had to fill Mr Ferreira in on developments.

"Dammit," Ma would say each morning once she was off the phone. "It's an update for the station master every blasted morning. I feel like a weather reporter on the radio. And I know the news doesn't stop with him either. When he's finished with me, he phones all the station masters from Cookhouse to Noupoort with his gossip about the Entertainer – and at the Railways' expense." Ma stuck her pencil behind her ear and glanced at the wall clock. "You'd swear Elvis was in town," she'd say.

One day while Ma was complaining like this, she found Mr

Jacoby standing right behind her. We thought he was still in the Zane Grey because that's where he always had breakfast. Reuben had to stack it all on a tray while Ma kept an eagle eye on proceedings to make sure everything was still warm. Then Reuben had to trot down to the rondavel. Everyone accepted that the singer felt more at peace in the privacy of his own rondavel. "The Port Elizabeth crowd are quite capable of asking him to smile for their box cameras first thing in the morning," said Ma.

But this morning he suddenly appeared at the front desk. The guests on the terrace craned their necks, almost choking on their English breakfasts.

"Wow, you scared me!" Ma snapped shut the book in which she signed out the tennis balls.

"I hope I'm not being a nuisance." Mr Jacoby smiled at me. He looked at the Arizona sheriff's star that I'd pinned to my shirt. His hand swung up from his hip quickly, he pointed an imaginary gun and said, "Kabam!"

"Oh, no, of course not," Ma fluttered. She was knocked completely off her stride. "Is there a problem with your breakfast?" she asked quickly. "Can I offer you a cup of coffee? Is everything in the Zane Grey still to your liking? I'm sorry that the hot water to the rondavel basins ran out so early last night, but now that you're here, guests suddenly want to wash their hair every night and there isn't enough pressure in the donkey for hot water to . . ."

"It's all perfect," Mr Jacoby interrupted her, his rings flashing in the light. The guests at the breakfast tables leaned this way and that to get a better view. Some drew cameras out from under the table and it was clear that they'd been prepared for a chance appearance by Mr Jacoby. They kept the cameras at the ready in case he should step out on to the terrace.

"Don't they know any shame!" sighed Ma.

Mr Jacoby laughed. "I'm used to it," he said. "Never mind, let them be. They're on holiday, and when you're on holiday, you're not as strict about good manners as you might be at other times."

He flashed a smile at me. "I thought," he said, tipping his lounge stetson at an angle on his head, "that someone might go in to town today? I wondered if I could go along?"

The Pastor appeared suddenly at Ma's elbow. "I'm getting on the nine o'clock passenger train from Cookhouse," he said "for evangelical work." He smoothed his oily forelock. "Then I'm coming back on the four o'clock goods. You can come with me. The conductors all know me and I don't have to pay. If they recognise you, you won't need a ticket either."

"Hold on a minute," said Ma. "It'll only cause a commotion if Charles Jacoby suddenly appears on a train. That train won't get further than Dynamite Krantz."

Mr Jacoby just laughed.

"I'd have thought a car would be more comfortable," said the Veteran, also appearing from nowhere.

"But I've never seen you behind the wheel!" shouted the Pastor.

"I was, upon occasion, Montgomery's personal driver."

The Pastor folded his arms. Since the Veteran had withdrawn from their speaking-in-tongues sessions, he'd eyed him askance. "I thought you were an infantry man?"

The Veteran drew himself up and said in his fiercest parade-ground voice: "I was only Montgomery's chauffeur for the duration of his visit to our Division. I am an infantryman by calling and by inclination."

But it was the decisive Tant Geert who didn't make a bid, simply announced a fact. "Mr Jacoby will come with me in the Borgward," she said firmly.

Everyone swung round. We hadn't even been aware that she was there. A while ago, she'd mopped up the yolk of her egg with a piece of toast. She looked at me. "And young Fabian will be our gate opener."

Before there was time to argue we were in the Borgward. "Ah, an Isabella," said Mr Jacoby, stroking the upholstery. He sat at the back, so that he could enjoy the view. As we prepared to leave, it was clear that even the guests' dogs realised that the man with the lounge stetson was an important visitor because they milled around the Borgward with arched backs and tails curled up and competed to see who could leave the biggest pee-splashes on the hubcaps.

The guests on the terrace waved their handkerchiefs and stooped over their box cameras as we pulled off. The Veteran and the Pastor stood dejectedly beside Reuben whose silver tray flashed in the sun like a Roman soldier's shield.

As we drove along, Mr Jacoby asked, "What do you call this gate?"

"The Heartache gate," I told him. "Pa calls it that because it's the first gate between Soebatsfontein and the plains."

"And that furrow? What do you call it?"

"The Scanlan furrow – it brings water from Lake Arthur and Commando Drift. One day it will bring the Verwoerd Dam water."

"Oh yes, of course. I've heard of that big scheme. Where does that furrow lead?"

"Down to Kranzplaas. There's an aquaduct over the dry riverbed. It's the Divisional Council servitude all along here. Look how green the grass is – no animals can get to it. Olive Schreiner stayed on Krantzplaas."

"Oh, I see. Really? I see. What bird is that?"

"It's a hoopoe. It's nest stinks because it builds with cow-dung."

"It's pretty. Look at its crest."

"I only shoot starlings and finches. Pa's forbidden me to shoot anything else."

"It's a good thing that your daddy is protecting bird life. What's growing like that on the rocks? When did it last rain? What type of lizard is that one sitting there? What vintage is this Borgward? How long have you been afraid of heights, Master Latsky? What are you researching, Miss Latsky?"

Ma reckoned you could tell Mr Jacoby had an enquiring mind. She said she felt sorry for the day the music world would turn against him, when he was too old, or when new singers stole the limelight because that's when the emptiness hits you like a fist – she spoke from personal experience.

Mr Jacoby did not often take his stetson off in public. He even went to the toilet with his hat on, even after dark. "Maybe the hair is thinning on top," teased Pa, but Ma decided it was more likely to do with maintaining the public image. And she pointed out that he had taken his hat in his hand the day he'd arrived at Hotel Halesowen.

And naturally, though we didn't know that yet, Charles Jacoby would also sweep his hat off with a flourish when Verwoerd arrived at the Cradock town hall. But that still lay ahead – Verwoerd's visit, the procession through the streets of the town, Dr Clark leaning against the door frame of the Karoo Café watching Verwoerd's white head moving through the crowds.

"An Entertainment Artist must have an image. Image is everything. The image is the man." Ma waved her cigarette, poured a drink and stuck her pencil behind her ear. She blew the dust off the plastic roses. "If you lose your image, the public gets angry and they stop listening to your music."

"Does he bathe in his hat?" Pa asked with a laugh. "Maybe we should ask Fabian to do a bit of spying down at the ablution block. Hey, big boy? You snoop everything out, don't you?"

"Ag," shouted Ma.

"Does he sleep in his image?"

Ma turned away to her book with the grocery statistics. "Twenty-five loaves," she read aloud, "thirty Sunlight soaps, ten Mrs Ball's chutneys . . ." As she went along, she ticked the items with her pencil. Pa went to the bedroom and the curtain rings sang. Everything stopped for a moment and Ma and I looked at one another.

But then everyone picked up their tasks again and Ma chased me outside to go and play, "Come-come, sonnie, why are you standing there rubbing your paws like a praying mantis again? Why don't you ever play with the town children? You could teach them so much about the veld – about all the animals and plants and bird's eggs, instead of avoiding them as though they've got the plague."

Mr Jacoby asked all about the station, the signals, the cattle pens at the loading ramp, Dynamite Krantz, the river, the hide shed near the town station, the turn-off to Swaershoek, and about the town and its people.

"He asks so much," said Tant Geert at one stage, "that you never get a chance to ask him anything."

"Ja, that's the basic technique of a star," Ma answered. "A star must never drop his defences – he must protect his privacy at all times. The public has a hungry eye." She poured herself another brandy and said: "Wow, I'd better start using that tot measure again, my hand is getting heavy."

Tant Geert laughed with Ma and asked for a brandy too. "He's very professional," said Ma. "And so humble. You get guests who complain about every crack in the rondavel ceiling, every squeak of the fan, every little insect in the cupboard. Let people just get a bit jolly in one of the rondavels, and there's some old sourpuss stumping up to reception with a complaint. If one of the town dogs barks at night, or Fabian's bantams start crowing too early because it's full moon, you get a hairy look at the breakfast table. But not Mr Jacoby. He's as polite and patient as a Dutch Reformed minister. Always a friendly word for everyone, and never too grand to give someone an autograph."

"Jacoby's signature decorates everything at Soebatsfontein," growled Pa, "except the Latsky cheque book."

Ma had had Mr Jacoby write on a tablecloth: *With country and western love from Charles Jacoby*. In the Zane Grey he'd had to write on the wall above the bed: *Charles Jacoby the performer slept here*. Ma had had him write in the register: *Charles Jacoby, famous Star performer, stayed in this Establishment and enjoyed it immensely*.

Ma dictated all the words to him – she'd written the phrases on the back of her cigarette box. She had had him write everything in English.

Pa was furious. "You're embarrassing all of us." But Ma tapped a balloon and said: "Ag, it's the festive season and everyone feels more generous than usual."

"I suppose you're also going to organise a white Christmas,"

Pa sniped as he walked away. "Did you dream up all these things from your fortune cup?"

All the odd guests disturbed Pa: the Veteran, who regularly polished the name plate he'd put on his rondavel door, made no indication of ever moving and continued to say he'd only go the day his war veteran's pension showed up; the Pastor, who'd cultivate everyone who came into his orbit and who'd pray out loud every afternoon with his stoep bedroom door wide open; Tant Geert, who wouldn't budge an inch over her ancestor research and who'd also not volunteered one more word about Antjie Provee; Dr Clark who sat on the terrace with notebook and pen and, during their sessions, questioned mercilessly, prying and boring ever deeper into Pa's donga-eaten heart.

And now the singer with the rings, the stetson, the silver spurs and the white horse, Valour, which he'd ride through the lucerne fields in the late afternoon so the flocks of white tick birds would rise up lazily under the horse's hooves, settling again on the pines, and all the animals raising their heads and looking round at the man in white, the white horse and the flock of white birds swarming up before them and floating into the trees with leisurely wing strokes.

Pa withdrew to his room and set about reading his *Path of Truth* booklets. He rang the water bailiff at Lake Arthur and threatened him. He rang the officer in charge of the police station at Mortimer and asked him what he was doing about the thieves who boarded the goods train and robbed it while it stood at Halesowen overnight so that the locomotive could be filled with water. Shaking with bottled-up frustration, he took out Grandpa's will and Ma had to call Tant Geert to come and discuss family matters: the complicated trust, the family farm, the mistakes which had been made, the rumour that, at the end, Grandpa had been found against his bed in the town house with an empty pill bottle in his hand – one of the Karoo's richest sheep farmers who had everything and yet nothing. How, Pa asked Tant Geert, can we break the trust?

There are other members of the family, Tant Geert reminded him. Those from Graaff-Reinet, from Pretoria, the Ceres-Karoo family; there's young Fabian who still has to go to school – they're all part of the complicated game Grandpa is playing from his grave.

"But I want out!" Pa shouted. "I want to be free."

"Never mind," comforted Tant Geert. "Never mind." She nodded at Ma and Ma brought the bottle of sleeping remedy closer. Tant Geert held Pa's pale head with the greying hair and they waited until the sweet soporific calmed him and he fell into a light sleep.

That's how much the strangers who visited the Hotel Halesowen that Season disturbed Pa. For Ma, of course, it was the best Season ever – for the first time since her days on the stage she found herself in the middle of excitement. Even the prospect of stone throwing and political unrest in the New Year stimulated her.

"It's a Bumper Season," she said frequently, but she was as pale as Pa when he went down to the Bitter Aloe for his sessions with Dr Clark and returned to the homestead an hour later to collapse on his bed, depressed and exhausted.

Then Dr Clark would take a long walk on the river's edge. "He's studying the monkeys' behaviour," joked the Veteran. Ma's enthusiasm for her Star Performer did not go unnoticed by him. He shared Pa's jealousy. But he didn't say much about Mr Jacoby. "Hold your tongue, soldier!"

Tant Geert was the only one who felt herself to be on an even footing with Mr Jacoby.

"Hello, Charles," she'd greet him the first day they'd met, when Mr Jacoby had dismounted and Reuben was busy with his tray and dishcloth, chasing the town dogs into the furthermost corners of the yard. "I'm Geertruida. Call me Geert."

Ma, cross and flustered, stood behind Mr Jacoby gesturing, her mouth forming the word "mister", and when it looked as though Tant Geert hadn't understood: *Mister, mister, mister, mister,* Ma's pretty round lipstick painted mouth spelled out soundlessly, but Tant Geert ignored it and, taking her friend Charles's elbow, led him up on to the terrace.

And so it was that Tant Geert and Mr Jacoby began a friendship that was built during morning-tea sessions at their private table under the bluegum tree halfway between the Wilhelmina and the Zane Grey, and during late-afternoon strolls to the milking shed because they were both fond of animals and enjoyed the peace in the milking shed.

There they would stand watching the cows lazily chewing the cud and enjoying the relief of having the milk drained from their swollen udders; watching the dairymen's clean, experienced touch-fingers shiny with udder salve; and the milk running over their brown hands until they got a rhythm going on the teats and the streams sang into the buckets.

Tant Geert and Mr Jacoby liked the smell of the shed – the warm smell of the cows and the steamy smell of milk, the workers' sweat, the smell of the rawhide thongs, and of ammonia from the streams of yellow urine that gushed suddenly into the drainage channel when a cow lifted her tail and you had to jump clear before you got drenched. All the smells were bound by the fragrance of chopped lucerne and the stench of manure that drifted in from outside.

In the gathering dusk, they would stand and watch the dairymen fill bucket after bucket, pouring the warm milk into the cans. Sometimes Tant Geert would bring along a cup from the kitchen and then they'd each have a drink of warm milk, but it made both of them shudder a little bit because it was so fresh from the teat.

It wasn't an intimate friendship but Mr Jacoby found in Geert someone who was not intimidated by his fame, and he realised that along with her easy manner and self-assurance went an aversion to gossip and scandal, and idle curiosity, and that made him feel safe with this person in her flannels and broad lapels who treated him as her equal and discussed worldly matters with him for hours on end – the difficulties of travel, being away from a home, hotel rooms, train tickets, compartments, late buses, poor taxi services, restaurants and long-distance phone calls.

For her part, she recognised in him something of the wider

world, the ability to leave behind, to move, to expose oneself to one's own vulnerability, to search out risks, the forlornness of the long road, the loneliness of foreign places and the humming telephone lines.

She was something of a performer herself, I realise now, looking back, with her big entrances and departures at the beginning and end of the High Season every year; the postcards sent from the far corners of the earth to the family in the Karoo – those who'd remained trapped in the safe patterns of farm or town life.

So the two of them found something in each other, there under the bluegums, at their table with the floral tablecloth that Ma had sent over the lawn with Reuben, watching after him anxiously. And the best cups had been taken out – Grandma's set – and Reuben was scolded if his tray tilted even slightly because real gold was painted on the porcelain, and lots of miners, Ma told him, had lost their lives in their efforts to dig that gold out of the ground. "Be careful now, Jack, be careful, calm down, they aren't going to run away. Look, they're still sitting under the bluegums. Oh, heavens, hang on a minute, put it down a second, I forgot the teaspoons. Do you think I should put some chocolate cakes on the tray, with the compliments of the establishment, Reuben? Jack?"

41

Tant Geertruida, Mr Jacoby and I had now reached the bridge over the Fish River. We were in Cradock. The station was behind us, and over the bridge you could see the long street, trembling in the heat as it stretched up to the church.

"The Great Fish is just a trickle at the moment, Charles," said Tant Geert, "but if it rains heavily, the brown waters push down from here and even up at Soebatsfontein the old Fish groans from all the trees and branches and stumps that it drags along with it to the sea. It's burst its banks before now and chased the people who live here in River Street out of their houses – shame, the poor, as usual . . . and look ahead there, Charles. Look at the old church – do you know it's a replica of St Martin's in the Fields in London, right next to South Africa House? It looks just the same. Down to the last pillar. I went past it again in a taxi recently to admire it. Unbelievable; it looks as though someone had lifted the church out of London and put it down here. We call this one St Martin's in the Veld."

Mr Jacoby asked Tant Geert to pull up at the kerb. The purpose of his trip to town this morning was to plan his forthcoming concert during Doctor Verwoerd's visit. He wanted to start by having a good look at the bridge and then go and look over the town hall. Before the concert, he'd arrive at the station with Valour and then ride over the bridge and up to the hall. Even though it was school holidays, the cadet band would march behind him – in any case, the cadets were to escort the Doctor from the landing strip.

We stopped and Tant Geert put a cigarette into her holder. She leaned against the Borgward and watched Mr Jacoby as he inspected everything carefully.

"Have a look at that, Fabian," she said. "Have a look at how thoroughly a true professional goes to work. See how he plans every step, anticipates every eventuality; just look at how carefully the man goes to work. You'd think that an established singer like him wouldn't need to plan any more, you'd think he could rely on his instinct, but just look at that thoroughness, Fabian . . . learn from this, pupiltjie . . ."

Once Mr Jacoby had written all the particulars down on the back of his cigarette box, we drove down to the town hall. "When did the river burst it's banks? When was the bridge built? Where did the Fish River get its name from? What fish do you catch here? What is your school motto, Master Latsky? Is the Culture Board a big organisation? Is there a lot of unrest round here? How many people do you think will come to the concert? What do the cadets feel about having to march in the middle of the school holidays, Master Fabian?"

So Mr Jacoby asked his questions as we drove up to the town library where Miss Marge Bruwer worked. It was almost next door to the town hall.

"I'm going to say hello to Marge Bruwer in the Schreiner Room quickly," said Tant Geert, "while you two go and pace off the stage."

I strolled over to the town hall with Mr Jacoby. Passing cars slammed on their brakes and people's heads popped out of windows. Mr Jacoby was wearing his white lounge stetson and I had my sheriff's badge. We went into the town hall by the side door.

I'd never been in the town hall while it was empty. Now I was amazed at how big it was with its high ceiling and the hundreds of chairs, the stage and the long curtains that seemed too heavy ever to move.

"Not too bad," said Mr Jacoby, casting an expert eye round the hall. "I wonder what the acoustics are like." He paced off the stage. So many paces in that direction, so many paces across, so many back that way. He took out his cigarette box and a gold pen and noted down the measurements. He squinted upwards, examining the lights, seeking and finding the two red fire extinguishers against the wall behind the stage and establishing to his satisfaction that they were still relatively new. He led me to the fire stairs and found the emergency exit and the small dressing room where he would prepare himself before appearing on stage. He took out a fragment of blackboard chalk and drew a cross exactly in the middle of the stage. That's where he'd stand.

He looked at me. "Let's go, cowboy."

Outside, the sun was warm. Mr Jacoby waited at the car while I went to call Tant Geert. He leaned against the Borgward and, as cars came past and surprised faces swung round towards him, he made a little salute with his right hand against the stetson, Western style.

"It's good advertising," Ma said later. "Cradock is such a tiny place, if just three cars saw him, the whole town will know in a tick that he's around. He showed just enough – not too much, not too little. He doesn't come cheap, but he's not too scarce either . . . Wow, but the guy is a professional! It's actually amazing that he doesn't also sing in America."

Ma was very disappointed that she'd had to promise the Cultural Committee to keep his visit as quiet as possible. "People are going to curse us when they hear he was at Soebatsfontein and we kept him to ourselves."

I went into the library. It was quiet and there was no one among the shelves. The counter was also deserted and a kettle boiled away, steam already gathering against the ceiling.

Cautiously, because Miss Bruwer was always very strict about silence in the library and notices all over the place demanded that you be quiet as a mouse, I made my way between the shelves, past the Langenhovens and the Trompies and the Agatha Christies and the Zane Greys. All seemed abandoned there and I felt lost in the sour smell of pages that had been leafed through by so many fingers.

I came upon them without them seeing me, in the Schreiner Room, which was next to the reading room. They were under one of the oil portraits of some ancestor or another of Olive Schreiner's. Tant Geert's jacket had been thrown down on the shiny table where one could sit and read. Her shirt was unbuttoned and pulled off her shoulders, slightly, so you could see the brown liver spots.

This was right at the beginning of the relationship between Tant Geert and Miss Bruwer – a relationship that was to last for many years, until Miss Bruwer died tragically in a car accident between Cradock and Graaff-Reinet, on the Wapadsberg, one windblown Sunday afternoon. The driver had underestimated the turn in the gravel road and the dizzying drop suddenly gaped beside them; the old Midland Library Service Ford plunged down and Miss Bruwer called out "Geert!" one last time as she rolled around inside the car and dust started to cake on the blood at the corners of her mouth. At last, all was still, the car lying upside down, halfway down the mountain, the dust cloud drifting off slowly and then settling; the frightful silence gave no hint of what had happened.

The chassis of the car creaked a couple of times and the driver lay dead still. He was already gone. Miss Bruwer lay there fully conscious and, through the broken glass, she could see the shimmering plains, the clouds gathering far on the horizon and a couple of rock kestrels that swooped and dived over the veld. I don't know what she thought of, lying there, pinned under the wreck, bleeding herself empty. But that's the way she died, within an hour or two of the accident. And it was only after a full day that a passing farmer on his way to a stock sale noticed the Ford's tracks veering so suddenly over the bank and down the slope.

But now, Tant Geert and Miss Bruwer were still full of the passion of newly discovered love. They couldn't display their love in public, walking round hand in hand at Soebatsfontein, for example. Everything had to be conducted in a hasty and clandestine fashion, and Tant Geert had a battle to get Miss Bruwer to go as far as agreeing to move into the Wilhelmina for the remaining weeks of her stay. "No one will suspect anything, Marge," she comforted. "We owe it to each other. One of these days I'll have to be off again and then it'll be goodness knows how long before I can return to the Karoo."

Tant Geert was bent over backwards and Miss Bruwer was licking the two brownish-pink scars on her chest. They were already shiny with her saliva and the breath grated in Tant Geert's throat. Before they noticed me, I turned into a shadow among the shelves in the adults' section.

I stood there listening to the sounds, the rasping breath, the table legs scraping slightly, the rustle of clothes, and I imagined that I could smell saliva. Then I crept over to the counter and stood irresolutely there, out of earshot. The silence was punctuated by sounds from outside – hooting cars and Mr Jacoby's "Howdy!" as he greeted his fans.

Then I rang the small silver bell you could use to call the librarian. Ping! It was as though the air suddenly thickened in the library. I heard sounds again, hasty, whispered voices. I looked up and Olive Schreiner stared sternly down at me from her portrait. Her eyes burnt into mine. I closed one eye and took aim at her. I saw nothing. I opened my eye and closed the other one. Olive's eyes bored into my open one. Tant Geert and Miss Bruwer appeared from behind the shelves. They cleared their throats and tugged at their clothes. "Hello, Fabiantjie," called Tant Geert shrilly. "My, but you were quick. Have you finished already? Where's Charles?"

"Tant Geert," I said. "I feel funny; I feel drunk in my head again, and I can't see through my right eye. It's gone blind."

Tant Geert fell to her knees before me. "Pupiltjie!" she cried. She smelt of spit. There was a red blotch on her neck. "Which eye, dear?" She gripped my shoulders. "Can you see nothing at all through it?"

"No, this eye." I pointed to my right eye. "It's blind."

"Oh, Lord in Heaven!" cried Miss Bruwer, grasping her forehead.

"Howdy!" we heard Mr Jacoby calling outside.

42

Gravel struck the bluegums as Tant Geert pulled up below the terrace. On the tennis courts, the guests stopped playing and craned their necks to see over the shrubs. The couple of people who were sipping beer and lemonade on the terrace to stave off the heat, came to stand at the railing to stare down at us. Ma was there in a flash, coming down the steps.

"What's going on?" she asked. "Mr Jacoby, is something wrong? Is everything to your liking?"

"The child is blind in one eye." Tant Geert got out and looked at Ma, who looked back at her. Tant Geert's words didn't seem to have sunk in.

"What child?" she asked slowly.

"Fabian," Tant Geert told her.

Ma swung round to me. She stared at me and I tried to smile. My eye felt like a cold ghoen in my head, like a dead river pebble that I wanted to pull out and throw away. I felt dizzy and the eye began to twitch and I couldn't control it.

He had come in the night and his saliva had dripped into my eye as he had bent over me. It had eaten the pupil away and got in through my eye socket to my veins. He'd snuffled about all over my room while I had lain there drugged by his saliva, with my head thrown back and my mouth half open, the way Pa always lay after he'd taken his sleeping remedy. He'd fiddled with my things in his paws, had picked up my catapult, had sniffed it and put it down again, had picked up my Dinky Toys one by one and studied them, feeling the little wheels and looking in through the tiny windows. He'd fondled my clothes and put my marbles in his mouth, tried to chew them and then spat them out again. He'd picked up my school books and tried to catch the red ants on the pages.

He'd gone over to the washbasin and tried to suck from the taps without knowing how to turn them on, and then he'd sniffed at the plug and pissed his steaming yellow pee into the basin because he'd smelt my pee on the plug, my pee that I splashed in there at night when Pa and Ma were already asleep and I was too frightened to go to the toilet in the dark. When he had finished, he'd slunk out of the room and left the house by the end dining-room door, the one that was left unlocked for guests on summer nights.

Pa was near now, and Reuben too, with the tray in front of his chest, as though he wanted to protect himself from the danger. The Veteran stood at the top of the steps on the terrace, upright as a Field Marshall, as Pa carried me up, suddenly strong and decisive, his own anxieties forgotten. The Pastor with his trembling evangelical touch was in the background, with a comforting hand on Ma's shoulder.

Mr Jacoby, in a gesture he was never to repeat in similar circumstances throughout his stay – perhaps he was confused or thoughtful – took off his stetson and exposed his forehead. It should have been a swaggering gesture that he reserved for very special occasions. But no one noticed, except me where I lay limply in Pa's arms as he carried me up the steps, barking at Reuben to get the guests to keep their distance.

I had to lie on a sofa while Pa shone a torch into my eye. I heard his voice: "There's a pearl on the child's eye."

"It's a cataract," said Tant Geert.

"But when did the thing grow?" asked Ma. "What does the other eye look like?"

"Heavens!" cried Tant Geert.

Ma pushed Pa's torch to one side. "Fabiantjie, here's my hand. How many fingers can you see?"

"Six," I lied, and, just before Ma burst into tears, Tant Geert broke in, "He's pulling your leg, man. No hand has six fingers."

"Fabian!" cried Pa. "Don't play the fool. Have you had headaches recently?"

I shook my head.

"Are you sleeping well?" asked Ma.

Tant Geert bent over me, "Why do you wander around the rondavels at night, Fabian?"

"What's this about wandering around?" Pa looked angrily at Tant Geert.

"Hush now, shush," Ma comforted, laying a hand on Pa's arm. Suddenly she had an inspiration: "Call Dr Clark!"

"No, he's a doctor of the soul," countered the Pastor, who'd appeared behind Ma.

"And don't you come here with your laying on of hands," threatened Pa. "None of your Anabaptist nonsense here."

"Okay, okay," the Pastor gestured with both hands raised, palms towards me. I looked at the scars in his palms where he'd burnt himself with a lit cigarette once, as a penance. He knew that the Creature had dribbled into my eye. He knew who snuffled about here at night, he knew about the droppings, trodden deep into the earth so you couldn't see them with the naked eye or smell them directly. You could only smell them at night when their penetrating stink hovered in the air – a smell you couldn't quite place, but that drifted restlessly through the trees and clung to the palate, so that guests brushed their teeth for longer than usual as they stooped over their washbasins in the rondavels, or Ma complained there was an after-taste in the milk.

Then the Veteran pitched up as well. "Corporal! I served for a spell in the Medical Corps in North Africa. It seems to me you're wounded, corporal."

"Medical Corps?" queried the Pastor.

But the Veteran bent over me. "Give me that torch." He pulled the eyelid back and looked in my eye. He examined my other eye. He straightened and handed the torch back to Pa, announcing: "The child is a G-3. He was born that way."

"A G-3?" Ma asked, frightened.

"That's someone who is unfit for Service to the third degree," explained the Veteran, dusting off his hands.

"For God's sake," growled Pa, "what rubbish." He pulled me upright. "Come on, Fabian." He looked at Ma. "Get the car. Lyell must have a look. We're going to town. And, if necessary, we'll go straight down to PE for a specialist opinion."

"But I can't just drop everything here!" Ma looked round anxiously, at her front desk, the telephone, the open bookings register with the pencil fastened to it by a string, her shelf with the record books full of rainfall, tennis-ball, grocery and other statistics, to her terrace with the guests sitting there, keeping their distance, but still craning their necks inquisitively to try to see what was going on in here.

"Call Reuben," Pa commanded. It was an Order and Ma hurried to fetch Reuben who was standing at the end of the terrace with his shield before him, his white cloth over his arm, silent, upright, motionless.

Reuben came to the sofa where I lay, but he didn't look at me because my relationship with him was something outside the relationships that bound him to Pa and Ma and the other adults. When they were around he and I ignored one another.

He stood upright, listening to Pa. "Reuben, you're now in charge here. Do you understand, my Jack? Put down your tray and tea towel . . . come, come, do it first so you don't get confused."

Reuben put his tray on the desk carefully. Taking his time, he took the white cloth from his arm and folded it. He put it on the corner of the tray. Then he came back into the circle around me.

"What do you say if someone rings?" asked Pa.

"I say, 'Hello, Hotel Halesowen'."

"Good boy, Reuben. And if they want to make a booking, then . . ."

"Then I say we are fully booked until 15 January. Then the Utrecht will be available. It takes three beds."

Pa looked amazed.

"But Reuben," cried Ma, "how do you know about our bookings?"

"The book is always open," answered Reuben. "While I am waiting for bar service, I read it."

"Commendable," said the Veteran. "We should have had him with us up North."

"He's really a sharp kaffir," said the Pastor. "He could become a lay preacher in the locations just like that." He snapped his fingers.

"Okay, fine, Reuben," Pa continued, "if you don't understand something, just . . ." Pa interrupted himself and looked indecisively from the Pastor to the Veteran, from Mr Jacoby to the guests outside the windows. ". . . then you ask Miss Geertruida. And if there's really a big problem, go and knock on Dr Clark's door, down there at the Bitter Aloe, but don't bother him unless you have to because he's busy writing. Only if there's really big trouble."

"Fire or a fight," Ma added.

"Come on," said Pa. "Let's get going."

Ma said she'd open the gates today. I was told to sit quietly on the back seat and to move as little as possible.

"Try to look straight ahead, Fabian," said Ma. "Or, better still, keep your eyes closed."

I sat with my eyes closed in the back of the Volkswagen. I felt the bumps in the strip road, heard the Scanlan furrow slide by, felt the scratching feet of the hoopoe, smelt the trains as we went past Halesowen. I felt Dynamite Krantz go by, heavy and dark, and I got goose flesh as its shadow fell over us. I smelt the Collets' orchard and the lime pit beyond Hasimara. I could smell the Veteran's Brasso and Miss Bruwer's spit on Tant Geert's chest. I saw Tant Geert's marks, shining with spit – eyes like the ones you get in a tree-trunk when you cut through it.

Dynamite Krantz jerked slowly open and climbed up into the air and the dust settled and the Fish was stained brown, for miles, to the south. As far as Golden Valley, we heard afterwards, people wondered what had happened upstream.

In the night an apparition clambered amongst the loose rocks and boulders scratching out dead dassies and shrivelled mice and flat beatles from the gravel and feasted so happily all night that he woke up next morning with a pot-belly to find the sun already high in the sky and that the SAR&H's gang had come with their picks and shovels to dig out the dead foreman.

Then I realised – there in the darkness in the back of the Volkswagen, with the gravel road rumbling under the car – that the Beast would never leave me; not while I was a child, not when I graduated to a bigger school, not while I was studying, no matter where I might go to civilise myself at Tant Geert's recommendation; and not when I was grown up, not even when I reached Pa and Ma's age.

He would stay with me through all my days, guarding over me, just as he was the shadow in the lives of everyone I watched through my good eye that summer – the eye that I thank the Lord for, because if that also died then it would have been just me and the Beast in the dark, from now until the end of days.

43

"It's an unimportant summer," Tant Geert comforted me. "A completely unimportant summer. One day you'll find you've shaken it all off, Fabian. You'll have forgotten all about it.

You'll grow out of it . . . What the hell, it's just the mad bluebeard Latskys and all the eccentrics that they always seem to gather round them who've disturbed you so much. That old Tantalus-daddy of yours.

"Pupiltjie, I must take you with me into the world. It's becoming a matter of urgency for me to get you away from here. Do you know how boys of your age live in Leiden and Utrecht and Amsterdam? You'll meet them one day because I know you'll travel. You'll meet your contemporaries from those cities . . .

"Fabiantjie, you must get out, you must get away from this shrivelled, stifling Karoo, out of this dusty country, out of Africa. God knows, I'm so fond of the sunsets and the tick birds and the smell of the veld and the awful wide open spaces, even the droughts, because there's a certain dignity in such a merciless reduction, in such a freezing of possibilities and enterprise . . . but, Fabian, it creates people who are as gnarled as the succulents that have to survive among rocks under a merciless sun, stingy in their thoughts and their dreams, prepared to do anything just to survive.

"This place makes one home in on survival, pupiltjie, and man cannot live on survival alone. You need more than that. A Breughel and a Hooft, a Shakespeare and a Coleridge, a Goethe. You need a Catallus, a Sibelius and a Nietszche, a Wagner and a Freud . . .

"I don't know whether you know who these people are or not, and I regret that I am mentioning only men's names, because women are always kept in the background . . . but Fabiantjie, how can I explain it to you?

"I'm not saying we don't belong here because white is just skin deep. You know. But I feel so nervous when I think of our ancestors – about the struggling wagons on the empty landscape, the reed houses, the hopeless battle to get seeds to germinate, to build up a flock, to stack a stone wall, to lay a roof, to get a document written by someone somewhere in the district who could write, to arrange a communion service or rally a commando to ride out against cattle rustlers, to hack a grave into the hard earth, three feet deep because the bed rock prevents you from getting to a decent six feet.

"I think of the villages turning their brave faces up to the harsh sun for centuries, the emptiness, the poverty of the blacks . . .

"God, Fabian, how many houses do you think have books in them? Paintings? Do they know who Botticelli is? Do they know about Nietzsche's crazy ideas? Do they know how . . . ag, leave it. I've had too much sherry. I love this place, but there's so little to do here that within a few weeks I fall to drink like your mommy . . . I don't know how the woman copes with that brother of mine and his lost soul. I just don't know . . . Go to sleep now, Fabian, go to sleep now, kiddo, off you go, back to the big house. And this night wandering among the rondavels must stop too, now, pupiltjie. You're seeing things you shouldn't be seeing . . . there, there, shut my door after you . . . Sometimes I think all the bloody-mindedness of all the Latskys has been bred into him. He's always suffering from the wrong rememberings. He stands there guarding over the flame under him, the flame that's never turned low, a foul pot of dark ground coffee, so dark, oh, so black, Fabian, you have no idea, pupiltjie . . .

"Fabian, have you gone, pupiltjie? Oh, Marge, Marge, why don't you come? Why are you so scared of the gossips? Ag Marge, it's just a summer like so many others, a normal summer in the old Karoo, an unimportant summer.

"That's what it is, a summer of no importance at all.

"And you're still there then, pupiltjie? Run along now, so drunken old Geert can get some sleep . . ."

44

"Goodness, but we are a bunch of specimens," said Ma, dabbing her cheeks with a tightly balled tissue. "A retired actress, a farmer working for an LSD experiment, an old war hero, a missionary, a head doctor, a lounge crooner and a travelling scientist . . . and now Fabian, too, blind as a bat in the right eye. And the only guests we attract are PE's sad sacks, this Hotel Halesowen . . ."

"Soebatsfontein," growled Pa, and then rattled off more of his favourite place-names: "God-se-oog. Verneukpan. Putsonderwater. Genadeloosrant. Pynlikheid. Perdvreklaagte."

We were driving home to the farm. Through her tears, Ma kept asking me things like, "Look at that windmill, can you see it, Fabian?" or, "My, look how strangely those hawks are circling. Are they rock kestrels, Fabian? Have a look, my boy."

Dr Lyell had said, "Take it easy. Take it easy now." He looked at Ma as we went into his consulting room. It stank of Dettol and medicines. "Hmmm," said Dr Lyell. He had me sit on the bed, sat himself on a stool in front of me and looked into my eyes with his light. "Look over there," he said. "Now over there. Turn that way." Then he had me sit in front of a reading card. "FMRSTYHTKZ," I read with my good eye. "Nothing." I shook my head when I had to keep my dead eye open and shut the other one.

Dr Lyell shone his light into my eye and I could see the spider's web wrinkles on the palm of a red hand. The hand took hold of my face and squeezed the breath out of my lungs. I shut my eyes and felt how it must be to go completely blind. A breath fanned my cheek, but I couldn't see what it was. Dr Lyell took his stethoscope and listened to my chest. "Hmmm. Hmmm," he said. Then he asked me to lie on my back and relax. "Haanow, haa-now," he said. "Haa-now, little champ. Haa-now."

I opened my eyes and Ma and Dr Lyell were bending over me. "Hmmm. Hmmm." The rock falcons circled in their eyes. "Did you know you were blind in one eye?" Dr Lyell asked.

"Did you know, Fabian?" asked Ma.

"How long have you known, Fabian?" asked Pa.

"When did you find out?" asked Dr Lyell.

I closed my eyes. "On the water tank," I fibbed.

"Oh!" cried Ma. "Oh, my child! When Mr Jacoby arrived?"

Dinosaurs lived in the Karoo; they say their skeletons still exist in the clay underground. Shells never let you forget. They rest in the banks of dongas. They crumble if you pick them up. Tides had tugged here, water swamps.

"Oh, my child . . ."

"Haa-now. Hmmm . . ."

"God's-eye," said Pa, looking through the Volkswagen's window. He looked far over the horizon. Only a Latsky, Ma always said, could look so far into the horizon, as though he could see all the suffering of all the years that lay ahead, as though he could see hell yawning.

"Can you believe it?" Ma shook her head and looked through her window over the tissue she was pressing against her nose. "Can you believe the child was born this way and he's been running around all these years without our finding out? Have we been neglecting our Fabiantjie? Our little one-eyed boy?"

Lucky for Ma there was a quarter-jack of comfort in the glove compartment. Pa let her be. He drove and looked the other way. Sometimes there's a throwback in the genes, he always said.

Now, I thought sitting there in the back, now I'll have to hear that it's Antjie Provee's blood; now Pa will drag that business up again and blame the slave woman; now Pa will go absolutely berserk because I've brought disgrace on the Latskys; now . . .

"Why are you shaking so much, Fabiantjie?" asked Ma, turning to me. "It's high summer, child. Here, have a little sip. Come, I'll pour a drop into the lid for you. It'll help with the shock. Come on, sip it. Won't you? Don't you want it?"

Back at the house they were all waiting for us. "Birth defect," was all Pa said when he saw Tant Geert, the Pastor and the Veteran waiting there. Then, bitterly, "His mother must have had a drink the day that eye should have been developing."

Luckily Ma didn't hear him. To this very day I'm glad that she didn't hear, although I think it's possible that he might have slung it at her another day because she was always conscious of my eye. From then on we had to sit to the right in the bioscope. So that everything would be on my left eye's side. I had to read less, because I shouldn't wear out my healthy eye. I had to eat a lot of carrots, finely grated, because they were good for the eye. I had to wear a hat in the sun. I had to get more sleep . . .

Now she sighed, "Ag, it's a sick time." But when she began to talk to Reuben, she praised him for his neat entries on the back of a shoe box lid about how many tennis balls were out and about everyone who'd phoned.

"Your spelling's up the creek, Reuben, but I must say, I can tell exactly what's been going on here at the desk while we've been away. I'd give you the evening off immediately if it wasn't that you're the only one who knows how to mix a Bing Crosby just as old Mr Summerville likes it. Fabian, come and look here. Come and see what nice columns Reuben has made on the back of this shoe-box lid. My, oh my, I'm pleasantly surprised."

I walked to the dining room with my good eye shut. I turned among the tables. I felt cloths brushing against my legs and I heard the faint tinkle of cutlery as I bumped into tables. I tried to guess which table I was near. Number eighteen or number seven? Number three or eight?

Suddenly I heard Ma's voice right beside me, "Ag, no, Fabiantjie. What are you up to now? No, man, it isn't natural for a child of your age to stand here spinning on his own axle. No, man, go and play outside. A person does have two eyes, after all, sonnie."

I turned to Ma. She blew her bottle breath over me and the Veteran stood a little way back, like a crow hovering over the white tablecloths. "The Beast has a row of eyes!" I shouted. "The labourers have seen Kikuyu!"

"Fabian!" Ma scolded. "You've had your nose too deep in the books again. Scoot now. Go and get some fresh air. Go and help Reuben to pick a bowl of fresh peaches for me in the orchard. And only the ones without worms, you hear?"

Ma and the Veteran went to sit at table seventeen while I went out. They sat in the corner where the light was dim. He bent towards her and the shadows of his black wings fell over her. I could smell Dr Lyell's consulting room: Genadebrood. Allesverby. Kommaarklaar. Godverlaat. Duiwelsbrood. God-se-oog-fontein. I could hear Pa muttering in the room as I passed by under the window.

In the orchard the peach smell fell over me and Reuben asked quietly: "Shall we each eat one ourselves, Kleinbaas Fabian?"

"Better not. But I'll bring two to your room for you to-night."

"And another *Reader's Digest*?"

"Hey, Reuben! You're reading too fast!"

He looked at me. "Are you going blind?" he asked.

I shook my head. "No," I said. "But I can only see half of what you see. That's all."

45

That night Ma made a mistake with the LSD Pa was supposed to get. By one o'clock in the morning all the guests were assembled in their dressing gowns in the yard in front of the big house. The mothers tried to chase their children back to the rondavels, but the children hid behind the ghostly white bluegum trunks. The dogs barked and nannies emerged in their blankets from the row of rooms behind the donkey. They looked strange without their head scarves, and when they moved and the blankets slipped from their shoulders you could see their bare breasts. Ma's dressing gown fluttered in the breeze and she held a lantern. We were all looking up because Pa was crouched on top of the gable of the big house. He was wearing striped pyjamas and blood ran down the side of his face.

It was when Tant Geert appeared beside Ma that Pa started crying. He threw down the knife and the blade gleamed in the lamplight. The knife fell on the lawn and the dogs rushed forward to lick the blood from the blade. Then they went off to lift their legs against the tyres of the cars which gleamed in the moonlight where they stood under the trees.

We kept the piece of his ear that Pa had cut off himself in a jam jar of formalin that Dr Lyell brought for Ma after racing along the dirt road from town to come and stop the blood.

"God, doctor," Ma had said over the telephone, her cigarette trembling between her fingers. "He tried to cut off his ear. Please bring something we can preserve it in."

That's Ma for you – practical right to the bitter end.

46

That summer? A different one? Or do things repeat themselves, so that day and year don't really matter, anyway? Isn't every story just a return to an earlier one, an addition, an amplification . . . or even a process of betrayal?

This is the currency of memory: betrayal of the past and of those with whom you shared the past.

This morning I was overcome by sudden doubt when I received the Schreiner documents from Miss Elsabe Bouwer of the Public Library in Cradock.

She'd gone to a lot of trouble: photographs of the stone grave on Buffelskop, an issue of the *Nuwe Afrikaner*, photocopies of documents. And, all at once, with the fragrance of sun-warmed rocks and bruised succulents rising from the array of documents, that sad summer rose before me, uninvited, with the discomfort of undigested memories.

My love for that piece of earth – our broken-down old Soebatsfontein – was formulated for the first time by a short newspaper report. Perhaps it was the first time that I had seen my world portrayed in words – the place where, as a child, I'd looked around me every day. Perhaps it was a kind of home-coming from the stories on the library shelves to the landscape I had known.

In the town library I read:

"Olive's body was embalmed and placed in a teak coffin, zinc-lined, and, after a simple service, laid to rest temporarily at Woltemade No 1. Meanwhile the sarcophagus was being built on top of Buffelskop out of ironstone, by a local stone mason, Joe Mann. When everything was ready, Olive's body was brought up by train, and at De Aar, Cronwright was waiting with two small coffins. One of the baby and the other of their beloved dog, Nita.

"On 13th August a little procession of friends climbed up Buffelskop, the coffin being carried by ten staunch natives.

"How good it was that Olive should sleep in Nature's open temple with its magical beauty and vastness of space.

"Cronwright Schreiner, who spoke a few moving words, ended by repeating a verse from Tennyson's 'In memoriam':

" 'Thy voice is on the rolling air,
I hear thee where the waters run,
Thou standest in the rising sun . . .' "

Miss Bruwer had already found me hanging around the door to the Schreiner Room earlier that morning.

"Have you heard of Olive Schreiner, boy?" she'd asked as she'd done many times before, peering at me over her spectacles. "Do they tell you about her at that school of yours?"

I had shaken my head. No, I'd indicated, as I'd done many times before, faithful to our ritual.

Oh, the open winds on Buffelskop! When the kestrels dive over rock ledges, the valley falls away at your feet as you stand high on the roof of the world, amongst warm ironstone and spekboom: nothing around you, just wisps of cloud and Joe Mann's stone paunch.

Miss Bruwer and I performed our ritual because I had to wait in the town library every afternoon until Ma fetched me for the drive back to the farm. Now, during the holidays, I sometimes waited here while Ma and Pa consulted Dr Lyell about Pa's remedies or went to see the bank manager about the family trust.

We sat again in the quiet, sour Schreiner Room, beside the hand-written manuscripts behind glass, the Victorian stiffness of Olive's portraits against the walls. I paged through the yellowed books Miss Bruwer pushed towards me. I didn't really listen to her continuous chatter in bastard English and Afrikaans, only picking up a word here and there that sounded familiar. Especially place names: Gannahoek, Kranzplaas (our neighbouring farm, where Olive lived after she married Cronwright), Leliefontein . . . At one stage Miss Bruwer grabbed my forelock and pulled it a couple of times.

"Wake up, boy," she said. "Wake up to your heritage. Your mother is from the Cape, isn't she? With English blood in her veins?"

And a little later, "Olive understood this country. She could unite. She could write life back into the country . . . not those soldiers out there."

Outside, the soldiers' boots stamped on the town square between the library and the Karoo garden with the droopy palms and dead frogs in the lily pond. They were practising for the parade planned by the city council for the visit from the Prime Minister and Mr Jacoby.

Later, when Miss Bruwer went off to make herself a cup of coffee (townsfolk gossiped that she always put in a splash of brandy), I tip-toed out over the creaking wooden floor. I leaned against the pillars in front of the library and thought about Pa with the piece ripped out of his ear, just like his stock grazing in the fields, ear-marked against theft and straying.

"The man is mad!" I remembered Reuben's words. "That boer is mad!"

I watched the soldiers. They'd fallen out and were lounging on the hot tarmac. They looked bored, smoking lazily, resting their heads on their helmets or winking at the town girls who ducked quickly in and out of shops and offices.

Suddenly the summer had acquired a different smell, a new

texture. From there where I stood against the pillar and looked out across the square, I couldn't put it into words. But something was on the go, I knew, or perhaps it had already happened, something that made me turn and go inside, to where Miss Bruwer was busy stamping books. I noticed that she'd put away the books we'd paged through. The highly polished table tops in the Schreiner Room stood empty. An ashtray waited in the middle of the main table for someone in the forsaken town at this time of stone throwing and foreboding, to come and read up on the writer who lay buried on the mountain behind Halesowen station and near the railway line between Port Elizabeth and De Aar.

47

It was inevitable that Tant Geert's wanderings at Soebatsfontein should eventually take her across Dr Clark's path – especially in the time before Miss Bruwer plucked up courage enough to move into the Wilhelmina with Tant Geert for the High Days.

It was the time when Tant Geert was walking so much that she was hardly ever seen sitting in the shade of the bluegums. "I'm walking my weight off," was all she'd say. "Here at Soebatsfontein you increase in weight but not in wisdom."

Tant Geert and Dr Clark were both walkers. With her jacket lapels flying away from her broad chest, she surged over the plains, a galleon on the brown waves of hills and shrubs. As she held her course to the next swell, her afternoons became voyages of discovery. The glint in her eye told you that, even at her age, Tant Geert still believed that life held surprises.

Dr Clark had his own style. With his nimble limbs, his eyes darting about as though to decipher the very shadows under the thorn trees, as though he were assessing the moods of the veld, measuring the moodiness of the rocks, he came across as more intense, also less at home in the monotonous plains. In his haste, he walked slightly sideways – Tant Geert said that you have to walk like that on New York City's pavements to make your way through the hordes of people. In comparison with Tant Geert he was no frigate – perhaps a streamlined yacht, too fast for his chosen waters, running close to the wind.

Fast people – clock people – have never felt at home in the Karoo; it is a world that breeds endurance and patience. Ma always said, "Only four things a year happen in the Karoo: Winter, Spring, Summer and Autumn. You have to match your pace to that, otherwise you'll go off the rails."

The two first met by chance and exchanged polite greetings, the patient's sister, the patient's doctor. Pa stood between them, Janus-faced. Turning his sad gaze on them, each in turn. Two loyalties that repelled one another, like opposite poles. After a courteous nod – or later, a remark about the weather – they each set off in a different direction, taking pains to ensure they didn't bump into one another again; until a subsequent, unavoidable, meeting under one of the belts of pines, beside a windmill, on the bank of the dam, or, suddenly, amongst the reeds.

In spite of themselves, their conversations grew longer. From one terse exchange, grew another, longer one, and friendship, too, grew like a crystal, every gesture of agreement or fellow feeling was a further crystallisation which grew on to the increasing mass.

"Is it the same old story," Tant Geert finally threw down the gauntlet one afternoon on the plains, "of parent and child? Of father and son? The Puer Eternus? Must I ask, like Parsifal, what ails him?"

"I can't reveal anything," answered Clark. The sun flashed on his spectacle lenses. He looked slightly befuddled here in the open, with his hair windblown, the sweat making his spectacles slide down his nose so he had to push them up again repeatedly, his skin reddening in the sun. He fiddled with his wristwatch, clearly uncomfortable with Tant Geert's question.

New York City, thought Tant Geert. What had they done

there to this clever young man? And what is he doing with his strange remedies in the isolation of the Karoo? A new breed of witchdoctor? A medicine man? A muti man? A juju from the concrete jungle?

"I'm his sister."

"You're unfair. I'm as discreet as the Sphinx."

The canny Tant Geert knew that he'd made a concession. He looked away as she challenged him. "The subtlest of friends," she tested him.

He smiled and glanced up at the sun. A clever woman, he thought. "Blank and pitiless as the sun," he quoted.

In that instant, Tant Geert saw a potential soul mate in him. Her cynicism about the New Yorker started to recede – and, in the days that lay ahead, it would dwindle even further.

Because she knew he'd given more than he'd perhaps wanted too, she raised a hand in salute, "Till next time then."

"So be it. Our paths obviously converge."

Tant Geert smiled. "All roads lead to Rome."

"To Rome, then."

"To Rome, Dr Clark. The New York of the ancient world."

He wasn't sure whether she was pulling his leg or not. "Just as you say, Miss Latsky."

"Good day."

"Good day."

Like two ants that had touched feelers momentarily, they drifted apart on the plains. From the slopes of Buffelskop they might also have seemed like two tumbleweeds propelled by the wind.

Neither of them had noticed the Veteran on a hill nearby, the row of medals flashing on his chest. For some reason or another he'd felt that today he'd needed to wear his medals for his walk.

He stood inert and upright, as though preparing himself to implode into the black hole of his own shadow.

48

When you're a child, things have to have a name. The hairier, the scarier, the more sharply defined, the better. How else was I to digest the things that were going on around me?

To add to everything, the Veteran began to focus his frustrated blood lust on the Beast and started taking me on endless expeditions into the veld. Only to tell me, where we sat somewhere on warm rocks with a good view out over the river, that I carried my mother's fragrance about me and, when we tackled the heights of Buffelskop and I began to sweat, that I smelt strongly of her.

And at night the workers sat round their fires drinking wild-honey beer (brewing it was strictly forbidden) and spun yarns about the Thing, and his slinking about and his troublesomeness on the thresholds of the huts where young girls lived. They talked of how he lay low in the dongas where the children went to relieve themselves because Pa wouldn't build toilets for the workers. The first lot of wooden toilets had been chopped up for firewood, said Pa, even though there was perfectly good firewood only a morning's walk away.

In addition, I'd come upon the conversations between Tant Geert and Dr Clark as I dawdled in the peach orchard. I don't know when they'd decided to get together regularly. But they'd made an arrangement to meet in the seclusion of the orchard, amongst the tall dandelions where they sat and talked endlessly.

The snatches that reached my ears haunt me to this day, and it's still difficult for me to weave them together into something that makes sense. And I can't be sure that I always heard right, or if I remember correctly the things that I did hear: Did the Veteran ever touch me, in a certain way, in his rondavel or there among the rocky ridges while we searched for the Beast, or was it all just talk?

What did I take in of the endless exchanges between Ma and Pa, when they thought I was asleep; when they thought that the whole of Soebatsfontein – perhaps the whole world – was asleep, and it was just the two of them and their growing despair?

Why, to this very day, am I still so wary of certain expressions, certain words and formulations. And why, in my later life, did I take the fulfilment of Tant Geert's wishes as inevitable – that I would travel continuously, always departing, always headed into the unknown, always seeking out a new kind of loneliness?

But fragments of phrases stay with me from those mornings in the orchard, when I lay near them, concealed amongst the weeds, while they exchanged phrases like, "The parent is the wound", or "Eye, foot, womb, breast, ear, heart . . . we all have to make the acquaintance of our own wound . . ." And, when they discussed the stories about the half-person, "Raka," Tant Geert would laugh, "Old Blackfoot", "Kikuyu", or "Kees", – that *something* that left knuckle marks in the yard and could be a werewolf or a tokoloshe or Antjie Somers. Then Tant Geert would shout, "Melampsos!" and Dr Clark would nod his head in a measured way and I would get the feeling that, afterwards, he'd hurry to the Bitter Aloe and open his encyclopaedia at M.

I was very observant, Ma always said, and I remember from my childhood the subtle shifts in relationships, the secrets and the unspoken fears, the insinuations and pre-judgements, the jealousies and all the other forces that built up during that summer after the visit of the Prime Minister and the Jacoby concert, and after that Christmas Eve and Christmas Day, and, naturally, New Year's Eve celebrations with its Midnight and its dawning of 1961 and the unjustified, pathetic conviction that the New Year must be celebrated because it could not help bringing an improvement on the previous year, the consequent pulling of crackers and the slurping of champagne froth, as though people didn't realise – and I already knew it – that it would only bring them closer to their own death, their own oblivion.

As though they didn't know that time is the hungriest of all creation, that we are its fodder, and that it feeds on us in order to live itself and drag itself forward, year after year, to the final day where God himself waits for it – that day when all watches stop and memory is unnecessary because past, present and future are one.

Or perhaps God is time. Perhaps it's God himself who feeds on us, who devours us, so that he can get the energy from his creations to create further – almost like the stories Tant Geert told about the great painters and writers: how, in order to create works of art, they fed on and mutilated their own lives and the lives of those around them, just to make time stand still in one book or one painting, as though they could buy peace and quiet through that.

I remember the nights in my room at Soebatsfontein. The moths circling my night light and the guests' crackly transistor music from the stoep room. I was too frightened to go to the toilet in the dark so I just stood and pissed into my washbasin. In the desolation of the night, I sometimes even wondered about God. Was he unhappy? Was he the Van Gogh of heaven? Was it his fault that the sun blazed down on us so mercilessly?

Under the peach trees, Dr Clark told Tant Geert about the Beat Generation and his time in New York City. She listened avidly. They were the Season's two intellectuals. Neither Pa, nor Miss Bruwer with her otherworldly, Anglophile preoccupations, nor Ma, nor Mr Jacoby, could hold a candle to them.

They played the pretentious little games all intellectuals are so fond of – alluding to texts, making connections, digging around in the mind. They gave free rein to their bored brains, which could no longer find stimulation in everyday things. Dr Clark referred to Achilles's tendon, Oedipus's swollen foot, the ankle wound of Alexander the Great, Ulysses' leg, even Philoctetes and Bellerophon who both limped.

"Everyone is weak in the ankle in some way or another," he said, slapping a butterfly away from his face.

Tant Geert remembered something, rested her head against the peach-tree trunk and quoted, "The deeper implication is the verticality of the spirit."

"Precisely," he cried. "And the knowledge of mortality is

bedded in every wound. But the wound can be a gift too. The very foot that made Achilles mortal gave him his power. You see, 'ourselves as epic stories' – we must heal the wound through narrative. That's therapy."

It was then than I began to slither away through the dandelions and the other weeds, a rifleman on elbow and knee, as the Veteran had taught me to do – sly as a snake, so that the movement of the plants would look like the stirrings of a breeze to Tant Geert and Dr Clark, still deep in conversation. I escaped by creeping down a furrow, leopard-crawling, gliding over ditches, until I was out of sight and could run, as I always did when I didn't understand, full tilt, with my elbows and knees pumping, recklessly racing, through the shadows of the pines and across the fields until, again, yes, to the waters of the Fish, that cool unbroken stream, and the cool sand, the donga walls with the teasing monkeys, the white speckles of shell fossils, the reeds bending with the wind: God, did you wound me? Was it you?

49

That night I dreamt that Joe Mann and I were rolling plump ironstones down Buffelskop. He wore a tatty khaki hat and his large workman's hands were calloused. We stood beside the sarcophagus.

The stones bounced wildly down the mountain, leaping close by the red candles of the aloes, ploughing furrows between the spekboom plants, singing like the church bells in town, down the mountain, to the railway line at the foot of the slope, right to the sleepers and the rushing, smoking locomotives with their dumb, faceless drivers.

50

You couldn't help wondering about Tant Geert, alone in a London hotel room. The grey city roared heavily round her, hundreds of thousands of people dragged their lives along through streets, factories and houses. She was aware of the small dramas they played out behind every window and closed door, in every hotel room, and, on the sixth floor, she sat alone in her small room.

She was familiar with this hotel, with the ringing tone of the telephones, the smell of the cleaning fluid they used to clean the baths, the insect powder smell, the glow of the small heater when the rain drew grey lines on the window panes and she had to arrange her evening among the furniture she knew so well and the mirror which reflected her wounded body reprovingly, the waiters who kept a discreet distance, the availability of news-papers, the special pitch of traffic noise, screams, rattling steam pipes, the whoosh of latrines . . . It wasn't as though she weren't at home here – it was just that you kept thinking of her white torso with the two orangey-brown scars, the lidless eyes, the unblinking eyes, and that you reminded yourself that she did it of her own will, and that they would stare out of her body for the rest of her life.

Even if she covered them with blouses, even if she disguised them with the comfortably broad lapels of a man's jacket, you'd still remember the absence.

And she walked easily through the streets of London, look-ing at the pretty young women with their breasts bobbing or standing alert under their blouses, those countless forms that the female breast takes: the pear, the apple, the bagpipes, the sagging bag of oranges, broad and full below, nipples up, the snouty rabbits' muzzles of the seventeen-year-old, the shaken-out pillowcases which swayed against the bodies of the hotel cleaners, the erect lambs-noses of the prostitutes she had sent up to her room.

And what, you might well ask yourself, did she see in the

freckled breasts of Marge Bruwer, that flabby pair with the limp nipples that Tant Geert rubbed and sucked and pinched in the Schreiner Room, amidst the stodgy portraits and patient spines of books?

Once Miss Bruwer had staggered off to the toilet, Tant Geert had returned to her Borgward. Triumphantly she had borne the smell of her lover on her fingertips and she had held her hand to her nose a couple of times while she set off along the gravel road to the farm.

In her rondavel, she had drawn the curtains and then had lain on her back on the divan and then she slipped her hand in through the fly opening of her flannels and had rubbed Marge Bruwer's musky smell deep into herself, grafting the other woman into her.

Did she also think, like Pa, that no descendant could escape the Latsky madness? That it was the madness that pranced on the family crest in those two rampant, bloodthirsty lions with claws extended and mouths open? That the current of Diep Rivier, the trailing spoor of the Beast, of the shaved scare-monkey, painted white to follow the troop and frighten them away, the yard baboon, the stuffed Kees in the family room, that these were the stories of our family, just like the stories other families repeated year after year, creating a family mythology?

I knew that, at night, there was a breathless shadow that hovered at Tant Geert's window. Were she to open the Wilhelmina's curtains, there'd be nothing but a diffuse invisibility, a taste in the mouth, a long shadow, the pinching in of the vagina and anus, the pinprick in the fingertips and a sudden whiff of boegoe in the armpit, that spurt of adrenalin . . . was that something limping away into the shadows of the moonlit bluegums, there where the leaves stir silvery and the white-splashed trunks stand like lepers?

When she opened the Wilhelmina's door in the dead of night (something she never did in her sixth floor London hotel room), she wondered what had brushed against her door and she was overwhelmed by the fly poison smell of half-eaten, rotting peaches in the orchard, because the troop of monkeys had been through there at dusk, shaking branches and only taking a bite here and there from the fruit that fell to the ground.

She looked round and saw her reflection in the rondavel mirror, that slight hump the Latsky women developed with age as the skeleton shrank, so that in time, with their broad shoulders and narrow hips, they became gnomish figures, those carefree summer nymphs in floral frocks and straw hats.

There she stood, Geertruida Sophia Latsky, doctor of science, world traveller, cosmopolitan, black sheep, a legend in her own time: in the rondavel doorway distressed, determined to follow the spoor to the end, to chart the intricacies of our blood, to give a name to every tree in the dark forest, to fell Grendel with the sword.

She stood there, her white legs with the branching, blue varicose veins, in men's pyjamas, shorty-pyjamas, with the fly skew over her lower belly, a vertical grimacing shadow mouth, a crooked gaping irrelevancy. Her hair was awry and her eyes were dark and perplexed with the deep sleep from which something – something – had roused her.

One hand was on the doorknob and in the other she held the heavy Second World War Luger, the pistol she'd begged off someone somewhere in her travels, and which she always carried with her without any customs official ever stopping her.

It was the heavy black pistol with the small black eye, that barrel that could press as coldly as an accusing finger against the temple, hesitant, curious, in those decisive, most private moments behind drawn curtains, when there was no wind in the trees, when she sat on her bed listening to nothing and waited: only the nothingness, the black spaces between stars, the trailing shadows in the dongas – the quiet, the absolute silence of choice.

She stood with her hand on the doorknob, with the door half open, she looked out, she listened, holding her breath. I stood behind the bluegum trunk looking at her openly, but it was too dark and her eyes were too lazy from her sojourns in Europe to see me. I hauled out my willy and kept my eyes on her while I pissed against the tree trunk. The wind took the smell to her and she raised her pistol hand. The Luger was clumsy in her grasp, black and heavy. But she raised it until it was squarely aimed at me. I looked down the poison eye as I stood in the steam of my own pee. A light breeze stirred the bluegum branches above me. She withdrew suddenly into the ring of light in her rondavel, slamming the door shut. I heard the bolt moving awkwardly, iron banging against wood. Her shadow groped over the curtains and the light was pinched out. Just like the others, the rondavel stood shrouded in darkness.

The next morning she didn't appear on the terrace for breakfast and, at eleven, Ma herself took a tray of tea, toast and marmalade down to the Wilhelmina. She came back to report, "Geert has caught a sudden cold. In the chest. She's staying in bed today."

Ma looked at me. "She's a Latsky," she told me. "I know it now. I just saw it in her eyes."

51

Hans Castorp's wound, his lung with his *petite tache humide*, made his life impossible, decided Tant Geert and Dr Clark.

That's why he had to retire to his magic mountain to live in isolation. And there, through the small flaw in the fabric of his lung, the huge world of the spirit poured into him.

Thus, they decided, the wound becomes the healer.

"The wound is a talking mouth," said Dr Clark.

And then Tant Geert made her confession. Under the peach trees, sheltered by the rank weeds, she confessed to Dr Clark that she'd had her breasts and her womb removed, years ago, by a Dr Maylam in London.

He almost choked on his own gasp. He stared at her speechlessly. Something between madness and lust flickered in his eyes. But when he finally found his tongue and asked her whether she wouldn't like to come and have some sessions in the Bitter Aloe – he must, he simply must analyse her – she refused.

"It's enough to have one member of the family blabbing everything," she said decisively. "If the Latsky demon gets hold of me, I catch a train, a bus or a taxi or set off on my own two feet and go on a journey."

"You're running away. Sooner or later you're going to have to confront that demon."

"Rubbish. With respect, that's New York City claptrap, Llewellyn." Because Tant Geert had started calling him by his first name, and he'd started calling her "Gert", and then, as the days went by, "Gerrie".

In time their friendship came out into the open. And in the long dusky evenings "Gerrie" was Anglicised to the terrace term "Jerry".

"Jerry!" the call would sweep across the lawns, from the Bitter Aloe to the Wilhelmina.

"Yes, Lew?" she'd call back.

That's the way the friendship between Tant Geert and Dr Llewellyn Clark, Chief Psychiatrist at the Somerset Hospital in Mouille Point, was that summer.

52

"Ag shame, poor Fabiantjie," said Ma. "The child is looking at the world skew. I hope he isn't going to see only one side of everything all his life."

Ma pushed a curl back from her forehead, glanced at the clock and decided to wait just fifteen little minutes longer before telling Reuben to open the sundowner bar. Her hand rested on the phone as if she expected a call.

"How is the fellow going to shoot if he's called up one day?

And what's he going to do in the cadets if he has to look right or march to the left?"

"Well," said Tant Geert, "Odin had to sacrifice an eye to gain wisdom. And then he went all over the world."

Pa ordered Tromp van Diggelen's book from White & Boughton. His muscular body had made him a folk hero. He taught Afrikaners to develop their muscles and eat healthily.

"Tromp van Diggelen," Pa explained to me, "was a sickly child like you. But we're going to get you right with this book, big boy. And we'll have a look at what he says about eyes, too."

White & Boughton telegraphed a priority order through to Port Elizabeth and when they rang to say the book had arrived, Pa got out of bed, put on his blue trousers and a white shirt, shaved, combed his hair, put his Parker and his cheque book in his shirt pocket, set his swanky hat on his head, called me and we set off for town.

I can't remember Pa and me ever driving into town on business alone like this before. There might have been times, but I'd forgotten them. Perhaps I remember the trip so clearly because it was specifically for my benefit.

Pa chatted the whole way as though we went to town like this every day. "Van Diggelen's exercises can be done while you're lying on your divan," he said. "You just lie on your back and tense your muscles one after the other. Tense, relax, tense, relax. It's so simple! Ten minutes a day, according to the paper, is all you need and you get muscles like that!"

Pa looked quite elated today and he told me about his rugby-playing days at the Gym in the Boland. He'd played for the Gymnasium's first team, and for Stellenbosch too. Wing because he was speedy. "Ag," said Pa, "those were the days! Intervarsity! Coetzenburg! The days of my youth were the days of my glory."

Pa and Ma had a new theme: my health. "He inherited weak lungs from his mother's family, from those English Van der Bijls from the Boland."

"No," Ma countered, "the weak lungs come from the Latskys – the intelligence comes from the Van der Bijls."

"That'll be the day," said Pa. "The Latskys were always

clever people. Just take my Uncle Hermanus, look how far he got in medicine. And Grandpa studied in Leiden."

"And what about my Uncle Bertie?" demanded Ma. "He transplants all sorts of organs. Lungs, livers, everything."

"Ja, but only in baboons!" laughed Pa. "And they never live longer than three days."

"Just you wait," said Ma. "One of these days Uncle Bertie will be on the front page of *Die Burger*. When he's transplanted something into a human."

"Seeing he's so good, let him transplant a new eye into Fabian," said Pa.

I looked down at my knife and fork. I wondered how it felt to be able to see with two eyes. Does the world maybe look different to the way I think it looks?

"Do you think Fabian can judge distances?" Ma asked. No one knew for sure so she got up from the table to ring Dr Lyell.

"Perhaps there are orientation problems to do with distances," acknowledged Dr Lyell.

"Sonnie, be careful with the airgun," warned Ma and gestured to Reuben to bring her plate back from the warming oven. Ma looked at me, her head tilted. "Fabiantjie, I wonder whether we shouldn't put the bicycle away for now?"

"Oh, rubbish!" Pa exploded. "That's typical of your family. Let the child ride his bike."

"And what if he crashes into a wall?"

"Has he done that before?"

"No," said Ma, drawing patterns on her cigarette box, little squares and boxes, as she always did when things started to go wrong for her, as though she wanted to pack everything into neat little boxes.

Suddenly she looked up. "Boytjie? How far do you think it is from here to over there where Tant Geert and Dr Clark are sitting?"

"Ag, cut it out," growled Pa.

That's the way things were round the time we discovered that I was half blind.

Now Pa and I were sitting in the Volkswagen, already halfway past Dynamite Krantz, and Pa told me that we were going to work through Van Diggelen's book together. Pa would make sure that I did my exercises every day.

"We must equip you for life, big boy," he said. "So few people are prepared for life. We Afrikaners must qualify ourselves. You must be able to speak English like an Englishman. And make sure that you come first in class, Fabian. Remember, you're a Latsky, you hear?"

At the Hennings' farm, long-necked ostriches drifted by. "You've got a lot going for you, Fabian. It was different when I was young. Grandpa sent me off to boarding school when I was only five years old. They shaved my head and I had to fight my own battles to survive."

Pa looked through the window and pushed his hat further back on his head. "But you can study from home. And once you've finished here at Boys' High, I'll send you to Stellenbosch. Perhaps you can write your matric at the Gym if you want to. At Stellenbosch you can study Law or Medicine. Uncle Boeta will organise you a civil service bursary from Pretoria. He only has to pick up the phone and it's done. Fabian, the world is at your feet. There'll be opportunities for the Afrikaner in the New Republic. Maybe you'll even end up in Parliament. You won't be the first Latsky in government, mind you.

"Look, look up there on Dynamite Krantz, look at those dassies in the sun. So fat! You could pick one off perfectly with a .22 from here. Can you see him, big boy? There, yes, over there, near the elephant's-foot. Oops, I nearly drove down the river bank. No, look back, look through the back window, man. Then you'll see him. Do you see? A beauty, hey?"

The book was waiting on Mr Crafford's desk. He was the manager of White & Boughton. It was wrapped in brown paper. Mr Crafford shook hands with both of us. He asked if he could take a drive out to Soebatsfontein, he and Miss Bruwer. There was something on his mind he needed to discuss.

"Yes?" asked Pa. Mr Crafford was a refined little man who always wore a bow tie. Pa looked dark and stormy beside him, with his black hair combed back, those Latsky eyebrows and his suppressed tension.

"About Verwoerd's visit," said Mr Crafford. "About the spectacle in the town hall."

"No, fine, then you must pop over," answered Pa. "Just give us a ring beforehand."

When we got back in the car, Pa growled, "It's Geert again, stirring things up."

"It's about the march from the landing strip," I said. "We have to go through the location and Tant Geert thinks that's a provocation."

"Is that her word?" asked Pa.

"Yes."

"She doesn't know what provocation is," said Pa. "She doesn't know our world any more. She knows nothing about the tough Karoo. She doesn't know Soebatsfontein." I could see that Pa's mood was changing. He revved the Volkswagen's engine so loudly when we pulled off, that Mr Crafford's bow tie popped up in the shop window.

"Provocation, hey?" said Pa. "Ag, can't Geert just leave us alone? What does she know about the heat and the struggle, of the Afrikaner who must shake off the yoke of the English? Has she any idea of Black Africa? No, she hasn't. Her head is full of the restaurants and galleries in all those cities of hers."

But he still took me to the Karoo Café. "Moordenaarskaroo," he sighed as we sat at the table. "This is why you must get educated, Fabian. Grab your opportunities, son. I didn't have the chance, you know, Grandpa's trust . . ."

But I wasn't listening any more. I was tearing the paper off Tromp van Diggelen's book.

". . . trapped by those stupid restrictions . . ."

We ordered cream sodas.

". . . loss of land . . ."

I looked at the cover. *Health through a healthy mind,* I read. A muscular man water-skied behind a motor boat with a pretty young woman on his shoulder.

". . . family griping non-stop, then . . ."

"Is this Tromp van Diggelen?" I asked, pointing at the picture. Pa looked up irritably. He doesn't have his *Path of Truth* booklets here, I thought. Or his sleeping remedy. Pa was breathing fast.

"How does anyone break free?" he asked.

"Look, Pa, here's Tromp van Diggelen. Look, here's his signature under the picture. Look."

Pa sighed and started paging through the book with me. There were lots of pictures of people holding their breath and sticking out their chests, pressing their hands together, tensing their necks, and bowing their legs so that the muscles knotted. There were more hearts and colons and lungs than in my biology book.

"Reuben will like this," I said. "All the blood vessels and stuff."

"No way," said Pa. "Reuben is only a kaffir. They believe in witchdoctors and things like that. We Westerners have understood the circulation of blood for centuries. Reuben will never believe you if you tell him that his heart works like a river pump."

"Reuben reads very fast," I said.

"Let's leave Reuben out of this. He's fit enough. The kaffirs are naturally fit. They don't need Tromp van Diggelen. It's us Afrikaners who have to build up our bodies."

He paged through the book with me. "Look, big boy, he says you must rub your whole body down with a towel every day. Remember, after your bath at night you must rub yourself all over until your skin is red. Skin friction, good Lord." Pa bent over the book. "Look there's even advice for constipation."

I looked up. "There's Dr Clark."

Pa nearly knocked over his cream soda. "Who?" he asked, confused.

"Dr Clark, there at the counter."

Dr Clark stood at the café counter waiting to be served. He slapped a fly that had settled on his neck.

"Don't move," Pa hissed. "Sit still, just as you are, Fabian."

Dr Clark obviously hadn't seen us. He bought the paper and a packet of peppermints and then left.

159

"There he goes," sighed Pa.

We sat in silence until I said carefully: "He's a funny man, Pa."

Pa stirred his cold drink with his straw. His hand shook slightly.

"He's very clever, Fabian. He's writing a book."

"Are you helping him with the book, Pa?"

"Oh, a little bit, certainly a little bit."

"The Veteran says dagga is nature's LSD."

"What!" shouted Pa. He looked suddenly angry; those coffee grounds stirring in his eyes, as Ma always said. "What? Answer me, Fabian."

He glared at me. I stammered. "H-h-he s-s-says d-agg-a . . ."

"I heard that. I'm not deaf." Pa leaned over the table towards me. "What do you know about LSD, Fabian? What? I want to know."

"It's medicine," I whispered.

"Medicine, yes, Fabian. Medicine." He sat back and pushed Tromp van Diggelen's book away. "Medicine that the doctor has prescribed for my problem."

I don't know whether by "problem" Pa meant "The Problem", because "The Problem" had always to do with Doctor Verwoerd, the radio news, the outside world and Reuben and them.

"Yes, Pa," I said quietly.

He leaned forward again. "Fabian," he said slowly. "I never want to hear you using the word LSD again. Do you understand me?" He leaned even closer and I could feel his breath on my face. His eyebrows bristled wildly and small hairs curled from his nostrils. "Do you understand, Fabian? Or I'll thrash the skin off your backside."

"Yes, Pa."

"And I don't want to hear anything about dagga either. If that major starts talking to you about things like this again, you come running straight to me. Do you understand?"

I nodded.

"Let's go." Pa got up and took hold of my elbow and we left.

160

The soldiers were rehearsing in front of the town hall again. We didn't look at them. We'd already gone past Dynamite Krantz when we realised that Tromp van Diggelen's book was still lying on the table in the Karoo Café.

53

The next evening we sat on the terrace waiting for Miss Bruwer and Mr Crafford from White & Boughton.

"The country's in its death throes," said Pa to Ma while he screwed the gas cartridge on to the soda siphon. It was a family evening, as Ma called it, when we Latskys gathered slightly apart from the guests on the terrace and the other people kept their distance.

Then Pa liked to take over some of Reuben's tasks. He squirted the soda into the plastic glasses, Ma added red cold drink, and we drank slowly, letting it bubble in our mouths, staring into the night. Ma wore a powder-blue summer dress and she'd pulled her hair up into a bun.

The stoep was still warm from the day's heat and I lay on my back with my cheek close to a blood-red geranium. I gazed at the stars, breathing in the perfume of the geranium, and I thought about Isabel, the fragrant girl in the pharmacy with tumbled hair who leaned down to hand me my cough mixture in a brown packet.

The night lay wide around us. Later, Ma said, "It's hard to believe this place – our country – has developed bad breath."

A shot cracked through the night and we all jerked upright. The Veteran was up on his feet immediately, as taut as a bowstring in his tunic with the gleaming eyes of his medals.

The shot echoed against Buffelskop and circled round the valley basin. "It's a 243," said the Veteran. "Fired three miles northwest of here."

"It sounded as though it were just the other side of the

huts," said Ma. She smiled bravely at the guests who looked worriedly across to our table. Should they rather go back to their rondavels? was the question in everyone's eyes.

"Sound travels well at night," said the Veteran. "You can see the burning tip of a cigarette two miles away."

"Reuben!" Ma called. "A round for everyone on the house." Reuben sprang into action. Pa started worrying about our two expected visitors. He stood with his hands on his hips at the stoep wall and stared down towards the gate.

We didn't know whether the shot had been fired on Hasimara or Green Acres. In earlier years Pa would have wasted no time in fetching his gun and his torch and jumping into the Volkswagen to go and investigate. Now he looked at Ma, "I think we should all go inside after this round."

But, as we gathered up the plastic glasses, there was suddenly a light on the road, and then two headlights at the gate. "It's them!" Pa cried out, pleased.

Mr Crafford had donned his sea-green bow tie for the occasion. Miss Bruwer looked severe in silk with a high collar. We greeted each other and Ma, Pa, Tant Geert and the Veteran went to the family sitting room.

"The bar will close early tonight," Ma told the guests. "It's better that way. If there's a bit of shooting, we're always extra careful."

The guests hurried off to their rondavels and a queue soon formed at the ablution block. Reuben cleared up unhurriedly. He shook out tablecloths, nipped candle flames between his thumb and forefinger and paused in the smell of lingering smoke. He took the last glasses through to the kitchen and then tipped the chairs against the tables.

We were all in the sitting room when he appeared in the doorway. His shadow on the wall gave Ma a fright. He could go, she gestured to him. An early night would do us all good. Ma would make tea and bring it to the sitting room herself.

Then I had to say goodnight and Ma walked me to my bedroom. She checked that my window was shut and fastened. I lay on my back for a little while, thinking about the months of practice the cadets had put in for the Prime Minister's visit. After a while, I crept out through my bedroom window and slunk round the house. I slithered on my stomach between the stoep geraniums and peered through a gap in the curtains. The windows were wide open so I could hear everything.

Pa sat on his leather chair with his hand against the ear with the plaster. Miss Bruwer and Mr Crafford were on the sofa opposite him. Ma and the Veteran sat slightly to one side – as though they realised that the real conversation would be between the brother and sister and the two bookish visitors from town.

I was stunned when Miss Bruwer took out a long golden holder and put a cigarette into it and looked expectantly at Pa. Flustered, he lit a match and jumped up but in his haste he let it go out, and he had to strike another. He retreated to the sideboard and poured a glass of sherry for each of them.

"And to crown it," exclaimed Miss Bruwer indignantly, in English, "here in Schreiner country, of all places."

Mr Crafford's spectacles misted over and he shook his head.

Tant Geert said nothing, but we all knew what she did with Doctor Verwoerd's portrait when she moved into the Wilhelmina every Season.

Pa topped up the glasses. The conversation did not flow. A little sherry splashed on the carpet, and Miss Bruwer ground it in with her heel, just as you'd crush a brown beetle.

"And we think we know our country," she said, suddenly sad. Tears slid down her cheeks. (I stretched to see better because I could hardly believe my eyes.) I knew Tant Geert wanted to get up and comfort her, but in this company she had to restrain herself. Miss Bruwer shook a handkerchief out of her sleeve, blew her nose and excused herself. I heard the bathroom door shut and immediately afterwards the whoosh of the cistern flushing, but above the sound of running water, I could hear her sobs.

Her cigarette in its long holder lay forgotten on the ashtray. There was a small red lipstick smudge at one end, and, at the other, a smouldering worm of ash that grew longer and longer as I heard Ma going to Miss Bruwer. Pa looked up at Mr Crafford, Tant Geert and the Veteran.

"Now the English are out of the room," he said. "Now we are all Afrikaners together and we're going to do some straight talking. What do you want from me?" He stared at Mr Crafford with those Latsky eyes and Mr Crafford's hand moved to his green bow tie.

"Uh-uh-uh . . ." said Mr Crafford.

54

"We must fence them off, raise a wall between us and darkest Africa," said Pa.

Mr Crafford's bow tie sat skew and Miss Bruwer's silk blouse no longer looked too fresh. Tant Geert leaned back, bored, while Ma and the Veteran watched their own shadows against the wall, as if they were watching a film.

"These plans of Doctor Verwoerd's are fantastic. A Commonwealth of nations. You stick every black into his own country and give him his own government. You build your factories on the borders of the reserves. Then each group can rule itself. And the Afrikaner stays free – a Republic for us at last, after all the years of British domination. Free too," he glanced at Tant Geert, "from the yoke of the Dutch colonials."

"Shouldn't we get another bottle of sherry?" Ma asked carefully. Everyone looked at her wearily, but no one answered. She got up anyway and came back with an unopened bottle.

"Civilisation is not a matter of compromise," said Pa. "And we have a duty to try and preserve civilisation here at the southernmost tip of Africa. Listen to the racket that comes from the huts night after night. Stabbings, drunken rowdiness, breeding like flies. No, I am one hundred per cent behind Verwoerd."

Mr Crafford looked up. "But we're concerned with the way

it's done," he said. "It's the holidays and yet every school child has been summoned to march. And the float-building – what's that going to cost the town council? And then the children have to march through the location. What if there's stone throwing? You know what it's like there in the location these days, with all the outside incitement. And the blacks are angry because they're going to be removed and resettled at Lingelihle, away from the coloureds."

"We mustn't show fear." Pa shook his head at the sherry Ma offered.

Ma sat down again, swallowed her sherry and looked at Pa. "You also think it's a stupid thing to do – the marching and the floats and Mr Jacoby," she said. "And you also think that Doctor Verwoerd has gone too far with the state of emergency and removing people. You're furious about what's happening in the location. Because it costs so much."

Pa looked at her, exasperated. "Don't tell me what I think."

Ma tilted her head, as she sometimes did when she knew she shouldn't give in, even though her natural instinct was to keep the peace.

"I'm only repeating what you said. If you don't think that way now, fine."

"I haven't changed my mind," said Pa. "I just think we mustn't show that we're afraid. We must stand together."

Tant Geert raised her sherry to the light. Up until now she hadn't said anything. "I smell trouble," she said.

"Big trouble," Mr Crafford nodded.

"Deep, deep trouble." Miss Bruwer banged her empty sherry glass down on the table.

"Don't you trust the armed forces then?" asked the Veteran, stroking his row of medals with his fingertips.

But no one answered him. Talked out, they sat there in silence, until Tant Geert leaned over towards Miss Bruwer and asked quietly: "Why don't you two stay the night, Marge?"

55

And that's how the ice was broken as far as the cautious Miss Marge was concerned. So many times before, when Tant Geert had tried to persuade her to come and stay with her in the rondavel, she'd said, "Oh, Geert, you know how I am. My indecision is always final." But in spite of that, she slept over that night with Tant Geert in the Wilhelmina, while Ma rigged up a bed for Mr Crafford in the sunroom.

The next day, Tant Geert drove to town with them to help Miss Marge with her last chores. Tant Geert brought Miss Marge back in her Borgward like a trophy and I saw them, as though in a sepia photograph, pausing briefly on the threshold of the Wilhelmina: Tant Geert with her broad lapels, the slight Marge Bruwer stooping to pick up her case, but not quite lifting it completely. Already she was looking in through the open door of the Wilhelmina, and you could just see the starched white sheets on the divan in there, and the bluegum breeze ruffled her hair and a shaft of sunlight fell over them, obliquely, as though it would bind them to that moment, for all time.

But then time slid forward again. They were in the rondavel, the door closed behind them.

Ma stood on the terrace looking down towards the rondavels. Dr Clark was sitting on a deck chair near his door. He watched the two women disappear into the Wilhelmina.

"Shame," said Ma. "Who's he going to talk to now that Tant Geert has got Marge Bruwer here?"

"He can talk to Mr Jacoby," I offered.

"Charles Jacoby and Dr Clark!" Ma laughed and patted my head. "They're worlds apart, Fabiantjie," she said. "That little doctor is fresh from New York and he's a snob. Charles Jacoby is a down-to-earth entertainer. He sings for us."

She raised her glass to the Zane Grey. "To the salt of the earth."

56

Years later, worn out from listening to hundreds of sad life stories, Llewellyn Clark would take an overdose of tablets in his New York hotel room.

He'd made a sentimental journey to the Big Apple, nearly twenty years after his first visit, and he was deeply disappointed that it had all changed so much. You couldn't even look up Ginsberg in the phone book. Rumours were in circulation that he'd withdrawn to the top floor of his house and few ever got to see him. Should you be lucky enough to track down the house, he would scrutinise you from above and, if he decided you could come in, he'd wrap the front door key in a sock and throw it down to you.

As for the other members of the Beat Generation with whom Dr Clark had sat debating so enjoyably in the smoky folk-clubs and restaurants at night . . . Some had become pinstripe-suited members of the establishment: publishers and newspaper or magazine editors. Others did the endless rounds of drug re-habilitation centres, hovering between withdrawal and full-scale addiction. Most of the young people with the long hair, the freedom slogans and dagga pipes had disappeared without a trace – apparently dead, or, nearly dead, sucked in by the rou-tine of family life in small-town America. And Timothy Leary, the guru of the decade that came to be known as the psychedelic sixties, was already picking up problems at Harvard over his experiments with mind-altering drugs.

Dr Clark's methods had become dated and he'd been over-taken by young psychiatrists with new techniques. The rebel began to seem eccentric and later plain boring. He was tolerated in the corridors of the hospital he worked in – the Stikland Neuroclinic in Bellville. He was the old man who, honest to God, gave his patients LSD in the sixties, permanently derail-ing many of them.

His book, which he'd partly written in the Bitter Aloe, was not well received. One short paragraph had referred to one of

Pa's dreams: the patient in the great Karoo and his dream about the parrot, painstakingly recorded by Ma.

Dr Clark had disappeared into obscurity and when I looked him up in later years, reports on his sessions with Pa no longer existed and his memories of the summer with "Jim Reeves" were sketchy.

Alas, Ma's dream book was gone too.

Had he only been to Soebatsfontein once, or had he sat there writing during other Seasons too?

One summer, or four?

Now there is no one left to ask, Pa is dead. He died slowly, going quietly from the inside out, until his body shrivelled up over him like a white shell. Ma was gone before I could say goodbye to her because I had obligations that I couldn't just drop. She died alone, which was actually just a manifestation of the way she had lived because hadn't she always been a past master at keeping everything to herself . . .

Everyone is silent and gone, and I have no one who can check my facts. It's all swept away, past, as though it had never happened.

The rondavels are ruins, overrun by kikuyu, destroyed by weather and time. The bluegums perished during the droughts.

Only the throb of Tant Geert's Harley Davidson is still to be heard among the broken buildings . . . until you discover it's a diesel locomotive that has replaced Halesowen's steam trains. That's the thundering engine beat that you hear.

But let me tell the story of Tant Geert's motorbike.

57

Tant Geert and Marge Bruwer would stroll in the dongas near the river of an afternoon. They would wait until they were out of sight of the big house and the rondavels and the tennis courts. Then they held hands as they clambered carefully about, examining fragments of bone and calcified shells. They pointed out animal tracks to one another and jumped in unison when something rustled in a bush.

Sometimes they took off their shoes and waded knee-deep in the Fish River. On the opposite bank, they'd sit quietly on sheets of rock and watch the monkeys that kept a wary eye on them from the trees. If the small circle of visitors to the guest farm made them feel claustrophobic, they'd wait until their feet were dry and then walk over to our neighbour's – Oom Bobby Greenblatt. He farmed with parrots and aviaries with birds of all colours and sizes were dotted about under the trees in his yard. The birds shrieked and called, clambering up the wire with their beaks.

One afternoon when they came up from the river to listen to Oom Bobby's stories about the irrigation farmers, they walked past an outhouse door which stood ajar. An old Harley Davidson lay inside, half covered by a tarpaulin.

"Damn me to hell!" exclaimed Tant Geert. "Marge, look at that beautiful thing!"

"Because you're a bloody interesting woman, you appreciate my parrots and you brighten my afternoons with your chat, you can have it for five pounds," said Oom Bobby once the sherry bottle had followed the tea tray. The parrots were complaining, the monkeys gibbered in the trees on the river banks and a sunset stained the horizon red.

"Done," said Tant Geert.

"My people knew Olive Schreiner," Oom Bobby told Tant Geert and Marge. "And the crazy Cronwright, as mad as a hatter." He glanced at Tant Geert. "Did you know that your sister-in-law's granny had a house next door to his, there at the Strand? Apparently she and Cronwright were always squabbling over the fence. He was stroppy until the day he died. Argued about dogs and postal deliveries. About overhanging branches and loquats that attracted the bats. That sort of thing. But also about his late wife. He was bitter to the end. Oh well, and now his wife lies up there on the mountain with her dog."

"The lot of all writers' families," said Marge Bruwer.

Tant Geert went to fetch the Harley Davidson next day and it roared like a tractor through the gate and into the yard at Soebatsfontein. She was wearing Oom Bobby's goggles – the ones he wore when he was winnowing wheat because he suffered from hayfever. Miss Marge sat in the sidecar with her knees up under chin. She clutched her straw hat to her breast. Her eyes were red from the wind and dust, but her cheeks were pink and she was laughing herself silly.

Tant Geert pulled up under the terrace in a slightly clumsy sweep. Taking off the goggles, she looked over to the Borgward and called out, "Don't worry, Isabella. I still love you."

When she looked up to the terrace, she found Reuben standing there with the sun flashing on his tray, and Ma, and Pa in his paisley dressing-gown, and Dr Clark who hurriedly stuffed his notebook and pen back into his shirt pocket.

"Five little pounds!" Tant Geert called up to them. "And you can smell the Karoo shrubs as you ride. Not like in a car where you only smell dust and petrol. My, what an experience. Hey, Marge?"

"Geert, you drive like a madman!" giggled Miss Marge.

"Whatever next!" said Ma. "The bossy woman, for heaven's sake. She looks so comical in Bobby Greenblatt's leather leggings. Just like a cowboy."

"Calamity Jane," exulted Tant Geert, and then I realised she'd had a drink – Oom Bobby had decided that they had to celebrate the deal all over again.

"The parrot-Jew's sherry and smooth-talk," growled Pa, swinging round and disappearing inside.

"So you've bought the thing, have you, Geert?" asked Ma.

"Cash!" crowed Tant Geert from below the terrace. "Oh my! Marge dear, shall we go for another spin? Down to the fields?"

"Oh, yes, yes!"

"But it's lunch time!" Ma was taken aback – but actually more jealous of their fun that anything else.

"Hop on, Fabian!" Tant Geert called to me and I was down the steps in a flash.

There was room for me on the seat behind her. I slipped my arms round her waist, and before I could ball my fists in embarrassment, I felt the folds on her soft stomach.

So off we went, with Miss Marge laughing in the sidecar, me clinging on at the back and Tant Geert opening it up as though she'd been racing Harley Davidsons for years.

"Go, Geert, darling! Go!"

We flashed through the lucerne fields.

There were still a couple of weeks to go before Christmas. The Prime Minister's visit was round the corner. The blacks hadn't started throwing stones yet, but we expected trouble any minute. And Oom Boeta and them were on their way from Pretoria in a black government Cadillac.

"Go, darling! Go!"

I nearly jumped out of my skin when Miss Marge groped between her legs, pulled out a bottle of sherry and held it to her lips. Brown drops trickled down her chin and the wind whisked them away. When she stowed the bottle again, her mouth was red and moist.

"Hold on tight, Fabian! There's a bend coming up, pupil-tjie."

58

"What's going to happen, Ma?" I asked. "What's going to happen?"

The days were churning round me. It was as though I were on a swing aiming higher, gaining altitude, hovering for a moment at the highest point, swaying down backwards to hang half upside down over a precipice, and then to dive down into emptiness again.

"But, Fabian?"

Ma pulled me close. It was quiet round us, that evening as we sat at table seven. Ma pushed the dream book away.

"Come, you and I are going to have a nice cup of tea," she said. "I think we deserve it. Things are all topsy turvy around us. One doesn't even get a chance to sit and read quietly any more. Look how the *Reader's Digests* are piling up. Tea for two. What do you think, Fabian?"

She left me in the quiet dining room. In the dimness, the round tables spun in formation like flying saucers. They drifted with the wind in one direction like swallows leaving before the winter. On the gable, the wind charger clattered in the night breeze that puffed around the big house. Buffelskop scowled irascibly in the night.

"Ma!"

I ran down the dark passage to the kitchen. She was standing at the coal stove with her back to me. There was a smell of congealed fat, smoke and steam.

"Ma!" I rushed up to her. She smoothed her hair. "It's a wild night, Fabiantjie," she said, "but at least we're together. And thank goodness we have a roof over our heads."

She made tea in the big kettle, adding two heaped teaspoons of tea leaves. Then she took her special fortune-telling cup from the shelf. It was broad and shallow so the tea leaves could spread out nicely when she wanted to read them.

In the sitting room we turned on the radio and Ma poured the tea – using the strainer for mine but not for hers. We sipped in silence while the wind tugged at the roof and trees. The windows rattled in their frames. Ma left dregs of tea in the bottom of her cup, and then suddenly, when I was not expecting it, she swirled the cup round three times with her left hand. Then she turned it upside down on to her saucer, holding her hand over it.

"Come, Fabian," she said quietly. She spoke in her deep, fortune-telling voice. "Concentrate. Come now, shall we look?"

The wind charger squealed on its axle as the wind changed direction. The single lamp in the corner of the dining room glowed brighter. Then, as the wind dropped, it flickered and glowered dull yellow again. In one deft movement, Ma turned the cup the right way up again. She bent over it. A curl fell down on to her forehead.

After a short silence, she spoke quietly. "Here, here near the handle. When the leaves gather there it is near to home." Ma bent right over the cup and stayed like that. It seemed as if she'd put her face right into the cup, as though part of her were disappearing among the tea leaves. I heard her gasp. She looked up nervously: "Fabian . . . !"

"Yes, Ma?"

"Get me the bottle from the dream-book cupboard. Quickly, run . . ."

"Ma?"

"Round in circles . . ."

"Ma?"

In circles round Pa in the yard, like drooling dogs, their shadows like the hands of a clock, they stepped round in a circle. Round him.

"Round him!" shouted Ma. The light in the corner flickered.

"When, Ma?"

I would have hidden in the fat arms of Boe, our head cook, near the stove's warm, open mouth, if I'd been on the farm. Where she shifted her pots and ranged her black smoothing-irons on the hot hob, I would have hidden if I hadn't been marching in the procession from the land strip to the town hall. In Boe's arms I'd have sucked my thumb and listened to their gravelly tread around Pa on his office chair in the sun in the yard.

I heard afterwards that Boe had had to fetch the office chair and take it out.

Early, while we had been still at school, straightening our berets and squaring up to one another, whose boots and bandolier were the shiniest? Who already had hair on his fore-arms?

While the band practised the National Anthem in the school hall, they came through the gate into the yard, yelled the workers into a mob and had Pa sit in the yard. While the school sergeant major issued us each with a flag and we ran jubilantly over the school grounds, they locked Ma into her bedroom and drove all the guests into their rondavels.

For hours on end they interrogated Pa about the meetings they reckoned he had held in the big house, with people like the man from the bookstore. They probed him about his programme of action designed to undermine the good faith of the young people. Boe made a mug of coffee and tried to take it to Pa, but they drove her back into the kitchen. With their dark glasses and the camouflage uniforms the troops had started wearing in those days, they walked round Pa, glaring now and then at the workers huddled under the pepper trees near the milking shed.

Our procession reached the townships at more or less the time when Boe went down the kitchen steps with the mug of coffee. We left the landing strip triumphantly, the cadet band and the floats with the Products of the District leading the way. The floats portrayed aspects of the agricultural industry: on the first one there was a cardboard merino ram among bales of wool, followed by a pyramid of lucerne bales, then a dairy float with a lowing Jersey cow surrounded by bags of buttermilk rusks, shiny milk cans and big red Goudas from the cheese factory, and, finally, a fruit and vegetable float, piled high with produce from the irrigation farms south of the town.

We expected to see impressed black faces when we entered the township. The town council had decreed that all employers should give their workers the day off. But the township was like a ghost town. Dogs yelped on their chains. Paper packets flapped against fences. Curtains were drawn, doors shut tight. A baby started crying in one house on a corner where we had to make a right turn.

In the town hall, the Prime Minister addressed us about the preservation of our Heritage and about the Onslaught on our country. Mr Jacoby, in his lounge stetson, sang to us and then a magician conjured fancy white fantails out of a hat.

When we surged out of the hall after the Doctor had been granted honorary citizenship of the town, it was Miss Bruwer's voice that rose up in me, raspy, sad. The band members stooped to pick up the instruments they'd left outside the hall. The farmers who'd pulled the floats with tractors and trucks, stopped dead in their tracks.

Only skeletons of the floats stood in the square. While we had been eating tea and koeksisters and singing folk songs in the hall, the blacks from the township had stripped the floats of everything that was edible – and of cardboard and wire and planks for their shacks.

And while I stood there on the square in the hot sun among my friends, staring at the stripped floats, it was Miss Bruwer's voice that echoed in my ears:

> Thy voice is on the rolling air,
> I hear thee where the waters run,
> Thou standest in the rising sun . . .

Ma looked up from the teacup. The wind charger clattered. The light burnt bright again. She pushed the curl back from her eyes and said in that voice that I can still hear. "Get that drink for me now, sweetheart."

59

Every period in a person's life has its own texture. With the Schreiner documents here before me, while I think back to the fear-filled nights in a bolted and barred house while railway tracks sizzled like red hot whisps of straw and the radio's alarm cry faded into the night, I recognise the texture of that summer: Ma's powder-blue summer frock, the warm fragrance of geraniums, the stony smell of Olive's sarcophagus where the Veteran and I had sat resting while he reassured me that we were hot on the trail.

And death's stinking breath, everywhere. But also life that thrust out from under death – the first mealie field that Pa sowed after the government ordered the farmers to plant mealies for the army, and the first mealie sprout lifted a clod, the wet calf that stood behind its bleeding mother on shaky legs . . .

And stubbornly the memory persists: round and round and round. Out of the past rises a heroic figure, the man who, in his own farmyard, perhaps gibbering, weeping, begged for the safety of his family, his name, his person.

60

And I remember Tant Geert and her Nijhoff. She raised the book so I couldn't see her face as she read. We sat alone on the terrace, Reuben waited behind his shield, motionless near the door, tennis racquets cracked against balls, bodies plopped into the swimming pool, but everything played itself out as though afar off, as though we weren't part of it all.

From behind her Nijhoff, Tant Geert read. She read while the Veteran sat in front of his rondavel with his tin of Brasso and his array of medals, while Ma wrote out long lists, ticking off something here and there, peacefully at work at the reception desk.

61

But that summer still had no end. I went to Helsinki and looked up a fortune-teller and I remember one particular moment, a particular stillness at Hotel Halesowen, the loneliness that brings the wind, the flickering light in the corner, the flying circles of the tables, the waning promise of a clear morning, and the remembrance of the past day that had melted away.

The Helsinki woman was a Russian who'd taken the ferry from St Petersburg to Helsinki after the dissolution of the USSR, travelling with only her crystal ball and a set of cheap fortune-teller's shawls in her bag.

She stared into her crystal ball and then looked up. "Your fortune has been told since you were a child. You grew up within the aura of a clairvoyant. A woman. Who was she? Your grandmother? An aunt? Your mother?"

"You are mistaken." The midnight sun lay low on the horizon. Her caravan was parked under trees close to Sibelius's statue. It was two in the morning and birds still twittered.

She rubbed her ball again and gazed deeply into it. "Something is turning," she said, "round and round. It won't come to rest, I'm struggling to follow it, I can't focus . . ."

I waited.

"You must not deny the past," she said after a while. "What work do you do?"

"I'm a writer."

"Then you must write about it."

"Is that a command?" I smiled.

"The sort of command that can only come from within yourself."

Ma bent over the cup. "The handle is the home," she said. "Tea leaves close to the handle are trying to say something about us, Fabian. The leaves closest to the rim are the closest in time."

She tipped the cup and turned it so the lamplight fell on it. "And these right down at the bottom are saying something about bad luck. That's where they always cluster, my boy – I suppose that's life at Hotel Halesowen for you."

The Finnish fortune-teller crouched over her crystal ball. "I see a figure," she said. "A woman. She wants to communicate with you. She . . ."

I tore the curtain back and banged my head on the roof of her caravan. A cat darted back, alarmed. It smelt of wine and stale cigarette smoke. I kicked open the door of the caravan, stumbled down the wooden steps and walked as far as the lake.

I had to take my jacket off as it was hot and I was sweating. Then I returned to my hotel.

"Ma . . ."

Ma took out her red fortune book that she kept under the dream book. "Only a warning," she murmured. "Luckily, only a warning . . ."

She looked up to me. "Oh, Fabian." She took my hand.

At three that morning in Finland, with a summer wind in my face and a lonely canoeist rowing away in the light of the midnight sun while I stood watching him from under a tree at the lakeside, I felt her hand clasp mine.

"It's yesterday, Fabian," she whispered, and the sun flickered like a lantern in the lowest corner of the earth. "It's yesterday that's unpredictable, lovey. It's yesterday."

She looked up, pushing the curl back from her forehead. "Now how about getting me that little tot, hey?"

62

But still that summer seemed to have no end. We suffered a great loss through the opening of the gates. In a protest action involving the whole district, every gate to every lucerne field was thrown open and the cattle were driven into the warm, lethally green lucerne which was in full flower.

When we came back from town, we found our Jerseys browsing hip-high in the lucerne. We ran to them. "Where is Reuben?" roared Pa. Here and there a cow was already lying groaning; others stood bloated and drunk. As he ran, Pa got out his pocket knife and the blade was ready as he took the last few strides. Cursing the citizen force and the shooting practice where he'd had to waste his time, he sank the blade up to the hilt into the distended belly of cow after cow.

Green stomach juices bubbled out as the cattle deflated like great balloons, and lay with rolling eyes, lowing in pain. We managed to pull some through like this, but others died in pools of blood and foaming stomach acid. As Pa cleaned the blade of his knife against his trouser leg, a patrol drove in through the gate.

A motorbike was in the lead followed by a pick-up with the bailiff at the wheel and Reitz beside him, then a truck, and then a strange machine that looked almost like a harvester cricket. It was the first time I'd seen one: the wheels were so high it seemed to be walking on legs. Above, higher than a man, were small windows, and on top, even higher, I could make out the bobbing helmets of the soldiers.

"There he comes," said Tant Geert, her eyes on Reitz, "the jackal himself."

63

It was a palaver getting Mr Jacoby to town for the concert at which Hendrik Verwoerd was to be guest speaker. The Culture Committee kept phoning and the strong-arm guys from Verwoerd's body-guard kicked their heels in the Karoo garden or clambered over the roof of the town hall.

Verwoerd had received a lot of death threats and six years later he was to be murdered in Parliament by the crazy Dimitri Tsafendas who would stab him six times. The first doctor who rushed to his aid there on the mat while the bells of parliament rang, would be Dr Morrison, Cradock's MP. Ma and Pa had voted for him because he was a Nationalist.

Mr Jacoby was very nervous about his appearance along with the Prime Minister – a man who'd challenged the whole Commonwealth. Early that morning, Reuben had hurried back and forth between the Zane Grey and the reception desk. Now for a flannel cloth, then a headache tablet, then again for a drop of orange juice. I wandered among the rondavels, already dressed in my cadet uniform. The beret sat jauntily on my head. Mr

Jacoby, I noted through his half-open door, was stooped over a basin of steaming water. He had a cloth draped over his head and shoulders and he was taking deep breaths of the steam. Ma had asked Reuben to crush a few bluegum leaves in the water, and the strong eucalyptus smell wafted through the rondavel door.

But the white guitar, polished to a shine, stood against the wall, the stetson hung ready to be placed on his head, and there was Reuben again with something else on his tray, oh yes, I see, a little something to settle the stomach.

The Veteran was also outside his rondavel. He wasn't watching everything as he usually did, but stood at attention, afraid that his uniform might crease. He raised his hand to me in a salute and called out, "Who goes there?"

Still in his dressing gown, with a book under his arm and spectacles skew over eyes that were thick with sleep, Dr Clark, looking somewhat bewildered, appeared in the doorway of the Bitter Aloe. He glanced down towards the Wilhelmina to see whether Tant Geert and Miss Marge had emerged yet, but their door was tightly shut, as were the curtains, so he turned back and closed his own door.

As I strolled up to the terrace, I suddenly found the Pastor beside me. "Master Latsky," he said. "We must pray for God's mercy for the Republic today. Emperors shall rule, it is true, but the Greatest Prince is the Prince of Heaven. Praised be His Name!"

And the Pastor wandered off dreamily towards the orchard where, among the rotting peaches shaken down by the monkeys, he kneeled and prayed out loud, so loudly that the guests were roused by all the excitement and now also came out of their rondavels unusually early. With towels around their necks and toothbrushes in their hands, they made their way to the ablution block.

In no time the smells of steam, soap, and bacon and eggs mingled on the kikuyu lawn where the town dogs romped and chased each other around.

Finally, with the terrace full of people and some of the

waiters polishing the cars under the trees in preparation for the drive to town, Mr Jacoby appeared on the threshold of the Zane Grey. He stood there, pure white, glittering, his cheeks red from the steam, his stetson at a jaunty angle on his head and the guitar which hung around his neck also at an angle.

The guests on the terrace clapped as he came across the lawn, with Reuben shooing the town dogs away before they could smear Mr Jacoby's white cowboy pants. Dr Clark reappeared on his stoep with a book under his arm and Tant Geert and Miss Marge emerged from their rondavel, self-conscious and still groggy with sleep. They stood there, smiling bemusedly as though the applause was for them.

The Pastor returned from the orchard with outstretched arms and prayed for a blessing on the day, and behind me, Ma said. "Will I ever forget this, Fabian?"

Mr Jacoby took a light breakfast and then the SAR&H lorry arrived and they began the delicate process of loading Valour. Ma left it all to Reuben because Pa hadn't emerged from the bedroom yet, and we were all waiting for the curtain rings to sing.

Then we'd know that he'd allowed the day to stream into his room, the day he and Mr Crafford had debated so long over, until Pa had had to acknowledge that the wrong methods were being used to foster the Republican ideal, and he had to agree that it would be an incitement of the voteless black people if the procession with Verwoerd at the helm should march through the location of all places.

But, in desperation, he had reaffirmed his love of the Republic, railing against the threat of a chaotic Africa and against the things that were swirling darkly in the bottom of Ma's fortune cup, and had declared, "For the foreseeable future I am one hundred per cent behind Hendrik French Verwoerd."

64

Had Reuben turned his eyes away when the gates were thrown open so the cows could graze the dangerous green lucerne? Or had he perhaps even opened the gates himself, obeying a command which had been whispered from the township and had spread along the railway line to all the farms in the valley?

The dreams of that time are clearer in my memory than the reality. And the night things – the things of the time after Pa had dropped into an exhausted sleep after his dream sessions; the things that clustered in Ma's fortune cup – grew larger late at night. Those things grew larger than the dining room where we sat drinking tea. They escaped through the windows on flying saucers, spinning round and round, as though they were tea in a cup and it was I who now, after three rapid movements with the left hand, to the left, turned the cup quickly over on the saucer, then held my hand over it and carefully turned it right side up again and stared in at the patterns of tea leaves.

I have Ma's red fortune book here at my elbow, I leaf through it, I am amazed at the arsenal of things that can be coming up, can go wrong, the dreams that can lie broken behind one, the endless succession of good fortune and mishap that can befall one – always in terms of symbols like a horse's saddle (an aptitude for travel and discovery), a satellite (submission to power, if it lies close to a bigger form), a ladder (the power of personal drive and initiative), a monkey (if it's close to the handle, a mysterious enemy; near the rim, an enemy in your own house), a kettle (in the base of the cup complications at home, thus discord and ill-feeling; if not, domestic aptitude and organisational ability), an apple (good health, the possibility of recovery), a bride (a symbol of grief), a cigarette (you allow frivolity to thwart your projects or initiatives), a clock (a warning that nothing passes as quickly as the years), a bat (an evil prognostication; mysterious enemies are closing in, be wary . . .)

"On guard, Fabian! Always on guard."

It was a long list of possibilities, but that's life, after all – a continual series of forks in the road – all the alternatives, but almost never a choice.

And whose is the hand that turns the cup, to the left, anti-clockwise, swiftly, deftly?

And why does a writer always feel, like in Sophocles' *Oedipus Rex,* the detective will discover at the end of all his painstaking investigation that he is the murderer himself?

65

It was a dreamed time, and will always remain so for me. Not because the domain of dreams is more beautiful and easier to cherish – but, perhaps, more likely because the dream interpreted reality better than I could do consciously as a youngster.

Night after night I dreamed the dream of the jail on the banks of the Fish River. Stony and rough, the jail where the workers were taken if Reitz's patrols caught them on main roads with knives or crowbars.

In my dreams we stormed this Bastille at night with flashing knives and swaying hurricane lanterns. Boe's son Willempie and I led the attack, and I carried the symbol of our struggle, brandishing it high above our heads: the writer Olive on a cross, with a scarlet turban topping her grimacing skull.

My troops wore gumboots – heavy was the tread of the workers' army! – and with our eventual victory, the author rose again and so did Windpomp, Boe's husband, glowing, laughing from the red incinerator of the haystack; brushing glowing straw from his garments, stepping through whisps of red hot hay he strode, with hands full of wheat that dripped, melting through his fingers.

Dancing joyously in the flames, we released the prisoners. Then we hauled the guards off to the tannery near Cradock station, over the river, which meant we had to drag them through the shallows of the Fish. Bloody and muddied, their spluttering heads swayed from side to side as we pulled them along by their boots.

We kicked the tanner's doors open and strode through the suffocating stench of meat and salt straight to the hanging racks where the freshest sheep- and cow-hides hung, still wet and freshly salted. The hides, with their fine lacework of veins and streaks of yellow fat, were cool and moist to the touch as we rolled each guard in one and then tied him up with rawhide thongs before loading them all into an empty truck beside the platform.

In the stillness of the night, we waited with our flickering lanterns for the first train. When the time came, we switched the points and hijacked the train, taking the guards by steaming loco to Halesowen, the station beyond Buffelskop, where we arranged them in a large swastika between the sisal plants, leaving them for the sun to bake dry, to melt the fat, shrinking their hide jackets so that their beastly tongues swelled as the contracting hides embraced them.

This was not a dream to boast about and I would not have dared tell Ma or Pa. Now, years later, I comfort myself that a child in his fantasies doesn't know the salty flavour of real blood or comprehend the ripping of metal through human flesh.

But I blame my dreams – the dreams of those days as well as my dreams as an adult – on what happened that day when Pa and I stood amongst the Jerseys and the patrol with Reitz and Fanie the Weed came rumbling through the farmyard gate.

Reitz and his company strode up to us, grabbed Pa by the shoulder and manhandled him up to the kitchen door. I recall a few soldiers, the son of the garage owner, Little Pete Specs from Altydsomer, Erwin Moolman. Reitz and Fanie the Weed blew shrilly on their whistles to summon the workers – who'd scattered in all directions. The rondavel doors slammed shut as the guests were herded in. Where was the Veteran? Where was Dr Clark? And the Pastor? Was Tant Geert there, and Miss Marge?

I don't know – I only remember the workers, ranged up against the shed, and the waiters who had to come to the farmyard from the terrace, still bearing their trays.

At first Reuben didn't want to follow the other waiters, but he came anyway, glancing neither to right nor left. He had to fall in against the shed with the others. They had to stand there with their hands raised above their heads while Reitz paced up and down behind them.

"Who opened the gate?" he yelled.

I pressed myself against Pa's leg. There were green gobs of stomach juice on his trouser leg. "Cut it out," said Pa. "Cut it out, Reitz. This is my farm. You're interfering on a neighbour's farm here. Look how you've scared my guests. Leave it now. I'll speak to my workers myself."

"Who opened the fucking gate?" bellowed Reitz.

Reitz farmed five sluice gates higher up the river and he knew our workers. Boe's husband, my friend Willempie's father, was not in the group against the stable wall.

"Where is Windpomp?" he demanded, and one of the soldiers clouted Reuben in the back with the butt of his rifle. "The one with a missing finger."

"He's out in the veld," Pa offered.

"Windpomp!"

Reitz set off towards the haystacks. Had Reuben's eye, deliberately or accidentally, flickered in that direction? Anyway, that's what the workers thought, we heard later. It was Reuben, he who lived with the whites in the back room near the donkey, it was he who had pointed to the haystack with his eyes. He, yes, he.

That was the beginning of the time when the other black people on Soebatsfontein turned their backs on Reuben. Perhaps it added to the frightening intensity with which he fell in love with Tsitsi, Oom Boeta's servant.

Because they were still to arrive at the farm.

Reitz stopped in front of the biggest haystack. He took out the matches he used to light his pipe. The kitchen door, which had been locked by the soldiers, burst splintering open. Boe ran out screaming. It was the first and the last time I ever saw Boe running. I was startled by the thick pads of flesh on her thighs, the strong shins that kicked her skirt and were finally exposed as she picked up the skirt and rushed at Reitz, howling, "No, baas, no, baas!"

The stack caught fire, flames darted over the top and up the sides.

No one said a word. Where was Ma? Still locked in her bedroom? Tant Geert couldn't have been there, could she? Was it a different summer that swam round in the bottom of the teacup, stubbornly, round and round?

No one spoke. Boe stood somewhere in the empty space between the kitchen door, which hung skew on its hinges, and the burning haystack. She did not weep.

Reitz circled round the glowing haystack. "Ants! Ants! Ants!" I screamed, with my hands over my ears, when he took up a pitchfork and stuck it into the red furnace and the fork began to glow from the tips thrust into the hot hay and the glow crept up to Reitz's hands and I knew: if hay was properly stacked, as ours was, it could smoulder for six months, charred on the outside, but if you scraped away the crust, it was molten red inside and if a wind came up, flames would leap up again, turning the haystack into a torch that the furthest neighbours could see at night. Reitz's hands were molten scarlet on the pitchfork and his body began to melt and he flowed into his glowing boots and became a strip of crackling, encircled by his pocket knife, his pipe and the buckle of his belt, while I screamed and pressed my hands to my ears so that I wouldn't hear the ants, and I felt Pa's strong arms pick me up and carry me away, and later, on Boe's lap, in her warm, plump arms, I forgot the revolvers and the men who carried pistols, splattered blood against the stable wall, and the scrawny workers, original inhabitants of the land, whose blood it was.

Boe comforted me, the white man's child, while her Willempie, suddenly thin and stunned, squatted in the shade of the pepper trees, watching us in silence. This action of Boe's, while the soldiers clambered up into their long-legged insect and roared through the gate in a swirl of dust, and the guests opened their doors a crack, is the most dreadful thing of all.

In the following days thousands of ants died, too stupid to turn round, obeying the instinct that drove them to their nest under the glowing haystack. Willempie and I watched them and, on the third day, we decided upon the resurrection of Olive.

66

Valour dropped steaming green turds during all the efforts to soothe and coax him up onto the back of the SAR&H Bedford. The driver had backed the lorry up against the loading ramp, so Valour only had to walk onto the back of the truck, but perhaps the train ride from Cradock to Halesowen had upset him so much that he wasn't going to let anyone load him on to anything again in a hurry.

Reuben brought a bunch of carrots from the kitchen, but that didn't help. Eventually Mr Jacoby was called away from the telephone at the front desk – the Culture Committee chairman yet again – and he came to stand at Valour's head, rubbed the creature's nose, whispering sweet nothings about the Kentucky hills into his ear.

As if bewitched, Valour let loose his steaming turds and stumped onto the Bedford. He stood with his neck against the railings and raised his head. He looked me straight in the eye and I saluted him.

"Parade! A-ten-tion!" bellowed the Veteran, who had strolled up from under the pepper trees. He took long strides with his crows' wings thrust back. This was how he would march later that day, uninvited and unknown, amongst the townsfolk who lined the streets and filled the square in front of the town hall. They'd point and ask one another about him, until someone uttered the word "war hero", and another the word "veteran" and "Africa Corps" and another "wounded in the Great War".

Quick as a flash, the bush telegraph took the news to the strings of people on the pavements and to the crowds on the square: the man in the strange uniform, the one with the row of medals on his chest, was Major Heathcote MacKenzie, honourably discharged after the conflict in North Africa. Thin and trembling from excitement in the wind, looking neither right nor left, the Veteran had created his own position five paces behind the school cadet band, and won himself the applause appropriate to a war hero.

I marched in the platoon just behind him, staring at his stiff shoulders, his straight back and his scrawny neck. In fact, everyone in my platoon looked at him, because we were still rookie cadets. We wore berets and not caps like the older children. We could scarcely march in time and kept getting out of step, and the rhythmic efficiency of the Veteran's stride served as an inspiration and a pace-setter to us.

Tant Geert had parked the Borgward under a pine tree and when we marched past, shortly before we turned the corner for the last bit of street before the town square, I saw her and Miss Marge sprawled on the Borgward's front seat, rocking with laughter and pointing at the Veteran, the old crow with the turkey neck.

Dr Clark sat in the Karoo Café, busy with Chapter Four of his book – in which he compared LCD with other hallucinogens – and only got up for a moment to come and lean against the door frame and watch the goings-on on the square.

He had no desire to even catch a glimpse of Doctor Verwoerd's white head, but it so happened that the black car arrived from the landing strip just as Dr Clark abandoned his Coke and came to stand in the entrance to the Karoo Café.

He saw Doctor Verwoerd get out of Pete Specs's black car and raise his hat to the crowd. He saw the cadets stand to attention for the National Anthem and he saw the orchestra's instruments gleam in the sunlight. Everyone stood to attention. Stunned with surprise, he looked at the Veteran standing in the middle of the parade ground, straight as a rod, as though he were the Commanding Officer of the parade. Dr Clark also noticed that a security man on the town hall roof kept his binoculars focused on the Veteran.

Then he saw Doctor Verwoerd walking amongst the floats with the Products of the District, shaking a hand here and there, exchanging a friendly word or two, before going into the town hall.

And then there was Valour who trippled into the square to a roar of welcome, and the cheer became deafening as Charles Jacoby took off his stetson and threw the white hat into the sunlight so that it went up like a flying saucer and made the crowd catch its breath because they were afraid the wind might take it.

But the nimble Valour was under control. Mr Jacoby caught it with a flourish, sweeping it back on to his head and then he trippled through the town hall doors where the mayoress waited to welcome him on this momentous day, the day of the Honorary Citizenship, that summer's day in Soebatsfontein's most profitable Season, the season of Reuben's betrayal.

67

"It was the women who noticed him first," Ma said of the Veteran's parading. Her tone was not without a hint of jealousy and she raised her drink and hula-hooped her hips. It was evening on the terrace and we were reliving Verwoerd's visit.

"He looks like the cat that got the cream," growled Pa, eyeing the Veteran cynically. Pa reckoned the Veteran had made a spectacle of himself. Why did he have to show off his marching talent in front of everyone like that?

"He's the town hero," said Ma, ordering a free round for everyone on the terrace. "On the house! On the house! And here's to Mr Jacoby!"

Mr Jacoby was not with us where we gathered on the terrace because he had withdrawn to the Zane Grey. He had a seriously funny tummy after the day's tensions and every now and then the white stetson was to be seen making its way up to the ablution block through the darkness.

"A cowboy with the trots!" said Tant Geert. "Nature's got our performer on the run . . ."

Ma surveyed the scene. "I'm satisfied," she said, "with the contribution the Hotel Halesowen made to the Prime Minister's visit. The Dutch can say what they like about Apartheid, but what a charming man he is!

"What a Season! And there's still Christmas to come! We'll have to work our fingers to the bone, but everything is going so well!"

She glanced at Pa who sat deep in his paisley dressing gown with a knee-rug over his legs. "This kind of self sacrifice raises you high on your cross," said Pa. But luckily Ma didn't hear him – she was too excited about everything that had happened.

"And your brother is already on the way, isn't he? Just think: all the Latskys together – that doesn't happen every day."

Pa gazed up at the Milky Way. "Putsonderwater," he intoned. "Soebatsfontein."

68

We waited until the spirit had returned to our bones. Like my brave ancestors, the Rebels, who would not bow before the British Empire, and the Voortrekkers, who turned their backs on the Dutch regime at the Cape, I led the assault with an ostrich feather in my hat.

The bandolier across my chest was made of a perished girth and old shoe-leather. My heart swelled undaunted, because we were going to abduct Death himself, away from the cold domain of stone. I would bring the authoress back to life.

Forward, rebels! For freedom and life and the colours of our flag!

Ma had made our flag from a large Piet Retief tobacco bag, with the Dingaan shield and assegais in the middle and below that the motto of our republic: *Choice Quality Assegai!*

First we went to the haystack. The wind had dropped. Beneath the heat haze and the black crust, the furnace was consuming Windpomp, the wandering shearer who'd come to put down roots on our farm with his wife and son. Then we tackled the long slog over the plains, clambering over the railway fence, hopping over the polished tracks, and then we started to climb up the steep slope of Buffelskop.

We had to zigzag to get to the cliff because the Veteran wouldn't have allowed us our expedition without wanting to come along. We'd waited until he lay down on his divan for a nap, before leaving stealthily, going up the river a little way first, knee-deep in water, to shake him off our spoor.

We sat and rested a little while on the sarcophagus to catch our breath, the rock warm under our buttocks. Then we went to work. Without any difficulty we moved the first two loose rocks aside. I crawled into the coolness within, gathered the bones together and passed them out. The bones made a pathetic heap in the sunlight outside the sarcophagus. Badly decayed, they lay on the open sack as if many hands down the years had taken hold of them, fingered them then put them back.

I carefully packed the bones into the sack while Willempie held it open. Sparks shot out of them, just like flint, when they struck or rubbed against each other. We could smell gunpowder! I wiped my hands on my khaki pants. We hid our terror from one another, for the sublime breezes of Buffelskop were playing in our hair and a flock of tick birds drifted dreamily below us across the floor of the valley, following the course of the Fish, towards the white speckle of buildings that was the Hotel Halesowen.

The bones tinkled faintly as we carried them down the slopes of Buffelskop. There's life in them, Joe Mann! sang the wind. Miss Marge was right! whispered the stones and thorn trees. It was a heavy load and we had to shift it from one shoulder to the other. At the track we had to wait for a train to pass first.

The engine came from the direction of PE, headlight ablaze, roaring past with pistons pumping. It was Verwoerd's train – en route into the Karoo, to towns without landing strips. His plane couldn't land everywhere in the wide landscape. Verwoerd was sitting in there reading or making notes, although Pa and them said that, as an experienced debater, he never spoke from notes, and his little wife, the dainty Mrs Betsie, sat beside him. They worked hard, specially at that time, and, at weekends, they escaped to their small farm.

It was called Stokkiesdraai and newspapers published pictures of Verwoerd playing with his bulldog under the trees there. Then the train staggered out of sight over the brown surface of the earth, chugging into other districts; carrying the man who would influence so many lives and who would eventually fall victim to assassination, carrying him further and futher away.

The conductor waved to us, we waved back. Two national flags flapped on the locomotive. We watched the fluttering flags until the train was gone and only the steam drifted low over the plains. The sleepers were still vibrating and the signal wires trilled, but Verwoerd was gone, leaving us to consider the consequences of his visit between us.

Beyond the avenue of sisal, between the stone cairns of workers' graves, we laid the sack down. From among the sisal aloes, we hauled out the cross we had made from a piece of cut-down telephone pole and old fencing droppers. We laid the bones out carefully on the sack. The sun was high and burning down. We argued over the precise position of every bone. Willempie had to go to the farmyard to get pliers and wire while I kept vigil over the bones.

Unease crept over me, while the skull stared fixedly in my direction.

It seemed ages before Willempie returned. "Did Pa see you?"

I asked anxiously. Pa. Something in him had died, with Wind-pomp's death. He wandered incessantly about the house. Once, while he was talking to the bailiff on the phone, he collapsed and Ma had to resuscitate him and carry him to bed with Reuben's help. His sessions with Dr Clark grew longer and longer; sometimes the door of the Bitter Aloe remained closed for hours, and then, when it opened, Dr Clark looked even more disturbed than his patient.

Willempie shook his head. He had come away without being seen.

He set to work. First he wove the shiny copper wire between the loose teeth, drawing the lower jaw up near the ear sockets, wiring a few loose cranial plates together. The ribcage was more difficult. Why were there so few ribs? "Because she's a woman," said Willempie. Lower down against the cross, the thigh and shin bones. Then the arms, outstretched with every small finger bone in place. Willempie had hardly finished, and already we'd fallen in love with her and worshipped her. We dedicated ourselves to her. Using my old pocket knife, I carefully cut open the dress I'd pinched from the back of Ma's winter clothes chest. Reverently, we wrapped it round her shoulders, her lovely slim neck, round her pretty hips, her legs, her delicate, tender feet. We folded the dress over her breasts and then I sewed it up painstakingly with a sacking needle and baling twine, finally smoothing the material properly into place, and raised the writer up.

Her silhouette echoed the shapes of the tall sisal flower-stems around us. We gazed at her. We waited. The smell of the smouldering haystack wafted to us on the wind.

"Will we ever catch the Thing, Willempie?" I asked him.

"Kikuyu covers his own tracks," Willempie told me.

"But we'll get him, Willempie."

I thought about the portraits in the Schreiner Room, the sour smell of the books Miss Marge opened before me. I thought about Pa and the Prime Minister and the shots that echoed against Buffelskop at night and Miss Marge saying, "She could unite. She could write life back into the country . . ." Was it true that the country was dying, without our realising it, and that the Prime Minister and the Headmaster and everyone at the parade just imagined that they knew the country and loved the land?

Because that's what Tant Geert and Marge Bruwer told each other on their long walks in the fields of Soebatsfontein. Sometimes they invited me to come along, and then Tant Geert would talk about Rome and London and Amsterdam. "Oh, Marge!" she'd exclaim when she got excited with the telling. And, "Oh, Fabian, little pupiltjie!"

Eventually Willempie and I got bored and wandered off for a swim in the river, splashing about in the clear water. It was late afternoon but I was afraid to go home; perhaps Pa would be lying as he had been yesterday – as quiet as a dead person in the bedroom. Ma was probably sitting, deeply involved in her tea cup, in the deserted dining room. Reuben was probably standing on the terrace with his tray, with no one ever exchanging a word with him and the bored waiters keeping their distance. The town dogs were probably yawning where they lay beside their owners' rondavels, and the guests' children were probably teasing each other on the lawns until one ran crying to a rondavel to rouse his parents from their afternoon nap.

The afternoons stretched out endlessly when it was too hot even to risk a swim. Everything waited. The bluegums were silent, the troop of monkeys lolled, exhausted, on the damp sand in the river bed, digging out cool hollows to lie in. The cows stood about with heads hung low, taking short panting breaths. The Pastor lay with his head under his pillow. Even in the shade the cars were baking hot. The waiters got bored and irritable because no one was placing any orders.

Everyone was waiting for the first cool breath of the evening breeze, waiting for the Milky Way to appear on the dark throat of the night like a sparkling necklace.

Willempie and I sat in the early dusk, with the river water stretching silvery before us, masturbating. We both worked vigorously but Willempie won, his shining seed spurting in an arc right into the evening waters of the Fish.

194

I thought of what Tant Geert had said, "The government is collapsing. Because only a man who is drowning drags everyone else down with him."

I glanced at Willempie, who was pulling his shorts up, sated. "That lady," I said, "she'll bring life again. Just wait and see."

But what we didn't see was the Veteran among the river trees, where he stood motionless in his black uniform among the reeds.

Tall and black he stood there, an upright bat, groaning with pleasure as he watched us working our small penises. He stared at us, transfixed, and he raised his nose. He smelt something of our heat. He had to suppress the grunting breath in his throat as he felt his veined penis begin to jerk in his hand and the seed spurted into the sand at his feet.

69

What more can I say now, nearly two decades later? Is the country, or this story, still dying in my hands? Two things remain certain: the authoress, motionless between the sisal aloes, where the winds of the Karoo howled stories through her skull that whole summer long. And the haystack, which glowed right through the rainy season and deep into the winter.

No one ever discovered Olive. On one of the last days of that Season, when Tant Geert was on the point of departure and everything was coming to an end, Willempie and I sat among the sisal aloes. We gazed reverently up at our crucifixion. The prickly pears near the sisal avenue had burst unexpectedly into bloom that morning and bees buzzed around the colourful fluff.

"Your wiring is holding out well, Willempie," I said.

He nodded.

Then we heard footsteps approaching over the dry veld. We froze. Our shrine was about to be violated! I heard the voices of Tant Geert and Miss Marge. They chatted as they picked their way through the sisal aloes. Had they seen us slipping in there?

We sat as still as mice, but when they came into a clearing, they saw us. They stood arms akimbo, looking at us. Miss Marge's face was red from the exertion, as it always was when she came walking on the farm.

I expected her to come closer to me and say, "Have you heard of Olive Schreiner, boy?" But they just smiled at us, waved, and, shaking their heads, walked on along one of the many footpaths that they had followed that summer on the neglected farm – in expectation of the Verwoerd water.

What can I say?

> Thy voice is on the rolling air,
> I hear thee where the waters run,
> Thou standest in the rising sun?

Yes, that too.

But there were so many things that remained unsaid: why were Ma and Pa absent from my memories of Verwoerd's appearance in the town hall? What had happened? Were they also sitting in the hall? What did Charles Jacoby have to say to Verwoerd behind the curtain of the Cradock town hall, while they waited for the excited townsfolk to take their seats?

"Howdy?"

Yes, probably.

One summer, or four?

I'm not even sure of that.

It was as Tant Geert had written, years later, from London, when my first novel was published. "Congratulations. Charmed. When you come to a fork in the road, Fabian, take it."

I mulled over her words for ages, turned the postcard round three times anti-clockwise and then read on:

"You know what Gorter wrote:

> I wish I could give you something
> of consolation deep into life,
> but all I have are words,
> names, and worldly things none.

"But, hang on! When (not if) I die, the Harley Davidson is yours. With Marge gone now (what a sad place to die – Wapadsberg, that God-forsaken mountain pass in the middle of the Great Karoo) I suppose you're the only one I can regard as, well, some kind of heir-in-law. Take the machine, pupiltjie, and ride the hell out of it. Do you remember that afternoon? You and Marge and I in the lucerne fields on old Bobby Greenblatt's motorbike? Oh, the sanctity of the Great Karoo."

Three months later she came to Nieu-Bethesda to visit the mad sculptor Helen Martens, and died.

A capricious wind blew during the funeral.

70

"Dynamite Krantz doesn't belong to anyone," Pa said when the Veteran asked him if he and I could sleuth around for dassies up there.

But Ma wasn't happy. "It belongs to the Railways," she said. "Or maybe it belongs to the Collets, or the Barbers, or Bennie van Rensburg over on Green Acres."

"No," said Pa, "that Krantz is no-man's land. And those dassies up there are so fat, they're asking to be culled."

And that was how Pa gave his permission.

"Right, corporaltjie," crowed the Veteran, "let's catch the cocopan when it comes past Halesowen and ask to be put down at Dynamite Krantz."

He winked at me to remind me not to let on that we were actually after the Beast. The Veteran was afraid that Pa would say what he'd said so often before, "What crap stories are these about that ape-thing again?"

And the Pastor, said the Veteran, would fall to praying if you so much as mentioned anything unbiblical. The Bible declared that the devil was invisible, the Pastor reckoned. "You search for Kees in vain."

"That's where he's wrong," said the Veteran, winking at me again.

Pa gave me the .22 and twenty bullets and we walked up to Halesowen. The Veteran had his 303 and a bottle of water at his hip. There were a hundred rounds in the bandoleer across his chest.

"Forward march!"

At Halesowen we had to wait until the cocopan showed up from Mortimer. Every morning at this time the workers who maintained the sleepers and signals on the line between Mortimer and Cradock came past. Two men stood pumping the cocopan. They came riding along like an insect out of the mirage. The bobbing figures of the men looked like the legs of an approaching insect.

When we were sitting on top of Dynamite Krantz, I could see Oom Boeta's black government Cadillac approaching from a long way off.

"There comes Pa's brother!"

I jumped up to wave, but the Veteran laughed at me. "Come off it, corporaltjie, those Pretoria types don't look around as they drive along. They're city people. Not interested in lucerne and ostriches. You'd need a heliograph, at least, to attract their attention."

The Cadillac swished past below us. The geese who'd settled on the river took fright and flapped up, honking. We'd been watching the dassies on the rocks below us, waiting for the fattest to emerge, but now they scattered. "My, but aren't we swanky," muttered the Veteran as he focused his binoculars on the Cadillac. "TP 2000," he read the registration plate. He looked at me. "Only fellows with real connections can get number plates like that."

"My Oom Boeta is very high up. He knows the Doctor personally. He works in the Union Buildings."

"I can tell from the car," said the Veteran, "and from the way he drives in the middle of the road. Just look at the cloud of dust." In the direction of Halesowen all we could see was dust as Oom Boeta raced along. "That car has wings," said the

Veteran. "It flies over the corrugations. No, fine! I can see your Oom Boeta is a high man."

I'd heard Pa tell Ma that his brother was the only Latsky who'd made it into the Broederbond. In his time, he'd been a mere clerk in the magistrate's court at Klipplaat, but he'd sat the civil service exams one after the other, and just look at him now: with a flashy black Cadillac, his sons at Boys' High in Pretoria, a pedigree boxer dog, a house in Waterkloof with a driveway and proteas, an office in the Union Buildings and a fancy title. And he was on a first-name basis with everyone from Paul Sauer to Ben Schoeman.

"That's one thing about our government," Pa was fond of saying. "There's always a job for a sharp Afrikaner man. And Boeta is the sharpest of the sharp."

"And the silent type," Ma liked to add. "He's a man of few words. While the other men around him were talking nonsense or conniving, Oom Boeta was climbing up as slowly as a mountain tortoise. And just as patiently. Just wait and see, he's still going to be a big big wheel."

"He's already a big wheel," Pa'd answered, "that brother of mine." Then Pa's mood would swing down again. "Ag, why wasn't I also born with his talents? Why did I have to be the black sheep of the family?"

"You're not a black sheep," Ma said. "I wouldn't like to be married to a man like your brother Boeta. He's out at the crack of dawn, off to the Union Buildings, and that Cadillac only comes back up the driveway an hour or so after dark. Your poor sister-in-law. And there in Pretoria you have to mind your p's and q's. You can't just say what you like. The poor women have to wear hats no matter where they're off to – Sunday best every day. No, they're too grand for me. I'd rather be here at the Halesowen Hotel where I can pop on a housecoat and put my feet up under the bluegums, corns and all.

"Who wants to go to a ministerial reception every Friday evening? Just imagine how much they gossip. They watch each other like hawks, stabbing one another in the back and walking all over whoever gets in their way to the top. Spare me!"

And Ma would shake the curl back from her forehead and light a cigarette, drawing the smoke in deep. She'd reach out to Pa, stroking the back of his hand.

"My old sweetheart," she said. "Everything's just fine."

"It's them that keep the country on the go," said Pa. "It's those Afrikaner menfolk who are going to make South Africa the strongest country in Africa. The world is going to sit up and take notice of the Afrikaner. Every one of the men around Boeta does the work of fifty blacks – those that lie around in the shade all day and then beat up their wives and stab each other at the weekend."

"Yes," Ma answered quickly, "that's why your brother Boeta had his first heart attack."

"Yes," answered Pa, "the tension is eating at us. We've shaken off the English yoke; we'll win freedom for the Afrikaner yet. It's not easy for men like Boeta to carry out Doctor Verwoerd's ideas."

"That heart attack!" laughed Ma. "It's all that merino mutton that we send up to Pretoria that's brought on his heart problems."

"It's the least I can do for him," sighed Pa. "And, on top of that, his share in the trust . . ."

"Ag, forget the old trust," said Ma, stubbing out her cigarette. "I must actually go and have a word with Reuben about slaughtering something for Boeta and them."

Every second week, Reuben had to select an old ewe for Oom Boeta. He was also responsible for cutting up the meat and cooling it down in the paraffin fridge. In the kitchen, Boe would wrap the meat in newspaper and pack it in a big cardboard box. Then Ma would rush it off to the Halesowen station, just in time for the express to De Aar, and, from there, Oom Boeta's merino would travel to Waterkloof by Transkaroo Express, and Boeta would invite all the big-wigs for a Karoo mutton braai.

"Nothing preserves meat as well as newspaper," Ma said. "And anyway, all Boeta has to do is pick up the phone and the SAR&H in Pretoria will give him priority service – chop-chop and the Merino chops are delivered to the front door."

"There go the Pretorians, corporal," said the Veteran. "My, just look at that dust cloud . . ."

71

"Fabian's got eye trouble," said Ma.

"What's that you're saying there?" asked Oom Boeta.

"Yes," answered Ma. "We only found out the other day that poor Fabiantjie can only see through one eye. Fabian! Come and show Oom Boeta and them the pearl on your eye."

"Dear God!" exclaimed Oom Boeta. "For heaven's sake, people. I live just round the corner from Willie Meyer! He's the leading Afrikaner eye specialist in the country. You must bring Fabian up to Pretoria so Willem can look at this eye."

Oom Boeta's house was set against a ridge in Waterkloof. The streets were lined with jacarandas. There was a full-time gardener, a Zulu, who wore a khaki uniform and tended the proteas that had been brought up from the Cape and had to be looked after very carefully in this climate. He was also responsible for the boxer dog and the fruit trees in the back garden, for the shiny Cadillac, for the big lawn that had made Ma say, "Now at last I know what a rolling lawn looks like." Then there was the Shona girl, Tsitsi, who lived in the servant's room behind the garage. "Boeta and them are really organised," said Ma. "And all the latest gadgets in the kitchen as well."

Every afternoon the Airforce Sabres practised over Waterkloof. They drew smoke trails across the sky, climbed into the blue of heaven, tumbling and diving. Sometimes the smoke was coloured with the shades of the flag, orange, blue and white.

"Just look at that," Pa always said when we were at Oom Boeta's. "Our airforce. Our boys in the clouds. Doesn't that make you feel proud, big boy?"

Sometimes Oom Boeta took us to the Voortrekker Monument in the black Cadillac. Even if it was summer we changed from shorts and sandals into long pants and proper shoes and socks. "It's a church," Oom Boeta would explain.

"A temple," Pa would add. "Sort of."

We looked at the panels with carved scenes of the Voortrekkers' fights against the Zulus. "Barefoot over the Drakensberg!" Ma cried and Oom Boeta eyed her slightly askance. Was she serious or only joking?

Oom Boeta told us how the Afrikaner had to bow to England, how the Boer War devastated our country. "Kitchener," said Oom Boeta, "that rubbish! How many of our women and children perished in the British concentration camps! Twenty thousand!"

"More," said Pa. "Twenty-two thousand."

"Then the poor Afrikaner sat in sackcloth and ashes in the slums of our cities," Oom Boeta continued.

"A scandal," cried Pa, looking up to where the Sabres ripped through the sky.

"But now the Afrikaner is pulling himself up by his boot laces," called Oom Boeta. "We're taking over the civil service, we're getting homelands on the go for the blacks, South Africa is becoming the larder of Africa!"

"No one will ever tell us where to get off again." Pa swung me up on to his shoulders, as though I'd be closer to the Sons of the Clouds up there.

"Specially not the English."

"Hear, hear. Nothing beats a Boer."

Oom Boeta arranged for us to visit the control tower at the Valhalla Airforce Base. We watched the lights flicker on the screens as the Shackletons and helicopters took off.

"Amazing!" cried Pa. "What an experience!"

"Oom Boeta is pretty high up," he said. "My brother Boeta only has to pick up the phone."

"How do you know for sure that he's a Broederbonder?" asked Ma.

"How else would he have done so well?" asked Pa. "There's

only one way to the top, and that is the Broederbond way. And don't you remember that night while we were visiting, when he rushed off in the Cadillac with all sorts of excuses? It was obviously a Broederbond meeting."

"Well, well," said Ma.

"One day the Afrikaner will understand what the Bond did for him," said Pa.

It was on the tip of Ma's tongue to ask him when he was going to be approached by the Bond then, but she bit her lip. She remembered where we lived, Hotel Soebatsfontein, the rondavels, and the row of rooms, the droughts and the lonely trains, the families from Port Elizabeth who came to lie around there, the emptiness and Pa's despair.

Why ever would they ask him – who in any event was so wary of meetings and old boys' networks and cliques?

And, in any case, he'd never be able to observe the rituals of the Broederbond. Oom Boeta, yes, he was a man who could take the initiation ritual into the Bond seriously – the promise that the Bond will not allow itself to be betrayed, that the Bond never forgot – and who wouldn't laugh at the two candles in the dark room, the drawn curtains, the flag against the wall and the way in which the recruit was led into the silent room.

Once he was left standing in the dimly lit room, the yet unknown members of the Broederbond-chapter came into the room and stood behind Oom Boeta. He was not permitted to look round and he didn't know that some of his best friends and closest colleagues came to stand behind him – people with whom he had daily contact without ever realising that they were members of the secret organisation.

The ones that were to read out loud carried torches and, after the hymn, Oom Boeta was told, "The Broederbond was born of a deep conviction that the Afrikaner nation was placed in this country by God the Holy Trinity, and that this nation will exist as long as God wills . . ."

Another voice took over, "It will be expected of you that you live on and work in the firm belief that the Almighty God decides the fate of nations . . ."

". . . and that you'll always be true to your traditions . . . that you will strive towards a community project involving motivated Afrikaners; to strengthen and develop the Afrikaner nation, to promote his culture and the advance of his involvement in the national economy . . ."

"You, Barend de Wet Latsky, do you understand the aims of the Afrikaner Broederbond, do you subscribe to the basis of our aim and struggle from the depths of your heart? What is your answer?"

"Yes," answered Oom Boeta. "I, Barend de Wet Latsky, answer affirmatively."

"I ask you then, in the full presence of the Broeders who have gathered here as witnesses, to undertake in all seriousness . . .

"To serve the Bond . . . never to tell any outsider anything you know about the Afrikaner-Broederbond or its members . . .

"What is your answer, Barend de Wet Latsky?"

"My answer is yes."

"Then I declare you a Broeder in the words of our slogan. I wish you strength. Be strong in your membership and the practices of the Bond. Remain strong in faith for when the struggle gets tough, stand strong in the love of your nation. Be strong in your service to your nation . . . My fellow Broeders and I will now welcome you with a handshake as our fellow Broeder."

"Hearty congratulations and welcome."

72

The lights went on and Oom Boeta turned to find himself surrounded by his doctor and his minister, the head of his children's school, his own private secretary with whom he worked every day, the head of his church council and the judge, the officer in charge of the local police station and . . .

Oom Boeta was a Super-Afrikaner.

Could you think Pa into that group, in a black suit, among all the men, making conversation?

That night when Oom Boeta climbed into the double bed he shared with Tant Retha, his wife, she stirred, "And tell me, why are you so late, then, Boeta?"

"Ag, just that little old meeting, Retha, my angel," he told her. They lay in silence side by side for a little while. Then she took his hand.

"Is it going to be a regular little old meeting from now on?" she asked carefully.

"Every month, my dear," he answered, "on a regular basis."

Tant Retha smiled drowsily, squeezed his hand and turned over. She fell asleep contentedly. Oom Boeta lay awake beside her for a long time.

"Hearty congratulations and welcome," he heard the voice of the man whose office was opposite his in the same corridor in the Union Buildings. "You're one of us now."

A Transvaal thunderstorm engulfed Oom Boeta's house there in Waterkloof, Pretoria, that night, in 1954 – a rainy year, with such unpredictable weather, the Sabres barely got the chance to practise. It was a heavy downpour. In the double bed Oom Boeta sought his sleeping wife's warm hand again and then moved to one side so that his son, my cousin, who was scared of lightning, could slip in between them.

A sense of contentment and certainty came over Oom Boeta, lying there with his pretty wife and his son. He remembered the stories of suppression and humiliation. Poverty and loss. He would make a difference. He knew now that he belonged to something, that the Settlement at the Cape in the seventeenth century was not an aberration of God. He would work hard, he'd honour his oath: let those who belonged together struggle together.

Faithful unto death.

73

Oom Boeta took us down a mine. We drove to the shaft and the black Cadillac waited under a lean-to while Pa, Oom Boeta and I descended into the bowels of the earth.

"The gold fields!" boasted Oom Boeta. "No other country on earth has gold deposits like ours."

The mine manager with his white safety helmet was waiting for us on level four. He greeted the gentlemen and Master Latsky, and then took us on a guided tour.

I thought of those stories about collapsed mine tunnels, shafts where cables broke and lifts that plunged hundreds of meters down, trapped workers a kilometer underground after a tunnel had collapsed. I remember Oom Boeta nodding and shaking hands with a dusty mineworker with a grey face – you could only see from his eyes that he was a black man. He looked like a clown with make-up. He took hold of the drill and his whole body shook and shuddered and Oom Boeta yelled over the din, "Look at the seam! See how the gold runs?"

Then Pa had to get out, he couldn't stand the confined space any more. Oom Boeta was disappointed – he wanted to show us the chalk crosses on the shaft sides on level seven where thirty miners had died in a cave-in the month before. Pa looked at me and I saw his face was wet with sweat. He took my hand and I knew I was standing in for Ma. I stroked his arm while the sluggish lift hoisted us up with its squeaking, groaning cables.

Then Oom Boeta took us to the public airport again and he was presented with a box full of golden lapel pins – golden springboks with wings.

"Hell, but the man has contacts," cried Ma, who was showing Tant Retha how to prepare a leg of Karoo mutton the proper way. Ma was impressed by all the beaters and mixers and cookers in Tant Retha's kitchen. "Nothing but the best," she remarked. "Wow, I feel embarrassed when I think of Hotel Halesowen's wood stove and my old pantry with its dripping cooler."

"Oom Boeta is the pride of the family," said Pa. "He knows everyone in the Cabinet. He only has to pick up the phone."

"Boeta is a dear, gentle man," Ma said to Pa, "but you admire him too much. He's only human."

"He works terribly hard," said Pa. "It's people like him who are winning the Afrikaner some status in the cities, who are breaking the English stranglehold on the economy. They're battling it out in our highest council chambers. We're going to be able to stand shoulder to shoulder with the Jews and the English. Just wait and see. We're going to order them around for a change. Just keep an eye on Boeta. He knows more than he lets on. He's a member of the inner circle."

His work made Oom Boeta so tired that in the evening he lay on the sofa while his children, my cousins, earned tickeys by tickling his feet.

"There's only one thing that makes Boeta relax," Ma always said, "and that's this foot tickling business."

"Ja!" laughed Pa. "Even the high and mighty need a tickle."

74

Behind Hotel Halesowen's kitchen and washrooms stood a row of pepper trees and behind them lay a row of servants' quarters.

"Hey," said Ma. "This Port Elizabeth crowd can't go on holiday without their nannies. They bring the poor maids all the way from the coast just to feed their mongrels! The way their cars shine! The fuss and bother over small things like swimming towels and keeping an eye on the children!"

Ma was very strict about the city children: Hotel Halesowen could accept no responsibility for a city child who fell into a dam of slurry from the stables or got lost in the river dongas. She'd smooth my hair. "The city children think they're like Fabian who knows every sisal plant, every meerkat burrow, every donga here on Soebatsfontein. Every Season I go through rolls and rolls of Elastoplast and bottles and bottles of Dettol. And do you remember how Fabian's heel swelled up and went black the time the snake bit him? Must I worry my head off now about all these other people's children? I'm sorry, it's out of the question."

Perhaps that was the reason why so many guests brought their servants along with them – mostly young Xhosa or brown-skinned girls from Port Elizabeth. The location women, as our waiters called them, sat listlessly around under the trees and hauled themselves slowly to their feet if they were called to the rondavels or the stoep rooms to perform some little task or other.

"Ag, no," said Ma," It seems as though fewer and fewer Port Elizabeth folk can go on holiday without their maids. The servants' quarters are full to overflowing this year. I don't like their windows facing the kitchen. That row of windows and doors must be broken out and put in again round the back. I'm sick of seeing that bunch of lazy maids through the pepper trees from here in the kitchen. Close up this side and put the doors and windows on the other side, so they can look out that way and we can get some peace too."

Ma was fed up because the PE servants drank and fought and generally misbehaved. They seduced the waiters away from their regular women and this caused many a fight.

Long before the Season had begun, Pa gave an Order. Before Soebatsfontein's bookings filled up, there was a flurry of banging and hammering and plastering in the row of rooms. It was a big expense, but no establishment worth its salt, according to Ma, would allow the maids' quarters to look out on the catering facilities in this way. Absolutely not.

"Thank heavens!" said Ma. "Now we'll be spared the racket this Christmas. What a relief! Anyway, Boeta's coming from Pretoria and he's not a man for this close cohabitation between whites and blacks."

Pa also gave the Order that forbade Reuben visiting the young girls there. We needed a head waiter who could keep his head at all times.

"Ja," said Ma, "he's always casting an eye round down there. Next thing one of them will be up the pole. Then we'll have a head waiter whose head keeps swivelling towards Port Elizabeth. No, they have to be told. They're not here for a holiday or to kafuffle.

"They're here to keep those town brats off the scorpions' tails and out of the thorn bushes. They can ferry tennis balls and mosquito repellents about, but let them in heaven's name please not get pregnant, courtesy of Hotel Halesowen's bar service!

"We're already battling with numbers in the black population. Look at the kids swarming around the huts. When Boeta arrives we'll get the latest population figures from him. He's always got that sort of information at his fingertips."

"And, another thing," ordered Pa, "in future there'll be no fraternising between the visitors' nannies and our people in the huts. They'll work each other up and I don't want to expose my lot to the Port Elizabeth influences."

When Oom Boeta and his family climbed out of their black Cadillac, all eyes fell on Tsitsi, the servant they'd brought with them from Rhodesia. Oom Boeta and his family had been across the Limpopo on holiday and the Shona girl had cleaned their rondavel there. He'd offered her a job and she'd accepted. Rhodesia was always full of rumours about the South – for them South Africa was the land of milk and honey where you got paid in strong money.

A bit before the Messina border post, Tsitsi had had to get out of Oom Boeta's car and make a wide detour to avoid the border police. She'd walked through the scrub and was surprised to come upon a well-trodden footpath. So she wasn't the only one to be smuggled into South Africa in this way. It had been a dry season and she could wade knee-deep through the Limpopo. A little further, she had cut across into the scrub again and the path took her in a curve back to the tarred road – this time on the South African side.

When she reached the main road, the tar was so hot, it shimmered in the heat. There was no sign of the Cadillac. Panic-stricken, she ran through the bush, losing the footpath. Had they forgotten her? Had there been a misunderstanding? Had the border police stopped them and were their bloodhounds already on her track?

Finally the Cadillac came round the corner, creeping along. They'd stopped at the curio stall on this side of the border and the children had bought dear little wooden elephants and hippos. Oom Boeta had acquired a handsome hippo sjambok and Tant Retha a cured springbok skin for the sunroom.

The family pretended that they didn't notice Tsitsi's tears. She calmed down eventually. Pretoria's jacarandas were blue when they drove into town. She stood at the door of her room: all this space, all to herself? A bed with legs! A thunderstorm broke, and her tears ran like rain down the windowpanes: not gratitude, not relief, not homesickness. Just tears, just because they'd dammed up in her and had to come out now.

"She's a Shona," Oom Boeta boasted, "from Rhodesia. They don't mix with Zulus or Xhosas, they're too proud a race. There's not a continuous stream of youngsters at my back door. She does her work neatly and faithfully and sits in her room on Sunday afternoons."

Tsitsi was pretty. It was her prettiness that kept her apart. Even when she was a little girl, the men's hands had wandered over her, later more demandingly. They reacted to her as Reuben did the first time he saw her, when she got out of the Cadillac: as though someone had thumped him in the small of his back. He lost his breath and spun for the rest of the day on his own axle, tray in hand, until Ma said, "The Season is hotting up and Reuben is starting to lose his concentration. What's the matter with you today, Reuben? Look, my boy, there's a raised hand, there at the furthest end of the terrace. Run, my boy. Buck up, Jack! My, what are you day-dreaming about, Reuben?"

Those weren't easy days for Reuben. He polished the shoes more brighly than ever. It was as though he wanted to recognise himself in every toe-cap. He bent to the brush, one hand deep inside the guest's shoe; he brushed hectically; he spat a fine spray and boned these shabby old holiday shoes until they had mirror tips. Was Reuben reading his own fortune, bent over the toecaps like that? What did he read in them? I wondered, while the other waiters and the cleaners walked past him without any greeting.

He read more and more, begging me for book after book. I brought him whatever I could. I smuggled them to the donkey under my shirt, where he drove the shuddering drum to the brink of explosion.

With steam sinking down on him, the red fire mouth behind him and a shining axe in his hands, Reuben turned to me where I sat against the trunk of the bluegum tree and said, "It wasn't me."

75

Reuben and Tsitsi didn't get the chance to talk to one another. But they continually walked into one another's smells, in the many passages, hallways and rooms of Hotel Halesowen.

He discerned strange lands in her smell, something of a world across a river, endless bush, stretching out to the horizon. She smelled of flint, of copper rubbing against skin, of fires and creams and places which he could only imagine. He lay in his room dreaming of them once he grew bored with the white boys' adventures in one of the books I'd brought him.

Reuben came into the dining room and walked into her smell as though he were bumping into her body. The smell of Mum, copper and light perspiration, the smell of the fireplace, it hung there between tables three and four. He stood in it a moment, deaf to Ma's "Hey Reuben, shake it up, my Jack!"

He drew in a deep breath.

He didn't know where Rhodesia was, but someone had told him it was beyond Colesberg and Bloemfontein, in that direction, a faraway world north of the mines. The girl from Other-land, he called her in his thoughts. He stood there with bowls of peanuts on his tray, a weakness in his knees, between tables three and four.

If he could talk to her, if he only got the opportunity, he'd tell her about the things he'd read in *Reader's Digest*: of mountains spitting fire, of distant tribes who pierced their noses, of a man who made a journey in the land of ice with dogs pulling his little sled in front of him.

He'd tell her about the misunderstandings at Hotel Halesowen, the fire leaping over the haystack, the other men turning against him, spitting in his face and saying, "You think you're white." He'd tell her of the days and nights that followed; how he'd cried like a woman in his room, how he'd held his pillow over his head and listened, terrified, for a footstep on his threshold, a fingernail against his windowpane, a knee scraping against the iron roof.

About Poqo, about the rumours and fury that rode up and down on the trains – this, I know, Reuben would have told her if he could only have persuaded her to sit somewhere with him in places he dreamed of: in the cool shade of a tree at the river's edge; of an evening, near the donkey as the first flames began to snap companionably. Up there on the aloe hillocks, among the warm rocks, he'd clear out a nest for them on the cool shaded ground and they'd be like two leopards, they'd stretch out against one another, licking each other, over each other and against each other and in each other, at last, gasping, quickly, pumping, her dress pulled high above her hips and her red tongue licking his, her mouth swallowing and gobbling his, her soft eyes, Tsitsi-eyes, Limpopo-eyes. Limpopo? Would Reuben know the name?

He'd tell her about the trains that moved like zip fasteners across the black breast of the land. The trains that carried their messages day after day, night after night, from south to north, from north to south.

Or did Reuben only think of her mouth and her almond eyes that narrowed at the corners when she laughed, her silence there under the bluegums?

Tsitsi sat quietly dreaming among the nannies from Port Elizabeth who gossiped and laughed noisily. She picked the last of the pink flesh from the watermelon peelings discarded by the Port Elizabeth children. Reuben ambled round the terrace with his tray, keeping an eye on her, quiet amongst the other nannies – they who talked and argued so much.

She noticed his gaze; she also walked into his smell: shoe polish, chopped thorn wood, vinegar, the smoky smell of the bar, the splashes of whisky and brandy on his hands. She licked the splashes off and was intoxicated, as he was, from the feeling in her heart, that gripped her like a steel fist and wouldn't let go.

The smell of his body when the terrace was crowded and he had to trot to keep up with the orders, lay like a river down the passage. She was there herself quite often too, taking care to avoid him, but testing the waters with her toe, withdrawing to go and complete a chore – fetching suntan lotion for Oom Boeta's children, trying to find the sunglasses Tant Retha had lost in the kikuyu, bringing Oom Boeta's fisher hat so his bald patch wouldn't get sunburnt. And on her return she was back at the river, wading in ankle-deep, standing dreamily in the passage.

There in the dim passage, with its framed prints of English country houses, hunters on horseback and hounds with stiff tails, their smells mingled until Ma came past, threw open a window and sighed, "My, but these blacks do pong. But then, people say that we whites stink to them."

Or his eyes took hold of her, those black urgent eyes of Reuben's with which he challenged the donkey. "Sit a little away, Kleinbaas Fabian," he would gesture, and throw in another piece of wood.

"You're making it too hot, Reuben. It's going to explode."

But he'd just laugh, stoop for the axe and split stump after stump. The axe would fall in one rhythmic movement from over his head, a shining arch that would split the white thorn-wood in two.

The steam fluttered like a flag. The donkey groaned – "Antjie Provee," Reuben sang quietly, and laughed at me. The

213

pipes running to the ablution block began to complain as the first guests turned on their showers. The bath taps of the ablution block shuddered from the steam pressure and a dull groaning filled the air.

I still associate that vibrating drone with the dairy herd, coming slowly from the farmyard into the milking shed, without being driven by anyone because they knew the way and walked in their own time. I associate it with the evening starlings that descended blackly on the reeds, with the city children changing their games in the gathering dusk, talking more quietly and dreamily, acting out secretive rituals at the furthest edges of the kikuyu, among the trunks flecked even whiter in the gathering darkness.

I don't know what they were up to. I didn't talk to them much. I couldn't stand it when they started questioning me, wide-eyed, about the river, the dongas and the slopes of Buffelskop. I watched them jealously when they set off into the veld with their knapsacks and freshly cut sticks. I followed their tracks without their knowing it and I was furious if they disturbed the troop of monkeys, or bent the fence, or stole peaches in the orchard.

The steaming water spluttered from the outlet pipe, spewed in an arch and took a handful of wind like a white-hot hand. Then it splashed on to the iron roof and steam trails ran down the sheets and into the gutters.

The trains went up and down, but Ma and the rest were unaware of what was going on. And who would tell them about the meetings in the location in town, the visitors who came and went secretly with the late-night passenger trains? The newspapers didn't report it, nor did the radio. The radio only reported rainfall statistics, swarms of locusts and Verwoerd's plans. They wouldn't have read about that in the *Reader's Digest*, let alone *Farmer's Weekly* or *Huisgenoot*.

And the brief items about these goings-on which Tant Geert usually sent from overseas were quickly crumpled up by Ma before Pa could read them and get upset.

Ma read the *Farmer's Weekly* match-making column and

giggled. "Geert," she teased after her third drink, "Don't you think we should put smalls in for you and Marge? I don't know about her, but at least you've got money – Pa's trust takes care of you, doesn't it?"

Tant Geert pretended she hadn't heard. Anyway, the trust was a painful subject – Pa and she seldom referred to it. Pa only dragged it out when he was feeling very disturbed. Why should Ma tonight, of all nights, refer to it, she who avoided conflict at all costs?

"Just think of all the old widowers who'll come and stay at Hotel Halesowen to look you over," teased Ma.

"And how about a small ad for the major?" Tant Geert hit back, at ease, her whisky to her lips.

Ma didn't answer, she bent over her glass.

"I'm stoking Antjie Provee until she groans tonight," laughed Reuben. "Move back a bit further, Kleinbaas Fabian."

"You're overdoing it, Reuben."

He threw in more wood and turned round to laugh at me. Behind him the red jaws devoured the thorn stump in a wink. The big tank shuddered and the pipes trilled and roared against the walls. Steam filtered out of the seams in the elbow joins in the pipes at the corners of the house.

Reuben glanced up at his flagpole. His stomach was a donkey and every time he saw Tsitsi, it was as though his fire were getting stoked up higher. It was that Tsitsi, that Tsitsi who burnt in him so. At night he lay in his room and thrust with his pelvis while he worked himself. He licked the seed from his hands: it was Tsitsi, Tsitsi who licked so. He imagined Tsitsi's tongue.

He leafed through a *Reader's Digest*. The new ones weren't passed on to him soon enough once Ma and Pa, Tant Geert and the Veteran were finished with them. Reuben grew impatient. The limp pages came too late and were too few.

"Reuben is pushing his luck with that donkey," said Pa. "Since that thing with Windpomp there's been a recklessness in him. I've already warned him a couple of times that the rust is eating at that tank and the day will come when it breaks up."

"Please, Fabiantjie," said Ma, "you mustn't go near the donkey when Reuben stokes it. You mustn't go any closer than the second bluegum tree – sit right near the trunk. We don't want a tragedy on Soebatsfontein."

Ma kept an eye on the Veteran. Her eyes raked through his oily hair like a comb. They lingered on those crow's wings. She watched the thin body with the worm veins and sat inside his stories, as though they were a uniform jacket that he put around her shoulders during an unexpected chill.

Reuben had now taken his shirt off. He'd unbuttoned his black bow tie and he hung his shirt on a bluegum tree branch. The evening fragrance of the kikuyu came over the roof, mingling with the smell of steam and Reuben's sweat. He split the thorn wood with his axe and the smell of it lodged in my nostrils.

Tsitsi stood watching him through the pantry window. She watched the steaming white water that spewed out of the pipe, the smooth muscles that raised the axe and swung it. She looked at the ridges painted red by evening and she heard the hadedahs calling. She stood there in the pantry, trapped in the smell of mealie-meal, soap and fresh cauliflower, and she heard the muffled clink of crockery in dishwater close by.

I could stay here, she thought.

She remembered the little room behind the Cadillac's garage, the quiet Waterkloof Sunday afternoons when the Sabres split the blue sky and thunderstorms gathered, humid and irritable, until the waters broke. The room had pressed in on her as the rain streamed down the window-panes and she had sat and watched the alarm-clock, waiting for six o'clock when she was to go back to the kitchen and put water on to boil for Oom Boeta's coffee.

I could stay here, she thought, because the grass smells nice under the trees and that man wants me and I can feel my body answering his. We can live in his little room. I can work here in the kitchen and maybe learn to do cleverer work. He'll be on the terrace or on the lawn among the rondavels or here near the donkey at night.

He is a clever man because he reads every scrap of paper the white people throw away. Some of the cleaners keep for him everything the guests throw out that has words on it, and every night he comes to get his papers when the leftovers are shared out among the waiters and the kitchen workers under Boe's strict eye.

Then she would see him bending over the crumpled-up papers. He would smooth them out and read. Tsitsi thought, he is the hungriest man on earth. He wants to eat me.

Like he eats those papers.

The day the Cadillac was packed, she must stay. But how was she going to arrange it? She thought for a crazy minute, I'll hide somewhere, there in the dairy, behind the lucerne bales. I could disappear in the dongas, in those wild gullies down towards the river, where people said the Ape person must live, there where the wild rains have eaten holes into the ground.

That hungry man, he with the teeth as white as the wood he splits, he can eat me. He can bite into me as though I were watermelon, right to the deepest sweetness. There where it's reddest, there, yes there, he must eat me, the hungry man, the man with the tray, the kikuyu man, the . . .

She murmured names for him; her own words with which she caressed him.

Time was running out for them.

76

"Jeepers, but you are a bunch of wayward Afrikaners here at Halesowen," said Oom Boeta.

"We aren't Afrikaners," growled Tant Geert. "We're a jolly mixture, as you well know, Boeta."

"You're the family's arch liberal, Geertruida," scolded Oom Boeta. "We don't count you as a member of the nation."

"What am I a member of, then?" demanded Tant Geert. "And what about Marge here beside me?"

Oom Boeta eyed the two women with that careful expression on his face. He rubbed over his bald head and pushed his glasses up on his nose. He rubbed his head again. "That's his Broederbond rub," Ma always said. "Quiet and thoughtful. Clever man – just look how small his hands are. Geert's brain without (thank the Lord) the lust for adventure."

Oom Boeta looked at Tant Geert. Then he looked away. "The lady of the lake," he muttered.

"Lake?" asked Ma. She was trying to diffuse the situation again. "There's only that old mud dam at Hotel Halesowen, the one where the servants and their kids swim. We're still waiting for your Verwoerd Dam."

"Well, you've already got Grasrug and Lake Arthur," said Oom Boeta. "And the Verwoerd water is on the way. I've seen the documentation – it's coming, it's coming."

"One day," said Pa. "One day. Always one day. Until then we just sit here on the plains, staring into space and pampering the city people. Maybe something will happen today, maybe tomorrow – maybe never. Nooitgedacht!"

"There you are again," cried Ma. "And on the brink of Christmas too. We're going to have to start getting into the spirit here at Halesowen – we can't sit around in sackcloth and ashes all the time."

"Dodge City. Crittur's Creek."

"Oh, shut up. Don't start now."

"Gatsonderput."

"Oh, no, man."

"Look where Boeta works," Pa continued. "In the highest circles. And look where sister Geert travels. The postcards come from all over the place. And me? I sit here on the veranda at Soebatsfontein, strangled by the trust and I can't do anything about it."

"Our late Pa thought it was right that you should be the caretaker of the estate," Oom Boeta said soothingly.

"Papa wanted to keep us all close," added Tant Geert. "He didn't want it all to fall apart."

218

"But you can escape. I had to stay. A third-class hotel on the Fish River. Who opens a tourist hotel in this neck of the woods? Only the Latskys. The Karoo is no place for holiday-makers. That's why all we get here are cranks and spongers and ducktails and nom de plumes."

"Excuse me!" shouted the Pastor.

The Veteran smoothed his hair. His fingertips ran along the row of medals.

"Ag, no," said Ma. "Now you're bad-mouthing the guests."

Pa looked away. Ma leaned forward. "Look how the young-sters are enjoying themselves there on the kikuyu. Doesn't it make you feel cheerful? Look at Port Elizabeth's young crowd romping on your lawns. Look at the cars all parked there. From as far away as Oudtshoorn and Queenstown."

"And the balloons hanging out in honour of His birth," added the Pastor.

"And Charles Jacoby has decided to stay on a bit."

"On our bloody so-called ranch," snorted Pa. "Someone please tell him this isn't Hollywood."

"But it's ours, our lives." Ma pushed the curl back. She leaned even further forward.

"Wild horses, wild horses . . ." murmured Oom Boeta, shaking his head.

Pa turned to him. "Who's a wild horse?" he asked. He was breathing fast; everything was turning against him. He glared at Oom Boeta, "You can't come here from Pretoria and abuse us. You descend on us, eating us out of house and home. And all day, every day, I have to listen to your stories about the plans you're cooking up there in the Union Buildings. You know, Boeta, all your jobs for broeders and meetings don't get us anywhere here on the borders of Kaffirland. Just listen to what will go on again tonight at the huts, and it isn't even Christmas yet. What are you going to do with them? Go and ask that of your Doctor, that bloody Dutchman."

Pa stood up and went inside. Oom Boeta remained seated, shaking his head. Ma put a hand on his arm.

"Never mind," she said. "Our crowd here at Halesowen is

used to his tantrums. You must remember from your child-hood, Boeta. It'll all blow over just now."

"He's worse," said Oom Boeta. "I've never seen him this bad before."

"Mr Latsky is suffering a lot," said the Veteran. "We must try to be understanding."

"If he'd only let Prince Jesus into his life." The Pastor cast his eyes up to the stars.

"And then?" asked Tant Geert. "That Latsky will send the saintly Peter out of heaven if things don't go the way he wants them up there. And undo the crucifixion while he's at it."

"Blasphemy!"

"What blasphemy?" asked Tant Geert. "What's blasphe-mous about undoing the crucifixion?"

"But where would we be then?" asked the Pastor, com-pletely at a loss. "Without the Sacrifice?"

Tant Geert wanted to answer, but Ma cut her short: "Ag, no, you, two, just cut it out now."

"And I take exception as well," said Oom Boeta, getting up.

"You Pretorians!" cried Tant Geert. "A little set of ten rules and if you break one, you'll be undone. Tell me, Boeta, tell me, is there a corner in that Bond of yours for an old duck like me?"

Oom Boeta swung round. The light flashed on his spectacles and his bald head. "What Bond?"

"Geert . . ." Ma got up.

"You are in the Broederbond, aren't you?" Tant Geert sipped her whisky. "Is that so or not? If I see Dominee Naudé from Graaff-Reinett's son, that young Bey, I'm going to corner him about this. He at least has an open mind."

"I neither confirm nor deny it?" Oom Boeta was so het up, he spoke his answer as a question. He rubbed his bald head. Then he turned to Ma. He drew a deep breath and said, "Ask Reuben to wash the Cadillac early tomorrow morning. I think we should push on to Bushman's."

"Bushman's River?" asked Ma. "But weren't you only going after New Year?"

"Things don't look too good round here," answered Oom Boeta. "I've had a hard year in the civil service. I came for a rest."

"Boeta . . ."

"I don't want to argue about religion and politics."

"Boeta . . ." Ma leaned forward, stubbing out her cigarette. She took his hand. "Listen, Boet, old man. In the evenings out here on the terrace we go at each other like cat and dog. That's just the way it is at Hotel Halesowen. But tomorrow morning at the breakfast table, we're friends again. One big happy family. There's nothing else for us here, you know."

Ma looked heartbroken. Tant Geert passed her a handkerchief.

Ma continued, "Ag, Boet, man. Everything will be forgotten by tomorrow morning and you can relax on a stretcher under the bluegums and listen to the doves. We're braaiing a leg of lamb tomorrow afternoon, Boeta. With sweet potatoes. Those tick birds you're so fond of, patrolling the green lucerne fields in the mornings. And the stars at night! So close, you can pick them. There's balm for the soul here, Boeta."

"Heavens!" cried Tant Geert. "You sound like a sales brochure."

77

"Nostalgia, pupiltjie, nostalgia is humanity's only true possession. Do you feel it, Fabiantjie, when the little fleecy clouds turn pink over the plains of the Karoo? Do you see it in your Pa's eyes as he gazes out into space? Do you smell it when your Ma takes her trunk down from the cupboard and opens it – that one from her theatre days?

"Nostalgia is what pulls us forward, forever forwards along the road between our birth and our death. Something must drag you to your death, not so?

"Once you lose the nostalgia, you can throw in the towel, pupiltjie. Even if your nostalgia is a longing for things that lie so far in the past that you can scarcely remember the flavour or the feeling, even if the nostalgia reaches so far back, it remains a sort of thrust forwards. Because if you're touched with nostalgia, you hope. And by longing for yesterday, you turn the past into a future.

"Why do you think the terrace and the kikuyu lawns are so subdued when dusk falls, pupiltjie? The time just before Reuben gets going with the drinks, just before the whisky and wine make us jolly? It's the heartsore of the blue hour, my child. Because a human being is a broken being. Human life is sustaining one wound after another. Eventually your system can't take the pain anymore: just look what Van Gogh did, look at your poor Papa running around with a plaster on his ear. You either crack like my poor old brother, or you wander like the major from small hotel to small hotel, in case, somewhere along the line, you might happen upon a rich widow. You kiss the bottle like your dear Ma, or you remain on the point of departure, always about to go, as I am, my child, like me: leaving, leaving, always leaving.

"Tomorrow's parting is yesterdays arrival. That, my dear pupiltjie, is your old Geert's terrible fate.

"And you, Fabiantjie? Those brown eyes look like autumn leaves again tonight. And you never play with the city children. Do they scare you? Do they tease you about your little dead eye? What is it, my darling? Come here. Come to old Geert. Come, I'll press you to my ravaged old chest. Here's a haven for you, my child, day and night. You must never forget that. There, there, little one.

"Look there, see how the evening bleeds. In Rome, you know, in the summer there's a stuffiness at this time of evening too. You smell stale sweat and the words of writers who have walked past, lovers who've whispered in each other's ears. You smell withered roses, crumbling walls, the breath of opera singers. Oh, the elegant decadence in that city of ochre walls and balconies, fountains and pickpockets!

"Fabian, we must go on a trip. I'm just going to hide you away in my suitcase, pupiltjie. You know, that big brown one, the one with all the labels stuck on it. You'll fit into it if you curl up and at the customs, I'll just say, oh dear, books are so dreadfully heavy, what a burden to be a book lover! The curse of reading, I'll say to the customs official, is a lifelong burden. And the customs man will stare at me with uncomprehending eyes because he doesn't know our secrets, pupiltjie. You and I are citizens of another world . . . We are not at home in this world. We have no rondavel. God help us, we are only wanderers. Restlessness such as ours never refuses a visa."

I left Tant Geert there on the terrace where she sat waiting for Marge Bruwer to come out of the ablution block so they could enjoy a nightcap together.

I walked past Ma who was sitting talking to the Veteran. "Geert is getting restless again," I heard her say. "I know the signs. She's started talking about the great cities of the world again. She's wandering around restlessly and her hand is getting heavier with the whisky. Look, she's calling Reuben again. Hotel Halesowen is closing in on her again. Ag, that Geert. She'll never put down roots."

The Veteran pressed his foot against Ma's under the table.

"Nostalgia always rages in those born in August," he said. "No matter what their country of birth. It has nothing to do with the star sign you're born under, but the fact rather that every month has a character of it's own."

Ma poured herself another drink, sat back in her chair and the Veteran's story wrapped itself round her shoulders.

"Where I come from . . ." (Ma no longer bothered to ask where because she knew she'd get some vague answer or another) ". . . August is the month of sad winds, trees on the verge of winter, like old women who have survived the cold but cannot be sure they'll make it to the summer. They wander on pavements, their hands bent with arthritis, with their walking sticks grown fast to those palms that had once stroked the bodies of young men.

"August is an unlucky month and lovers have to restrain

their love in November. With an eye to a birth free August the following year.

"In November the wombs of our country's most beautiful women are as receptive to seed as the freshly ploughed earth of the Fish River valley in a good rainy season. It's obviously nature's way of trying to tame August, to force wild, melancholy, windy, dusty August, the month that's neither winter nor spring, to fall into the parade of more obedient months."

The Veteran sighed and stroked his row of medals. Marge Bruwer had now joined Tant Geert and the two women sat with their drinks and watched the river scrub get darker and darker. The groups of children wandered about in the dark like white snow flakes, singing quietly and teasing one another. The guests strolled over the lawns to the terrace adjusting their (in Ma's words) "smart casual" clothes and checked that their hair was combed for dinner.

Tant Geert and Marge Bruwer didn't talk much. Something had happened. Had the fire gone out? Or had Tant Geert indicated that she was longing for those far-away cities again?

"I met her in another country, in another place. In November, the month of abstinence. I sat on a tiled stoep in a foreign country and I ordered calf's liver and enjoyed the tinkle of expensive silver cutlery on the restaurant table and I thought back to the dead on the battlefield and how lucky I was to survive . . ."

"Was this before the blind telephonist?" Ma asked eagerly. But the Veteran didn't answer, just continued with his story.

"When I looked up, she was at the table opposite mine, under a red-and-white umbrella, in a light cotton shirt, snow-white, with a ribbon in her hair, one of those wide hair ribbons that would make some women look ridiculous, that only the strongest and most beautiful women can get away with. The legs that stuck out from under the table reminded me that some women, with just a small detail of the body, can make men drown in the fantasies of a lost age.

"I thought of the exquisite fountains of ancient Italy, of the piazzas with their memories of a time when beautiful women had egged on the gladiators of Rome.

224

"Without our exchanging a single word, she made me feel like a gladiator. And something told me she'd noticed me too, that she was aware of me.

"Without looking directly at each other, we ate particularly slowly, both on our own, enjoying the sun on our skin and the light breeze in our hair – without our eyes meeting. That meal at our separate tables was an extended caress. She was in the wine, in the fragrance of the pot of flowers before me, in the heavenly food, in the breeze that played with my hair.

"And I realised, two people can love one another without ever touching, could caress one another without hands or lips, can reach the highest pleasure in a way which had been unknown to me at that stage – a virile young soldier . . .

"Who would stand up first? She or I? What would her first words to me be? Or mine to her? Would I follow her, or she me, winding through the street market, until we brushed against each other lightly, looked up, apologised, and then began talking?

"But it was unnecessary, the game came to its own conclusion, there at our tables.

"August was fended off once more."

Ma had sunk deep into her chair. The jacket of the Veteran's story sat heavily on her shoulders. She looked round when she heard Tant Geert ask Marge, too loudly by accident, unexpectedly, so that other guests also looked round, "Marge, dear, can I make free with your body? Shall we stroll down to the Wilhelmina, you and I?"

And Marge Bruwer drew herself upright, got to her feet and stepped off the terrace with the hair bun bobbing indignantly behind her.

78

Reuben thought up all sorts of plans to lure Tsitsi into his room.

Tsitsi and the Port Elizabeth nannies didn't understand each other's languages very well, so Tsitsi didn't sleep in the servants' rooms, she slept in the Cadillac. At night, Oom Boeta pulled the black Cadillac up right under their bedroom window so that he could hear if Tsitsi ran around at night.

"We can't afford to have Tsitsi getting up to anything," said Tant Retha, "because I can't manage without her. Next thing she'll run away in this valley. What would I do at Bushman's without her? Three weeks in that bungalow with only a wood stove and a primus and no black hand to lend strength to mine? You know what Boeta's like. When he's on holiday he insists on meat three times a day – eggs and chops for breakfast, braaied leg of mutton for lunch and meat balls in the evening. For him chicken is a vegetable. I refuse to stand at the cooking pots all day and every day. That's no holiday. I'd rather stay here at Hotel Halesowen. Boeta and the children can go to the Zuurveld without me."

Tsitsi was given her blanket at eleven every night, after the last guest had drifted away from the terrace. She would put it on the backseat of the Cadillac and then go to pee behind the tennis courts because she was too frightened to go in the dark to the servants' longdrop behind the donkey.

She would squat in the night and think about Rhodesia. The evening breeze would touch her buttocks coolly. It was nice when the warm urine flowed and steamed warmly into the cleft of her buttocks. The grass would tickle her thighs and long after she'd pinched off the last drop, she'd squat there in her own steam.

She remembered the days she cleaned the white family from the south's room in the game reserve and how they persuaded her to come and work for them. She looked up at the stars and wondered what was going on in her own country now. She thought of bougainvillaea and dry plains and paper flapping in bushes. She didn't understand what she longed for.

She didn't miss the poverty and the struggle. She missed, yes, she missed the friendliness of the people, so different from the sulky Xhosa women from Port Elizabeth to whom she couldn't get through, try as she might.

As she squatted there rubbing her thighs with her warm hands, she longed for the smells, from beans in a wooden bowl, a sack with white mealie-meal pouring from its spout, of paraffin as you pump a primus, and sounds: the broken old radio that only worked if you slapped it on the back, the singing round the fire at night . . .

Eventually she stood up. When she walked back, round the tennis court, across the lawn and up to the terrace, a worried Tant Retha would be standing there with her hands on the railings. Why is she taking so long? she would wonder.

When they'd arrived, Tant Retha had shown Tsitsi where the servants' longdrop was, but Tsitsi had been terrified of that dark hole under the planks. She had shuddered at the blue-bottle flies clustering in the corners of the wood and iron building and the sound of her own excrement falling and splashing like clay against a wet dam wall.

Ag, sighed Tant Retha, these girls from the bush, squat in the bush once and you want to do it for the rest of your life. You can't always get it out of them. "Are you there, Tsitsi?" she called impatiently as Tsitsi came walking up. "Come, come, come, my girl. It's bedtime. Get into your car."

When Tsitsi opened the door, the ceiling light came on. She crept in onto the red backseat and the light remained on a little while after she'd closed the door. She sat there in the lit cage for a long time, while, behind her back, Reuben was busy clearing the last dirty glasses off the terrace, wiping the tables and tipping up the chairs.

Tsitsi listened to Reuben with her whole body: how the glasses tinkled quietly in his hands, how his cloth slapped the tables as he swished stray crumbs away, how the broom swept over the paving.

So it went every night until one night he realised, with absolute certainty, that she was sitting listening to him, even though her back was turned, even though she pretended not to see him. Then his feet started to drag, the cloth wipe-wiped seekingly, the broom nosed its way slowly under the tables. One night he even dropped a glass and Ma, already in her dressing-gown, came out to the terrace to see what was going on – this wasn't like Reuben, was it?

"Ag, Reuben, how could you? And it had to be one of my long-stemmed glasses, I suppose. Are you tired tonight, my Jack? And we have to slaughter tomorrow and there's scarcely a vegetable left in the pantry, so we'll have to go over to Bobby Greenblatt's and ask if he can help us out with carrots and lettuce."

When she saw his face, she softened, "Reuben, I must say that in all the years it is only the fifth glass you've broken. I remember the exact number, it happens so seldom. It must be a record for any establishment. Come, bring the dustpan, I'll help you. It's been a long day for all of us."

Tsitsi listened to how Reuben and Ma (for her no more than "the other white woman") cleared up the broken glass together. She heard Ma's comforting tone, heard her thank Reuben for a hard day's work well done, heard how she wished him good night and how the key turned in the lock on the terrace doors.

She listened to Reuben's footsteps on the terrace steps behind the Cadillac, but she also kept one ear on the noises in Oom Boeta's room. She'd opened one window – the one nearest the wall – and she could hear someone brushing their teeth and spitting into the basin. She heard Tant Retha's whining voice, but she didn't really understand what it was about, just made out something about "the strangest collection of people" and "that retired soldier" and "Geert and the English woman".

But she couldn't put it all together. She didn't understand that Tant Retha was viewing the nightly goings-on on the terrace from the heights of Waterkloof. For Tsitsi the whites' evenings on the terrace were a dream world: drinks which were drunk at leisure, waiters who ran up at the snap of fingers, money that was pulled recklessly from pockets as though the source were inexhaustible, everything accompanied by the smell of perfume and aftershave, everyone dollied up in clean, pressed clothes, the fruits of many a servant's ironing and deft fingers.

She was too young, I know now, to realise that no one is ever free and that prisoners often enjoy greater space than warders, that the rich man is trapped in his own prison, that everyone is finally up against the limitations of their own existence.

She waited for Reuben to come down the steps, but it was his habit to wait until Ma's footsteps faded after she'd locked the terrace doors and drawn the curtains. The coloured lights on the stoep roof went out. This was the sign that Ma had reached the passage leading to her bedroom because that's where the light switch was.

Now, for the first time the whole day, Reuben felt free – as he did every night at this time. He stood there on the terrace as he'd done for years. He gazed up at the stars, trying to guess what the weather would be like the following day. He smelled the first dew that had settled on the kikuyu and he heard the sleeping cry of a river monkey. When he heard footsteps on the grass he glanced towards the rondavels and saw the Veteran going barefoot to the ablution block, sleepily and with hair sticking out sideways, like the feathers of a black cockerel. His tunic was unbuttoned and you could see the white cleft of his chest as he walked.

Reuben also imagined that he could smell the girl in the Cadillac. He turned his head slightly – he had to be careful because he knew that if Oom Boeta drew the curtains, he'd be able to see him on the terrace and Tsitsi in the Cadillac right there under the window. Reuben was nervous of the man with the big black car; the man who worked – as he'd heard on the terrace while waiting for orders – in the same building as that Boss-man Verwoerd.

Reuben tipped his head a little to one side when he listened. Tsitsi sat in the Cadillac in the dimness because the ceiling light was out and only a little light came through Oom Boeta's curtains. He had his back to her and she had her back to him. Still in the night silence of Hotel Halesowen, under the spread-out stars, what happened between them in those few moments, was the sweetest love that had been made that Season at the Hotel Halesowen.

And that included the honeymoon room, the one furthest from the donkey, the one with the pink sheets.

79

Everyone rushed out of their rondavels.

Oom Boeta stood up near the top rock garden, his white civil-service legs shown off by his shorts, his bald head exposed to the Karoo sun. He was out first – he'd recognised the sound at once. Hands on hips he stared into the sky. The sun flashed on his spectacle lenses.

Afterwards, Tant Geert was to say, "You'd think it was the Second Coming, the way Boeta stared into the heavens with such unbounded respect . . ."

"Oh, Barend!" cried Tant Retha when she ran out too, after grabbing something for the sun. "Do you think they know we're here? Do you think they saw the Cadillac?"

"Are you crazy, woman?" asked Oom Boeta. "Get hold of yourself. You aren't in Pretoria now."

The guests emerged from the rondavels, still drowsy from their afternoon sleep. Dr Clark who'd been busy writing his book, came to stand on the Bitter Aloe stoep with one hand shading his eyes. Tant Geert and Miss Marge came out of the Wilhelmina and Miss Marge's hair clung sweatily to her brow. Their blouses hung loose and Miss Marge wiped her face.

Children poured out of the milking shed, appeared from behind lucerne bales, or came running up from the haystacks, where they loved to poke long sticks into the smouldering haystack and wait until the tips of the sticks caught fire in the black lump. On the tennis courts, players let their rackets hang limp as they gazed up into the sun. The dogs started barking and chased their tails without knowing what had upset them or what it was they could hear. The kitchen workers all gathered at the door, shading their faces with their white dishcloths while they looked upwards.

The three Sabres cut low over the Karoo a third time and it seemed as though their engines were tearing the veld open. They were already past, just tiny dots flashing in the distance, when their sound gushed in on us as though it were something – a thing with weight – that they threw back to us, over their shoulders.

"They're trying to break the sound barrier," murmured Oom Boeta with upturned face. He stood there in an attitude I had never seen in him before. Forgotten was the man who lay on the garden bench bribing his children to tickle his feet. Gone was the carnivore who ate meat as though it were vegetables, gone the Broederbond pussy-footing, as Ma called it, the Waterkloof diplomacy, the civil service caution with words, the Union Buildings circumlocution.

"God, isn't it marvellous!" murmured Oom Boeta.

"The Republic!" cried the Veteran who'd crossed the lawn. He'd paced up from his rondavel raising his knees high as though a parade had been called. Now he stood beside Oom Boeta saluting the dots that glinted like horseflies. He'd been so eager to see the Sabres that he hadn't stopped to pull on his socks and shoes. The white feet with their blue veins stuck out of the bottom of the pants.

"An air raid," I'd heard him call out sleepily when the first droning of the Sabres had become audible. Then the dogs had started barking and at the same moment, like a drawn-out gunshot, the jets had torn over us.

"Just look! Ag, isn't it beautiful . . ." said Tant Retha.

And while we stood there gazing northwards, in the direction they'd disappeared, to see whether we could catch another glimpse of them, unexpectedly, from the south-west . . .

"Look!" yelled the Veteran. "At nineteen hundred hours!"

While we pulled our heads into our shoulders in anticipation of the sound-wave that would break over us, they flashed silently over us again, fast as dragonflies, shining like bullets on a battlefield.

There was sudden silence. Everyone stood with upturned face. The dogs crouched whimpering in the shade of the bluegums. The waiters' hands sweated on their trays.

The moment stretched too long. I heard Tant Retha's breath push out over her lips, from her throat that was unnaturally stretched and bowed to hold her head backwards, like someone drinking thirstily from a jar.

And just when we started thinking we'd imagined the second fly-past, that nothing had happened or would happen, just when the wind was about to start blowing again and the cicadas to resume their summer screeching, just then the coming Republic fired its most powerful shot.

80

So loud that Valour staggered in his stable and squealed confusedly in panic, so that Mr Jacoby, who was in the Zane Grey still sleeping off the excitement of his meeting with Verwoerd and the accompanying stomach problem, woke with a fright and grabbed his white stetson. He got up on trembling legs, all gooseflesh from dehydration and fever. Then he decided he must have been dreaming, that he was caught up in a nightmare in some hamlet or other in the Wild West so he turned over and went back to sleep and the afternoon passed him by.

Pa hadn't heard properly either. Bent over his *Path of Truth* tracts with his blunt pencil, he battled with the complex question of predestination. It had been explained with long words and contradictory formulations in Tract number 243 of October 1960, on pages eighteen to twenty, inclusive.

How could God be so harsh, wondered Pa, to cast out some from the word go, denying them their citizenship of heaven? The bang came out of his innermost being, it was a sign, it was God's mightiest thunderclap, it . . .

Pa sank back against the pillows, exhausted. Why was that cowboy's horse squealing so?

And why was everything suddenly so quiet?

Outside, I ran to Oom Boeta. I ran to him as he murmured the first words of the national anthem: "Ringing out from . . . ringing out from our . . . from our blue heaven . . ." over and over again. He stood there in his ridiculous shorts and I ran into him.

"Oom Boeta," I cried, "I want to join the airforce when I grow up!"

He swung round to me. His spectacles shone. "Fabian! What a terrific idea, my boy! I'll arrange everything for you when the time comes. Just be a good boy and grow up nicely and then, when you turn eighteen . . ."

"Your Oom Boeta only has to pick up the phone," confirmed Tant Retha.

Oom Boeta went down on his haunches in front of me. For the first time I noticed his eyes up close. I was surprised when I saw the big, soft, patient eyes. Excited eyes, I think now — excited about the possibilities of the Republic, of the dreams that were coming true, about the power of the Afrikaner.

"Oom Boeta has owl's eyes," I whispered that night when I couldn't sleep and crept in with Ma and Pa. Ma snorted gently, her hair spread out on the pillow and one hand open with the palm up as though she were waiting for something. Pa was still awake and the night-lamp was on — they lit it when even the sleeping-remedy didn't put him under. Pa stroked my head.

"He is high up," whispered Pa. "He is a very important man. We rely on him."

"Pa?" I asked quietly. "What is an important man?"

Pa didn't answer. We lay watching the lucerne moths bounce off the ceiling. Their shadows were bigger than they were. Their shadows tried to swallow them.

"A big man throws a big shadow," said Pa as we watched the shadows of the moths moving across the ceiling.

"Pa?"

"Shush, go to sleep now, big boy . . ."

Pa's mouth was against my forehead, his breath fanned my face. It smelt of pipe tobacco and sweet sleeping-remedy.

"Away in a manger . . ." he whispered. "Go to sleep now . . . go to sleep . . ."

81

Reuben thought: I could give Tsitsi a bottle of oil, then she could oil the hinges of that black car's doors, then that man with the spectacles won't hear when she gets out of the car in the night.

Gently, Reuben dreamed in his room. He dreamed that he waited for her round the corner and then led her to his room. He'd bring her in and light a candle and show her everything: the magazine pages stuck on the walls – mostly from *Farmer's Weekly;* scenes with herds of sheep or show cattle with great red ribbons round their bellies, farm dams and windmills. And he'd show her the newspaper pages clipped into patterns to edge the shelves, and all his possessions which were arranged there – his tin of Mum, his pipe tobacco, the ring he'd filed from a piece of copper piping, his passbook with a photo of himself when he was younger (a man of the hills), the framed portrait of someone he didn't know (a portrait that one of the guests had once thrown in the rubbish bin), the tin where he kept his tips, the Joseph Rodgers knife which Ma had given him for ten years' faithful service, his shoe polish, the key to the wood room, shiny from being handled, the key to the ablution block, keys Ma had entrusted him with in his fifth year of service, years ago, when he still sometimes pushed me round on the terrace on my tricycle, when Pa still farmed hard, when there was still water in the valley, before the droughts, the unrest, the burning down of school halls and churches, before Ma grew so fond of her drinks, before I knew about my one eye.

He also showed her the piles of *Reader's Digests* with the crochet cloth thrown over them, the pile of neatly folded pants, shirts, the two waiter's bow ties, the socks, his town hat, the comb and the glycerine for his hair, the tin of clothes pegs, his town shoes, shining like the flanks of the Cadillac. It was all he owned and the things were always arranged so he could look over them once the day's work was done, and so he could keep everything clean and tidy.

He showed her everything and while she was still looking, perhaps picking up the ring or stroking the toe caps in which she saw herself reflected, while she was looking so admiringly at all his things, he took her gently by the shoulders and stroked his cheek against hers. He smelt her hair oil and the sharp tang of sweat. She was afraid, he realised, the hollow at the base of her throat throbbed. She had a long slender neck. He had never seen a neck like it before. The skin was a rich brown with dark shadows in the creases. It looked like polished wood, shining with the oil.

He caressed the neck gently with his lips, moving his mouth slowly to her throat and his warm breath fanned her skin. She stood quite still and he didn't know where her hands were. He brought his lips slowly up to her ear and took the lobe of that little shell in his mouth. While he gently bit and sucked it, one of her thighs pushed between his legs, carefully, tentatively. Then she got a fright from her own movement and jerked the leg back. The smell in the room changed, the silence was different now. She stood there before him, she'd pulled herself loose, her nostrils flared with each breath, her eyes looked as though she'd been gazing into a smoky fire. They had contracted to two tight dots over something that wanted to come out, something she didn't know, something she was afraid of.

He left her there and went to sit on the bed. He was older than her; he knew what young women were like. He waited for her to turn away and hide her face.

She peered under the crochet cloth at the *Reader's Digests*, she picked up one of his bow ties, she opened the passbook, bringing the photo closer to have a better look. She didn't turn to him laughing, to say something about his youth in the picture, she didn't behave as he'd expected her to. She stood there with her back turned to him and her sides rose and fell. A drop of sweat appeared in the nape of her neck, where the hair began, rolled down her neck and disappeared between her shoulders, under her dress.

He sat and wondered how much she knew of what had happened: the white man Reitz, that day at the milking shed, the day everyone was trying to forget by carrying on as normal and living as though nothing had happened. Only Mr Jacoby had looked very disturbed. He came back from the concert in town and they brought his horse in a lorry. When the horse was off-loaded, he asked Reuben, "What's going on? What's that funny burning smell?"

And Boe was boss of the kitchen and she didn't let on anything. Every morning she walked from her hut to work. She walked right past that smouldering haystack without glancing at it. She walked to the kitchen thinking about the roast she had to get into the roasting pan that day, the pumpkin that had to be cut up first thing to be cooked soft by twelve, she thought about the cleaners who couldn't do their work properly because their heads were full of their boyfriends, and of the things they got up to with the terrace waiters at night behind the sisal plants.

Boe didn't let herself go, she kept a firm reign on herself, she forgot and suppressed, but she couldn't really forget. At night she woke and the smell of the burning haystack was everywhere in her blankets, her clothes, in her dreams; she couldn't shake it off.

Reuben wondered whether Tsitsi had noticed that the other waiters turned away when he came by. Would she have heard from the other nannies, would she know what they thought of him?

Was she too young to know how people can suspect you of

something and build on that suspicion and how the suspicion becomes you, so that in the end you can't extricate yourself from it, so that you also started believing in the suspicion, so that you lose yourself?

The drop of sweat rolled in where the small sinews of the shoulders lay as thin as a dove's. He wanted to catch the drop with his fingertip and paint it down her back, down the spine, in a shiny line that ran to where the hip fat began to swell, there where the back sinews on either side of her spine joined the buttock muscles.

He wanted to draw the sweat stripe right down lower to the tip of her spine, deeper, softer, moister now, he drew the trail between her buttocks, he drew it past her anus where the hair grew thinly, to the wetness beyond where he pressed it in, in so that she started to turn on his finger, and to rock gently back and forth and her legs slowly spread wider until they were wide apart, and with her back arched and her face raised and her mouth opened to the roof, and she shone with the fat she rubbed into her breasts and her stomach and he pressed a second finger in and she turned and tipped and a strand of saliva ran from her lips and traced a fine line on her face and he put out his tongue to lick it off and then pressed his hard tongue against one nipple, gently, gently.

Then she sank down and crouched over his member and she rode him with the beautiful words of her own country on her tongue and he made her listen to the language of his mountains as she reared over him, beautiful, her breasts looking up and away, the dale of her stomach where the navel swelled like a budding fruit on a fig tree, the breadth of her hips, with it all before him and for him, and when he thrust in deeply she farted and he breathed in the smell, then he came, jerking, spurting like hot fat up into her, she rose and fell, rose and fell, their shadows undulating against the wall like a giant ostrich's wings.

82

No one seemed to be able to tear themselves away from Hotel Halesowen that summer. The heat, the humid afternoons trapped under the bluegums, the comforting rhythms of English breakfasts, tennis tournaments, lunches, afternoon snoozes and terrace evenings . . . it all created a lulling rhythm against all the threats out there. The radio was turned off when the emergency bulletins began, the station master's stories about the blowing up of train lines and the burning down of yet another building were ignored, and conversation centered rather on the roll of English comics for Fabian, the latest *Reader's Digest*, and why the postal service was so lousy this month.

Dr Clark indicated he would be staying on longer, he was making good progress on the book. Mr Jacoby didn't want to take the risk of loading Valour onto a train while things were so rough out there. Marge Bruwer phoned the library for more leave, and Tant Geert sank back into a kind of frustrated vacuum. Everyone was waiting. The Veteran was the only one who got friskier and friskier. He held night parades, he kept his shoulders straighter than ever, he tried to embrace Ma in the pantry, but she pushed him away and ducked off to the front desk, where she took up a pencil with trembling fingers and checked the tennis ball list.

Reuben and Tsitsi continued to circle one another, but made no progress because Tant Retha's watchful eye never left them, and Oom Boeta with his all-wise eyes constantly hovered nearby, an ear cocked for the Cadillac's door even when his eyes were looking heavenwards, waiting for the Sabres.

They'd also decided to stay on because there was stone-throwing on the route to the Zuurveld. Perhaps it would be better to go to the beach after New Year. It actually didn't really matter – the food was good at Soebatsfontein, the children could swim in the pool, or splash around in the Fish River. And Boeta was getting a rest, reported Tant Retha and Ma looked relieved.

"I'm so glad," she said, smiling her best smile so that for a moment she looked as she had in her stage days, before everything began, when she was still young. Then she went to make sure that Pa had remembered his appointment in the Bitter Aloe. She helped him to get dressed, and she watched him as he walked over the kikuyu like a lamb to the slaughter.

"I'm so glad," she repeated her words to Tant Retha. "I'm glad," she said to herself, standing there alone.

"And what are you so glad about?" asked the Veteran, appearing suddenly behind her.

Ma swung round. "Why do you keep creeping up on me these days?"

He tried to embrace her.

"This has got to stop," she said. "This has got to stop."

He stood looking at her. "But it won't," he said. "You know that as well as I do."

83

There they all stood – the cars from Port Elizabeth, from Oudtshoorn, from Queenstown, from Colesberg and Aberdeen. They stood between the rows of white-washed rocks, the Dodges and the Plymouths, the Valiants and the Studebakers, the Ford Fairlanes and the Chevrolets, the Borgwards and the Volkswagens.

"Jolly, jolly," said Ma, "it looks like a second hand car lot here again. Do you know how much money is dotted about there among the whitewashed stones?"

Pa waved at them scornfully. "It all belongs to the bank." He gazed out over the plains. "City people get cars on tick, they aren't like us, saving first and then paying cash. All those cars belong to Volkskas Bank."

"Ag, you," said Ma, rubbing her thumb and forefinger over her lips. She pushed back a curl. "Why don't we ask Reuben and them to wash and polish all the cars as a Christmas Special? A surprise for everyone, what do you say?"

Pa nodded. "Nice idea." But when Ma got up he growled after her, "As if there weren't enough work already . . ."

Ma clapped her hands. "Jacks! Jacks!" she called and the waiters trotted up. Ma explained nicely. On Christmas morning when the guests came across the lawns, once they were close to the terrace, they should see their cars "polished to a shine, newly spick-and-span," gestured Ma, "each one sitting in its own patch of moisture."

"Just picture it," Ma continued when she came back to sit with me and Pa, "the guests come over the lawn, still wet with dew. They leave tracks on the kikuyu."

And so it was already Christmas in Ma's head, in her thoughts, she was so desperate for excitement and pleasure. Even though so much was still to happen before Christmas, Ma imagined it all: the city children bubbling out over the rondavel window sills with pillowcases filled with toys swearing high and low that Father Christmas had landed on the roof of the cowshed, the guests milling around their shining cars and some falling on Ma's neck to thank her and wish her a happy Christmas, others with tears in their eyes.

Others pressing tips on Reuben and the waiters and vowing to come back next year because this was surely the Karoo's prettiest and friendliest holiday farm, here at the foot of that dark mountain, in the curve of the river, in the valley, with the rondavels dotted about amongst the trees and the peach orchard and the plains, and of course the unexpected dongas and monkey routes through the river reeds – the places the children would be bragging about to their city pals for months to come.

High in the bluegums, the white tick birds preened their feathers. The sun burnt the last mist out of the river hollows. In the silo, the workers struck pitchforks deep into the silage and when they raised the forks, the damp straw steamed and they held their breath against the acrid vapour rising.

Then the workers and their families came from the huts and

packed together on the gravel between the terrace and the cars. They'd come to dance for us. The guitars were out and not everyone was sober, even though the visitors hadn't even had their breakfast yet. The workers shuffled and jived and waltzed up a cloud of dust and the guests clapped and threw small change to the dancers at the front. Here and there a tussle broke out but it was more for show.

Finally Ma arrived with presents for the workers and their families, packets of sweets for the children, bright headscarves for the women, boots for the men. Everything had been ordered wholesale from *Farmer's Weekly*, where an ad had announced "Christmas goods for the workers".

It smelt of heat and dust and the guests' eggs grew cold on their plates, but Ma poured sweet wine for the workers from a plastic can she'd ordered by rail from the Western Cape. It was already too hot and sweaty, but the Saviour was born and to finish off, the Pastor led a prayer and a pretty hymn, which brought tears back to the eyes of the tender-hearted. In Ma's eyes, of course, in Tant Geert's and Marge Bruwer's, in Pa's eyes, and in Boe's where she stood in the background with a kitchen cloth, thinking, when on earth is that haystack going to stop burning, when will the thing inside it die, when is the fire going to be quenched?

"Thank God for his Son, for his Lamb," called the Pastor , "born in a stable, in a humble farm shed."

It was lovely to see everyone together there, thought the guests, all those loyal workers, while out there it was all stone-throwing and burning churches and plotting murder and revolution, the poor government trying its damnedest to maintain law and order, while black Africa shouted "uhuru" and the winds of change threatened to brew up to a storm over the plains.

And just look at how happy everyone was, gathered together here, how the workers came to press Mrs Latsky's hand, how the men raised their hats to the guests, how the women kept their hands respectfully folded and tried to keep the children in order at the same time.

"Is this the way you want your Christmas to be?" Pa asked Ma once she had come to sit down again and the waiters had gone off with instructions about cleaning the cars on Christmas day. "This bunch of townies is going to be so bleary-eyed they won't even notice that the cars are clean, or they'll reckon it's part of the deal. One of these days they'll get up some morning and ask, why haven't the Jacks cleaned our cars this morning? It was done last week."

"Always so cynical," Ma hissed through her teeth. She looked tired now, after the excitement of the inspiration and instructing the waiters, and also after being put down by Pa so unexpectedly again. "The whole world chokes on the Latsky cynicism."

Ma tossed her cigarette butt into the geraniums and got up. "The way you see the world, everyone should just pull the blankets over their heads. But I'm telling you one thing, I'm not hiding in no bed. This girl's a showgirl. She likes a party. And goodness knows, this Christmas I've got itchy feet."

Pa began to tremble. He was used to her comforting him and letting his moods wash over her without any sign of resistance. On the odd occasion that she let fly like this in her English stage language, it was as though he was finally collapsing, as though he couldn't choose between heartache or rage, resistance or surrender.

Tant Geert appeared out of the blue. She helped Pa upright and linked arms with him. "Come, big brother," she said. "When did you last walk through your fields? You're a son of the soil, man. And Fabiantjie, trot along pupiltjie. You can keep an eye out for snakes." She slapped me playfully on the back. "Or tokoloshes or whatever else is roosting in your brain. Come, you two Latsky men, let's go and see how the lucerne is blooming."

84

Pa and Tant Geert linked arms and walked down the pine avenue. A surprised Dr Clark watched them from the terrace. In the Wilhelmina, Miss Marge was bent over the basin, washing her hair. The Karoo dust filtered in everywhere, collecting in her bun. She bent over the porcelain and studied her hair, splayed out over the basin.

Dr Clark took out his notebook and made a note: "Sibling rivalry?" he wrote. In his rondavel, the Veteran unpacked his bullets. He executed campaigns, he drew up the columns and his ears were filled with the rumble of tanks. He smelled dust and the winds of North Africa whistled around him.

"Zero hour," he whispered and his hand swooped like a fighter plane over the bed, the bedside table and down over the surprised columns of soldiers, who broke ranks and dashed about confusedly and Major Heathcote MacKenzie, or whoever he was, fired machine-gun bullets there in his rondavel with splatters of saliva.

In the Zane Grey, Charles Jacoby stood in his boots again at last. He took his stetson off the nail and put it on his head. He stood before the mirror to look at himself. "Howdy, cowboy," he said in his melodious voice; and because it had been so long since he'd last spoken, because he'd actually been completely silent since the frightful events, his own voice startled him. Could such a voice still find a place to sing in a country like this? he wondered.

But he pushed the idea away along with the rondavel door in front of him. And stepped into the sunlight just in time to see Marge Bruwer appear on the Wilhelmina stoep with a towel round her head, clearly amazed at the sight of Pa and Tant Geert and me strolling down the pine avenue, casually, as though we did it every day.

The starlings scolded us when we passed the reeds. On the other side we paused at a heap of monkey droppings. Tant Geert poked them with her walking stick. "Is this your and the major's apeman, Fabian?" she teased. When we walked in the fields, she paused on every contour bank to pull the blackjacks from her socks and turn-ups.

Pa looked up towards the hills. His face was dead white. "Ag, forget about the damn cars," Tant Geert scolded him. "It's just a pile of tin."

"I'm depriving that woman of life," Pa said. "She's so vital. I'm smothering her. I'm not worthy of her."

"Oh, come on now," Tant Geert put an arm round Pa's shoulders. "It's nearly Christmas and you're still so down in the dumps. When are you going to see Lew again?"

"This afternoon. But the therapy is draining me. God knows, I can't go on much longer."

Tant Geert called me. I was walking behind them, listening to it all. "Fabiantjie! Run along, boytjie, and pick a couple of nice quinces for us there in the hedge, and I'll bake them for you and your Pa tonight, just like we used to do in the old days."

They walked away from me, through the waving lucerne with its blue flowers that grew as tall as their thighs. Today Tant Geert looked taller than Pa, her shoulders broader. The wind seemed to blow him against her, as though they were wading through waves of blue flowers, as though they'd been swept away on the blue.

I called to them but they didn't hear me. The wind pressed against my face, and a quail rose screaming at my feet. I searched and searched until I found the nest with the two eggs. They looked like two brown leaves with their flecks making them almost invisible. I stamped with my left foot so the egg yellow splattered and one foetal chick's skinny neck oozed up round my shoe.

In the yard, Ma had called the waiters together. She wanted to make certain that everyone understood the instructions properly, that there were enough buckets and cloths. "At Christmas," she said, "the guests must come over the lawn and be stunned by their cars. The cars must shine like showroom models. Reuben, you're in charge. And you, Tsitsi, you and the other nannies must clean the cars inside. Tsitsi, do you understand my Afrikaans, girl? You must keep an eye on the others, you understand? You Rhodesians know what clean means, not like those street walkers from PE."

Ma looked at Reuben. "Reuben, my Jack, you and Tsitsi must take this project over and organise everything between you. Okay?"

Reuben looked at Ma in surprise, but he remembered not to show too much. And she behaved as though it were the most natural instruction on earth, this working together. She looked away from his expressionless face where only the eyes blossomed in gratitude.

Just a little loving, she thought. Just a little excitement. Just the feeling that tomorrow will bring something nice. Is that too much to ask?

85

I'd already realised as a child that so many things remain unsaid, things that are raised but then left there to brood, to hang over conversations like leaves on the terrace, to drift through the mind like the smell of morning kikuyu and bacon and eggs.

That was the secret of being grown-up, I reckoned that summer, the ability to leave things be and not ask unnecessary questions, to let things run their course, to live contained and not always be dragging everything out into the open: neither Tant Geert's Antjie Provee, nor Windpomp's death in the haystack and Reitz's frightful crimes, nor the relationship between the Veteran and Ma, nor the many questions about Tant Geert and Marge Bruwer in the stuffy heat of the Wilhelmina, nor the content of Dr Clark's endless sessions with Pa, nor the origins of the major, nor Reuben's possible betrayal, nor Oom Boeta's membership of the Broederbond. Let it be, surrounding us like the smell of the burning haystack which was always with us those days, everywhere, on the tennis courts, in the swimming pool, in the sitting room and the rondavels, everywhere, the smell of the things that remained unsaid, of that which was kept silent. Actually for the good of all, because it was holiday time at Hotel Halesowen and who wanted to pry, as Ma always said: "Who wants to poke and pry? Isn't life hard enough anyway?

"I'll be with you in apple blossom time . . ."

86

The Sabres never left us that summer.

After that first day, whenever the guests came out of their rondavels, they first looked up into the sky and pricked their ears before glancing at the children squabbling over the tricycles or niggling with one another over the swings under the mulberry tree.

When a train came over the ridge from the Cookhouse side and the dull drag of iron on iron began to echo in the distant emptiness, they'd glance up. Was it only the goods train from Port Elizabeth or was it the Silver Falcons?

Oom Boeta was always outside too, so that Reuben, on Ma's instructions, was constantly trotting out with a cloth hat for his bald patch. "The man's head is already peeling," Ma told Boe in the kitchen, "and he hasn't even got as far as the sea yet." She said to the Veteran, "We must preserve that brain because Boet and the Doctor are going to fend off the Black Peril, so help us God. Jack! Jack! Wake up, my boy. Look, that guest's hand is already yellow-white from hanging in the air. Get his order, my Jack. Ag, you Xhosas really don't have a sense of time, and the concept of service is as foreign to you as a wristwatch to a monkey."

But Ma only carried on like this after Pa's curtain rings had sung and everyone else was sitting sipping orange juice on the terrace in bright summer shirts with faces tipped up a little to catch the sun. They watched the children squealing round the tree trunks and it was only Pa returning to bed, with the footfall all the servant's ears were pricked for; the footfall that brought silence to our living quarters – a silence that spread down the passage and into the guests lounge, and from there through the dining room and into the kitchen.

Pa's sigh blew through the house like a desperate draught. It grew and brushed against bodies and made shirts and dresses flap. It pressed against the dogs, making them raise their heads. It eddied among the haystacks, grabbing the burning smell and spreading it further. It pushed dust over the plains, carrying with it the steam-sigh of weary locomotives. Pa's sigh took up in him the metal-scarping sound of railway trucks, raked together the silences of the dongas and pushed further into the valley, gathering up everything that moved: the scrabbling legs of ants that dragged a dung beatle, the plungers of windmills that groaned into the earth, the poverty-stricken workers' families who'd lost their jobs and lived on the road with their possessions – driftwood cast up against the road fences.

Pa's sigh swelled out and funnelled through the mountains and pushed its heartache over the Karoo plains. It spread, sank and evaporated and then we could carry on again. Ma rang the bar bell for a free round. The guests clapped and called, "Thanks. Thank you very much!" And Ma, at the front desk with her books of statistics before her, picked up the phone when it rang, "Hotel Halesowen, hello."

The curtain rings sang and Ma brushed the curl from her eyes and everything started happening again. Ma clapped her hands and it was Reuben, always Reuben, she scolded first. "Jack! Jack!" But Reuben, who never missed a beat, made the best of it, hoisted his tray shield parade-ground style, shook a leg, and the tips streamed in until his trouser pocket bulged with the pennies and the other waiters' eyes narrowed at him in jealousy.

The gleaming breath of the airforce came sweeping over the

valley. Inside, small and motionless as match-stick heads, sat the pilots with their round helmets. But all you really saw was steel and speed and wind. They tore Pa's chest open as he writhed in bed. His heels thrashed in the sweaty sheets and he bent his back so that he made a bow and Boe yelled for Ma and Ma desperately called for Dr Clark.

"They're tearing through my chest," Pa foamed at the mouth. "They're tearing my heart! Am I going to die? Oh God, I'm dying!"

"Dr Clark!" Ma screamed and rushed out to the stoep. Tant Geert banged the door of the Wilhelmina and came charging over the lawn, her jacket lapels flapping wide in the wind. Dr Clark's rondavel door opened and his perplexed face appeared round the jamb. The Veteran stood to attention on the terrace, turning his back on the commotion. He looked out over the plains like a commander surveying his troops. Oom Boeta turned from where he stood on the highest rock garden with his hands behind his back. He felt he should come closer, but what could he do? In any case, he didn't understand what it was all about, he'd never been able to understand. There was so much to do, so much to build, so much to feel positive about. Why did the man lie around so much?

I shot over the terrace, down the steps, past the cars and the tennis courts and took the river path until the breath burned in my lungs. I chose the path that turned through the dongas and eventually wound through the reeds. I stood there in the damp and humidity, then wandered on to see if I could find the troop of monkeys.

Later I veered down to the river bed and when I came round a tree, I saw Oom Boeta standing at the water's edge. He heard me and turned. The cloth hat was perched on his large round head. He watched me with his owl's eyes.

"Fabian, boy!" he exclaimed in surprise. "I came down to the river hoping I'd bump into you. Why are you sweating so, my boy? Are you training to get fit for the Airforce?"

I jerked round, swung off the monkey path, cut through the reeds and began to clamber up the river bank, where the fossils clustered in the lime and the fragile shells powdered in my hands.

"Fabian! You're going to fall!" Oom Boeta came stumbling over the sand and crashed through the reeds. "Did I give you a fright, my boy?"

But I was through to the top, past the first dongas and over the meerkat burrows and I spread my chest wide for the Sabres in case they came over the torn plains, low and urgent as angry wasps. I stood pulling my chest open for the winds that cut through me like steel. I knew that nothing would ever frighten me again. I had seen fear stand bowed on a sheet, I'd seen the drumming heels, the dark eyebrows quivering on the forehead, I'd seen fear and I'll be able to wear a medal because I'll be able to defeat it.

I started to march across the river flats. The meerkats watched me with their inquisitive bobbing heads and two crows dive-bombed me. Oom Boeta struggled up out of the river behind me and stood watching me from afar. His spectacle lenses were two bottle bottoms. He held his hat, hanging like a dead meerkat from his hand.

"Beyond fear!" I called. "Right turn! Left march in threes, left turn! Forward march! Halt, one two three! Parade, parade, right turn!"

Oom Boeta came running up. His paunch bobbed above his knees. Although I wanted to duck away he caught hold of me and pressed me against his belly. "Fabian!" His voice came from far away and the Sabres flashed past behind his head. "Fabian, my boy! Calm down, little fellow. Calm down. Deep breaths, deep breaths now."

I struggled in his arms, butting my head into his stomach. I heard the breath jerk out of his body. Oom Boeta staggered and fell, but took me down with him. We landed in the dust and he pulled me down on top of him. The earth swung and I tasted soil in my mouth and I opened my eyes and looked into his soft eyes. The crows flapped away, the breeze pushed softly against us.

"You can choose, Fabian. You are either one kind of Latsky

or the other. One kind lies like your Pa there and is destroyed by his own imaginings. The other sort gets out of this Karoo and stands upright. Feels a calling. Knows that everyone can win. Do you know what that means, my boy?"

He helped me up and brushed the dust from my clothes. "You know what, Fabian? I think you must come and live with us in Waterkloof. There's everything for you there – opportunities, a big city. Book shops. Extra lessons. You can develop as you should. You can study whatever you want to. Opportunity beckons every intelligent young Afrikaner boy. But here, here in this derelict old valley . . . No? Fine, I can see you're not in the mood for this, my boy.

"Must I ask your Pa and Ma if you can come back to Pretoria with us? We call it the Jacaranda City, did you know that? If you think lucerne flowers are blue, you should just see those jacarandas blooming on the streets. What do you say, Fabian? Boys' High for you, one of the top schools in the country. Your Pa wants to send you to the Gymnasium, but those Cape schools are a hotbed of liberalism. Then a year or so in the Airforce – I'll see to it that you're called up for Valhalla – and then Law or Medicine at university. Pretoria. Then it's all yours for the taking. Before we can count to three you'll take your place in Parliament as one of our young lions. Hey, my boy?"

Oom Boeta pressed my head against his paunch. He smelt of the Cadillac's seats. "Pa is working for America," I said.

"What was that?"

"Pa works for America."

Oom Boeta took a step backwards. He tipped his head a little to one side and put the floppy hat back on, once he'd shaken the dust out of it. "For America, you say?"

"For the CIA," I said.

"Is that so?"

"That's why he has to swallow LSD every third day."

Oom Boeta squatted down in front of me. He took me by the arms. "CIA, LSD," he smiled. "All the abbreviations! I've already told your Ma she should forbid Geert from sending you those American comics. How about that, for the CIA! And LSD!"

Oom Boeta stood up again. He looked into the wind. "Fabian," he said. "Too much imagination is also a handicap. It smothers sane thought. It affects pure judgement. You have to see your imagination as a horse. It's your wild stallion."

He crouched down in front of me again. "Do you know, when I was your age I was just like you. I watch you and I think: Ah, that little Fabian could be my own son. He's just the way I was. But you know, Fabian, I quickly realised: that stallion can only gallop if he has a strong rider in the saddle. With a tight rein. A tug on the bit. Heels in the flanks. A strong girth. And at night he must be stabled."

Oom Boeta stroked my hair. "If the horse gets out of hand, it goes the way it has with your Pa, my boy. You can, I see it in your eyes. Your Oom Boeta can see it in your eyes. Come, let's go back home. It's the time for the orange juice to be set out on the terrace. And perhaps you'll tickle my feet today, for a tickey. What do you say to that? How many niggerballs can you buy for a tickey? A whole handful, my boy."

87

"Partyville!"

Ma raised her drink to the sunset. It had been a hard day. Dr Lyell had had to come out from town. Tant Geert had spoken harsh words to Pa. Dr Clark and Dr Lyell had stood debating under the terrace for ages, and Oom Boeta had argued with her about my upbringing and the opportunities up North.

But now, as part of her build-up to the Christmas and New Year celebrations, which were just around the corner, she'd changed into her powder-blue summer frock. Her hair was caught up in a bun and when she turned her head the light gleamed on her pearl necklace and earrings. The guests queued at the buffet or snapped their fingers for Martini, brandy and water or a Bing Crosby. Reuben and his team ran around, their faces shining with sweat.

Some guests had thrown rugs and cushions down on the lawn under the trees, and some had even dragged a divan or two from the rondavels for the smaller children so they could suck their thumbs, drunk with sleep under the watchful eyes of their nannies, while they waited for Charles Jacoby, completely recovered from his tummy bug, to come across the kikuyu from the Zane Grey to the terrace for the concert that Ma had negotiated with him so many days earlier, right after his arrival.

A small stir went through the guests when Pa appeared and took up his place at our family table. He looked pale and shaky but he ordered a tomato juice with salt, Worcester Sauce and a slice of lemon, sank back in his chair and stared out into the night. At least he was there and Ma fussed over him. She'd learned ages ago to make the very most of the smallest happiness. She organised the tomato juice herself, clucking over the drops of Worcester Sauce and grains of salt and gesturing with her cigarette because, in the final analysis, wasn't there always a ray of hope, a silver lining to the darkest cloud?

And although Dr Lyell did think Pa must go back to Mouille Point for shock therapy, Llewellyn Clark supported Ma's refusal. Tant Geert was there, and Oom Boeta, should things really go off the rails. And naturally, Charles Jacoby, the singer. He was in his rondavel and she knew he was already standing before his mirror preparing himself for his appearance.

"The dew will fall early tonight," Pa told Tant Geert. "Can you smell the lucerne?"

"You're the only one with a nose for lucerne, brother of mine," she laughed. "All I can smell is perfume and pudding, leg of mutton and mayhem! My, what a beautiful evening! Just look at the evening star, Fabian. Do you see it? The very big, shiny one. In London you can crane your neck as much as you like but you'll never see a sight like a December's evening here. Not so, dear Anglophile?" She nudged Marge Bruwer, who was laughing at her side, all got up in a silk blouse.

"Oh, dear Geert, do shut up!" But it was all in good humour, and it seemed that the inhabitants of the Wilhelmina had ironed out their problems. With the rituals of Christmas ahead, Tant Geert also had something to occupy herself with.

"Er . . ." Oom Boeta glanced towards his strict wife. "I wonder if I should also order another little brandy?"

She nodded reluctantly because she'd slept badly the night before and the business was not yet sorted out to her satisfaction. Earlier there'd been a scene about the nannies sleeping in the kitchen. Ma had tried in vain to explain: It had been the custom for years at Hotel Halesowen to let the guests' nannies sleep in the row of rooms behind the kitchen. But this year, as was always the case during a good Season, the rooms had filled up quickly and then those who weren't accommodated had to sleep on mattresses on the kitchen floor.

Boe chased them out at the crack of dawn when she came in to stoke up the wood stove, put out the buckets for milk, and opened the pantry windows to let in the last of the early morning coolness.

Sometime in the night Tant Retha had gone over to the kitchen to get a glass of milk from the fridge for Oom Boeta's heartburn and she'd come upon, as she'd complained that morning, "a pile of nannies on the floor, and one could hardly believe this was the place where the hotel food was prepared."

"But where else must the nannies go at night?" Ma was desperate.

"Anywhere, as long as it isn't here where the food is prepared!"

"But I can't forbid guests to bring their helpers with them. We can't look after all their needs like a city hotel. Reuben does the shoes and we help with washing and ironing, but I can't take on their children as well – and there are so many nooks and crannies in those dongas . . ."

"I do understand. But one wants to be able to put the food into one's mouth with confidence."

Ma lost her temper. "Are you suggesting that our kitchen is

dirty? You can scrape your fingernail over Boe's pots and you won't get a scrap of grime."

"No, no," Tant Retha immediately countered. "It was just such a shock in the middle of the night, all that black breathing in a heap on the floor. And so scantily clad – all naked Xhosa bosoms and thighs, oh Lord, I got such a shock . . ."

"Please take a flask of iced water to your room tonight, milk too for Boeta's pigout-heartburn." Ma was livid. "The extra maids have to sleep somewhere. I can't let them camp on the lucerne bales in the dairy. Those days are gone. And the way you make that Tsitsi of yours sleep in the Cadillac! In the morning she's so stiff from curling up all night it's a wonder she can do a scrap of work."

Tant Retha took Ma's hand. "Oh, let's make peace," she sighed. "I am sorry. Boeta and I are under so much pressure in Pretoria. Our nerves are on edge by the time we get to Soebatsfontein. The Lord knows, there are only so many of us whites in this country and we're expected to do everyone's thinking for them. Running an African country is too terrible for words."

But now Ma had shaken off the day's aggravations and deliberately hidden her tot measure behind the plastic flowers on the reception desk. Tonight she poured with a free hand. "Merry, merry!" she cried, moving from table to table.

The Veteran came striding across the lawn. He wore full regimentals with a red cummerbund and his cap under his arm. An officer's staff swung in his left hand.

"Ooh, swanky!" cried Ma and some of the guests clapped for the major. Ma got him seated and before he could wink an eye Reuben had set a dry Martini down before him.

"Praise His Name!" The Pastor appeared on the steps.

"Hallelujah!" whispered one of the waiters.

"Get thee behind me, Satan," Pa growled into his tomato juice.

Dr Clark bent over his notebook. "Freud identified the struggle between father and son, between *senex* and *puer*, as the nucleus of our culture. That is why Christianity insists on the healing unity of the Father and his Son. But why then Christ's words on the cross? The wounded *puer*?"

"A little tract card for you, Fabian?" asked the Pastor, giving me one of his leaflets with a picture of Christ on one side and on the other another picture of Christ with a white dove rising up towards heaven over his head. "Something to read after a wicked day, oh, a very wicked day."

Tant Geert tried to get up, but Marge Bruwer pushed her back. "Never mind, dear," she said comfortingly. "Let's just enjoy the occasion now, shall we?"

Tsitsi sat against a bluegum, watching Reuben as he moved among the tables. She saw glasses of all shapes and drinks of all colours moving through his hands: small glasses with dark yellow liquid, a tall, narrow glass that fizzed palely, a long-stemmed glass with red wine . . . "Reuben," she said quietly. "Reuben . . ."

And far away under the thorn trees where the darkness of night was gathering in pools, a paw pushed the branches back quietly. He saw Ma throw her head back and laugh, the shiny things on her ears. He saw Marge Bruwer bend and pick a red geranium which she put, unobtrusively, without even my noticing, next to Tant Geert's hand on the table. He saw Reuben glance every now and then to where the nannies sat on the kikuyu in their white caps, and he knew that Reuben caught Tsitsi's eye.

He saw Dr Clark push his glasses up and watch Pa and write something in his notebook. He saw the Pastor who opened his little white Bible and bent to point a verse out to a guest, and the Veteran who observed everyone and stroked his medals with his long thin fingers so the nails made a slight scratching sound on the metal that became more urgent when Ma's perfume wafted towards him and when she bent over him while Pa's eyes rested angrily on them. Then the Beast stiffened and withdrew deeper into the bush, but still watched, because a moon-white figure came from the rondavels.

His white lounge stetson sat at a jaunty angle. His arms were fringed to the elbows. His silver spurs jingled as he strode across the kikuyu and a silver Colt with a mother-of-pearl inlaid butt hung low on his left hip. This was the Colt he wore only for special private appearances because Charles Jacoby did not wish to inspire more violence in a violent country.

Jacoby appeared on the kikuyu with his guitar and the guests burst into spontaneous applause. The children went mad under the trees and the small ones, who'd already dropped off during the long wait on their divans, sat up, confused and tearful. Everything came to a halt as the waiters gathered at the railings and then stood to one side, smiling, so Charles Jacoby could take up his position near the glass door, there where Reuben had removed a globe from the light fitting so that the star could plug in his guitar and amplifier.

The paw took hold of his pizzle and pulled back the hairy foreskin so that the wet pink head was visible. The piss was yellow and it stank, marking this place where he stood against that cowboy who held the guitar before him so nonchalantly and called out to the terrace guests in his golden voice, "Howdy, folks! Happy Festive Season!"

"The Saviour is born!" cried the Pastor, but no one paid him any heed. His gospel concerts on the terrace were forgotten because, as Ma was to say later, he was "totally upstaged by Mister Jacoby".

Mr Jacoby's fingers stroked the first chord on his instrument, making everyone's skin tingle with gooseflesh.

"Superstar!" Ma shouted.

Tsitsi slipped a hand into her overall. She took her left nipple between thumb and forefinger. She pressed and rolled it while she kept her eyes on Reuben. Tant Geert had kicked off her sandals and her big toes nuzzled against Marge Bruwer's white ankle. I lay on my stomach where I liked to lie in the evenings until the last of the day's heat had oozed out of the stoep paving; and as I lay I saw how Tant Geert's strong sinewy toe made red marks on Marge Bruwer's white ankle. It must have been hellishly sore, but Miss Marge just reached forward, took a sip of sherry, and sat back again, bland and innocent. She looked as though butter wouldn't melt in her mouth.

Ma leaned towards me. "Isn't this the most wonderful

evening we've ever had at Hotel Halesowen, sweetheart? I'm sure you've even forgotten about your eye now. You don't need two eyes to get the festive feeling, boy."

Her eyes filled with tears and she had to pull the hankie out from under her watch strap when Mr Jacoby began to sing "Silent Night". The Pastor, afraid he was losing ground, let his deep voice be heard. Pa's tenor chimed in and the guests' heads turned in amazement.

It was the sign for everyone to overcome their shyness and sing and Miss Bruwer's shrill voice even got Tant Geert going with some bravado – and then, suddenly, clear as a bell, the fresh young voices of the nannies under the bluegums washed over us. The trays quivered against the waiters' chests, and the stoep trembled under my stomach from the deep chords thumping from Mr Jacoby's amplifier.

Far away, over the scorpion ridges, the Beast loped off. He glanced over his shoulder once and squeezed out a turd that he scraped into an old meerkat burrow so that the Veteran and I would not come across it. He lumbered through the dongas, over the sisal plains and clambered with difficulty up Buffels-kop, further and further from the single pool of golden light in the valley bed – that pool of light where the small group of people who'd shared their lives at Soebatsfontein that summer were drawn together in song during the endless night of the Great Karoo.

88

Tsitsi struck on the inner thigh. First the shiny black skin with a yellowish layer of fat beneath it. Then muscles, sinews, blood. Over the kikuyu, as she was dragged, her pelvis forced wide open, her eyes turned back, white in terror. Only Shona on her tongue now, moaning, white flecks of salt at the corners of her mouth.

The door of the Cadillac was thrown wide open and city mongrels licked her blood from the gravel. First one dog and then eventually all of them – the spaniels and the fox terriers, the collies and the pavement specials, the boerbulls and the mongrels. They licked and nibbled at the grass and then went to vomit under the bluegums.

Tsitsi, raped.

89

It could have been one and all, anyone. Because Ma had seen it circling round in her fortune cup earlier and also in the lifelines on the palms which she was forever examining: the black Cadillac, in tea leaves washed down right near the bottom, the paw reaching out, the wind charger clattering more loudly and then the lamplight swelling and shrinking.

Tant Geert . . . it could have been her because she hadn't been able to sleep that night, after the Charles Jacoby terrace concert. Her *femme fragile*, Marge Bruwer, slept skew on the divan, with her night-shirt pulled high above her buttocks. Tant Geert stood gazing compassionately at the white English legs, illuminated by a strip of moonlight. When Tant Geert moved round the bed, she could see the dark cleft and the triangle of hair where the upper thigh arched from the torso and the dark purple blotch where the capillary veins had burst under the sucking kiss at the high point of the previous afternoon's passion behind drawn curtains. The mark of the mouth would remain there for a good ten days, changing colour in stages from livid purple to blue, to green and finally, a less attractive, sickly yellow.

Tant Geert pushed the door open slowly and when she looked out, she could see the black Cadillac gleaming against the white wall of the big house, with the dark patch of Oom Boeta's window behind it. As black and shiny as an undertaker's hearse, she shuddered. And Boeta could also sometimes deal with things as though he were an undertaker: so controlled, so obliging and correct.

She turned back to her Marge.

Or it could have been Oom Boeta himself because he guarded Tsitsi so jealously at night, there under his window. He who'd offered her a job up in Rhodesia and then smuggled her into the country at considerable risk. He, too, was restless after everything that had happened: the evening's buffet, the excitement, Country & Western mixed with Psalms and Hymns and the couple of FAK numbers thrown in later, and, along with it all, the brandy and water and the steamed pudding and strong coffee, the day's tensions with Pa's anxiety attack and me running away to the dongas until Oom Boeta came to find me at the request of Ma and Tant Geert. Everything was forced together into a sour blend because in the small hours of the night he'd had to get up, and once he'd checked to make sure Tant Retha was still asleep, he went over the lawn and fumbled his way through the silent house, with only streaks of moonlight that crept in between the half-drawn curtains; through the tables in the dim dining room in search of a glass of cold milk for the sour burning of the stomach ulcer that would worry him very badly in later years and finally burst open one night so that he'd bleed to death in the loneliness of a hotel room because he was away from home, representing some minister or other at a congress somewhere – Cape Town? I can't remember now.

In any case, he hovered in the kitchen doorway, a sleepy man, bewildered by the sight of the sleeping nannies, surprised by their breath, taken off balance by what he saw, the voluptuous shadows, tones of black and brown and ochre in all sorts of shapes, mouths open against palms, thighs pulled up high, a full breast with a large erect nipple, a knee and the sole of a foot, a buttock and an elbow in the folds of a blanket.

Oh God! Oom Boeta thought when one of the women raised a drowsy head and looked at him. He turned on his heel and fled back to his Retha. So it couldn't have been him.

Pa had refused his sleeping remedy that night because he

wanted to think. His head churned with thoughts. There was an oil lamp deep in the core of his brain, it had attracted the moths that circled around and around it. Swinging and circling and turning and he had to keep his eyes open or the moths would flutter against his eyelids and the sound would drive him crazy.

He came to my room once and bent over me because he imagined he'd heard me mumble, and then he stood there watching me. He imagined he heard something, but reckoned it must just be a guest going to the ablution block with a runny tummy after all the festivities.

He pushed my curtain back a little and looked out over the lawn. To the left he could just see the nose of the Cadillac. Why were the dogs milling about so restlessly over there near the guests' cars? He glanced towards my bedroom door, the one leading to the short passage that opened out into the stoep room, and from there it was a short distance to the front entrance and the terrace.

But Pa went back to his room. He watched his shadow on the wall. He sighed, and the bed creaked under his weight.

And then there was the Veteran who'd circled Ma after the concert, making a crude grab for her whenever he thought no one was looking. But the ever-observant Reuben was there, too. Through the foliage of a pot plant, from the terrace, through the glass doors, he saw what he had long suspected.

I was naturally also present, in the dark outside, and I looked in, because at this time of night the house looked like the brightly lit aquarium at the Dolphin Park in Port Elizabeth.

You could stand outside in the night and look in at where the fish swam round and round one another and you could see the mouths opening and closing, but you couldn't hear any words – you could just see the perpetual finning of limbs, the body language, the withdrawing and coming closer, the ceaseless swimming round each other, alone or in shoals, the taste-taste of people and things. From here, the eyes resembled fish eyes as they glanced out into the darkness.

After everyone else was asleep, the Veteran, still in his evening uniform, sat in his rondavel. He oiled his pistol and then the 303. It was a ritual he enjoyed, alone like this in the night, just him and the smell of gun oil and the pistol's weight in his hand.

He had nothing to be afraid of. If the door should swing open suddenly, there would be time to load a round of ammunition, click off the safety catch, and he'd fire before the intruder was upon him.

And afterwards, after he'd inspected the corpse, he'd fire a second shot into the rondavel's roof, so he could tell the police he'd first fired a warning shot, and when the attacker paid no heed, he'd had to deliver the fatal shot in self-defence.

This is what Heathcote MacKenzie sat thinking in the small hours of morning, until, compelled by unavoidable necessity, because his prostate always bothered him, he had to go out and pass water against the white trunk of a bluegum. It always gave him satisfaction to see the dark blotch of his urine stain the ghostly white trunk, and to smell the salty tang of his previous urinations from the grass at the base of the trunk as it rose and the wind blew through his hair.

He stood thus with his penis in hand looking up to the big house, at the black Cadillac and the glow of light from Ma and Pa's room. Did he imagine he heard something from the Wilhelmina: a sob, a groan? He smiled: as though we couldn't imagine what those two old birds were up to in there . . .

The English can be really decadent behind their cool front, and that Geertruida Latsky – the old soul recoiled from nothing. That he knew all too well as a citizen of the world and a man of experience.

And Reuben blew out the candle at his bedside, but tossed restlessly on the mattress. Then he lit the candle again and looked at the shadows of his belongings. The candle moved and then flickered the enlarged forms of his hat, his shoes, his Mum tin . . .

He heard something. No, it was just a bat fidgeting in the ceiling, or the donkey cooling down.

But there it was again. Imagine if it were Tsitsi, the girl from Rhodesia, standing there at his door? Because he'd seen how she looked at him. Or it could be one of the waiters, one of those who didn't greet him any more, or jostled him deliberately in the passage, who, the other evening, when he was called away from the donkey, had thrown a pile of thorn wood into the burner so when he got back Reuben had to scratch it all out again hastily before the great tank burst.

He hadn't told anyone. He'd bear it alone. He was a man. He came from the mountains. He knew how to cover his back, and his front too, he'd be on guard.

He snapped open his Joseph Rodgers and stood against his door, with his ear to the wood. It was his own breath that he heard. It was the wind whistling in the open mouth of the donkey and the pipes that sucked and gargled and sighed now that everyone was gone and everyone was asleep. It was the bats snuffling amongst the roofing sheets, the cattle in the farmyard grinding their teeth as they chewed the cud . . .

Reuben pushed his door open. It was light outside. The moon hung in the night. He smelt the dewy kikuyu and got a fright when he saw a row of shining eyes. At first he wanted to call out, but his voice stuck in his throat. Then he saw it was the Veteran, emerging from behind a bluegum. He was wearing his evening uniform and the row of shining medals was pinned to his chest, as if he were on his way somewhere.

90

"Do you want to know who the hyena is who leaves those tracks on your doorsteps?" Tant Geert asked Boe and them when she carried her own dirty cup to the kitchen as she liked to do sometimes. She enjoyed a bit of leg-pulling with the young girls. She'd tease them about their boyfriends and the racket at the huts at night.

Pa didn't like Geert chatting to the kitchen staff. "You're too familiar with the maids, Geert," he said. "They don't respect you for it."

But Tant Geert wasn't put off. It was her little bit of contact with the real citizens of the Karoo, she said, the ones who'd always been there and always would be, even in the days to come when the wind would whistle through the broken frames of the rondavel windows.

"Do you want to know what the Thing is that plagues the young girls so? I hear Boe calls him Aboenawas." They laughed and turned to Tant Geert and waited. "Answer me just one question," she said, revelling in their attention. "What animal walks on all fours in the morning, two in the afternoon and three at night?"

They looked at her without saying anything, giggling nervously.

"You don't know?" They shook their heads, confused, fidgeting with the cooking pots, scraping something out of a pan, fiddling with a dishcloth.

"No, Miss."

Tant Geert turned. "Ask Fabian," she said, walking out with her cigarette. "He's known for ages."

91

And when Tant Geert asked Marge Bruwer why she loved her, Marge answered, "It was you, it was Rome, and I'm a housewife from Philadelphia."

"Or a librarian from Cradock!" Tant Geert laughed, flattered.

Marge Bruwer had soon learned how to handle Tant Geert's mood swings – and references to Rome, which Marge had only visited in conversation with Tant Geert, was the best tactic.

Because Tant Geert hankered after other latitudes; there was something in her blood, she said, that had to circle the globe:

Oh, God, I know not where I go
But let me leave this land
Set me free of all recollections, oh!

And singing, enter the third space.

"Oh, Geert!" sighed Marge Bruwer, and they called me to accompany them on an afternoon walk through the fields of Soebatsfontein. Miss Bruwer and I had never been outside the country's borders, but, in our mind's eyes, the canals of Amsterdam, the trees of the Maliebaan, the piazzas of Rome stretched before us. And when she noticed that I had my ears pricked, Tant Geert's stories got even more colourful.

"And at the top of the Holy Steps, lies the Sancta Sanctorum, the holiest of all holy places which you can only look at through railings. The portrait of Christ that hangs there, the most precious of the precious," sighed Tant Geert, while the lucerne swished against our legs, "was started by St Luke and completed by the hands of angels. That's why it's called the portrait that was completed without hands. Isn't that marvellous, Fabian?

"Tell that to a bunch of mealy-mouthed Calvinists and what do they understand by it, hey? Ag, the dictates of the virtuous!"

I know Tant Geert was having another dig at Oom Boeta and Tant Retha because they always looked away when she started talking about Europe's cathedrals. "Roman Peril, old Boeta and Retha always call it," snorted Tant Geert. "And one day they'll have to explain everything to St Peter at the gates up there."

While we walked through the tall lucerne in a cloud of bees and butterflies, with a hare leaping up in front of us every now and then, our eyes straying to the brown distances with their stony ridges beyond the fields, vistas of Europe unfolded. There was no stopping Tant Geert at moments like this. She was an evangelist. The gospel was Europe, the third space we must strive to reach.

"Fabian! Florence's sun on a summer morning, the wind ruffling your hair while you sit at a pavement café, the espresso shooting through your system like electricity, and then, once you've scraped together all the energy you need for sublime beauty, then: the Uffizi with its Botticellis, those doe-eyed angels with their chiselled features – pupiltjie, you'll go back again and again. And forget about the old centaur who haunts everyone at Soebatsfontein . . ."

"You know, Martin Luther got his calling on that Scala Sancta. You may only climb the 28 steps on your knees because they're the steps Christ used when Pilot had washed his hands of him; they were brought from Jerusalem to Rome by Constantine's mother Helena, and to this day you can only go up there on your knees, and there's a dark stain on every second step which they say is the blood of Jesus . . ."

"Did you hop up there on your knees, Geert?"

But Tant Geert was not to be put off her stride: "And Martin Luther, they say, was a little way up the steps when he heard a voice. And there and then he got up and walked away to go and found a new church."

We stopped to watch the meerkats ducking in and out of their burrows on the river flats. "So, Fabian," Tant Geert continued, now fully into her stride, "Behind conventional history there are other stories, my child; you can lose your way completely amongst all the things."

"Pretentious horsy old woman," growled Tant Retha when Tant Geert went on like this, and transformed the whole of Hotel Halesowen into a fairy story. The terrace steps became the Spanish Steps – "There goes Reuben up the Spanish Steps with his tray." The Fish River became the Arno, the water furrows the Heerengracht, the ablution block a Roman bath house. She called Miss Marge Pomona, the kitchen women became the Amazons, the Karoo Garden in front of the town library was Central Park . . .

"And you must visit Caracalla! Oh, Fabian, to hear opera there, among the old ruins! Shelley wrote *Prometheus Unbound* there, so romantic amongst the vines and creepers and the ancient ruins of the walls . . . Do you know who Prometheus was, Fabian?

"Why would you let an old wolf bother you so much when you can move out into space?"

"Travel, books and bad weather, that's what we need," Miss Marge intoned the well-worn refrain, not without a touch of irony.

"Ja," sighed Tant Geert, "not the sunny, godly days like we get here at Soebatsfontein. Ag, just look at the old Karoo . . . also created by God, hey?"

Then she hugged me again, "Nothing goes by as fast as the years, pupiltjie."

"Onward, Fabian, ever onward."

92

The Chinese man who delivered the sweet-'n-sour take-away in its foamalite box, slapped a green apple into my palm. He held out his hand for the money. "You'd better leave that leather jacket in your room when you go out. Here in New York they'll shoot you clean through the head to get the jacket off your corpse, undamaged."

He put out a hand to touch the jacket, but I was already pushing the door shut. I was cautious. It's a big city, and I was alone. I sat cross-legged on my bed, eating with my bottle opener because the pale green plastic spoon that came with the food had broken with the first scoop.

I leafed through the *New York Times*, stopping to read an article on the Beat Generation. There was also a photo-essay on Cadillac tail-fins from 1948 to 1958. The 1958 was the swankiest model, the one that had brought Oom Boeta and them to Soebatsfontein in 1960.

I read that a seventh man in five days had been robbed of his leather jacket near Times Square. Maybe someone would try to rob me too. It was hard to decide whether it would be frightening or exciting, or how the combination of fear and excitement would feel.

I flushed the half-eaten pork concoction down the toilet and threw the foamalite box and broken spoon in the bin. I wanted to throw the apple out of the window so I could watch a piece of fresh fruit tumble the twenty storeys down to the pavement.

But the window was sealed as a precaution against suicide and I was at the mercy of air conditioning and the stink of a cheap take-away.

I rang my agent. He was unenthusiastic about our first meeting. A small publisher had made a modest bid on my first book. The advance, he told me, had been processed via his bank to South Africa. He hoped that there would be enough left for a bottle of whisky once all the commission and conversion fees had been deducted. My agent was a frustrated writer whose texts had never reached further than the regional magazines of the Mid-West. He'd also written TV soap operas and had been Professor of Creative Writing at an unknown college on the West Coast.

He invited me out for a meal, adding that I didn't need to wear a tie because it wasn't a fancy restaurant, and he warned me to keep away from the subways.

"Don't try to fuck anyone. You'll get yourself killed," were his last words before I zipped my leather jacket right up under my Adam's apple, put the fruit into my pocket, took up the file with my most recent manuscript, and set out.

If you approach New York airport at sunset, the aircraft waiting to land are ranged on different levels against the horizon. They look like a swarm of bees in battle formation.

On Broadway the illuminated buildings are stacked like rock strata. Rocks made of electric light. They broadcast messages about Coca Cola and the Johnny Carson show on giant video screens.

I looked up to the rocks of light. How would it be to clamber up there, to the top – until you could look out over the street where the cars flowed like a river? How would it look if everything were blown up with dynamite and those rocks rolled down into the river? How far downstream would people be able to see those pictures drifting past?

I stood near a sidewalk-wristwatch salesman.

I waited until the mounted policeman was close to me. He was dressed in black and wore a stetson. He sat high on his skittish stallion. The night before, when the town had quietened down for a brief half hour at around five in the morning, the clip-clop of horses' hooves through the quiet canyons had echoed up to my hotel room.

Now the policeman looked like a cowboy with pistols on his hips in his Wild West of skyscrapers, flashing neon, and the milling stream of people who moved past Times Square and the hooting long yellow cabs.

"Dodge City . . ." I murmured.

I waited until he was close to me and I knew I wouldn't miss. I reached into the pocket of my leather jacket and took out the cool apple from the Chinese take-away. I stood with feet planted wide, ignoring the watch salesman who was trying to palm a Gucci watch off on me for only five dollars and I flexed my shoulders wide.

93

Tsitsi didn't die the night of Charles Jacoby's concert when she was dragged out of the Cadillac.

She died years later, in her small room in Waterkloof, with the rain streaming down the window panes, the alarm clock that would announce coffee time while she was growing cold, her shadow swaying on the wall, a death in motion.

What had Tennyson written?

Oh Sorrow, cruel fellowship,
Oh Priestess in the vaults of Death,
Oh sweet and bitter breath,
What whispers from thy lying lip?

I'd often thought it was a printing error. Shouldn't it have been "dying lip"? Or was death the final lie of life? But just a few lines later, Tennyson wrote:

And shall I take a thing so blind,
Embrace her as my natural good;
Or crush her, like a vice of blood,
Upon the threshold of the mind?

I obviously feel obliged to bring most of my characters to their end! And, in all fairness, I'd like to describe my own death too. After all, I've already mentioned Pa's death, Ma's, Tant Geert's, the Veteran's – did I? No, I didn't. After Ma's death, Major Heathcote MacKenzie had his uniform ironed, slid his 303 into his gunbag, packed his leather case and walked out of my life. I never heard from him again. Ma had set up a trust that took care of him, wherever he sat arranging his bullets on a table, or imitating fighter planes with his hand in the small hours.

In his own way, he'd already died in North Africa, years earlier.

Reuben's virtual death? Let me save that up a bit longer.

My own? Of course, it's impossible to stage your own death in advance, that's why I chose the one sort of story where you aren't obliged to do so – the autobiography. Because it is, after all, the genre in which the main character can walk out alive at the other end, if not exactly inviolate.

And even telling all this is also a way of dying, not so? To turn the hand against oneself?

The *Freitod* is the terrain of the writer, the eternal *suïcidair* who declares: "I die by my own hand, therefore I am."

94

Three hours later I was sitting in my agent's office.

He looked just as I'd expected. He had a crumpled, cynical face. A man who'd once hoped he'd be an Updike and then worn himself out hoping that an Updike would walk into his agency.

He'd read my book but understood nothing of the world I came from. He criticised me for not writing more accessibly. "Ease out," he'd written in a letter to me. "These days people would rather go to the movies."

I wondered why he didn't just open a pizza parlour on Forty-second Street.

Now he whined, "Why did you have to chuck an apple at a cop?" He'd had to respond to my call from the police station with a taxi ride. I could see I aroused a variety of emotions in him, but he was trying to maintain the veneer of New York cynicism.

"I wanted to see what a New York police cell looked like from the inside," I said. "I wanted to know how it felt to be guilty. And anyway, you said I shouldn't mess around with the women here."

"So you chuck fresh fruit at a mounted policeman!" he said, getting up from behind his desk, and taking his long grey jacket from a hook behind the door. "Nice leather," he remarked without looking at my jacket. "Do you hunt a lot there in Africa?"

We left. The documents given to us at the police station remained on the desk.

There were three people waiting in his office foyer, a girl with long hair and a disquieting look in her eye – something between Joan Baez and Sylvia Plath. There was a ring in her nose. A neat young man, he could be a young Saul Bellow, with a crew cut and a jacket and tie. He looked as though, at this stage, he was still selling life assurance. The third was a chap with "male menopause" written all over his face.

All of them held a manuscript on their laps.

The receptionist tried to attract my agent's attention, putting a hand out to him as we walked past quickly. But my agent made as though he hadn't heard. I saw the anxious upturned faces of the three supplicants. The menopause man's lips formed the agent's name soundlessly.

I felt good. I was on first-name terms with my agent, at his invitation.

We were going to eat at his expense.

95

Tant Geert asked Reuben to take the tarpaulin off the Harley Davidson and then push the motorcycle out on to the lawn.

Reuben took an orange duster and polished the machine and cleaned out the sidecar carefully – as though the cycle weren't about to make the ten-mile journey to town on a dirt road.

Tant Geert emerged from the Wilhelmina. She was dressed in Bobby Greenblatt's leggings and the goggles were already over her eyes. But, contrary to what everyone had expected when Tant Geert had announced she was off to town to see Dr Lyell for a "conversation between scientists", it was not Marge Bruwer who came out of the Wilhelmina and climbed into the sidecar, but Llewellyn Clark – Somerset Hospital's First, most daring psychiatrist.

He and Tant Geert had obviously discussed the trip in advance because he'd come over from the Bitter Aloe with a whole lot of notes and books under his arm. How on earth were they going to load it all on to the old Harley?

But they pushed and shoved and packed it in and finally roared off. Dr Clark held a handkerchief over his face against the dust. He'd removed his spectacles for fear that, with all the bumping over the corrugations, they'd be swept off his nose to disappear for ever in the dust and gravel. Now he sat there, blind as a mole, his study-room eyes defenceless and watering in the wind before they'd even picked up speed.

"Ag, man," said Ma on the terrace. "That odd couple – the New Yorker and the Amsterdammer – what on earth are they up to now?"

She'd heard Dr Clark and Tant Geert arguing on the terrace the night before. Dr Clark had begun with a reference to Albert Hoffman, the man who'd first discovered the effect of LSD on the brain – "brain candy", Dr Clark had called it, slightly light-headed from all the ideas and the evening breeze. "He also discovered psilocybin and psilocin in the magic Mexican toad-stool, and the hallucinogens in ololiuqui, the American morning glory," he had enthused while Tant Geert had watched him cynically.

She was careful not to ruin the new-found friendship, but with Pa's drumming his heels on the sweat-stained sheets she'd seen enough. Now she pestered the little doctor. He must explain. And if the explanations didn't set her mind at rest, she warned Llewellyn Clark, she would tell Barend Latsky – Oom Boeta – about the LSD experiment here on the holiday farm in the Great Karoo. "And that man will not tolerate it. You know that even marmalade is an alien product for him, Lew."

Dr Clark was sophisticated enough – after all, he still had a fighting career ahead – to see the veiled warning, or even stronger, the threat, as a challenge.

And so began night after night of debate, explanation and declamation. With Ma picking up something here and there and then withdrawing again, escaping to her emergency drink in the cupboard near the reception desk. Writing up all those dreams – the parrots and melting bodies and flying ploughs and monster faces and exploding colours that sounded like music – was it all for nothing?

The humiliation of seeing her husband creeping around the bedroom on all fours at midnight, begging her to throw a rope to him so that he could escape from the funnels of Mozart's music and get above them, before the kaffirs came, before the waters broke, before Noah sailed away on the . . . all for nothing?

Llewellyn Clark had already explained to her what it was about.

"Why," he'd asked, "do you call it 'prayer' when you talk to God, but when you say God is talking to you, you call it madness?"

Ma didn't understand what Tant Geert and Dr Clark were on about. She went and unpacked her theatre trunk, or played her 78s, or counted the spare sheets in the linen cupboard and made a new list of Hotel Halesowen's moveable assets.

"Joey Versluis," she murmured, and the fact that Tant Geert's departure was now imminent too, upset her. The Season was drawing to a close. One of these days, Charles Jacoby would place his rondavel key down on the reception desk, raise his stetson and leave. Oom Boeta and his lot would load the black Cadillac full of merino mutton and vegetables – until, as it did every summer, it creaked on its axles. Dr Clark himself would have to resume his duties at Mouille Point seeing his leave had run out. Perhaps (did she hope or fear?) the major would also grow restless when the rondavels and stoeprooms emptied one after another and the waiters hung about with nothing to do and the cleaners swept out the rondavels, removing the safety pins and cottonwool balls and empty matchboxes and old combs and cigarette butts, and the door to one rondavel after another was shut as soon as mothballs had been sprinkled about and fly poison sprayed all over.

Suddenly there would be leftover food and the cement reservoir overflowed and Reuben only threw a couple of thorn stumps into the quarter-full donkey's belly. Weeds started sprouting in the cracks of the tennis courts, kikuyu runners started lifting the tiling on the terrace and the swimming pool bubbled with green algae.

There was no one now who would be stung by an insect or bitten by a spider; the first aid box remained locked and dust gathered on the record books. Ma stood at the telephone and did endless crossword puzzles and rang Station Master Ferreira three times a day to find out whether the post had come yet.

273

That's the way it was every year after New Year when the city cars rumbled out through the gate, one after another, when Ma stood on the terrace, waving one family after another out of the yard. "And every time," she always said, "it feels as though you're saying goodbye to members of the family."

This is what built up in Ma, even before Christmas. And that's why it was so important for her to get as much information as possible from Dr Clark before the clever man disappeared to Cape Town leaving her with her husband and his nightmares, those nights when he suddenly appeared in the doorway when she was busy with her dream book or her fortune cup in the dining room, when he appeared there with a long shadow behind him, and declared, "Deus absconditus."

Now Dr Clark leaned towards Tant Geert, and spoke in a low whisper, so that I wouldn't hear. "Have you watched little Fabian, Jerry?" he asked. "In him we can observe the process that causes everything to go awry in a person's life while you're growing up. You know what Mallarmé said: *L'enfant abdique son extase* – to fit in with his world, the child has to abdicate ecstasy.

"You know this morning I read in the *Tibetan Book of the Dead*, the texts Jung studied so closely . . ."

Tant Geert leaned forward, "Lew, tell me about LSD. Come on, forget the theories. Just give it to me straight."

"The brain is an under-used, self-conscious symbol factory whose primary task is directing the body."

"And?"

"The brain, Jerry, is an uncharted wilderness. We've only just started discovering what's there. Take this Beast everyone around us has conjured up. How long ago was Beowulf with its Grendel written? We tell one another the same stories over and over again. I want to know why. Why do they talk in Zanzibar about the popobawa, a name derived from the Swahili words for bat and wing? Just like the Soebatsfontein workers' tokoloshe, the popobawa only has one eye. Antjie Somers?"

"And?" Tant Geert looked up. "Reuben, two whiskies, please. Fabian, dear, run along and play now, off you go."

"Look, De Quincey was one of the few people who didn't experience a dull inertia when he used opium. Alcohol, the sanctioned substance, is actually only a depressant. But we're not interested in delirium or sedation or normal stimulation like that provided by nicotine – rather in other more interesting dimensions – Jerry, listen to me . . . spheres of observation and experience that swing from the most exquisite emotions of mystic elation to the most frightful concretisation of anxiety and madness and despair . . . there where the tokoloshe roams . . ."

"But, Lew . . ."

"It's nothing new, Jerry. Every subculture on earth has some leaf or root or berry they use, from the ancient Egyptians, to the Sioux, to the Greeks of Delphi, where the old woman, in order to gain the power of prophesy, must drink of the underground river Kawsotis. In his Odyssey, Homer refers to Telemachus' visit to Menelaus during the search for his father, Odysseus. They drank nepenthe. And what about . . ."

"You can't con me with mythology, Dr Clark," said the sly Tant Geert. "Give me the hard facts."

Llewellyn Clark sighed. "The so-called theobotanicals interest me particularly," he continued, "plants used during religious rites. Have you ever heard of the holy toadstool, or God's Flesh? No?"

Tant Geert shook her head. "Tomorrow you're coming with me to Dr Lyell," she said firmly. "All you're doing is quoting chunks from your book and it doesn't fool me. I'm all for research but definitely against dosing up some poor Karoo farmer with brain candy or whatever you want to call it, Lew. I must say that right up front. And you know I'm a broad-minded woman. No anal retention here."

So the conversations continued. Every night Tant Geert threatened that they were leaving at the crack of dawn to consult Dr Lyell, but then Dr Clark would win more time by seducing her with more facts and coincidences. Like the story of how one spring afternoon in 1943, in the Sandoz Laboratories in Basel, on the Rhine, Hoffman accidentally ingested a small quantity of the materials LSD was to be made of. The dizzying kaleidoscope of colours, sounds and other manifestations that took possession of him for two hours, spurred him on to further experimentation . . .

But it was the attack on Tsitsi that caught everyone on the wrong foot. Everyone felt uncertain, threatened and, yes, guilty. No conclusion could be reached because she shook her head and refused to speak anything but Shona or even so much as point a finger. The police came, stood around listlessly and then left again without coming up with anything. There were so many tracks, the maid refused to co-operate, they said. Everyone was a bit under the weather the night of the Charles Jacoby concert and clear explanations of everyone's actions and movements were not to be had. Further, Oom Boeta wanted to get the police off our backs as soon as possible because he was afraid Tsitsi's illegal immigrant status might come to light.

There was not too much permanent damage, was the general consensus. She probably wouldn't get pregnant, they told one another. And she was a bit shocked. But time would sort that out.

That's how things stood after Tsitsi's rape, the woman every man had secretly desired from the moment her slender hand had opened the door of the Cadillac for the first time, and she'd climbed out onto the gravel of Hotel Halesowen's yard like a steenbuck – truly a woman from across the Limpopo, nimble, attractive, unsullied. Tsitsi. Reuben's flame.

"The eternal now," Pa told Dr Clark there in the Bitter Aloe when he was asked about his experiences of a hundred microgram, a speck you could hardly see with the naked eye. Within an hour the substance started to work properly, and about eight hours later Pa surfaced again, in time for eleven o'clock tea on the terrace, with Ma clucking over him and, if time permitted, sit holding his hand.

"The eternal present. Time stands still. The second hand on my watch freezes."

276

"Subjective time," Dr Clark wrote, "cannot be equated with clock time." He looked up, "And?"

"And you see with three eyes," said Pa wearily.

"With three eyes?" asked the same Dr Clark who sat squinting mole-eyed in the sidecar while Tant Geert crouched over the throbbing body of the Harley and they flashed past the ostriches at the Hennings' farm, past Dynamite Krantz and the tannery.

Ma sat biting her nails on the terrace, Marge Bruwer pored over Tennyson, enjoying the peace in the Wilhelmina. Pa's blunt pencil travelled over his latest tract booklet. Charles Jacoby lay on his bed in the Zane Grey, checking his roster of appearances for the coming year. The Veteran looked for me among the rondavels because he wanted to press-gang me into a final sortie against the Beast-Rapist, and Reuben stood with his back to the kitchen door and looked at Tsitsi who leaned against a bluegum tree, tired and withdrawn while a foxterrier sniffed at her leg.

She didn't even notice the dog, and didn't wave away the flies that clustered at the corners of her mouth.

96

Tant Geert swept to a halt with a flashy curve under the pine trees in front of Dr Lyell's consulting rooms in Dundas Street. She pulled the goggles off her face. She was not an attractive sight with her slight hump, the man's jacket, the leggings and red marks where the goggles had pressed in around her eyes, with sweaty hair clinging there.

She actually looked ready for a bout of wrestling but her appearance was deceptive because she gave Dr Clark a hand getting out of the sidecar.

He'd been wedged in with notes and books; and the ride had left him stiff and fuzzy-headed – after all, he was only a Capetonian who'd gone astray in New York, a city person who couldn't get to grips with the surprising switches between force and indolence that characterised Karoo life.

Or understand the gap between care for one's own and recklessness with others. Or the somersault between hope when it rained and despair when the rain stayed away. In the same way that the temperature could soar and then drop so suddenly that it split rocks, the forces of nature here could have broken him too if he hadn't left again in a hurry, back to his refuge of the mild Cape.

He tottered up onto the pavement when Dr Lyell came to stand silently in the shade on the veranda, surveying them. What could he say to these two aliens, the one as eccentric as the other?

Nevertheless he welcomed them cordially into his consulting rooms. He was a prudent man, and a respected practitioner. He wasn't one to be bamboozled by smooth talk.

"LSD!" cried Tant Geert during the conversation. "One can scarcely believe it. The hippies use it in America."

"There's a whole school of researchers at Harvard . . ." Dr Clark offered.

"No," Dr Lyell shook his head. "It sounds as odd to me as it does to Miss Latsky. In any case, I don't feel that my patient should be subjected to experiments any longer. We don't know what the long-term effect on his psyche will be."

"Backwardnes-s-ss!" hissed Dr Clark, storming out. He only arrived back at Soebatsfontein at eleven that night after he'd begged a ride on the last goods train, sulking in the guard's van, having to endure the bored conductor's friendly chatter about the weather and politics, and then stumbling up the dust road from Halesowen Station in the dark, surprised by his fear that something was shuffling along behind him, something was stirring in the shadows. Ma and Tant Geert were waiting up for him on the terrace, very worried. Reuben was still standing with his tray like a pillar against the glass door. Everyone else had gone to bed. The feast days lay ahead and the guests were preparing themselves for the big moment with plenty of rest.

Ma walked to the terrace steps to wait for Dr Clark. He looked dusty and dishevelled. Tant Geert stood up too. "Lew!" she called out in genuine concern.

After all, the man was a soulmate – someone who swam upstream like her and wasn't to be put off by conventional attitudes.

Llewellyn Clark collapsed into a chair. "One hundred micrograms!" he called to Reuben, and Ma and Tant Geert burst out laughing while Reuben stood there perplexed, until Ma saved the situation by ordering three double brandies on the house.

"He's my brother," Tant Geert explained later to Dr Clark when the three lingered on the terrace after Ma had sent Reuben off to bed.

And Dr Clark accepted that.

97

Ma had read it all in her fortune cup, alone there in the dining room of an evening. Sometimes I was with her and then she'd lean right over the cup and say, "Fabiantjie, I see distant roads, I see a woman in your young life, and I see heartache too. I must warn you. Life is hard, you know, and it tempers you, my boy. Go and feel the skin of the plants there in the rock garden, tough, tanned like hide, callused by many seasons . . ." She bent deeper over the cup. "Child!" she cried, frightened. "You can bring that little tot with you now."

My agent took me to an Indian restaurant. There was no New York food in this city. Just Korean, Japanese, Indian, French, Chinese, Mexican, Brazilian, Peruvian and Surinamese.

While my agent never took his eyes off his plate, even when he asked me a question, I told him about the psychiatrist who'd sought inspiration here years ago and then returned home to try the techniques of psychedelia on my father, the Karoo farmer, after he'd hung up a poem in the shape of an apple in his rondavel.

He listened without reacting. My impression was that his brain was like a radar scanning everything in search of something with commercial potential, a flying saucer or jet fighter, anything that could move my fiction, quickly, into the stratosphere of the best-seller list.

"And what made you a writer?" he asked.

It swirled in the bottom of Ma's fortune cup, I wanted to tell him, because I know she'd seen it, that one night with the clatter of the wind charger and the rising and falling of the light in the corner of the dining room.

One night, or more? Did she see it repeatedly? "Oh, Fabian, bring me that drink, child!"

And I told him, without his looking up, about that spring day that first made me an artist, more than all the other things that dammed up, that one moment.

99

With twenty springs in my blood, I was programmed for this one. The blood fizzed in my heart like warm beer.

I'd hired a timber cottage on the Transkei Coast. At that stage, I still wanted to be a poet. You could smell the braaivleis fires even early in the morning. Here at the seaside people braaied for breakfast.

We were still in bed and I rolled over towards her. Her lithe, sun-tanned body was tangled in the white sheet. I stroked her stomach. It was the strong, flat stomach of a woman who hadn't born children. I nuzzled her hair, breathing deeply of her sleep-odours.

They reminded me of the stutter of her body the previous night. The patio doors were wide open and there were red geraniums in the moonlight. The flowers appeared purple – like mulberry stains.

You could smell the sea, and the patch of kikuyu lawn in front of the cottage, and the wet sand as the tide went out, and, from inland, the acrid smell of the bush in this part of the world.

We were in the Heart of the Sunshine Coast.

I got up and, as I breathed in the morning air, I felt her eyes on my back. Then I ambled, whistling, to the kitchen to pour orange juice and put fresh fruit on a plate. She was in the habit of eating a peeled apple every morning.

She'd arrived in the afternoon with the half bag of apples bought from a street vendor. Apples were scarce round here.

I leaned through the kitchen window to pick a geranium. I wanted to put everything on a tray and carry it through to her, the golden orange juice, the flower, the fruit.

Then the shot rang out.

The Magnum bullet slammed against her temple and forced a piece of her skull through her brain and jammed it against the inside of her right temple. The damming up of blood and the force of the explosion in the restricted space of her skull forced one eye out of its socket so that it lay there still connected to the tough wires of the optic nerve, on the pillow near her shoulder. That clear iris, ice-blue as the fjords of her home in Norway, forced out of the face, was still as clear and penetrating as ever.

Where had it all begun, that story about Grendel, the toko-loshe, the limping werewolf, the steppenwolf, Kikuyu, which Ma wanted to catch and keep as a yard baboon near the terrace where the guests' children could tease it, where it would sit, chained fast, day in, day out, so that you'd continually hear the chink of the chain, realising, there he is, there to see and know.

Had it sprung from my own thoughts, the tokoloshe of my childrens' stories that had come to life that summer, finding fertile ground, an incubator for his mischief? Did I simply want to play Beowulf, a sort of cowboys and crooks?

Perhaps it came to life around the workers' fires at night, in those dark hovels where they lived, too many in one house, with close-packed bodies and nightmares that slipped from one sleeping head to another at night and emerged over the thresholds with the hung-over workers in the morning.

Or was it a beachcombing brown hyena from one of the Veteran's tales of the Foreign Legion, a dune creature that had drifted down from North Africa to the Fish River? Or it could have sprung from Pa's mind, in those days when the curtain rings sang out and he tried to give names to his nightmares in the dark room, in that morass that his life had become – where evangelism and Dodge City cowboys and Verwoerdian doctrine and the terrors of the Black Peril surged ceaselessly.

He went to sit with Dr Clark every day and sometimes Herman Hesse's *Steppenwolf* lay on the table. Perhaps when Pa attempted to give form to the blurry mass of lucerne moths against the gauze windows of his mind, he saw a form build up outside the window, an apparition that also visited me as I lay in my room and everything was quiet and black and I knew it was somewhere in the house.

I listened to my heart and I knew his row of shining eyes was half blind, I heard him softer than a sob right near my door, in the passage, and in between the ticks of my alarm clock. And as time went by, in years to come, wherever I travelled through cities or books in fulfilment of Tant Geert's wishes that I should escape from the stifling nights in the Karoo, wherever I was, he stayed with me, the Grey One, and I heard his tread and felt his pale eyes there behind me.

101

I turned around. The smell of gunpowder and the smell of her exploded head made me feel dizzy. I walked to the fridge, took out a cold beer, went to pull on my bathing trunks in the bathroom, picked up a bottle of suntan oil, put it down again, brushed my teeth, washed my face and then picked up the suntan oil again. Then I went out to the stoep, unfolded a deck chair, put on my sunglasses and lay back in the sun.

The sun shone with increasing fierceness. Her vaginal smell steamed slowly up from my lap. I could feel it tickling in my nose.

I thought about the previous night. How she'd loved me. How, as lovers who already knew each other's bodies well, we had excited each other with practised moves. How, after a while, I'd lit the candle and seen the veins in her eyes contract and how she'd spread her hands on my hip bones and pushed me away, pulled me in, pushed me away. We'd tasted the traces of a lovely day in one another's mouths and her soft shoulder blades had folded under my hands like the shoots of a young, tender willow sapling before her pelvis had started thumping wildly against mine.

As I lay in the deck chair with her smell in my nose, I remembered how we'd fallen asleep in one another's arms. I got up to get out of the sun and go to the bathroom.

At the bedroom door I saw that her face had gone a peculiar purplish colour. The other eye had also started to swell out and her tongue was blue and grotesque, sticking out between her teeth. A butterfly flew in through the patio door and fluttered over her.

I went to stand at the washbasin in the bathroom. I pulled my bathing trunks down to my knees and washed my penis. The water was icy cold and I added a bit of hot water. As I soaped my penis, under the glans and down the shaft, washing her off me, I started to shake.

I realised that I must use the phone.

102

So, many years ago, I told my agent, my first love affair had ended. I'd wanted to marry her. Many people would say that life had dealt me a lousy hand with those events.

"You're like a candle flame," I'd always told her. "That's why I love you."

It had never crossed my mind that she might take her own life. I could never fathom what had caused it.

My agent ordered only Diet Coke. Maybe he was diabetic or a rehabilitated alcoholic. He had never looked up once during my story.

"Some story," he said now. "You should put it on paper."

Sex and violence, he told me, was what people went for – not my stories about struggling Africa or hovels in the Great Karoo. "People of the Free World," he said. "After all, it's New York. And New York is all of America."

Reuben could smell departure when he walked past Oom Boeta's rondavel.

The rubbish bags they put out contained the crumpled papers, bent hairpins, empty powder boxes, used tissues, blunt pencils and flattened toothpaste tubes of a holiday that was coming to an end.

He saw the disappearance of Tsitsi in the way in which they withdrew themselves and discussed safe routes home, but at the same time sat closer to Ma and Pa and Tant Geert on the terrace. He could smell her too, as he followed her, without her knowing. Through the passages, over the stoeps, down the garden path.

He stood over the warm steam of her excreta after the iron door had scraped shut on the servant's longdrop there behind the pepper trees and she'd walked back to the big house. Tant Retha made sure that Tsitsi used the longdrop now. If Pa caught Reuben here, he'd be out on the gravel road, yet another of the unemployed and homeless people on the servitudes beside the main roads, waiting for rain because then the farmers would hire extra hands again and accommodation could be found along with the job.

Here under the pepper trees, the servants' longdrop was a deep pit that had been dug years earlier. Over the pit, there was a seating plank with a round hole in it and a wad of newspaper they could use to wipe themselves with. In her younger, kinder days, Ma had put toilet paper out there, but the workers had stolen it to roll tobacco in, or snipped patterns in it and hung it on their hut walls, or just used it to light fires. – used it for everything "except cleaning their arses" as Ma had once said furiously.

"Now they have to wipe themselves on Verwoerd's face from the front page of *Die Burger*," Tant Geert mocked, ignoring Ma and Pa's shocked expressions. After that Ma instructed Boe to tear out all the pages with pictures of Verwoerd before the week's papers were carried down to the longdrop.

Reuben would obviously have loved to get his hands on those newspapers, that pile on the floor of the longdrop, there where spiders and earwigs made their nests and sometimes, in summer, a snake would slither in.

But he knew he'd get it from Ma – the longdrop was forbidden territory for all the men employed on the farm. It was for the maids' private use and had to remain so. When they came out (Ma sometimes checked on them from the kitchen window) they had to go and wash their hands at the outside scullery – there was always a bar of Sunlight soap to hand. "I'll teach these maids hygiene," said Ma, "even if it takes a century."

But Reuben followed Tsitsi now. Drugged by her bodily smells, he stood there after she'd left, he clung to it. He hoped to remember it, her warmth, the smell of her humanity; the fact that her excreta smelled so like his own filled him with compassion.

He thought of her soft eyes, her careful steps on the path, the way she sat eating slowly, thoughtfully, so different from the greedy, noisy Port Elizabeth nannies. He bent over her footprint in the sand and watched an ant hover on the edge of the little crater and then slide in.

Then he looked up to find Pa staring at him through a window. Pa's eyes burnt dark holes in his head and his hair stood wildly on end. He was wearing his paisley dressing gown. He stared at Reuben as though he wanted to hold him prisoner with his eyes. He didn't turn his head away.

Reuben bolted round the corner and stood panting between the washrooms and the row of stoep rooms. His breathing was laboured. He heard the guests chattering in their rooms. Actually he wasn't supposed to hang around here either: Ma didn't want the guests to feel their privacy was being infringed, so all the workers had to keep away from their back windows.

Reuben saw a hand come through a window to shake out a towel. Snipped beard hairs spread silver through the air. Reuben heard people sigh, hands caress bodies, lips kissing and tongues moving in the mouths of others; he saw elbows on mattresses. Reuben stood there and he smelt kikuyu and dust and he cursed the Great Karoo.

Perhaps he should take a train, perhaps he should take Tsitsi by the hand and drag her away from here. Perhaps he should go and investigate those places on the other side of Buffelskop.

Then he heard Pa's footsteps. Pa walked and stopped and listened. Then Pa walked on and listened. Reuben slid round the corner. "Kaffirs melt into the landscape," Ma always said. "Day or night – if a lazy kaffir decides to become invisible, you'll never be able to see him."

Pa's chest heaved under his dressing gown. He stood trapped in a haze of frustrations and suspicions. It churned round him like a swarm of gnats. He spun on his own axle. There were still six years, seven months and three days to go before his death as a relatively young man. The time ahead would be very like that day for him, days that melted into one another: days. Day in, day out, anxiety eating away at him. No strength in his arms. What did it help? Everything was vain, man was made of dust.

And Reuben always a step or three ahead of him. Everywhere the laughter of children. Pink and green watermelon skins on the lawn. The chatter of the nannies under the bluegums. Washing flapping on the line. Sometimes the sheets cracked like gunshots when the wind came up over the plains. The dogs pissed against the hubcaps at night. Steam rose from their urine – if you listened carefully, the stream sang tinnily against the hubcaps. Pa didn't sleep. Pa waited for the darkness to recede. Pa waited in vain. "Reuben!" he shouted now. He roared. But there was no answer. Was he imagining it, or did he hear footsteps? Fast? Yes, it was me.

"Fabian!" he cried anxiously.

I dodged him and ran to the orchard where I came upon Reuben. "Look," said Reuben. "Look, the Thing comes to the orchard at night. He picks a peach, takes one bite and then throws it down. Then he picks another one. Look at the mess of fruit here under the trees."

"Is it true that he's got a row of shining eyes?" I asked.

Reuben stood back under the peach-tree leaves. I saw only his calves under the dark green canopy. "He looks like this," said Reuben. He growled and limped out from under the leaves. He'd pulled up one shoulder and his left hand hung loose before him.

"Reuben! You look like Quasimodo!"

But Reuben didn't know who that was and he pulled a face. "One eye," he said. "Here." He pointed to the middle of his forehead. "And that eye shines at night. It's a night eye. During the day, the Thing lies in the shade. In a donga. He comes out at night. Here through the orchard, to the dairy, to the huts. He drinks the cows' teats dry. He lies on his back under the cow and drains her dry. Then he goes sniffing at the doors of the huts. He likes young girls, the ones that have never been with a man."

Reuben emerged from the leaves. "Like Tsitsi?" I asked.

"Look," said Reuben and he held his forearm towards me, his elbow pressed to his stomach. "That's how thick his prick is."

104

It wasn't only Pa who watched Reuben suspiciously, or kept an eye on someone else.

In the Zane Grey, Charles Jacoby held one curtain back a little and watched the Veteran who stood proudly before his rondavel, straight as a pole, as though he were listening to the National Anthem. Mr Jacoby stood frowning for a minute or two after dropping the curtain back to cover the window.

Ma went to check on the Pastor who'd been very quiet in the stoep room recently. She found him deep in prayer, using two bits of cardboard torn from a shoe box under his knees to reduce the skin damage.

That's how the Pastor spent the last days, although he did appear on the terrace to hand out tract leaflets now and then. He looked increasingly sloppy. Something was unravelling in him. The greasy quiff was no longer slicked back. The little Austin's battery must surely have been flat after standing idle under the furthest bluegum tree for so long – where it would later rust away. His guitar was forgotten, pushed in under his bed.

And when he appeared on the stoep, it was as though he had eyes only for Charles Jacoby. He watched the singer as though waiting for him to make a mistake, as though he was determined that Jacoby would slip up and then he could say, "I knew it all along – he's a false prophet."

Because Jacoby had definitely stolen "Silent Night" from the Pastor's guitar strings, as it were. And on top of that Tant Geert had forbidden him to hold any more revivalist meetings on the terrace. "We are revived enough already, thank you, pastortjie. And that goes for speaking in tongues, too."

It was difficult for me to measure the shifts backward and forward, the assessments, the suspicions, and the whisperings, but when Tsitsi came slowly by, from the kitchen to the pool, or from Oom Boeta's rondavel to the Cadillac, it was as though she trailed silence behind her, like a bridal veil.

The silence rose and fell in her wake, a gauzy fabric that lay white on everyone who looked at her, until she'd gone, and then the conversations were resumed. But now about her, about the mysterious attack, about whether it could happen again. Whether it could have been one of the guests, or one of the permanent lodgers, like that crow of a major, the old soldier. Or even the eccentric Mr Latsky; maybe one of the soldiers who were posted out on the gravel roads until the stone throwing abated; or one of the reservists who rode in the guard's vans of goods trains and sometimes had to wait to change trains at Halesowen Station.

Maybe even one of the political activists who hung about the locations, inciting people against Verwoerd. Or just one of the labourers who'd drunk too much home-brewed beer and had come into the yard looking for trouble.

Of course, there were the waiters too, the guests reminded one another. Specially that strange quiet one who was actually too neat for a kaffir – it made one smell a rat automatically – that Reuben, yes. The one there with the tray. The one who came to fetch the shoes from the rondavel steps in the morning and saw people in their pyjamas, women and young girls. Who knew what fires that could stoke in a black's emotions?

Things were all topsy turvy since Verwoerd had visited the town. The smouldering lucerne stack was a permanent monument to the simmering rage and frustrations of the black people that year. Sometimes guests' children went at night and stuck long hay forks into the black crust of the stack. The strongest would lift some hay up high and then you could see, below the black lucerne, the glowing inside, as though the haystack were a hot coal. You'd reel back from the surge of heat and let the gaping red wound close over again.

Pa forbade everyone to go near the haystack. "The thing will burn for months still," he said, "without your knowing what's going on under the crust." And it would just be a waste to pour water on it, because it would also splatter the other haystacks and then the lucerne would rot and there wouldn't be enough stored for the harshest of droughts.

Pa considered suing Reitz for the damage to the haystack because it was a huge pile of lucerne that lay smouldering away there. But when he'd phoned the lawyer in town, he decided against it. Reitz commanded the citizen force, it was a time of emergency – unusual circumstances in an unusual country, a summer like no other.

Those, anyway, were the placatory words spoken by the lawyer. Because who hadn't already learned in this world that some things were best left unspoken; that you should know when to turn a blind eye; tread cautiously when you walk on eggs.

Times were tough, the rainfall figures were dropping, the Verwoerd scheme was not coming on line, the whole world was turning against us, no one understood.

And the Veteran called me to his rondavel. His 303 lay

shining on the bed. His medals were pinned on. The bullets were arranged on the bedside table, the bandolier laid out.

He carefully unfolded a flannel cloth to reveal the shiny bullet it concealed. It looked different from his normal ammunition. "This is the bullet we'll use for the death shot, corporal," he said.

"A silver bullet because tradition has it that the werewolf can only be killed by ammunition made of precious metal."

105

Why I didn't withdraw from the hunt, I don't know.

But I was only a child, I console myself now, and a child realises things without knowing them sometimes. I was young, tumbled by happenings and times, overpowered by time, yes, a tide of unexpected power. Unexpectedly, as freak waves do, it had risen out of the bottom of that year with curving chest and flying white mane, and the days that I describe now were the days when that wave reared up over us, a horse or a dragon: yes, a dragon who reared up so furiously rampant, a wave dragon of brutal strength.

The rhythms of a holiday hotel had created the illusion of a mirror-smooth sea. Who would have imagined that so much power lurked beneath the peaceful surface of English breakfasts, tea at eleven, tennis tournaments, drinks at noon, lunches, afternoon snoozes before coffee at four and then the buzz of the evening terrace?

And, in addition, each guest had set up his or her own rhythms: a stroll every day to the nearest rocky ridge, or a nice little sit-down on the river sand each morning while the birds were still singing full tilt, just before the heat of day chased them to the nearest patch of shade. Or a regular round of tennis, or the mosquito repellent at the right time, or the vitamin drink or the headache pill every day at five, when the children came to shatter the peace in the rondavel with their whining and bickering and bath time with all its dramas lay ahead.

A wave yes, that reared up like a cobra, venomous, unexpectedly out of the flat, ankle-deep water where feet had paddled: Windpomp, Reitz, Tsitsi, the ape-man, Pa.

You could actually put all the names in a row, mine included.

106

I should have withdrawn, yes, because the evil was not to be known.

Even the oldest civilisations had felt the need to moot the existence of a dragon. A monster guarded the Gardens of the Hesperides, and one of Hercules' seven great tasks was to kill this creature. Ancient scientists had no problems with the existence of the dragon species and displayed specimens on occasion – although, admittedly, only dissected ones.

Now we know that they arranged parts of different animals and showed them with the allegations that these were the limbs, the tail and the head of a dragon. It was all trickery.

It seems to me that the dragon is more of a marker of memory. As an actor in antique mythology, he has become a reminder of old fears, old feelings of guilt, old wraiths and demons. Peoples with a long memory, a history that stretches back a long way, can comfortably refer to the dragon as the one whose paws walk through many centuries, and is portrayed in paintings, carved on the backs of chairs, engraved on the handle of a dagger, tattooed on a brave chest, glazed onto gracious meat platters.

In the mythical memory or legends of almost every people the dragon stands rampant as symbol of anarchy and destruction, of suppressed animal passion. That's how he's regarded in the forests of Java – as something with bat's wings and a bladder under the throat where poisoned urine is accumulated.

In the Americas you see the dragon cast in antique bronze, from the iron age. In Europe the Romans had the Draco, in Sanskrit you can read of the Nâga, and even Aristotle wrote about the dragon as enemy of the eagle.

In China there's the Pa, the snake of the Great West, and, according to the *Shan-hai-king*, the ancient Chinese work, the Pa could swallow elephants, digest them for three years and then spit out the bones. People who ground up and ate these bones would be cured.

I should have withdrawn from the Veteran's ridiculous expeditions. All that I've retained of them, is a schoolboy's fascination with dragons, and a vague feeling that the hunter becomes the prey, always and everywhere.

If nature has one law, that's it.

And then the fondling of the bones.

Also your own because those who go hunting the past, might find it to be a completely different hunting season, and who has the sites fixed on them?

107

"I think that it's better if Fabiantjie doesn't go on any more expeditions with that major fellow," said Tant Geert to Ma.

"Why ever not?" asked Ma. "It keeps him out of mischief. He refuses to have anything to do with the city children, and at least if he's with the Veteran, he won't go and hang about the huts. No, I think it's good for him to get out, and it keeps him fit. Anyway, he needs a father figure he can look up to."

"Are you out of your mind?" asked Tant Geert. "Do you want Fabian to make a father figure out of that nomad?"

"He's an officer."

"Officer, my foot. He's a hobo from the Cape, a Van Helsdingen, that's all. I'll eat my hat if Heathcote MacKenzie is his real name."

Ma stared at Tant Geert. Her face was white, the cigarette shook in her fingers. She'd already lost so much, loss and longing had exhausted her, and the Season – the one that was going to mark Hotel Halesowen's peak of success – was threatening to fall apart.

And now she stood there, too tired to fight against the loss of her last handhold: her major, the fine, upstanding man who might have been full of hot air, but was always there for her, who sent his rent regularly up to the reception desk on a tray, who always had a story to tell during the long winter evenings when the biltong was sliced – a tale of lost love, but told so that you felt the love were still there, still hovered somewhere, something that would never be lost. The major, who always comforted her, things will get better, listen, do you know the old story, why don't we have a glass of juice on the terrace while Mr Latsky has his sleep, shall I replace the old lamp globe?

Stripped of her last refuge, Ma stood there, weary and trembling. Tant Geert had never spoken to her so gruffly before, "There's horse froth on his lip and you know what that means."

"Geertruida!"

"Mind what I say. At least I'm not blind."

Ma stood there feeling everything crumbling around her. She gazed deeply into the fortune cup of that summer and everything she wanted to deny, that she tried to drown in Oude Meester, that she tried to pass off with her jokiness, everything went sour and threatening and like the smell of that smouldering lucerne stack, sharp, smoky, with, somewhere deep inside it, the stink of a body slowly turning to red ashes.

She didn't see me behind her where I paused on my way to the Veteran and our expedition to Dynamite Krantz. I stood there like a child peering down into a borehole who saw black water and frogs stirring in the depths, and who'd move out into the sun with the Veteran uneasily, knowing somewhere in my conscious that this was a game, but also not a game – that we were going into a strange land, one that couldn't be christened with one of Pa's names, Noupoort, Bitterfontein, Godverlaat, Bloedson, Kwelkaroo . . .

Tant Geert noticed Ma's tired eyes. She suddenly realised how she was talking to Ma. She remembered cries she'd heard in the night. That's my brother's voice, she'd thought sleepily, ag, it's too frightful, it's the after-effects of that shaman Lew's experiments. Then she'd turned over, uncomfortable on the narrow divan, and pull Marge Bruwer closer to her, her hand on one of Marge's breasts, and with her nose in Marge's neck fall asleep again, with the thought, Thank God for the breath of another, so close to me. I'm an ugly, crazy old woman with no breasts, yet I have so much to be grateful for. And I have an eye on the horizon again. I'm already planning to pack up, to push open that yard gate and swing the Isabella's nose into the wind . . .

Tant Geert saw Ma as she stood there: the one who'd stay behind when the rondavels were empty and the first winter winds howled over the plains. The one who had to push forward through the long empty days when the kikuyu turned winter yellow, when the orchard trees trembled like sticks, when the rooms were silent, the doors closed, and the voices only memories. Only the deserted terrace remained and Reuben's back as he stared out over the brown hills, the silent telephone, the plastic flowers gathering dust, the bottle of brandy, and finally the comforting tot once the clock hands stood at twelve and a numbing of the senses was legitimate.

Tant Geert stepped forward and clasped her sad sister-in-law against her scarred chest. She heard the single, tearing sob and she thought, God, I've never once seen her cry properly, and now it's just a single jerk of the body, like a windmill that pulls a bit up from a dry borehole and brings nothing to the surface because everything has sunk down so deep under the calcified layers of the earth, deep, deep down.

And Tant Geert, with Ma's desperate empty body against her, realised how much the Great Karoo claims, how it strangles with its merciless sun, its cicadas, its wind and its crows, its stones and its frugality, its silence and its remorselessness.

With its illusions: those sunsets, the clear mornings, the first rains.

"You must close down, you must sell up here," she said quietly.

Ma shook her head. "And then where to?"

108

Reuben stood trembling in front of the donkey.

It was the last wash-day for bed linen before Christmas. Reuben had to stoke the donkey in broad daylight to heat enough water for the laundry women who trotted from rondavel to laundry to clothes line with stacks of sheets, pillowcases and towels – "washing out the last stains before the arrival of the Bridegroom", as the Pastor put it from where he stood at his bedroom door observing all the hustle and bustle.

Reuben stood trembling with his back to the blazing mouth of the donkey. The Veteran and I had already set off for the railway line on the long journey to Dynamite Krantz. "There goes Hearn's Hunt," remarked the sardonic Marge Bruwer to herself, when she saw us marching out of the Veteran's rondavel fully kitted out.

Tant Geert was still comforting Ma at the reception desk, when one of the workers rushed in with the news from the stable. Charles Jacoby charged out of the Zane Grey and ran to the terrace looking shocked and dazed – the cowboy of the Great Karoo with the tassles on his arms swaying in the wind and the spurs clattering on his heels. He'd been trying on his outfit to see whether, after all those English breakfasts and buffet luncheons, he still looked like an inhabitant of the mythical Wild West, when he got the news that Valour had escaped from his stable and that the hoof marks – those chopping, powerful half-moons – led in the direction of Buffelskop.

Reuben kept his back to the donkey and he was holding a piece of wood. The labourers, the waiters and the stable hand, who'd brought the news, formed a semicircle in front of him. Boe and her team came running from the kitchen with their hands still dripping dishwater and Ma and Tant Geert hurried from the dining room. Tant Geert shouldered the screen door so roughly, she nearly took it off its hinges.

"D-day," murmured Tant Geert when she saw Reuben there with his back to the roaring donkey and the steam spitting dangerously from the overflow pipe, and noted how the elbows of the hot water pipes spewed out dangerous puffs of steam.

She saw Reuben cornered, and Tsitsi's face in the kitchen window. The laundry women, with sleeves rolled high on arms still gleaming with soap suds, screamed in unison with the labourers and waiters, "It's him, boss, it's him."

She saw Pa standing there with his paisley dressing gown hanging open and his hair on end and his hand stretched out to Reuben.

"Who opened the stable door?" asked Pa. "Was it you, Reuben?"

But Reuben shook his head. The sweat poured down his face, against his neck, into his shirt. He was too close to the fire.

"Reuben!" Ma shouted, tearing herself out of Tant Geert's restraining grasp.

"It was him, meisies." Boe was wild-eyed. The smell of the burning thorn wood, the smoke and the sweat drugged her, sweeping her back to the day when the flame had licked over the lucerne stack and everyone's breath had frozen in their chests for the man hidden in the stack, the man who'd dug a grave for himself in the heart of the lucerne stack.

"How can you say that?" screamed Ma.

Pa swung an arm to her. "You keep out of this." He was put off for a moment when he saw her tear-stained cheeks, but the workers egged him on.

297

"It was him, boss!"

Reuben stepped back, closer to the mouth of the furnace. The flames bubbled red under the paunch of the tank. The steam flag flapped in the wind, the steam cast a shimmering black shadow on the yard in the cruel sunlight. It looked like the flag of a pirate ship, and I knew now that there was a skull and crossbones deep in the heart of it. The workers of Soebatsfontein wanted a sacrifice.

Reuben threw the thorn wood into the furnace. Almost immediately the flames swallowed it up. He had another piece of wood in his hand. "Reuben!" Ma called. "The tank is going to burst! Move away! Reuben!"

"It was not me," said Reuben desperately but his voice was not audible above the ululating of the black women.

"Was it you?" thundered Pa.

Reuben threw another piece of wood in. The petrol-tank stomach of the donkey gave a groaning bellow like a beast whose back is broken, or like the winter-fattened slaughter ox that Pa shot right between the eyes on the first of July every year.

Ma saw something come to pass which she had long feared. She saw it coming. The steam tank tearing open, ripping apart, boiling water pouring over Reuben, burning the clothes off his body as though they were skin. She rushed forward, she had to stop it. Pa grabbed at her but she'd reached Reuben.

She planted herself in front of him with her back to him with her arms out protectively, and she looked at the people before her. Pa and Boe and the waiters and the labourers and the laundry women and Tant Geert and Charles Jacoby and the Pastor and, somewhere behind a pillar, Dr Clark, and she shouted, "No one takes Reuben away from me. No one."

109

That moment, with Ma standing there defending her head waiter, her champion mixer of Bing Crosbys – that moment was the real end of the Season of 1960. The year of Doctor Verwoerd's visit; the year Tant Geert made Marge Bruwer succumb to desire and felled her in the afternoon dimness of the Wilhelmina; the year when Ma excelled in her promotional activities with the visit of Charles Jacoby and his evening concert on the terrace, during which he sported his 45 colt with the inlaid mother of pearl butt; the year Dr Clark came and completed his book and Ma finally realised that Pa would never get better because he was too deeply corroded by the shadows, the dongas had eaten in to the quick, the hyena's spoor was all over everything, as well as the poison piss: Pa was lost, Ma was lost, Tant Geert was on the point of departure, Miss Marge longed for the silences amongst her library shelves, Dr Clark was wondering how things were going in the Somerset Hospital, Mr Jacoby's agent was ringing every day to find out whether the trains were running towards De Aar again and whether the Karoo blacks were still throwing stones and behaving turbulently.

Ma stood there defending Reuben at the blazing furnace, and thus she ended the greatest Season that Soebatsfontein had ever experienced in its days as a holiday farm.

110

Tsitsi left sooner than Reuben had expected.

Just after New Year, Oom Boeta decided on a sudden whim: the rondavel, into which they had moved after finding the rooms in the house too stuffy, had to be cleared up, the Cadillac's water and oil checked, the last shots taken with Ma's home-movie camera – long, longing sequences that I sometimes watch now and sense how Ma, camera in hand, couldn't say goodbye: on the river bank with the shining, meandering stream and visiting children playing in the sand with their colourful hats and buckets and spades, Oom Boeta up to his hips in lucerne, in his enthusiasm for the coming Republic, his hand was raised to wave at the blue sky and the wide open spaces behind him; a stolen shot in through the open rondavel door with Tant Retha jumping up from the divan, laughing and trying to smooth her hair; Tant Geert, Pa and Oom Boeta with their heads together over a trust document, on the terrace, with guests in the background – people we'd wonder about in later years and whose names we'd search for in vain in our memories.

But then the Pretoria family's longing for the sea and the dunes of Bushman's River Mouth became too strong. It was time to go, Oom Boeta announced one morning on the terrace. Ma got such a surprise, she let the movie camera drop to her lap. She looked at Oom Boeta as though she'd been stunned. She'd never been good at partings. There was always that nagging feeling: it's the last time.

"But Boeta, man, you were going to stay another three days!"

"Ag," said Oom Boeta rubbing his bald spot. "I want to smell salt water now. It's that time of year."

And so it was settled. When Reuben came to Oom Boeta's rondavel with the polished morning shoes, he saw the bulging cases, already strapped up. Tsitsi bent to dig something out from under a bed; he saw only her buttocks and the curve of a leg; and he was taken by surprise by the lust and longing surging through him, the rage and desire drumming in his ears as his nostrils were assailed by the morning smell of kikuyu; and by the realisation that things would take their course and there was nothing he could do about it. Tsitsi looked up suddenly and met Reuben's eyes where he stood wordlessly, holding the shoes before him as though he were bringing a present, hands slack from surprise; then the shoes falling to the ground and Reuben bending to pick them up and blow the grass off Oom Boeta's Broederbonders, as Ma called the black shoes.

That's the way Tsitsi would remember him: the surprise, the silence, because there was never talking in front of white people, the turning and the rushing off to his room, with just one last glance over his shoulder.

And the eyes. He's asking, she thought. He's asking so much. He never says anything.

"Come on, Tsitsi." It was Tant Retha whose sharp eyes missed nothing and who stuffed something else into Tsitsi's hands. "No, into that case, my girl."

Reuben hurried to his room. Out of the corner of his eye, he saw Pa, Ma and me coming from the terrace to say goodbye to the Pretorians. Ma was carrying one last bag of apricots and a piece of biltong for the long road. It was her surprise every summer when the Pretorians left, a surprise that was now expected.

I must give her something as well, thought Reuben as he strode up to his room, she must have something of me with her. He tripped over the threshold as though he'd never been in this room before. He stood looking at his things, his mind in a whirl and with his heart thudding: the passbook with his photo, the Mum tin, the copper ring, the tin with tips. Yes, the ring! He picked it up; she could hide it in her clothes, the white people would never know.

But then he remembered her fingers: the slim ring finger that ended in the long pinkish-white nail. Those fingers that threaded Oom Boeta's shoe laces once Reuben had polished the shoes bright, the mornings when he was very busy, struggling with wet wood at the donkey, when the shoes piled up and Tsitsi came to get the Pretorians' shoes herself because Oom Boeta couldn't wait another minute for his breakfast of kidneys and eggs.

The ring was too big. Reuben turned in his room. A picture! The one he'd clipped out of *Farmer's Weekly* – the one of the windmill and the pretty dam and sheep drinking. But then he shook his head, breathing heavily. Then Ma called him.

It was only a picture. And in time it would go dull, moths would gnaw at it. In the end Tsitsi would have to crumple it up and throw it away. Then he heard Ma's voice again. "Where are you, my Jack? The people want to go!"

He grabbed the Joseph Rodgers and ran from the room. The Cadillac was parked in front of the rondavel.

The car was polished to a shine – Ma had seen to it, as always, that the waiters buffed every inch of chrome and glass and paint.

"Reuben! Do we have to load the cases ourselves?" Ma scolded. Just once, Tsitsi's eyes flashed to Reuben's, behind the group of people saying goodbye – Tant Geert in her slippers, Ma who was fighting the tears by scolding Reuben, tousle-headed Pa exchanging a last word with his brother.

Then Reuben had to pick up the first of the heavy cases and juggle the luggage around in the boot, on Oom Boeta's instructions, in order to fit everything in. There was still a big box of mutton: Boe and her team had wrapped the chops and ribs in newspaper against the long journey. Oom Boeta wanted to eat properly at Bushman's. Reuben turned and looked for Tsitsi over the heads.

Oom Boeta slipped a shilling into his palm. "Until next year, Reuben," he said, shaking Reuben's hand. "See you look after my people nicely, my boy."

"Goodbye Reuben," said Tant Retha, "stoke that donkey properly, you hear? We'll see you again next year. Thanks for the shiny shoes. Come Tsitsi, what are you standing there staring at? Jump in."

Reuben wanted to push past. The Joseph Rodgers burnt in his hand, but he bumped into me by accident and half staggered. Tant Retha already had Tsitsi by the shoulder and was ushering her into the Cadillac. The sun flashed briefly on one of the rearview mirrors and blinded Reuben momentarily. Then Ma was in front of him and he saw Tsitsi bend to get into the car. There was so much luggage that she had to hold a case on her lap. "Hold that, Tsitsi," said Tant Retha when Reuben tried to push past and give the Joseph Rodgers to Tsitsi. The doors slammed. "Wind up the windows for the dust!" scolded Tant Retha. Oom Boeta was still leaning through his window. "The Airforce is waiting for you, Fabian!" were his last words.

Tsitsi disappeared behind glass. Through the window, Reuben could hardly see her face. She was concealed by the case she had to hold. Then the great engine purred into life and we had to stand back from the exhaust gasses as the Cadillac crept forward over the grass.

Some of the guests got up from their breakfast tables on the terrace to wave. On the gravel, Oom Boeta put his foot down and Pa said, "It's a powerful engine, that. Just listen to that horse power." Then the Cadillac swished away through the dust and gravel, disappearing in the first heat haze of what was to be one of the new year's hottest days.

Reuben felt something give way inside him. He turned round to the empty rondavel and looked at the sheets that lay in piles on the beds, a pillow on the floor, a tennis racquet against the wall. He went in, but couldn't smell anything of Tsitsi, just Oom Boeta and his family's sleep breath and candle smoke.

He picked up the racquet and when he went past Ma, she said, "Well done, old Reuben, go and hang it near the desk. And tell Boe to send the cleaning girls down here."

Ma rubbed her eyes. "Right," she said. "Right. That's that." She linked arms with Pa and Tant Geert. We all went up to the terrace and when we got there, Reuben was already standing at the glass door with his tray. He looked out over the guests waiting for one to raise a hand and summon him.

III

The Veteran and I forged ahead, armed to the teeth with the silver bullet wrapped in the flannel cloth in his knapsack.

We struggled up the slopes of Dynamite Krantz, over rocks baked hot by the sun. The dassies scurried into their crevices

303

and crows flapped overhead as though they were waiting for something to die.

We looked for droppings, or a trace of a spoor, or a wisp of hair caught on a thorn. The Veteran sighed and complained about the hole in his heart, told me stories about the Foreign Legion, then ordered silence. We stalked, we slithered, and the attack came suddenly, violently: something was crashing through the bush.

A Great Body was thrusting through the vegetation close by, we could hear its heavy breathing. Trembling and off-balance, the Veteran dropped to one knee in the firing position, and shoved the silver bullet into the breach of the 303.

The shot echoed across the valley and geese flapped up from the river; Station Master Ferreira's head jerked up at Halesowen; the ostriches at the Hennings' farm fled with wings outstretched, but the thrust through the bush didn't stop. The Veteran had missed. Then we saw the creature force its way through the bush and gallop away, stumbling down the krantzes, with mane waving in the wind: the beautiful white horse, Valour, Charles Jacoby's stallion.

112

"Mr Jacoby wants to slip away without any fuss and bother," Ma informed us all. She was pale because Dr Clark had left the day before and Pa had slept badly. Before the cleaners started in the Bitter Aloe, Ma went to check it. She hadn't crossed the threshold in all these weeks and now she could smell Pa's words; it smelt like it does when a swarm of locusts has gone past; the air hung thickly round the ceiling fan and Ma switched it on. It began to turn slowly. She threw the windows open wide.

Then her eyes fell on the waste paper basket full of

crumpled papers. She sat on the unmade bed with the basket between her feet. She picked up a ball of paper with Dr Clark's crooked writing going over the folds. She wanted to smooth the paper on her knee and read what was written there.

But the ceiling fan lifted her hair and stroked her shoulders. The breeze came in from outside. The smell of freshly mown kikuyu and the scratch-scratch of the workers' rakes as they gathered the clippings into stacks, wafted round her. She took up another paper ball, and another, piling them on her lap. She embraced them and they scraped against the soft inner flesh of her arms. Then she stood up and pushed them all away from her, so that they rolled away across the floor. Outside the Bitter Aloe she called so loudly that she startled herself, "Reuben, send those maids down here with the brooms straight away now."

A shadow fell over her. It was the Veteran. "Leave me alone," hissed Ma, tossing her hair and making for the terrace. "The Performer is leaving today," she told the guests. "He has made a special request that we let him go without any fuss." The tone of Ma's voice made the guests look at each other in surprise, specially when she added, "Please."

So the guests looked the other way when Charles Jacoby appeared in the doorway of his rondavel. He was a bit taken aback by the lack of attention and called to the terrace, "Ahoy!" but the guests kept their attention on their kidneys and eggs while they gossiped about Ma's uncharacteristic outburst.

Three waiters followed Mr Jacoby with the cases in which his clothes were packed – apparently a new outfit for every concert. His guitar was carried with tender care, as were the hat boxes containing those pristine stetsons.

Mr Jacoby was heading for Victoria West where the church hall was already booked out and the whole town agog. The first song he'd sing there would be, "Far in the old Kalahari" and he'd think back to Soebatsfontein; to all of us; to the summer nights under the clear stars, with the clink of cutlery on the terrace; to the smell of dew and bluegums; to the sleepy bark of a monkey in the troop at the river's edge.

And to the woman who'd personally supervised the loading of Valour on to the SAR&H lorry. Ma was numb from all the goodbyes, exhausted from trying to hold everything together. In his room Pa was reading his *Path of Truth* tracts again. One after another the rondavels and rooms were emptied and people left to take up their lives elsewhere. The Veteran sat in the sun on the kraal wall, a little way from the loading ramp. He watched everything like a crow. He saw Ma gesture and then pick up a couple of thongs herself and wind them into the railings; he watched her run her fingers anxiously through her hair and then stroke Valour's neck, calming the horse. Eventually he approached to say goodbye to Mr Jacoby.

"Happy soldiering," said Charles Jacoby to the Veteran and pinned a sheriff's star to his chest beside the row of medals. Even Ma smiled and we all clapped. Then the lorry pulled off slowly and Ma drew the Volkswagen up, so Mr Jacoby could climb in. His luggage was strapped to the roof rack. The Pastor appeared out of the blue, staggering under the weight of his heavy case. He pulled a comb through his hair before asking, "May I beg a lift?" Ma looked at Mr Jacoby who stood with hat in hand. He nodded and the Pastor gave me a quick slap on the back. "Put your hand in the hand of the Lord, discipletjie." Then he stooped to get into the Volkswagen, struggling with his case, one hand keeping his oiled hair in place. He'd left his room in a disgusting state, we discovered later. There were dozens of tract cards strewn on the floor. There were pages ripped angrily from the Bible with some verses scratched out in pen. We found a heap of dirty shirts in one cupboard, and Ma exclaimed, "But we don't even have a forwarding address for this man!" She ran a finger over the basin in the room. "Morning after morning he turned the cleaners away," she said. "Just look at the mess." More discoveries were to be made later – including the set of five pictures of naked women that I discovered under the Pastor's bed and sneaked into my room.

Now it was time for Ma's Star Performer to leave. Charles Jacoby waved to me. "Cheers, cowboy!" he called. "Don't forget what I taught you. Remember Ben Hur!" In the car, he said to Ma, "You should get a horse for that young fellow. Think how much he'd enjoy riding down to the river."

Ma just laughed, and counted her blessings – no one had told Mr Jacoby about the shot the Veteran had fired at Valour that day when we'd made a final attempt to kill the Beast. When we returned, we had to say we'd seen the lost Valour on Dynamite Krantz, and everyone was galvanised into action. Seven labourers were sent out with bridles and thongs. They returned late that night with Valour, a sudden apparition in the night – seven exhausted men and the stallion, whinnying mildly, his temper burnt out. Everyone sat replete on the terrace and Ma kept assuring them that the workers would bring Valour back safely.

Ma was furious when I told her the next morning about the gunshot with the silver bullet. "Just think of the national scandal it would have caused," she scolded, "if you shot the most famous horse in the country. Fabian! What am I to do with you?"

But Pa and Tant Geert and, more importantly, Mr Jacoby didn't know a thing about it. The Veteran and I were regarded as heroes because we'd tracked Valour down. "Maybe you weren't able to tame the Beast, but at least you tracked down the white stallion," said Tant Geert.

"I really must thank you again," Mr Jacoby told Ma now in his silky voice as the Volkswagen rolled along to Halesowen station, "that you caught Valour so efficiently that night on the krantz."

Ma looked away, out over the veld. It was a Godsent miracle that we survived this Season, she thought.

She said goodbye to her Performer on Halesowen station platform with grace and dignity. She waited until Mr Ferreira had organised everything nicely: the horse in his truck, with enough straw and a railway worker to keep an eye on him; Mr Jacoby in the guard's van, with a packet of dried sausage Ma had pressed into his hand.

The Pastor stood forlornly by, waiting for Ma to say goodbye to him too. He had a feeling he hadn't been her favourite guest. He and Ma had never made each other's hearts beat faster. "Ag, Mrs Latsky," he began now, "our dear Lord . . ."

But Ma shut him up with a quick handshake. Then she turned back to her Performer.

Mr Jacoby bent over her, the woman standing so sadly before him. He was not surprised by her open heartache, here on the platform with Mr Ferreira and the conductor trying to look away and no one else watching. He did shows all over the Karoo and was used to seeing loneliness. What people in these parts hid away from each other, they were prepared to show him because he was not bashful about singing of dreams and love.

Ma gestured that he shouldn't say anything. "I'll play your records," were her last words when the steam engine began to hiss and the great wheels ground on the tracks. Mr Ferreira flipped the signal beam and the train pulled off with a sighing release of steam and rattling trucks. Ma stood so the shadow of her waving arm fell over her eyes. She was a veteran at saying goodbye; she knew how to hide her feelings.

The train steamed away and Ma stared at the shining tracks shimmering in the sunlight.

Until Mr Ferreira's voice jerked her back to the present, "There he goes."

"Ja," answered Ma in the non-committal way Karoo people fill in silences. "Yes, there he goes."

She crossed the track and climbed into the Volkswagen. She drove back to Soebatsfontein slowly, where the breakfast eaters were already strolling away from the terrace and disappearing under the trees with tennis racquets or swimming towels. Before long the smack of balls could be heard in the distance and laughing children splashed in the pool. No one noticed the Volkswagen chugging slowly in through the gate, or how long it took Ma to emerge from the shed where she parked it.

Perhaps Pa saw her because he stood waiting at the window of their bedroom.

113

You carry your parents' heartache around with you just as you do the colour of their eyes, their tones of voice, their hair or their little habits. You can't free yourself from them. As you get older, you recognise more and more of them in yourself, you catch yourself with one of your mother's formulations on your lips, your father's rage in your chest. You realise that you are of them, from them and, as you get older, the way you take after them becomes more marked, you grow more like them, and thus more yourself.

Perhaps this is how genes pay tribute to the stream that flows through all of us down the centuries, the Great Fish River that meanders through the landscape of time, dragging its debris along, bearing memories and fears and dreams of past times, forwards, into the future.

Perhaps it was this realisation that encouraged Tant Geert to busy herself with family genealogies.

I didn't go to Waterkloof with Oom Boeta and family, and I didn't curl up in Tant Geert's leather case so that she could smuggle me past the world's customs officials to some exotic latitude.

I said goodbye on the terrace and at the gate. I stayed behind. Pa and Ma and I, and Reuben, and the Veteran, and the whole phalanx of unnamed waiters and kitchen workers who also stayed behind with us when the State of Emergency was lifted and everything settled down again after the cars departed.

My place was on Soebatsfontein and years lay ahead of me before I could get to the point where I could look at myself in the mirror, smiling, and call myself mockingly "Old Odin". And I brought a story home. To the ruins of Soebatsfontein's rondavels, to the tennis court where stinging nettles grew in the cracks, to the terrace where the rank kikuyu runners entwined with lost conversations, faint cries, laughter, guitar chords and the shuffle of feet.

Here I leave it, at the foot of the Spanish Steps.

It's my inheritance and I carry it with me, yes Tant Geert, wherever I roam.

114

It was time for Tant Geert to go. The Borgward's nose was already pointing towards the gate and the road beyond. I waited at the gate, while Ma and Pa and Tant Geert finished saying goodbye on the terrace.

Everything was over, the subdued Christmas and the quiet New Year celebrations, the guests who were disappointed that the time of balloons, sheep on the spit and high jinks had been spoiled by so many unnecessary incidents, the visit of bored detectives that had come to nothing, the tension among the waiters on the terrace, the food from the kitchen that wasn't always what it might have been – specially in the days following Tsitsi's rape.

I waited until Tant Geert was in the car before unchaining the gate. Now the soothing gestures and parting were done on the terrace. Ma pressed a handkerchief to her nose, looking into the new year like a person looks down a long hospital corridor in the sure and certain knowledge that bad news is waiting at one of those doors. Pa didn't so much as raise a hand, a black shadow on the landscape. "Good luck," were his last words to Tant Geert.

I pushed the gate open as the Borgward came roaring up to it. As was our custom, Tant Geert didn't stop to say goodbye, but drove through without looking at me. She and I were citizens of the world, she said, we were always travelling, we'd always bump into each other again in the loneliness of some latitude or another, so there was no need to say goodbye.

I didn't shut the gate because I knew it had to stand open for the known and the unknown. In the years to come, many people and things, many days and nights, were still to come and go.

The Borgward rumbled away, and then it was just dust and the bare plains, the smouldering haystack and the empty terrace. Ma and Pa had already gone inside. On the lawn between the terrace and his rondavel stood Major Heathcote MacKenzie Esquire with the row of shiny eyes on his chest.

I wanted to raise my hand and say something, point a finger at him, but then I realised Reuben was watching me from the terrace. His tray flashed before his chest: a shield against what lay ahead.

LITERAL TRANSLATIONS
OF AFRIKAANS PLACE NAMES

Allesverby: all is past
Allesverloor: all is lost
Altydsomer: eternal summer
Amenslaagte: amen valley
Bitterfontein: bitter fountain
Bloedson: sun of blood
Duiwelsbrood: devil's bread
Gatsonderput: hole without a well
Genadebrood: bread of mercy
Genadeloosrant: merciless ridge
God-se-Oog: God's eye
Godverlaat: God forsaken
Kainsdeel: Cain's share
Kommaarklaar: surviving
Kwelkaroo: tormented Karoo
Moedverloor: the end of hope
Moordenaarskaroo: murderer's Karoo
Nooitgedacht: never thought of
Noupoort: narrow gateway
Perdvreklaagte: plain where horses die
Putsonderwater: well without water
Pynlikheid: painfulness
Soebatsfontein: begging fountain
Verneukpan: cheating pond or mirage
Wurgdroogte: dry to the marrow

ACKNOWLEDGEMENTS

I am very grateful to James Hillman for his insights – particularly as summarised in his essay "Puer wounds and Ulysses' scar", published in *The Puer Papers* (Spring Publications Inc., 1979). James Fadiman and Donald Kewman's *Exploring Madness* (Cole Publishing, 1979) and Sidney Cohen's *Drugs of Hallucination* (Granada, 1972) were useful sources, as was Ivor Wilkins and Hans Strydom's *The Super-Afrikaners: Inside the Afrikaner Broederbond* (Jonathan Ball, 1978) and Nicholas Meijhuizen's "The Nature of the Beast: Yeats and the Shadow" (*Literator*, August 1994). John Varriano's *Rome: A Literary Companion* (John Murray, 1991) and Jean Améry's *De hand aan zichzelf slaan* (Atlas, 1995) were very helpful. It was a pleasure to re-read Van Wyk Louw – especially *Raka* (Tafelberg, 1974) – and to draw closer again to Nijhoff's *Verzamelde gedichten* (Bert Bakker, 1976), as well as Tennyson's *Poetical Works* (Oxford University Press, 1954). *Die Halleluja* (NG Kerk, 1957) was read along with Charles Gould's classic work *Mythical Monsters: Fact or Fiction?* (Studio Editions, 1992) and one Mercury's *Tea-cup and Card Fortune-telling* (W. Foulsham and Co. Ltd., no date given). Other texts were involved, especially the wilderness tales and mythologies from different cultures referring to werewolves, dragons, monsters, bats . . . Readers who consult the works mentioned above, will recognise my debt to the different authors and their formulations. Draft studies for this novel were published earlier as short stories: "Die wederopstanding van Olive" first appeared in *Liegfabriek* (Tafelberg, 1988), while *Die gas in rondawel Wilhelmina* (1995) appeared as an occasional publication in Afrikaans and Dutch by Kairos in the Netherlands. The story "The Big Apple" appeared in *Heerlijk weer verhalen* (Meulenhof, 1995).

EvH